August 3, 2013

Janelle,

Enjoy!

PASCHAL
MOON

Kathy D. Wooten

InspiringVoices®

A Service of **Guideposts**

Inspiring Voices books may be ordered through booksellers or by contacting:

Inspiring Voices
1663 Liberty Drive
Bloomington, IN 47403
www.inspiringvoices.com
1-(866) 697-5313

Because of the dynamic nature of the Internet, any web addresses or links contained in this book may have changed since publication and may no longer be valid. The views expressed in this work are solely those of the author and do not necessarily reflect the views of the publisher, and the publisher hereby disclaims any responsibility for them.

Any people depicted in stock imagery provided by Thinkstock are models, and such images are being used for illustrative purposes only.

Certain stock imagery © Thinkstock.

ISBN: 978-1-4624-0608-1 (sc)
ISBN: 978-1-4624-0607-4 (e)

Library of Congress Control Number: 2013907429

Printed in the United States of America.

Inspiring Voices rev. date: 04/30/2013

I'd like to dedicate this book to my church family, my family, and friends who have supported me the last four years of writing this novel. It's been an amazing experience and I deeply appreciate those who put their time aside to help me write and edit this book.

Many thanks from the bottom of my heart to L.M. Kupiec, and Kris V.

Special thanks to my dearest friend, Kelly Mucci for your encouragement!

Last but not least, thank you, PED for inspiring me to write this!

CHAPTER 1

SCHENECTADY, NEW YORK

Melody Savoy spied the sign Matarazzo Law Firm and pulled into the parking lot and gingerly parked the rental car. It was a warm day in June in the downtown area of Schenectady, New York. Mentally noting the law office stood on the corner of Clinton and State, she checked the address Hal sent her on her cell phone. Gathering her pocketbook, she stepped out of her car, consciously smoothed her skirt, and gathered her confidence. It was her first day, and her first assignment away from the Quad in Seattle, Washington. She walked boldly towards the large double doors, stepping inside the scene gave way to a busy lobby. Sheila, the receptionist peered over her glasses from her desk and observed the newcomer. She could see the woman had purpose here. *"Perhaps, the new secretary?"* she wondered. The woman would fit in. She certainly had the physical presence. Gorgeous long black hair against her ivory skin and a lean slender build, *Yes, she'd fit in.* She gave her a momentary look. Melody's piercing blue eyes bore into her.

Melody strode over to the desk and said, "Hi, I'm Melody Savoy. I am the new secretary for Mr. Blake Matarazzo." Melody glanced over to the name plate on the receptionist's desk while anticipating her response.

Sheila answered, "Of course. I'll just call to let him know you've arrived. You may continue through the double doors ahead." The receptionist points towards the doors as she lifted the receiver.

"Thank you, Sheila." Melody walked through the doors just as Blake Matarazzo was hanging up the receiver. She had noticed an empty desk to her right. *That must be my desk* she thought.

"Oh, come in! You must be Melody?" He walked from around his desk to greet her. He extended his hand and firmly shook her hand. "Welcome. Please call me Blake." Letting go of her hand, he thought of the phone call he had to make and how he had no time for a proper welcome. "Normally,

1

I take a few minutes so we can talk, but honestly, I need to make an important phone call. So I'll show you to your desk, let you settle in, and in about," Blake looked at his watch, "say twenty minutes from now you can come back and we'll discuss your duties for my office further."

"That sounds fine. No need to show me; just point the way to me." Melody was wondering about the call he was making.

"Wonderful. Go back through the door and to your left. Your desk awaits your arrival."

"Thank you. I will be back in twenty." Melody gave him her most official smile, turned, and was ready for her first assignment. While she exited his office, she couldn't help but notice the long history of legal accomplishments tacked to the walls. She shut the door behind her, and she noted her desk stood studiously to her left, beckoning her attention.

Melody sat into the high-back cushioned chair behind the desk and opened the bottom drawer to her right. Finding it empty, she put her pocketbook inside for safe keeping. A few moments later, Melody heard some hellos. She looked up from her desk and saw a couple of employees quickly walk by with an enthusiastic wave. Melody smiled their way, but apparently it was just a knee jerk reaction to wave to anyone sitting at the desk. She chuckled to herself, thinking, *does Hal really believe there is something unsavory going on here?*

Okay, focus now. Blake Matarazzo is sitting just a few feet away. You are here on assignment. I appreciate Hal sending me here. It'll be no problem watching after a handsome man. What a smile, and his eyes with that soft brown hue accenting his olive skin, and that hair, wow jet-black soft waves barely touching the collar of his Giovanni suit, tailored to his perfect, slender build. Melody shook her head and reminded herself again to focus. Yes, I must focus; she had to focus on the legal files on top of both sides of her desk, focus on the humming of the computer, and she had to check out the drawers which she did so expeditiously. Then the blinking caught her attention. She realized the phone was lit up like a Christmas tree. Quickly she thought, *"You can do this, Hal would not have given you this assignment if he did not think you were capable of handling it."* Breathing in and out soon she felt calm. The buzzer on the phone made her jump. It was the intercom. Blake. *Okay, girl you are on.*

"Ms. Savoy, would you bring me the Laurent file? It should be on top of the stack on the left side of the desk." Melody glanced down and quickly spotted the file. "Yes, sir. I'll be right in." Melody glanced at the time on the computer; her assignment was about to begin.

"Thank you."

Melody entered into his office and walked directly to his now outstretched hand and handed him the Laurent file.

Football memorabilia and family photos surrounded Blake's desk. His L-shaped desk was piled with legal files needing some sort of attention one way or another. He smiled as Melody walked into his office. Her beauty intrigued him as well as his curiosity. For a fleeting moment, he wondered why a woman of her candor was doing secretarial work. He brushed that thought aside. He was grateful he found a secretary as quickly as he did. His other secretary, Delilah, was out on maternity leave. He quickly opened the file and examined it before speaking to her. "Ms. Savoy," he held out the file to her, "Could you set up an appointment with Mr. Laurent for next week? We need to go over some things." She took the file and held it to her chest. "Yes, sir, and please call me Melody." She gave him a brilliant smile.

"Okay, Melody it is." Blake returned the smile but felt a striking sadness, as he could not help but noticed the scar on the left side of Melody's neck. He wondered for a moment what troubles laid behind her piercing blue eyes. His deep thoughts were rattled by a loud voice.

"BLAKE!"

Melody heard thunderous walking and observed a tall, distinguished man walking long strides towards Blake's desk. Before Melody left Seattle, her research revealed the law firm was well respected and operated by a father and son. *That must be his father, Stephen Matarazzo* thought Melody. *I'll just slip out.* But Blake was too quick for her.

"What time are we meeting in court today?" Stephen asked.

Blake deferred his boisterous father by saying, "Have you met my new secretary, Melody Savoy?"

Stephen spun around and extended his hand to her. "Hello, I'm Blake's father, Stephen. Welcome!" Melody shook his hand. Stephen's handshake was firm, assured, and exuberant, whereas Blake was more low-key, his father was abrupt.

"It's a pleasure to meet you sir." Melody smiled. Blake nodded to her and she excused herself by turning to Blake saying, "I'll get right on that sir, good day, Mr. Matarazzo."

"Stephen, please. It's a pleasure, my dear." He immediately turned to Blake while Melody walked out of the office and spoke to him as if she hadn't been there at all. "What time are we due in court, my boy?" Melody smiled to herself as she closed the door on their conversation.

Blake was used to his father's ways. He made an entrance wherever he went. It was why he was the best lawyer for several counties throughout New York State.

"1 p.m. We should head over." Without any further conversation, Stephen headed towards the closed double doors.

Blake smiled to himself, shaking his head side to side. *He's a flip of a switch,* he thought. Just as Stephen turned abruptly towards him, Blake sobered up and reached for the doorknob for him. It was expected.

Melody watched as they left for court. Having located the Gus Laurent phone number she held the receiver in her hand and waited. He answered on the second ring.

"Hello?" a gruff voice answered.

"Hello, this is Melody Savoy from the Matarazzo Law Firm. May I speak to a Mr. Gus Laurent?"

"This is he. Who did you say you were?" Gus was skeptical and gruff.

"I am calling from the Matarazzo Law Firm, and my name is Melody Savoy, Mr. Blake Matarazzo's secretary. His other secretary, Delilah, is currently on maternity leave." She felt the need to explain; perhaps he was speculative of her. "Mr. Matarazzo wanted me to call and set up an appointment with you for next week. What day would be good for you?" Melody's heart was racing; she was really doing this. *Okay, girl, get a grip.*

"Oh, um, how's Tuesday morning? That works well into my schedule."

"Okay, I have a 10:00 a.m. open. Is that okay for you?"

"Yes that's fine." Gus abruptly hung up.

Melody muttered a harrumph and notated his appointment on the computer. *Okay that was interesting.* She thought. She made a mental note to herself to add her conversation with him to her assignment blog. She set his file aside and gathered her thoughts.

Melody's cell phone next to the computer suddenly vibrated a text message. She quickly picked up the cell and read the text.

It read, "Call me Hal."

CHAPTER 2

SEATTLE, WASHINGTON

"Does she know?" Todd Riley was stunned with the news Hal just announced to his team. Hal Sampson stood staring at the four men otherwise known as the Quad. They were special FBI agents that most FBI agents within the agency had not even heard of. Walking around the conference table, Hal stared out the window. The sun's rays bounced off the crystal blue lake known as Lake Washington, which gave way to Puget Sound. It was a popular area for boating and fishing. His forehead wrinkled in deep creases, and his right hand was deep into his pocket. He absently ran his left hand through his now gray hair. His lips puckered several times before speaking.

"No, she does not know. I sent Arvidia on a dud undercover assignment to a law firm in Schenectady, New York. She's under the assumed name of Melody Savoy. I wanted her as far away from here as possible."

"Good. She doesn't need to find out Jim Mason escaped from prison!" exclaimed Todd. He suddenly stood up from his chair. He and the other members remembered all too well just how dangerous Jim Mason is. "We need to find him before he finds Arvidia!" The other members of the Quad nodded in agreement.

"Yes, we don't need another shoot-out like last time." Another agent, Mark Smith interjected his opinion, "Jim Mason took one too many innocent lives, and an unbelievable amount of man-power just to haul him in and lock him up. He is one evil man and I would not hesitate to put a bullet between his eyes."

The Quad, as they were affectionately named by Arvidia consisted of four FBI agents who had watched her grow up before their eyes. All of them thought of her as their daughter but none more so than Hal. They taught Arvidia skills one could only learn in the FBI academy. Her talents were extraordinary. All four men, Chris Magin, Mark Smith, Mike Lawson and Todd Riley were fiercely protective of her. They all knew the

5

devastation she survived and how shockingly disturbing it would be if she were here now that Jim Mason escaped.

Hal Sampson had been with the Seattle FBI division for 30 years. He knew all too well the horrors Arvidia went through. He sat down and placed his hand on Arvidia's file. The well-worn papers had always been locked away in his safe, away from her eyes. Over the years, he'd add more materials. He really just wanted to burn it, but he knew he couldn't until he found the answer to her past. She made it clear to him she did not want to know or see the contents of the file. She had no recollection of what had happened to her. Her only memory was of the day she was found. He knew somewhere deep in those papers they held a key to Arvidia's past.

Hal took a seat and motioned for Todd to do the same. He exhaled, and nodded his head, "I agree we need to find him immediately. I want to be kept informed of all new developments. He is considered armed, dangerous and you're to approach with caution. Most importantly, I do not want her to know about this." Arvidia's case still sickened him and his worst fears had come true. Jim Mason was hunting her down for revenge. All four men nodded their heads in agreement.

Hal's cell phone shrilled. Arvidia was calling.

"Hello Arvidia, how are you?" Hal hoped she did not detect the tension in his voice.

"I'm fine. I'm calling and checking in as I promised. Did you think I would forget?"

"No, just wanted to make sure you were settled in." Hal asked slyly. Hal planned every step of her arrival to New York through former colleagues in Albany. He wanted Arvidia to settle in without her realizing that the people helping her were agents keeping an eye on her.

"Actually, it was probably one of the smoothest transitions I've ever had!"

"What do you mean?"

"Well, quite literally, I found a cab immediately and he drove me right to the hotel. It just so happens that while I was checking in, the desk clerk's brother has a sister who's looking for someone to sublet her furnished apartment. She's going to be in London for a year. I was quite amazed how everything just fell into place!"

"Is the apartment in a nice area?"

"Oh yes, it's right on the Mohawk River. It has a nice view and it's quiet. There's a park nearby and a hamburger joint. It's not far from the office at all."

"Good. I'm glad things are going well. Sounds like you are off to a great start on this assignment. Remember to keep me abreast of any news big or small. You will do fine and you'll be home before you know it." Hal almost groaned saying that, but he was thankful for the many reliable eyes watching out for her in New York.

"Well I don't have much to report on now, but I'm sure I will in time. How's the Quad?" Arvidia missed them terribly. Their constant ribbing and teasing made her ache for them more. She knew someday she would have to branch out on her own but she didn't expect it to be so soon or so sudden.

Hal chuckled, "Oh they are fine. I'm keeping them plenty busy." Hal's tone turned serious, "Does this guy suspect anything?" He tried to be confident in his lie.

"No, he doesn't seem to detect anything." She asked hesitantly, "Hal, I did some research on this guy and from what I can tell he's clean as a whistle. Are you sure this guy is the guy I'm assigned to?"

"Yep, I got this assignment from the higher ups, Kid. Keep your eyes and ears open. You never know what you will find." Hal felt a pang of guilt as he spoke. He knew this law firm was clean, but he had to get her away from Seattle as fast as possible. Between my colleague in Albany and the Quad we hatched the quickest plan to get her out of Washington State and out of harm's way.

"And you're serious about me calling every night to check in?" Arvidia was perplexed by his request but she would honor it.

If you only knew Hal thought. "Yes, I'm serious. I need you to keep me abreast on this case. This is your first assignment away from the Quad and I need to be kept informed of your progress. You are on your own. I know you will do fine." Hal nervously paged through the file while he spoke.

"Okay Hal. I understand and I will do a written report as requested."

"Yes, that is fine." His voice trailed off. He'd only half heard her. She had no idea all the guys were in the same room with him discussing her very own nightmare, Jim Mason.

"Okay, will do. Give the Quad my love. I'll talk with you tomorrow."

"Okay Kid. Please be careful." Hal almost whispered.

"I will, Hal. Talk to you later." She hung up with a smile in her voice.

Hal clicked his cell phone off and exhaled a troubled sigh. He was not sure how long he could keep lying to her before she would figure things out. He knew when she questioned him about Blake Matarazzo he would have little time to find Jim Mason.

Hal placed the phone onto the table and put his hands to his face. Tension wore deep. A dull headache was coming on. Dropping his hands on the table he said, "Guys, we need to find him before he finds her. Todd, contact the Walla Wall prison, talk to the warden, and the prison guards. Find out exactly how on earth this insane guy escaped from there. Keep me informed."

"Will do, Sir." Todd answered. He and the other agents stood to leave the conference room.

Chris Magin stopped and turned to speak to Hal. He spoke softly, "Sir, are you going to let Will know?"

Hal looked up at Chris. "Actually, I am heading up to Lummi Island in the morning to inform Will of the news. I would not be surprised if he already knows. He forewarned me this day might happen; but it still doesn't make it any easier."

Chris turned and followed the others out.

Hal stayed in his seat until the crimson sun fully set behind Mount Rainier.

CHAPTER 3

LUMMI ISLAND, WASHINGTON

Hal silently prayed for guidance to deliver this delicate news to Will. He drove his battered blue Volvo up north on Interstate-5 towards Lummi Island. He gripped the steering wheel and slowly sipped his cold coffee. He glanced at the time on his dashboard. He had a two and half hour drive and was not looking forward to telling Will the distressing news. As he stared through the windshield his thoughts drifted back to the day he met Will Miles.

Will Miles was a respected and well known Indian chief of the Lemaltcha tribe on Lummi Island. He often tended to the sick and was faithful in his daily prayers. Many of the locals and tribe members went to him for advice. Even the members of the Quad sought him for advice with the daily difficulties in their lives. Hal was not sure how old Will was but he possessed incredible wisdom for a man that never seemed to age.

It didn't seem like 20 years had passed since that fateful day Hal received a call from the Whatcom County Sheriff's Department about a little girl they were unable to identify. It was a highly unusual case that didn't come across his desk often. He was more of the drug dealers and high alert type of assignments. He nearly told the sheriff that this was not his area of expertise. Yet, there was something haunting about the picture of the little girl. Her piercing blue eyes seemed to plead for help from within the image. The decision was made to look into the matter and see what he could do to help. He told the sheriff he'd come and meet with him. The sheriff sounded relieved. Hal could never have anticipated the horrific scene about to unfold nor how this little girl would attach herself to his heartstrings.

Hal met the sheriff at the end of the dirt road that led into Lummi Island Reservation. He looked into the rearview mirror and noticed a trial of red dust which billowing into the air. He rolled down the window and instantly his nostrils were stung with the pungent smell of the ocean. He

d to hear how loud the ocean waves roared over the rocks.
er the steering wheel and observed the seagulls flying above.
ched over some gravels, and rocks. Hal could see the once
well-kept homes that had seen better days. Directly ahead, he spotted a
brown house that leaned to the left and observed an older man rocking in
a white chair on the front porch.

The sheriff pulled to the side of the road and allowed Hal to pass. He
slowed as he was rolling down the window and pointing to the brown
house that tilted to the left, he said, "That is Chief Will Miles. The man
I spoke to you about on the phone. He will explain the situation. If you
need anything further help here's my card. I sure hope you can help that
little girl. It's such a sad situation." The sheriff shook his head sadly.

"Thanks for your help, I will do my best." Hal pulled ahead and
parked off to the side of the road. Will's home was the first one you see
when you come upon the reservation.

Hal stepped out of the car and looked around before approaching
the porch. There was a slight breeze that seemed to come with each roar
of the ocean as the waves slapped the shore. The air was thick with a
salty mist. Hal scrunched his nose from the smell. His shoes crunched
loudly on the gravel as he made his way towards the brown house. Time
seemed to stand still as the others tribe members stopped their activities
and watched Hal make his way towards Chief Miles. They all hoped the
stranger would be able to help the little girl.

Hal stopped at the foot of the stairs. "Hi, I'm Hal Sampson; I am the
Director of the Special Division of the FBI in Seattle." Hal showed him
his badge. Will glanced at the tattered badge; it had seen better days but
probably nothing like he would see today.

"Yes, I have been expecting you." Will spoke softly and stared straight
ahead as though he was keeping watch. His rocker squeaked as he moved
slowly back and forth. Hal noticed a long spear decorated with stripes and
feathers leaning against the porch railing.

Hal watched Will. He was a well-built man. His black hair pulled
tightly into a pony tail trailing over his white T-Shirt and topping the
well-worn Levis. His hands were calloused from long hours of fishing,
he supposed. Seagulls could be heard cawing high above the ocean. Will
glanced over towards Hal. His dark brown face creased in concern. His
eyes oozed fear and anger.

"Please sit. I have much to tell you." Will folded his arms across his chest and nodded his head towards the trees that lined the reservation in the shape of a U as if it were protecting the tribe.

Hal took a seat in the well-worn rocker next to Will. He followed Will's gaze in the same direction. He was surprised to see an enormous bald eagle perched on an evergreen tree branch almost directly above a little girl who played with a rag doll quietly under the tree. Lying nearby was an unusually large grey and white wolf with the white fur stretched behind his ears resembling a bandit type mask. He seemed to sleep with one eye open. Hal sensed these animals were in protective mode.

"Do you see the eagle?" Hal nodded. "Her name is Baldy. The wolf's name is Bandit." Will's voice softened as though he did not want the little girl to hear. "Her Indian name is Sqimi, which translate in our language young bald eagle. I gave her that name because when I found her, in her hand was a single eagle feather. All I know about her is from the night I found her. About 4 full moons ago, I woke up suddenly to an unusual amount of howling from the wolves. A screeching eagle was circling around my roof top. There was terrible screaming that came deep from within these woods. We are used to hearing wolves howl, but there was something different about that night. It's difficult to explain. When I came out to my porch, I saw dark black smoke billowing high into the sky." Will points towards the eagle, "That eagle kept flying around my house and then back into the woods. She was obviously agitated and I felt the eagle was trying to tell me something." Will sat back and took a breath. He continued by saying, "In my culture, we deeply respect the animals, in particular the eagle and the wolf." Will began again with his story, "I took my spear and followed her. When Baldy saw I was following her she went straight into the woods. I could feel the heaviness of the bad spirits within the forest." Will paused looking at Hal. Hal was practically on the edge of the rocking chair. "She finally led me to a cabin that was still smoldering. The fire seemed to burn in an odd perfect circle. I thought it was rather strange it did not spread to the trees. The evil spirits that lurked there were overwhelming. I did not know what to expect. Baldy suddenly perched herself onto a tree limb. She screeched loudly and fanned her large wings. As I was walking closer to her I was startled to hear a low growl. I then noticed the wolf, Bandit. I had thought the wolf was injured. As I approached him, he eyed me very carefully. I was

11

not sure to what his injuries were. He did not make an attempt to move. There are many hunters that come here to kill for the joy of killing." Will closed his eyes and he shook his head in disgust. He took another deep breath and continued, "I slowly laid my spear down away from him, as he watched me closely. I kneeled down bedside the wolf to examine him and just as I did, he jerked away and that's when I heard a lamenting moan. I pulled my hands back in shock." Will's anguish was written on his face as he recalled that moment.

"It was her," Will choked back tears and pointed towards a little girl playing nearby under the tree. "Sqimi."

Will had to prepare Hal for what he would tell him next. Hal could feel the tension in the air shift as Will took another long deep breath and looked towards the heavens while he spoke. "You must know everything. Please prepare yourself."

Hal's natural instinct was to lean in, but like Will, he took a deep breath and remembering all his training over the years, his senses were now heightened. He sat back and waited.

"She was near death. I did not know her name. She has not spoken since I brought her home." Shutting his eyes Will allowed the memory of meeting Arvidia to surface. Again, he recited, "I was amazed at the bonding of these two enormous animals that protected her. After Bandit moved, he stared at me then sat down. I could sense he was giving me permission to examine the little girl. During that chilly night, Bandit's fur had kept Sqimi warm. Baldy screeched warnings throughout the night. I looked down at Sqimi with her bruised eyelids swollen shut and blood pooling under the crescent slash above her left eyebrow. Her long black hair was matted and stained crimson. Her neck had numerous bruises and cuts. It was easy to see every bruise, cut and gash on her tiny raw form. Her arms and legs showed licked areas of where she'd been burned." He remembered how she moaned and writhed in pain. "I tried to comfort her by singing to her in my native tongue, Salish. I removed my shirt and wrapped her battered body. I gently lifted her into my arms and carried her home." Will's hands balled into fists while his eyes blazed with anger. He looked at Hal whose face had paled while Will explained what had happened. Then he declared, "An evil man left her there to die."

"I picked her up and carried her back to my home. Baldy and Bandit followed closely behind. My tribe was just as shocked as I was. They stood

12

guard for many days while she lay in the sick room. Baldy sat upon my roof and kept watch. Bandit lay on her bed while she healed. Even though she hadn't spoken a word I believed she trusted me. My tribe prayed over her. Slowly her wounds started to heal. Eventually, her raccoon eyes began to open. They had been swollen shut for many days. Her eyes are as beautiful as the ocean out there. I am still amazed she survived. My Sqimi has a strong will. The Great One has a special plan for her. You wait." Will's voice quavered as he spoke. His voice was full of emotion. It was obvious to Hal that Will loved this little girl. With a thick voice Will spoke, "We kept watch for the evil man but he never came. He is still here." Will took a moment and exclaimed, "He seems to be afraid of Baldy and Bandit." Will paused and regained his composure, "I called the Sheriff's department to inquire about her family's whereabouts. They allowed me to keep her until they can find her kin. Fliers were passed out, the news stations posted her picture and the radio followed, as well. There wasn't a town, city or county in a 100 miles radius that hasn't seen her picture. No one has stepped forward. That is why the Sheriff contacted you."

Hal cleared his throat, "Yes, I received the call yesterday." Hal thoughtlessly swiped his face.

Will pointed his crooked index finger to Hal, "I believe the evil man brought harm to her family." Resting his hand back into his lap he continued, "Sqimi, she trusts me. She is still suspicious of others and screams in her sleep. Bandit often nuzzles his head against her and this calms her. I stay close by and let her know she is safe from the evil one. Many of the tribe members have made her gifts and hang the dream catchers around her room. It was once believed that they stop the evil spirits from entering the room. She is starting to sleep through the night. Her broken spirit is healing."

"You and your tribe have done an amazing job protecting her." Hal was deeply touched by this man's compassion and kindness.

Will extended his arms towards the sky, "The Great One united this eagle and this wolf together and then guided me to her. Physically, she is nearly healed, except I have yet to hear her voice. She has a unique bond with the eagle and the wolf. They have not left her side since the night I found her in the woods. It is a rare sight to see these two animals united for a human."

13

Hal glanced over at the area where the little girl played. Occasionally, the wolf would stand and look about. The eagle's eyes were constantly searching. It seemed they expected the evil man to jump from within the woods. Hal could sense their purpose.

Curiously, the little girl stood up and tucked her rag doll under the pit of her arm while walking towards Will and Hal. Bandit followed close behind her. Baldy sensed she was heading for the house and flew over to the roof. As the child approached the porch Hal watched her cautiously step up the stairs and walk past him. Glancing his way out of the corner of her eye she nearly jumped into Will's lap. Instinctively, he encircled his arms around her. Bandit stood at the base of the steps, cautiously eyeing Hal. Hal's hair stood on end as he observed the enormous wolf lumber up the porch stairs with his mammoth size paws. *Stay still,* Hal thought, he is just doing his job just as you would.

Hal looked at her and noticed the angry; red crescent scar Will spoke of. Then the twin scar could be seen on the left side of her neck. The old burns were apparent on her forearms. Her arms and legs were still stained with the numerous bruises now healing. Hal's sharp eye knew instinctively they were defensive wounds. Despite them, he thought she was the most beautiful child he had ever seen. She smiled shyly at him. Will softly whispered into her ear that Hal was there to help her. Will was right about her eyes, they were the most beautiful piercing blue eyes he had ever seen, just as blue as the ocean.

Will whispered to Hal, "He is still out there. I can feel his evil spirit lurking." Will looked into Hal's eyes with pure intent saying, "You must find him!"

With a definitive stare, Hal return the intent to Will by saying, "We'll get him." Taking a deep breath, He said, "I'll need to see the area where you found her. May I use your phone?"

"Yes, it is in the living room area." Will sat quietly with Sqimi in his lap until Hal returned several minutes later.

"I have assigned my top four agents for protection. They'll arrive before nightfall." Hal stood over both of them knowing this was the right step to take.

"Hy'shge siam" Will bow his head. "It means thank you."

CHAPTER 4

THE WOODS

Todd whistled and kneeled down, "Wow, what happened here?" He closely examined the charred ground of where a cabin once stood. Towards the back of the cabin, he found some mud-filled imprints of boots and tiny bare feet. Todd assumed the smaller footprints belonged to the mysterious little girl. His sharp eye caught the presence of yet more prints. He knelt down and lightly fingered the surface. They were larger. His eyes followed the direction of the prints and came to an abrupt halt as the prints did alongside where the cabin had once stood. Standing and slowly pacing his steps toward the prints he spied fresh tire tracks leading into the thick of the woods. To the naked eye the footprints looked as if they belonged to several people but to Todd's trained eye he knew better. He knew in the pit of his stomach, this was the work of one person. He spoke aloud not to anyone in particular but Will was standing nearby and heard him exclaim, "If I didn't know better I'd swear whoever was here presented quite a temper tantrum!"

"Evil man is angry at Sqimi for having survived. He didn't count on Bandit protecting her or Baldy leading me to her." Will pointed to the sky and as if on cue, Baldy screeched as she flew by. He and Hal were standing near where Sqimi was found.

The agents were there to sift through the remains of the 'home' that once stood. "The evidence here will be thoroughly examined by our lead forensic expert, Joe Rizzo. We'll collect as much as we can. He's a whiz at pulling evidence from nothing. The tire tracks and footprints we can cast and go from there. There is no doubt in my mind the cabin was torched." It was Mark Lawson, the detail oriented agent who spoke this time. He placed his hands skillfully onto the badly burnt beam. He had years of experience and knew there was something odd about this fire. It had burned in a perfect circle. Even the evergreen trees surrounding the cabin weren't scorched. It seemed as if the tall trees stopped the fire from spreading.

Mike and Chris reappeared from within the woods. "The tire tracks seemed to have stopped part way thru the woods where the tree line narrowed but no vehicle." Mike scratched his head, "We looked for more tracks but it was as if they just disappeared." He looked at Mark and asked, "What do you suppose could have happened?"

Mike looked around and said, "Never mind the tracks, what happened here?"

"That's one question I think, only Sqimi can answer." Mark said.

Hal was riveted to the spot where Will found Sqimi. The leaves and grass were still matted down where she had lain. But the rain from the night before had washed away the blood that had once stained the grass. Hal kneeled heavily to the ground. He found tuffs of Bandit's fur and strands of the little girl's black hair. He placed them carefully into the evidence bags. So many questions swirled in his mind. He wondered how long had she lain there? How did she escape from him? What happened to her? Who attacked this little girl and why?

Unbeknownst to Will or Hal, Sqimi had left her protective corner of Will's truck and quietly crept up on them. She stood trembling near a very quiet Bandit; and fumbled nervously with his fur. She knew it was time. "He's bad. He's a very mean man."

Both men nearly jumped out of their skin. One because she was there and had snuck up on them and two, she spoke. Will gasped and looked at a surprised Hal. He quickly kneeled before her, "Sqimi, you can speak?" He touched her hand gingerly and asked, "Why are you here? You should've stayed in the truck."

She loosened her hand from Bandit's fur and pointed toward the four men in suits standing near the burned cabin. She spoke again, ignoring Will's questions. "Are they going to take the bad man away?" Arvidia pointed at the four men and Hal, her lips quivered now that she had spoken.

"Yes, they are. You're safe, my Sqimi. No one will ever hurt you again. I promise." Will spoke softly into her ear and pulled her close to him. She clasped her hands behind Will's neck and looked shyly at the five men that stood staring at her. Will gently lifted her up into the crook of his arms and slowly turned around and faced the startled men.

Sqimi leaned her body back so she could face Will. "I watched Baldy and I was afraid you wouldn't come back. Bandit came with me." She touched her small hand to Will's cheeks. She starred into Will's gentle face and whispered, "My name is Arvidia." Her beautiful blue eyes seemed to smile her name.

"I would never leave your side, Brave One;" Holding her to his stomach with his hands linked behind her. He was able to free one of his hands to stroke her long blue-black hair. "Your name is beautiful, Arvidia." He wanted her name spoken in love. Arvidia smiled shyly while the others looked on.

Elated, Will silently lifted praises and thanks to the Great One for answered prayers. He hugged her tightly then placed her lovingly on the ground next to Bandit.

Hal had heard the entire conversation between them and the way Will said her name. He turned to his men and hailed them over toward him. As they approached he thought to himself what an amazing step forward for Arvidia and a sad discovery of where she was found. "Gentleman, this is the little girl I spoke to you about. Her name is Arvidia." Hal signaled with hand signs to keep their demeanor low key, not too excitable.

Because of their boss, they knew exactly how and what to say. It was Todd that spoke for all of them. "On behalf of all of us special agents, it is a pleasure to meet you, Miss Arvidia." Todd gave a slight nod to her. She smiled and stuck next to Will for the time being.

"Let's sit and wait together Arvidia, for these nice men to finish their work. Come with me. We'll wait here on the tailgate of my truck." Will knew Hal would want to discuss more details with his crew. Without a word, she reached her hand into Will's as they walked away.

"Men, come look over here. Be careful. Comb thru this entire area." Hal looked into their eyes and said, "This is where Will found Arvidia with the um wolf." No more words were necessary.

The men, Chris, Mark, Mike and Todd were stunned once they laid eyes on the little girl. Despite her physical scars she was quite a beautiful little girl. *She survived this?* Thought, Todd. He had small kids of his own and he couldn't imagine harm coming to them. All four men seemed to be deep in their own thoughts as they looked at each other in disbelief.

Slowly Hal turned his attention away from where she was found and walked towards the truck where she and Will sat on the tailgate. Arvidia grasped Will's arm. Bandit emerged his enormous head from behind Arvidia's arm nearly pushing her off the tailgate. Suddenly, just as Hal began to approach Baldy flew sharply over his head. She screeched loudly at her displeasure. Startled, Hal nosedived into the ground flapping his arms wildly above his head. Baldy flapped her wings vigorously warning Hal. Bandit's lips parted slightly and he jumped off the truck and stood before Hal.

Arvidia put her hands to her mouth and giggled. Will looked at her and smiled. It was the first time he had heard her giggle. He had longed to hear her speak, laugh, and play. Will knew she was deeply afraid to part from his side. He'd told the other kids no when they had come to ask if she could come outside and play.

"Baldy is just teasing you." She signed some words with her hands to Baldy who immediately calmed down.

Will explained, to the surprised men whose jaws dropped, as they watched Arvidia "speak" to the eagle. He said, "I had taught her some simple signs so we would be able to communicate. One day, I turned and saw her "talking" to Baldy and Bandit. They seemed to understand her at a greater depth where we humans cannot. Sqimi has special gifts from the Great One."

The men joined in laughing with Arvidia much to Hal's annoyance. He stood up and wiped the dirt from his suit. "Darn bird!" He exclaimed.

Hal now stood in front of Arvidia and Will. Then just as she began to speak, it was Bandit's turn to protect his charge. Bandit let out a low growl. She pointed to his side. His suit coat had unbuttoned when he fell. "He does not like guns." Arvidia stroked Bandit's fur and signed to him to "sit" Bandit promptly sat, though he continued to bare his teeth.

"Oh." Hal handed his glock to Chris. Beads of sweat glistened on Hal's face and sweat seemed to pour out of his shirt. Being this close to an enormous wolf rattled his nerves to no end. He'd rather stand before a much wanted man with his glock than be this up close and personal with a wolf. Carefully, again, he stood to face Arvidia. He gently asked, "Arvidia, do you remember what happened here?"

Her face paled, her eyebrows flew up toward her hair line and her eyes widened in fear. Bandit's fur bristled up as he stood and bared his teeth ready to attack. Her hand shook as she pointed past Hal. Baldy screeched and flew off in the direction where she pointed and said, "That's the bad man!"

The hair on the back of Hal's neck stood up just as Bandit's did. His first thought was his holster was empty, he silently cursed himself. He then spun around and placed his body in front of Arvidia. He could now see the evil glint in the Bad Man's eyes even from forty yards away.

Bandit leapt into action just as the Bad Man sneered and sprinted into the woods. Chris threw Hal's glock his way and at the same time he hollered to the other men, "Quick! He's getting away!" It was a matter of seconds before they all scrambled in pursuit of both wolf and man towards the woods behind the burnt down cabin.

The men chased after him into the pines until they heard a jeep roar off deeper into the woods. Todd spoke gruffly, "I am betting money that this guy had to have had military training. He knows these woods well!" Todd's chest heaved as he kneeled to the ground.

Chris's shirt was soaked in sweat as he kicked the ground in frustration. "As long as that man is roaming free, this little girl's life is in danger. Did you see the look on his face? Wow, evil, pure and simple. I got chills just looking at him. Arvidia may know something that he does not want us to know."

"He's right." Mark leaned against the tree. "She needs our protection. I know we all may have grumbled about baby-sitting at one time or another. But there is obviously something more going on here." They all nodded in agreement.

Walking back to the charred remains of the cabin, Hal noticed Will and Arvidia were no longer on the tailgate but in the cab of the truck. Hal's eyebrows arched a bit," Where is the uh wolf?" Hal asked warily.

They'd almost forgotten about him. Bandit suddenly reappeared from the woods and stared cagily at the men, then walked arrogantly past them heading back to the truck. Hal and the Quad kept their distance behind him and followed.

"You guys finish up your investigation over to where she was found, and I'll ride back to the reservation with Will and Arvidia. Joe's going to need to come in with a crew and investigate the area with a fine tooth comb." The men did as Hal ordered without question. As they returned to the spot, Hal walked over to the truck.

Tapping lightly on the driver's side window, Will opened the door. Hal noticed a small knife in his hand as he laid it under the seat. Arvidia sat close by still slightly trembling. Hal asked, "May I ride back with you to your place and make a call?"

Will knew exactly what he wanted to do. He needed more help so he nodded his head in agreement. Hal walked to the front of the truck and climbed in. Arvidia seem to calm down. The ride back to Will's house was quiet.

Having parked the truck in front of Will's little brown house that tilted to the left, Hal got out first followed by Will with Arvidia in his arms. He waited until Will started up the steps and then he tagged along trying to keep his anxiety level down for Arvidia's sake.

Hal phoned Joe. Gave him the details, then hanging up the phone he returned to the porch where Arvidia sat on Will's lap. He thought it is now or never. I must get whatever information I can from this child.

Hal took the remaining rocking chair and rocked slowly even though his inner peace was anything but peaceful. Will knew instinctively Hal had to ask Arvidia questions so he started by saying, "Brave One, Hal needs to ask you some questions. It's okay. I trust him." She looked into Will's eyes and nodded agreement.

Hal watched the connection and realized again what a precious bond they shared. He would be respectful of that. "Arvidia, could you tell me what you remember?"

Arvidia hesitated and responded slowly, her eyes darted at Will who nodded his head in assurance she was safe. "The bad man hurt me. He was very angry. I was trying to hide." She rubbed her head where the crescent scar showed, "I have blips."

Both, Will and Hal wore confused looks, moments later, Hal asked, "What are blips?"

"They are like blinking, watch." Arvidia demonstrated by blinking rapidly.

Hal knew immediately she could see bits and pieces of her traumatic memory. This was not going to be easy. He signed and said, "Okay honey, I understand. We'll talk some more later." Hal could hear the Jeep Cherokee coming in now with his men. He stood and Will knew what to do.

Will placed her into the chair as he stood and spoke softly to her, "Sit here Brave One. I will say good bye to the men for now."

Meeting Hal at the jeep with the others he caught part of the conversation.

"Guessing we're staying put?" Todd was saying.

"What?" Will asked.

Hal answered, "They found a hunter's knife with blood." He showed Will the bag with the evidence tag taped to it. "I'll be taking this back to Seattle and see if our man, Joe Rizzo or his team can lift some prints. "I've ordered the men to stay. He's still out there. You and Arvidia need protection."

"Of course, I have room for two. I am sure Running Bull who lives next door to me can house the other two." Will look, relieved.

"Excellent. That will do. I will return as quickly as possible." Hal looked towards Arvidia and gave her a short wave, said his goodbyes, knowing both Will and Arvidia would be safe.

The following morning Todd woke suddenly to the roar of the ocean, the loud cawing of the seagulls, and the aroma of scrambled eggs and toast. He kicked his snoring partner's foot who sat up suddenly, tossing his head side to side, he continued to wake up.

"Wow, I can't remember the last time I slept that soundly!" Mark said running his hands thru his tousled brown hair while placing his bare feet onto the floor; He stood and stretched. He yawned loudly and strode over to the window which rattled with his approaching steps. He stretched again, "Must be the fresh air or something."

"Yeah, I know what you mean. I almost forgot where I was!" Todd's stomach gurgled as the scent of the eggs and bacon assaulted his senses. "Hey, I'm going to check on Arvidia and see what is up with that amazing smell."

"Okay, I'm going to take a shower first." Mark noticed a stack of neatly folded brown towels on the dresser. He grabbed them and headed for the shower.

Todd peered into Arvidia's room. He saw the various dream catchers that hung around her room. It wasn't hard to miss Bandit sprawled out on her bed. Todd searched for Arvidia who slept soundly with her Indian rag doll all rolled up. Bandit quickly lifted his head and stared hard at Todd. Todd was tempted to stare back, but decided messing with the mammoth size wolf wasn't worth it. He partially closed her bedroom door and tiptoed away.

He found Will busy in the kitchen making an incredible size breakfast that could feed an army. His stomach gurgled loudly. Will turned and smiled at him. "Sit! Eat! There is plenty left!"

Surprised Todd said, "Left?"

"Yes, Chris and Mike walked out just a few minutes before you got up. They went back to Running Bull's house."

Todd hungrily looked at the table and sat down. He gleefully scooped up a big helping of scrambled eggs and bacon. Hearing the shower turned off he knew Mark would be joining him soon.

"How long have you been an agent Mr. Riley?" Will asked as he cleaned the kitchen counter.

"Please call me Todd." He swallowed hard and cleared his throat, "Mark and I became special agents a few years ago. I met him, my partner, during an investigation of a large drug ring we busted six years ago in Spokane, Washington. We clicked right away and have been partners ever since."

"Are you married?" Will inquired.

"Yes, I am happily married to my beautiful wife, Pam for almost seven years now. We knew each other in high school."

"Wow, that's great! Your job must be tough on her at times. What about kids?"

"She's incredibly supportive of me, especially when I first went to college and then to the academy. I know she worries about me but she knows I'm doing something I love to do." Todd took a swig of milk and swished it around his mouth before he spoke again. "I have two kids. Joshua is 4 years old and my daughter, Michelle just turned 2. I'm sorry I don't have any pictures of them, I don't carry them with me due to my job."

"I understand. I will most certainly keep you fellas in prayer while you look for this man."

"Thank you, sir." Will nodded his head.

"Hey! Bro, save me some!" Mark smacked Todd in the back of his head as he walked into the tiny kitchen. "Showers open. This smells delicious! Thank you for making this Will."

"Not a problem fellas. The eggs are fresh from the chicken coop but bacon, not so much." Will whispered, "Please sit and enjoy. I am going to go check on Arvidia."

Todd shoveled more food into his chipmunk size cheeks. "This has to be the best darn breakfast I've had in a while! Shh, don't tell Pam I said that!"

Mark laughed, "Imagine all this for us."

"Chris and Mike ate before we did!" Todd mentioned.

"What? You mean there was more?" Mark looked around the kitchen, "He's got enough to feed an army!" Mark soon felt full as did Todd. He set his fork down and looked at his watch. "When do you think Joe will get here?"

"I would not be surprised if he is on his way up with all his equipment." Todd chuckled.

They always ribbed Joe for overdoing it as far as what equipment to bring to a crime scene. It always looked like a portable lab. Despite their ribbings, they knew Joe was a thorough investigator and could always count on him as far as digging for evidence to levels most investigators would not attempt to or had not thought of. All he needed was one piece of evidence and Joe is able to pull a story out of it. Hal knew his gifts were rare and recruited him to his team about the same time Todd and Mark were hired.

Little footsteps could be heard as Will encouraged Arvidia to enter the kitchen. "Come say hello, Sqimi."

Todd and Mark turned their heads towards Arvidia who walked into the kitchen pigeon toed with her rag doll dragging on the floor. Behind Will was an anxious Bandit who pushed his head around Will once he spied Arvidia. He then promptly sat down panting tongue hanging out and all.

"Hey little one, how are you?" asked Todd. Arvidia starred hungrily at the bacon. Todd handed her a piece of bacon. She happily crunched onto it while Will reminded her to say thank you.

"Thank you." Her voice was soft. She shifted her feet and looked at the two men. She promptly grabbed a handful of bacon from the plate and gave it to Bandit, who happily gobbled it up wanting more.

Observantly, Mark stated, "She's so fearless of him."

"She trusts him. If it weren't for him, she wouldn't have survived the night." Will shuddered at the thought of Arvidia alone in the woods.

"Hal told us about that. It is amazing she survived. Rest assured Will, we will get him." Todd stated firmly.

Will inhale sharply, "I have complete faith in you, gentlemen. You'll catch him. When you have finished eating, I would like to show you guys around the reservation and introduce you to our people since you'll be here indefinitely."

"Actually, I'm quite full. What about you Mark?"

Mark patted his stomach, "Ditto. I'm ready to walk this off!"

A few moments later they all walked out together. Will started speaking with much pride. "The Lemaltcha Tribe consisted of extended families. Most of them have lived on the reservation all their lives. Some of the young adults enrolled in the military, others went to college and the rest stayed behind and carried out their forefathers traditions." The sound of his voice faded a little as the agents observed how the tribal members treated him with deep respect. Mark noticed a small leather pouch around Will's waist. At times when anyone approached he would pull something out of it and hold their hand. He would close his eyes and speak in their native Salish language. Arvidia walked beside him carrying her rag doll, still in bare feet.

Mark asked, "Sir, if I may, what is that pouch you're carrying?"

Will looked down and patted the pouch. "These are various herbs to heal the sick. They grow wild all over the island. I was taught by my great-grandfather about the healing effects of herbs. I not only serve as their chief, but I am also their Shaman man. As a matter of fact, I used some of the herbs on her." Arvidia slipped her hands into Will's. Out of the corner of his eye, he noticed Bandit walking swiftly towards the woods. He knew his pack would be waiting to hunt. He knew Bandit would not stray far.

"Hello, Chief Miles!" an elderly Indian woman sat on a stoop. Her hands swiftly hemmed the nylon ropes into the weave of the net-like material which served as seines net for fishing.

"Hello Annie, how are you doing? How are you feeling?" Will approached her with Arvidia by his side.

Annie smiled a toothless grin and laughed softly, "I'm fine Chief. The darn knees ache like they always do but the Great One blesses me with another day." Her hands continued to hem as they spoke.

"You are quite right Annie." He lightly patted her hands. She stopped briefly and clasped onto his. She bowed her head and Will prayed in their native Salish language. It became apparent to the agents observing that Annie was blind.

"Amen Chief, Amen." Annie boldly asked, "Who are the strangers?"

"Annie, these four gentlemen are FBI agents from Seattle, Washington. They are here to help Sqimi. This is Todd Riley, Mark Smith, Chris Magin and Mike Lawson." Each of the men shook her hand.

"Welcome gentlemen. I do hope you catch that evil twisted person!" She whispered excitedly saying, "Chief, I hear she finally spoke!"

"Yes she did, her name is Arvidia." Will was surprised to see Arvidia approaching Annie who set down her net and held out her hands towards her. She lightly touched her face.

She softly spoke her name, "Arvidia, what a pretty name for a pretty girl."

Arvidia responded in a soft voice, "Thank you." She stepped back slowly and slid her hands back into Will's.

"Stop again, Chief, and bring Arvidia with you." She silently returned to her netting.

Will continued walking around the reservation with the agents, introducing them to various tribe members. The agents were continually looking around the reservation observing the men, women, and children milling about their daily activities. Word spread fast among the tribe members that Arvidia was finally speaking and that the agents were there to help protect her and them.

Eventually, Will brought the agents to the heart of the Island, the docks. Just before ascending onto the beach, Mark noticed several beautiful decorated canoes lined up with the oars neatly stacked up against the wall of the building where fishing and crabbing equipment could be bought. Todd walked over and lightly rubbed the sides of the canoes.

"Do you make these?" Todd asked.

"Yes, with the other tribe members. We usually use them to visit other tribes."

"That's amazing work." Chris said as he rubbed the sides of the canoes as well. Many of them were painted with the eagle's face throughout the entire canoe.

"It's called, Paddle to Lummi." Will, cleared his throat, and begins to speak again of the Lemaltcha Tribe. "We have an annual event called, Paddle to Lummi. Our sister tribes join in the celebration of peace among our people. All our canoes are brightly crafted with the eagle symbol, while others have their own."

"What's the meaning of the oars?" Todd seemed captivated by the canoes.

"Is this the common way to come onto the reservation?" Mike asked.

Will chuckled saying, "Slow down boys. Regarding the oars, I stand out in the sea with both hands raised showing they have permission to come onto the island. They lift their oars in an upright position meaning, they come in peace. To answer your question, Mike, there are two ways to come onto the reservation. One is the road next to my home the other by boat, which is quicker."

"What kind of fish do you catch?" Mike asked.

"King Salmon is our bestseller, but we also catch Trout, as well as crabbing for shellfish and King Crab."

"I wonder, if our guy passed through here?" Mark asked.

"I doubt that," said Will "He seems to prefer, hiding in the woods. Besides he'd be noticed."

Mark responded sarcastically, "Easier to blend in no doubt."

Suddenly, Todd remembered, "Speaking of woods, we should see if Joe has arrived?"

"Is this the Joe Rizzo, the one Hal spoke about?"

"Yes."

"I will show you the way back to the house." They proceeded up the slight hill where Bandit stood waiting for Arvidia.

CHAPTER 5

JOE RIZZO

Joe stepped out of the Jeep Cherokee and straightened his glasses. He was a wiry kind of guy whose brain always seems to be on the go. He is quick to think on his feet and has the unique gift of being able to extract evidence, even from the most minuscule of samples. He rarely leaves his sanctuary of the lab. When Hal ordered him he left. Hal wouldn't order out of the lab until he really needed his expertise.

He wasn't sure which direction to head once he stepped outside of his jeep. He felt awkward due to the suspicious stares darting towards him from the residents of this remote island. He instinctively went to the back of the jeep and rechecked to make sure he brought all the equipment he needed. Knowing he had more than enough, he also knew without a doubt, the guys would rib him about it.

While Joe was moving some equipment around inside the jeep he heard rustling of tree branches and he had the distinct feeling someone was staring at him. Hal had warned him about the eagle and the wolf. He carefully shut the hatch of the jeep and glanced sideways towards the trees. Sucking in his breath, he watched as Baldy sat boldly on the tree branch staring hard at him. Hal was right, she was an enormous bird. He heard and recognized the voices coming over the hill. The guys were waving at him.

"Hey Joe, how was the drive up?" Todd peered through the windows of the jeep, "I don't think you brought enough equipment!" The other agents laughed. *And so it begins.* Joe thought. He smiled and chuckled to himself.

"Joe, this is Will Miles, he is the Chief of the tribe here." Mark quickly stated. "The little one hiding behind him is Arvidia." Joe nodded his head and craned his neck to get a glimpse of Arvidia who shyly peered around Will's leg. Joe looked into her blazing blue eyes and noted the scars on her forehead and neck. He thought of the knife Hal had

27

processed and was thankful to put a stat rush on the knife. He was able to lift a print from the knife.

"Hello Sir, it's a pleasure to meet you." Joe said with a firm handshake. He squatted down and peered around Will's leg. "Hello, Miss Arvidia. I'm Joe." Joe was about to stick his hand out to shake her's until he noticed the enormous wolf. *Whoa! Wow, he's huge!* He thought. He almost tumbled back but regained his composure.

"Hi." Arvidia said quietly, she giggled at his glasses which had slid down his nose due to the sweat dripping off his face.

Mark gently slapped Joe on his back, "Will, this is Joe Rizzo, our chief, if you will, of forensics. This guy can do forensic research like no other. I know he will be able to identify and put a name to, whomever it is that is terrorizing this little girl."

"Welcome to Lummi Island. Whatever you need, do not hesitate to ask. You are welcome to stay with one of my tribal members until your work is done." Will offered.

"How long does Hal want you to stay?" asked Mike.

Joe stood up slowly and turned towards Mike, "He said three days max. I need to see the site so I can better assess how much time I need. Oh, before I forget to mention this, I did manage to lift a print off the knife and put a rush on it."

"Good. How long do you think it'll take?" Todd asked.

"It should take a few days. I'll call the lab tomorrow and see if anything has come back."

"Okay let's do this, Chris and Mike you stay here with Will and Arvidia. Mark and I will take Joe up to the site and show'em around."

Joe spoke to the Chief saying, "Chief Miles, thank you for your hospitality, I'll probably work through today and tonight. I'd like to get as much work done as soon as possible. I heard on the radio that there was a chance of rain tonight. I plan to come back here in the morning and check in with the lab about the fingerprint. Is that okay with you, Sir?"

"Please call me Will. Anything you need." He gently rubbed Arvidia's long black hair as he spoke. Her hair shone in the sun with a hue of blue. Joe starred at her before turning back towards his jeep. She smiled at him and hid behind Will's leg. He looked at the other guys as they knowingly nodded their heads towards him.

Todd shouted to Chris and Mike, "Maybe we'll be back before dusk. If you need anything, use the talkie. Fire a warning shot or use deadly force. Until we find out who we're dealing with, we've no idea what we are up against." Todd sat down inside the jeep as Mark muttered to himself trying to find a seat in the back while shuffling Joe's equipment around.

"Not a problem." Chris answered.

Joe put the jeep into drive and once again, starred at Arvidia before driving off into the woods. He shook his head and said to no one in particular, "I don't even want to know what happened to that beautiful little girl. She really doesn't remember anything?"

Todd shook his head. "Nope, she remembers what she calls 'blips'. She really couldn't tell Hal much about what happened to her. He is going to send Louanne to see if she can help her." Todd turned to look at Mark in the backseat, "Remember her?" Todd chuckled.

"Yeah," Mark made a face and looked out the window then said, "I haven't seen her in a long time, almost forgot she works with kids," Still longingly looking out the window, he asked, "when's she coming?"

"Hal mentioned that to me too. She is coming within the next day or so." Joe grinned and looked in the rearview mirror. He knew Mark had a special liking to Louanne. Mark was busily looking down and mindlessly checking his gun.

A sly grin crept across Todd's face. He too checked his gun as Joe was almost approaching the site. He wouldn't razz Mark any longer, it was time to work. "Joe, I sure hope you find something. I have a gut feeling whatever she knows it's more that what's here." He clicked the chamber shut on his gun and said, "Ready Mark?"

Mark returning to the present, answered sternly, "I'm back. Let's go."

Joe jumped out of the jeep. His adrenaline was running high through his veins. He quickly scanned the site and opened the hatch of the jeep without a word and set to work. Mark and Todd never interfered with Joe or his equipment. He was territorial on the crime scene and even worse in the lab.

"I assume this is where Arvidia was found?" Joe was walking to the site where her body had lain as he spoke.

Astonished, Mark asked "How did you know?"

"I know you guys. You're protecting the area as you do with all victims whether they are here or not." Joe said observantly as he squatted down. He carefully looked around before touching anything. Pulling out some tweezers from his carefully packed plastic bag, he began to part a pile of leaves beneath the tree trunk. "Hmm," Joe became excited as he held up a leaf. It had a familiar and distinctive odor. Placing the leaf into the evidence bag he looked up at the guys and declared, "This leaf has dead tissue on it as well as follicle hair. It definitely does not belong to Arvidia." He continued to place markers and crawled around the ground crouching for more evidence.

Mark and Todd weren't surprised at Joe's findings and decided to wander around the immediate site again. "Hey, Mark." Todd called, "More fresh footprints." He squatted down to take a closer look. Mark joined him.

"Looks to me like, he's carrying something or rather dragging something, heavy, like a trunk or a box or something of that sort. It seemed to have come from that direction near the cabin door."

In unison they both said, "A safe!" They both had seen a huge black box not ten feet from where they stood. After checking it out they found it empty.

"You would think he would have to have help but he did this himself." Mark agreed. They both walked towards the woods while following the tracks. Unbeknownst to them and hiding in the evergreen trees, was the Bad Man.

Meanwhile, Joe had approached the blackened walls of the cabin and peered inside. He carefully stepped onto the charred remains of the cabin floor. Parts of the floor had collapsed into what appeared to be a basement. He lowered himself onto the burnt steps which creaked as he put weight on them. He slowly crept down. He flashed his flashlight about and was startled to see something strange that caught his eye in the corner of the basement. He walked over to it and placed his gloved hands onto the badly melted steel bars, he thought, this had to be the origin of the fire. *This wasn't just a basement, it was a jail!* Joe exclaimed to himself. He climbed carefully over the partially collapsed bars. His adrenaline running high again, he knew he was onto something. He squatted down and slowly flashed his light around the stone foundation. His trained eye caught something odd about one of the stones, not wanting to disturb any potential evidence he carefully stepped over to the rock and noticed it wasn't a rock but rather dirt. He immediately deduced how Arvidia may have escaped. *A tunnel! How did she dig herself out?* Joe was puzzled. The tunnel was small and short. He peered through the tunnel and could see daylight and smell the pine. Pulling out his tweezers again and more evidence bags, he placed strands of black hair, a piece of cloth and samples of dirt into each bag. Stepping back, so he could take some pictures of the tunnel, he stubbed his foot on a partially hidden, what he assumed, was a bag of with a wet cloth inside. Leaning down and carefully picking up the bag he attempted to open it but decided against it. The bag was too fragile. *I'll examine this in the lab.* Joe thought.

"Joe! Where are you?" Todd hollered.

"I'm downstairs in the cabin. You guys got to come and take a look at this." Joe said solemnly.

Todd and Mark carefully made their way down into the barren cabin. They were both shocked to see where Joe was standing.

"Is that a . . ?" Mark stopped speaking when he saw Joe shaking his head yes.

"I think I know how she escaped." Joe stated. He turned around and showed them the tunnel.

"Is it possible she dug herself out?" Todd scratched his head.

"She must've been here a while, for a child her size it would've taken time to dig this out." Joe stated.

"Did you find anything else?" Todd asked.

"Just this bag, it's badly damaged by the fire and water most likely from the rain. I'll analyze it in the lab." Joe answered.

"The fire definitely started here." Mark pointed towards the burnt entrance of the cell. The stench of the gasoline still hung heavily in the air. "The fire spread quickly up this wall and over the ceiling. She's lucky to have made it out alive. This was one big fireball."

Todd peered again through the tunnel and looked back at Mark. He was fuming.

Mark shook his fist. He was just as angry as Todd, "Hang in there man, we'll get him."

"We need to find out who it is first before we can hunt this guy down." Todd spoke just as Joe looked up at them.

"I'm pretty sure we'll find out soon who's behind this. I'm positive the print on the knife will tell us. Did you guys find anything out there?" Joe nodded towards the woods.

"Yeah, we found an empty safe not far from the cabin." Todd raised his hands at Joe, and said, "Don't worry, we didn't touch it, the door to the safe was left open. I'm sure Mark and I can carry it back to the jeep."

"It's starting to get dark. I think we should head back to the reservation and return in the morning. Joe, if you are thinking what I am thinking, I don't think it's a good idea for you to stay here. He's obviously still around." Mark stated firmly.

Joe knew he was right. "Yeah, yeah, I know you're right. Let's go."

The three of them paused at the base of what was left of the scorched steps. They turned, looked at the remains of the cell and then looked at each other. No words were needed. They proceeded out of the cabin and headed towards the safe. Joe took pictures and carefully dusted for prints.

While Joe did his thing, Mark and Todd walked over to the back of the cabin where the opening of the tunnel was. They both tried to piece together the possibilities of what may have happened.

"She had to have tried to run away from him. I think these are her footprints, but they stop?" Mark shook his head quizzically.

"Maybe he grabbed her, but wait, look here, footprints start up again. They go towards the tree where Will found her. Whatever's happened, the injuries she sustained, happened between here and where she was found."

"I agree." Mark said solemnly.

Joe approached. "Guys, I'm all set. I'll move some stuff around in the jeep to make room for the safe."

Mark and Todd went to retrieve the safe. As they squatted down to lift up the safe, Mark spotted something lying in the grass. "Wait a sec, Todd." He quickly walked over to it and could smell it before he got there. The ember of the cigarette burned slowly on the ground, it poofed itself out and Mark quickly placed it in the evidence bag. He hurried back to Todd.

"What's wrong?" Todd could tell something spooked Mark.

Mark, wild-eyed and alert spoke in a near whisper saying, "We need to get out of here fast, he's here. That was a cigarette butt I found. He's watching us." They both looked and listened for a moment. All that could be heard was silence except the rustling of the tall trees.

Strategically they moved quickly and with precision to carry the safe back to the jeep as fast as possible. Joe was headed towards them but their eyes told a different story. Joe knew something was amiss. "What gives?" Joe grumbled.

"Get into the jeep now!" Todd spoke with authority. Joe obeyed as Mark and Todd placed the safe in the back of the jeep and they both drew their weapons. Joe watched and knew trouble was brewing. He turned the key and the engine hummed. Both men climbed into the jeep and Todd stated, "Floor it, Joe." Joe shoved the gears into drive and drove off fast with the dirt spinning behind them.

The Bad Man sat in the tree watching them. He flicked another cigarette to the ground and climb down from the tree. He strode over to where his jeep was hidden. He almost let out a cackle as he thought how stupid these agents were.

Joe drove quickly back to the reservation and parked in front of Will's home. Will was in his usual rocking chair. Bandit lay at the foot of the stairs and on the steps was Arvidia holding onto her Indian rag doll, listening to the red-headed lady sitting with her. Chris and Mike stood at the entrance of the porch. They both waved to the other agents and walked down the porch steps.

Joe said, before exiting the jeep, "Mark, Louanne is here."

Mark cleared his throat, his voice croaked as he spoke, "Yeah, I see her."

Todd laughed, "Man, go talk to her!"

"Hey guys, you find anything interesting?" Chris asked.

Todd beckoned them over to him and he spoke softly about the findings of the cell as well as informing them that they were being watched closely.

"What! Are you serious?" Chris was shocked and Mike quietly shook his head.

"I am not going to tell Will about this, I'll let Hal decide. I will say this. There is something fishy going on out there. We need to find out what it is."

Chris decided to change the subject when he noticed Will had moved from his rocking chair to the foot of the stairs. He obviously knew something was up. Chris slips Todd a bill, "You think Mark is ever going to ask her out?"

Mike laughed, "Five bucks he doesn't." He also slapped a five dollar bill into Todd's hand.

"I don't know, he just might ask her." Todd chuckled.

Will was no longer at the foot of the stairs but standing at Todd's side.

"Todd, is everything alright?" Will asked.

"Yes, Sir. We found a few things that may help us in our investigation but we won't know for sure until Joe analyzes it. He is going back up there in the morning. Then he'll head back up to Seattle."

"Hmm," Will silently nodded his head and returned to his rocking chair.

Todd spoke under his breath to Chris and Mike, "Someone please tell me he bought that."

"Nope . . . he knows something is up." Mike stated.

"Like I said, I'm leaving that up to Hal. I don't think it's my place to tell him. In fact, I'm not so sure I would want to tell him. Speaking of which, I need to call Hal. I'll be right back." Todd walked towards the porch and asked to use the phone once again. Will nodded.

"Okay Arvidia, you did a good job. I'll talk with you again tomorrow." Louanne gently touched her hand. Arvidia stood up and went to sit with Bandit. There she sat and played with her doll.

Mark rubbed his hands together and shoved them into his jean pockets. "So, how's it going?" Mark caught Louanne's attention as she stepped from the porch.

"She is going to be one tough nut to crack." Louanne stated, "She's been severely traumatized and honestly, it may take years for her to deal with the trauma she has suffered. I do find her intriguing to talk to and observe. How've you been? I haven't seen you around the office lately."

Mark slightly blushed, "We've been up here investigating this baffling case. We did find something up at the site which may help you counsel her. We believe Arvidia may have been locked in a cell in the basement of the cabin. She may have dug her way out through a tunnel. Joe collected as much evidence as possible and I won't be surprised if he wants to head back tomorrow to work on it."

Louanne gasped and quietly stated, "A cell?"

"We think so. The only person that can tell us that is her." Mark pointed at Arvidia. In the distance, the phone was ringing from Will's living room. Todd came out and beckoned to Joe. The call was for him.

Joe bounded up the stairs quickly. He hoped this was the news he was waiting for. A few moments later he returned to the porch and cleared his throat. Most everyone turned their heads and gave Joe the attention he commanded. A woman from the tribe appeared at Will's nod and whisked Arvidia away.

"I just spoke to Glenn from the lab, we have identified the suspect. His name is Jim Mason. Hal is running a background check as we speak and he hopes to be here tomorrow with more information."

"Well, 'Bad Man' Mason we know who you are. We know what you are. It won't be long before we have the whole story. We'll catch you." Todd stated with certainty.

CHAPTER 6

JIM MASON

Once Hal learned who he was dealing with he immediately contacted the local authorities. He briefly explained who Jim Mason was and why the situation was of great importance. The sheriff agreed to meet with his staff at the docks at six the following morning. Together they would begin a full investigation of the suspect. Who he was, where he had come from and most importantly, where would he be now. Capturing him would be another task put before them that had to take top priority, for obvious reasons. So, while Hal put his men at the station gathering that information he headed back to the reservation. After the phone call from Todd, he believed the whereabouts of Jim Mason was too close at hand. The life of that little girl was at stake and he was still an hour out. The only thing he knew right now was his name, the fact he had been in the Army and that he was an avid outdoorsman. His men would find out more on his family history but at this moment there were too many holes to fill and not enough time. He'd worry more about Jim Mason when he had him in custody.

There was something else nagging at Hal in the back of his mind. It was about the two kidnappings. He felt there was a connection with Jim Mason and the recent disappearance of two small girls as well as the introduction of a new street drug called, Blue Dust. Perhaps it was the fact the Mason didn't run. According to Todd they were sure he was close by. So why wouldn't he run? He had a chance to get away, to make a clean break, for now anyway.

He made a call to Louanne from his car phone to find out if she collected anymore information from Arvidia. After the third ring he hung up. The phone rang a few minutes later it was her.

"Hal, it's me, Louanne. Are you on your way?"

"Hi Louanne, Yes I should be at the rez in about 40 minutes. What do you have for me?" Hal watched the road carefully as she spoke.

"Not much I'm afraid. She's pretty traumatized, but did make a statement about the big moon. I'm assuming she is talking about the full moon. She mentioned how the Bad Man became mean when the moon was big."

Hal felt the hairs on the back of his neck stand straight up. He had to quickly pull over. "Louanne, what did you say?" He knew but he had to hear her say it again to be sure.

"She said the Bad Man was mean when the moon was big." She paused then asked, "Is that significant?"

"It very well could be. Thank you for your help, Louanne. Keep talking to her. She has no idea how much she is helping even with the smallest detail." Hal took a breath and said, "I'll talk to you soon. I better get moving'." Hal hung up and quickly put the gearshift into drive and took off, leaving dust and rocks flying in his wake.

Hal knew there was some kind of connection and the puzzle pieces were coming together, it may only be one, but it was more than what he had started out with this morning. He remembered reading about the other two disappearances, it had happened during the full moon. But that drug, hmmmm . . . what else had he heard about it? Searching the findings within his mind, he recalled the drug was indeed a very bad one. It caused severe cyanosis of the skin and severe respiratory distress. Some local kids had died and others were lucky to be out in the world searching in vain to buy more. The DEA agents tried desperately to track the pushers, but it seemed they too disappeared as quickly as they came. It was never the same people selling it and they had no clue as to who was processing it for sale on the streets of Bellingham moving towards Seattle.

Hal phoned Will's place and Todd answered, he simply stated he was at the docks and hung up.

The air was thick with fog, the mist silently passed over the docks and as this happened, and footprints remained on the docks and were easily spotted as they effortlessly tracked him. He waited, patiently pacing, for his agents to arrive. The ocean lapped the rocks quietly as if it knew what was about to transpire.

He heard the car pull up and out stepped his agents. As they walked in unison towards Hal he noticed there was something different about them. When they came closer he could see they had black stripes on their faces. His eyebrows arched a bit and he gave his men a curious stare, and says, "Not even going to ask." He pauses, "Yet."

The men shrugged their shoulders and grinned before getting serious and taken hold of all that Hal had to share.

"We have an important matter to attend to." Hal stated. Almost in an instant the air was charged with energy. Shortly thereafter, many members of the local authorities showed up in droves. Hal was quick to direct and disperse the photo of Jim Mason and their assignments. Once the authorities were in place Hal took a moment to explain.

"We will execute our public duty to capture this man, Jim Mason, today and/or within 48 hours." Hal paused as the men and women watched with unknowing eyes. "There is reason to believe," Hal knew it was merely his gut that was the "reason" but he trusted his gut time and time again. He continued, "Jim Mason has a connection with the two local kidnappings, sorry, 'alleged' kidnappings, and alleged association with the distribution of 'Blue Dust'. This makes him more than dangerous to not only Arvidia, but to all of us. He will be armed and he may possibly be using. He knows the woods well." Hal pointed towards the tree lined area away from the beach. "He knows how to kill and he apparently has no remorse about doing so. Todd, give us what you know." Hal stepped back as Todd made his way forward.

He stepped up to where Hal stood and keeping his voice monotone and direct he spoke at a level just about a whisper. "Sound travels on the docks and we don't want Mason catching wind of our words. He may already be watching; so I'll say this once, he's making mistakes. While we were at the crime scene last night, we, well, we felt him there and a burning cigarette butt confirmed this. None of us smoke so we high-tailed it out of there. We have sent our CSI, Joe Rizzo home this morning." Todd pointed out to Chris and Mike, "Chris and Mike took first watch last night and reported all was quiet." Todd nodded to his partner, Mark. Mark and I have been awake since 2 this morning and again, we didn't hear or see anything out of sorts, but walking to one of our vehicles to join all of you we did see fresh tracks. They were approximately 20 feet away from Will's home. We also spotted fresh cigarette butts burned out and they were damp. We were confident to call on several local tribesmen to stand guard until our return." Todd took a breath and said, "He's tripping up and seems more concerned with something, perhaps more Arvidia than he is about getting caught. She's safe. We removed her from her safe house about 10pm last night, after our umm, well, warrior gathering." Todd glanced at Hal's surprisingly, understanding eyes. Hmmmm . . . He thought he may just have known this would happen, we'll talk later.

Hal took over again, "Okay here's the plan. As Todd has stated, he's slipping up. The approximate location is 10 minutes north of here. It's all woods, Men. If we encircle this area we will," Hal placed the map on top of Todd's jeep, "be able to cautiously surround him. Let me make this plain and simple, if you get a sight of 'em, take 'em out. Vests! Ammo! Partner up! We move in five." Hal folded up his map and stuck it in his back pocket. The crowd quickly dispersed and Hal walked over to Todd. "Where is she?"

"She's in one of Bandit's caves. I have two tribesmen nearby the entrance of the cave and two in the trees and of course, Bandit and Will are inside the cave with her." Todd grinned he knew he'd done well. "Will is going to tell her they are on an adventure." Hal grimaced slightly when he mentioned Bandit, but he knew deep down within him she was perfectly safe and hopefully by the time lunch came she would be back at Will's safe and sound.

Hal and the four agents walked deep in the woods that skirted the edge of the reservation. Not a sound could be heard except the occasional cackling of the crows high above in the trees. Hal knew the other authorities were at their posts. The air was thick with tension. Todd put a finger to his mouth and pointed to the ground, fresh tire tracks and prints. Hal knew Jim was in close range. They quickly moved to their posts, guns drawn and whispers of prayers as the unknown unfolded.

Shots rang out echoing off the evergreens. It was difficult to distinguish exact location but Mike was positive. He signaled Hal that it had come from the west where they stood. Slowly and in rhythm they progressed. Crouching down, guns drawn it was Jim that became impatient.

"She was not supposed to live!" Jim's voice echoed loudly throughout the woods. The men froze. "She ruined my plans. She will pay!"

Hal took the lead and shouted back, "Jim, let's talk about this."

"There's nothing to talk about."

"There's no need for blood shed. We just want you to come in and talk to us." Hal waited. He watched Todd and Mark slither by and crouched behind the trees just past where they assumed Jim stood. His chest heaved in anticipation as he watched daylight slowly approaching, beads of sweat dripped down his face. He could also feel a sharp prickle of bark brushed against his shoulders bringing with it a pinch of pain.

"NO! I have to have that girl." Several shots are fired again this time aiming towards Hal.

Hal watched two of the local authorities clutch their chests and fall to the ground, two more move over to them and placing index fingers to their necks, they signaled to Hal they were gone.

"Surrender your weapon. You are totally surrounded. Throw out your weapon and come out with your hands up!" ordered Hal.

Todd signaled to Mark that he had a visual of him and to follow his steps. Having spotted Jim behind one of the trees, they were able to position themselves behind him and together they slowly aimed their glocks at him.

Jim swung around when he heard the twigs snap. His eyes were black as coal. His skin was nearly as gray as his hair. He laughed.

Todd and Mark ordered, "Drop your weapon!"

Realizing he didn't have much of a choice, Jim tossed his gun off to the side. Todd and Mark approached weapons still drawn, as Mark glanced past Jim he watched Hal approached. In a blink of an eye, Jim lunged at Mark knocking him to the ground. Todd charged at Jim blindsiding him to the ground just as he did when he played ball. They had him cuffed and flipped over before he ever knew what hit him.

"Mark, you okay?"

"Yeah," He groaned as he slowly made his way to an upright position. "Read him his rights and haul this jerk in." Hal walked over as Mark stood, "We got him." He wiped the sweat off his forehead and breathed heavily.

Hal heaved a sigh of relief saying, "Good job, Men."

Todd spoke, "We heard shots fired everybody okay?"

Hal shook his head, "He got two of the locals." He paused and said, "He'll pay for as well."

The rest of the local authorities gathered around surrounding Jim as they dragged him out of the woods. "We'll take good care of him." the local sheriff, Sam, sneered.

Hal stood next to Todd and Mark just as Chris and Mike joined them, Hal had some questions for all four of them. "So, you guys did the warrior dance?"

All four guys touched their face in unison, but it was Todd that spoke up as usual. "We've never experienced anything like it." Todd looked at the others and they all nodded in agreement as he continued. "Once we agreed we would participate, Will took us over to the hill and they were all ready to set up. They had bright colored costumes, made of buckskins, large headdresses and huge drums."

Mark could not contain himself, even though the pain in his back from Jim's attack, he had to interrupt. "Yeah, the music and the songs were so peaceful. It was absolutely an amazing experience. Will came to each one of us and while he spoke in his native tongue he marked our faces with these black stripes. He told us afterwards he prayed for our safe return. Then he had us get up and dance with them."

Hal grinned, "You guys danced? I would've paid money to see that." His agents smiled and shook their heads.

Mike puffed out his chest and stated, "I feel like a new man. It may have been strange but I'd do it again." The others nodded in agreement.

The men made their way out of the woods.

Jim Mason's trial spanned over three months. Hal firmly told the well-respected Judge Karen Shately that Arvidia had no memory of what happened. He did not want her further traumatized by testifying in court, as recommended by Louanne. The judge concurred. Hal and his agents attended the trial daily until the jury found him guilty of all charges. The Judge sentenced him to life in prison without possibility of parole.

As the deputies approached Jim to handcuff him and haul him away to the federal prison Jim turned and sneered at them. "I'm not done yet." Deputies quickly escorted him away from the media frenzy that stood outside the courtroom.

"Man that is one crazy dude. I hope he rots in prison!" Todd angrily shook his head.

"I couldn't agree with you more." Mark turned to Hal "How did it go for Will in family court?"

"Great! The judge signed the adoption papers and she is officially Will's daughter." Hal smiled.

"Fantastic! Perhaps we can stop by and give Will our news before we head back to Seattle?" Mark grinned and looked at the others. They were saddened to leave the island they had grown to love. Arvidia gripped each of the men's hearts. It was hard to believe a few months before they had originally grumbled about this assignment. Now they could not imagine their life without her.

Arvidia's family whereabouts remained a mystery. Her 'blips' haunted her at times. She tried to remember. Hal had hoped her family would step forward and claim her. He put out constant alerts, notified television stations, radio stations and newspapers. To no avail, no one, not even the top-notch FBI agents seemed to know where this little girl came from.

Meeting up in the central hall of the courthouse, Hal and the others were drawn to Will and Arvidia standing nearby the center fountain.

Will invited Hal and the agents to the reservation for a celebration of his legal adoption of Arvidia. He wanted to make the day officially her birthday. Hal informed Will of the judge's punishment for Jim Mason. He was thrilled. Hal and the guys, accepting the invitation, all walked out of the courtroom together.

There was much celebration among the tribe members. Many of them made beautiful handmade gifts for her and ceremoniously pronounced her as one of their own.

Hal stood on the front porch with Will as they watched her run and play with the other kids. The scars on her forehead and neck were no longer reddened, they had begun to whiten. Will had taken her to a renowned plastic surgeon in Bellingham. He was able to repair the damage to her face but the scar on her neck would remain visible.

Arvidia ran past Hal. Her long black hair shimmered in the sun's rays. She turned to see if the kids were still behind her. Hal saw her blue eyes sparkled like the ocean. *She is going to be a beautiful woman.* Hal thought.

"Will, may I speak with you for a moment?" Hal could barely contain his news.

"Certainly," Will beckon him to the white rocking chairs, "Have a seat."

"I was wondering if you would agree to let us train Arvidia. The agents believe she has great potential and shows much athleticism. And we all know she's inquisitive and has special natural abilities especially with animals." Hal put up his hands, "I have also put in an inquisition to continue her counseling with Louanne. We have never attempted this before, but there is something quite different about Arvidia."

Will silently rocked in his chair and looked at Hal, "Yes, I agree. The Great One has given her special gifts." Will stood and called Arvidia over. She came breathlessly and sat comfortably on Will's lap.

"Hi, Hal! Will's my new daddy!" She smiled and hugged Will.

Hal's eyes brimmed with tears. He looked at the other agents who quickly looked in other directions and pretended to find the air interesting to stare at.

Will chuckled and smiled at Arvidia. She looked up at him with bright eyes and listened intently as Will asked her, "Arvidia, these men would like to come back and show you some karate moves. How does that sound?"

Arvidia crooked her finger to Hal signaling for him to come closer, and then she whispered, "I have a name for them."

Confused, Hal pointed at the four agents, "Them?"

"I call them, the Quad."

The agents looked at each other as did Hal. Todd gave Arvidia thumbs up. Hal promptly changed the agents long winded titles and they became known as The Quad.

Hal could not believe how much time had passed. Twenty years seemed like yesterday. Hal saw the exit sign for Lummi Island, he had to refocus his thoughts and come back to the present. Jim had escaped, and he needed to inform Will.

The freeway soon narrowed as he passed the Samish Way exit. Mt. Baker soon came in glorious view with the Pacific Ocean sparkling below. The beauty of this area is indescribable. Hal was always in awe whenever the city of Bellingham came into sight.

He dreaded telling Will the news.

As Hal pulled up to Will's home, after all these years, it still tilted to the left, he saw Will in his rocking chair on the porch with Bandit by his feet. Hal had wondered where Baldy was. The Appaloosa horses neighed loudly within their fenced arena. Hal knew as soon as he stepped out of his car. Will had been expecting him.

Hal parked and exited out of the car, slowly he walked towards Will. Baldy screeched loudly and flew closely over his head. He perched himself on the roof of Will's house.

"That darn bird sure doesn't like me!" Hal's arms waving about.

Will fought hard not to grin. Baldy never liked anyone. She seemed to have a particular dislike of Hal. He cleared his throat and his face turned serious, "I have been expecting you. Baldy and Bandit have been quite agitated the last few days. Is Arvidia okay?" Will's face turned hard as though he knew something was dreadfully wrong.

"Yes, Arvidia is okay. I sent her away on a dud assignment to do some undercover work at a law firm. She's working as a legal secretary in Schenectady, New York under the assumed name of Melody Savoy. I had to get her as far away from Seattle as possible. I have some former colleagues of mine watching her. Hal sighed as he sat into the rocking chair next to Will. He wiped his forehead and became quiet. Hal was unsure how Will would handle the forthcoming news. He knew Will was a strong Christian, but even this news could break a man. The smell of the ocean stung his nostrils. He inhaled and looked down at his hands.

Boldly, Will ask Hal, "He escaped, didn't he?"

Hal was startled but not surprised. "Yes. That is why I sent her away. She has no knowledge of Jim's escape. I have instructed the Quad to find out how he has escaped and they are working feverishly to capture him. I have strict orders no one is to tell her of this. I assure you, Will, Jim will not find her."

Will rocked back and forth and stared straight ahead. He slowly stated, "I knew this day would come."

CHAPTER 7

MATARAZZO LAW FIRM SCHENECTADY, NEW YORK

"Good Morning, Sheila!" Melody stopped briefly at the receptionist desk. It was barely nine in the morning and her phone lines were a buzzing. Melody swore she had eight arms going with the filings and answering multiple lines. Yet, she was very professional and always got the job done. "Good Morning Melody! It is going to be one of those days!" Sheila rolled her eyes, and answered an urgent buzzing from Stephen. "Yes, Sir, what can I do for you?" Melody laughed and walked to her desk.

Melody sat down at her desk. She was adjusting quickly to the demands of working for Blake Matarazzo. She flipped her computer on and clicked on Blake's schedule. She quickly scanned the day's events and noted he would not be in until after early in the afternoon. Blake's demanding schedule made it difficult to search his office. Today maybe the opportunity she has to check out his office. *Good that will give me some time to check around.* Melody thought. She noticed Mr. Laurent would be coming in at two pm and a new client, Holly Stearns at three.

Melody briskly walked into Blake's office and placed Mr. Laurent's file onto his desk. She knew Blake would want to review his file before his meeting with him. She listened carefully to anyone that maybe approaching Blake's office. It was eerily quiet. She sat in his leather chair and swiftly checked his files, glanced through his notes. As she expected, she did not notice anything out of the sort. She clicked on his computer but it was locked. *Darn. I wished Joe Rizzo was here. He would know how to get into his computer.* She carefully glided her hands underneath his desk and gingerly opened his drawers. Melody was startled when Terese, a paralegal poked her head in the door-way. "Hey! Want to join us for a coffee break?"

"Sure." Melody casually swung out of Blake's chair and smiled at Terese. She had hoped she had not seen her looking through his drawers. She followed her into the kitchen area where Krista, another paralegal was busy making coffee.

"Krista, this is Melody. Blake's new secretary." Terese grabbed her coffee mug. Krista turned and shook Melody's hand.

"Oh! Hi nice to meet you! Where do you hail from?" Krista asked.

"Oh, I did some secretarial work in Utica, NY and I saw an opportunity to move here." replied Melody. "What is it like to work for Blake?" Melody sat down at the table and sipped her coffee. She eyed the two very carefully. She was not sure who she could trust. She felt comfortable with Sheila.

"Blake is a nice man. He has been divorced for a few years now. It was rough working for him while he was going through all that. He is much happier now that situation is done. He does not see her much. I guess she does a lot of traveling with her business." Terese smiled at Melody and sipped her coffee.

"I agree. He does have a cute eight year old son name Jake. Blake simply adores his son and he's a great Dad to Jake. Did you meet Stephen? He is Blake's father and Angelo Matarazzo is Blake's cousin. Overall they treat us pretty good here." Krista sipped her coffee, "How do you like working for Blake so far? He can be pretty demanding at times."

"Oh I can handle that. I do enjoy working for Blake. I don't know how he keeps his head on straight with his crazy schedule. I did meet Stephen briefly the other day. As far as the job, it was the challenge I was looking for in a position. I am adjusting. Thank you for your help the other day." Melody glanced at Terese.

Melody noted the time, "I should be getting back to work, Thank you for the coffee. I need to get a few things done before Blake gets here. It was nice to meet you both." Melody waved and walked back to her desk. Melody sat down and decided to search her headquarters database on her laptop for information about Blake. Melody was growing concerned she was not progressing as far as she thought she would with this case. There was something odd about this assignment Hal sent her on. She could not put her finger on it. It was irking her but she did not want to disappoint Hal.

Blake arrived late and rushed into his office with Angelo Matarazzo trailing behind him. "Can you believe that ridiculous offer by the insurance company offered?" Blake huffed.

"Yeah, that was a pretty bad offer. I am glad our client turned it down. She was upset and rightly so. Hopefully those guys will come to their senses and make a better offer that will be acceptable to her."

Blake paced around his desk not sure what direction to go. He turned and looked at Angelo. His face was beet red. Blake did not like it when the insurance companies made low offers to settle despite the severe injuries his client suffered. He pointed his finger at Angelo, "You are right. They will. Listen I have to meet with a client in a few minutes. Can we discuss this later?" Blake grabbed Mr. Laurent's file and tucked it under his arm. He did not know why, but Mr. Laurent made Blake very uncomfortable.

"Sure, we can discuss this later." Angelo turned and headed for his office.

Melody escorted Gus Laurent to the conference room. He sat in the chair, crossed his legs and stared alluringly at Melody. Melody caught the look he was giving her and shuddered. Melody smiled through her gritted teeth. The hairs on her arms stood up.

"Mr. Matarazzo will be in shortly. Would you care for some coffee?" Melody paused and looked at him. His hair was long overdue for a cut. He spoke with a raspy voice, "No, thank you." He smiled at her curtly. Much of his teeth were missing. She could see details of various tattoos on his hands and she noticed a strange looking tattoo on the back of his neck.

Melody shut the door quickly. Her skin erupted in prickly goose bumps. Will always told her to trust her gut. Melody knew instinctively this guy was bad news. She saw Blake walking briskly towards her, "Mr. Laurent is waiting for you in the conference room."

"Thank you, Melody." He swiftly walked into the conference room and shut the door.

Melody returned to her desk and studied Blake's files. The more she explored into Blake's history the less she found to prove Blake was guilty of anything, she was starting to wonder what it was she was really looking for or was she missing something somewhere? She could not shake Gus Laurent out of her mind.

Sheila, the receptionist buzzed Melody's line. "Melody, Holly Stearns is here for Blake."

"Oh, I almost forgot! I will be right there!" Melody gasped, she grabbed a legal pad and headed towards the lobby. She walked by the conference room Blake and Gus were in. She was startled when she heard shouting and Blake suddenly yanked opened the door and nearly collided with Melody. Blake's face was red and he walked quickly towards Angelo's office. After Blake exited the conference room, Gus Laurent abruptly left towards the lobby and disappeared into the streets. Melody tried to catch up with Gus but he was gone before she reached the doors.

Melody greeted Holly Stearns and beckoned her to follow her. She apprehensively followed behind Melody who led her to a smaller conference room next to Blake's office. Melody noticed she looked very frightened and her face was stained with tears. Holly nervously fidgeted with her tissues in her hands. She sat absolutely still in her chair and gingerly put a tattered piece of paper onto the table. "Would you like some coffee?" Melody asked softly. Holly did not answer. Melody decided not to push it. The poor thing looked as if though she would come unglued any second.

Melody walked towards Angelo's office when she heard rustling within Blake's office. She turned and walked towards Blake's office, "Blake?" She peered in and was startled to see Gus Laurent standing over his desk riffling through his files. "What are you doing?" demanded Melody.

"It's none of your business!" Gus hissed. He quickly hustled out of the office down towards the nearest exit. Melody quickly followed. She stepped outside to see a gold Lexus sped off too fast for her to read the license plate.

Melody looked at Sheila. "How did he get back in?"

"He said he left his wallet in the conference room. Why?" Sheila was surprised at the abruptness of this man. "I showed him the conference room and his wallet was indeed on the table. Then he said he needed to use the bathroom and I didn't want to leave the phone lines too long."

More like he planted it there. Melody's hair on her arms was standing at full alert. "It's okay. No harm done."

Melody returned hastily to Blake's office. Blake seemed oblivious that Gus had been in his office. Melody blurted out, "Are you aware that Mr. Laurent was riffling through your desk?"

"What?" Blake shouted. His face reddened once again. "That is one strange dude. He wanted me to make his DWI disappear. He does not want to appear in court or accept the plea offer by the DA. He wanted to pay me cash to make it go away! Can you believe that? I am not jeopardizing my career for him. No way! I will be calling Mr. Laurent and I will terminate our contract. He can find himself another attorney. I do not have a good feeling about him."

Melody nodded in agreement. "I definitely agree with you on that point. Your three-o-clock appointment is here. She is in the room next door."

Blake slapped his forehead. "I forgot!" He picked up his yellow legal pad and quickly went into the next room where Holly sat.

Melody returned to her desk and sat down. She placed her hands into her face. She was troubled. Why was Gus Laurent in Blake's office? What was he looking for? She thought to call Joe or the Quad. They would be able to help her. Melody heard the conference room door open.

Blake was flustered and spoke loudly at Holly. "I am sorry. I cannot help you. I do not understand what you are saying." Melody looked up at Holly who was pleading with Blake. She kept placing the tattered paper into Blake's hands. Melody instantly recognized the unusual voice and her rapid hand movements. Melody stood and walked towards Holly. "Blake, she is asking for help. She is saying I did not do this. She wants you to read this paper." Holly read Melody's lips and instantly gave Melody the tattered paper. Melody studied it.

"I read it, it's legit. I do not know what it is she wants from me. I can't help her." Blake, exasperated with the day's events thus far, he nervously ran his hand through his hair.

"Oh, yes you can Blake! Read it again. Read it out loud." Melody thrust the tattered paper, which was a police report and she firmly placed it into Blake's hand.

Blake surprised by Melody's boldness, huffed and read the tattered report out loud, "Okay, Twenty four year old female suspect was arrested for resisting arrest and placed under arrest. Suspect handcuffed. Badge #71 stood behind female suspect and read her Miranda rights. Female suspect was placed into the squad car and taken into custody. Yeah, so pretty basic nothing unusual what's the problem?" Blake shrugged his shoulders.

Melody was exasperated and she glanced at Holly whose eyes had brightened with hope, "Okay, I will demonstrate. Her hands are handcuffed right?" Melody stood in front of Blake with her hands behind her back.

"Yes, go on." Blake put his hand on his chin and tilted his head. His eyebrows arched and attention piqued.

"The report said Badge #71 stood behind the suspect and read her Miranda rights. Holly is profoundly deaf and mute, therefore, she is unable to hear or speak with her hands due to her hands being in handcuffs. How does she know her rights were read? How did these officers know she understood those rights? There was no interpreter provided. According to what she just said, she had no idea what she was being arrested for or charged with. She was kept in the jail for two days without an attorney present. Blake, these police officers violated her civil rights!"

She looked at Blake and noticed his brown eyes sparkle and a grin slowly spread over his face. Blake was impressed. He quickly read the report again and realized Melody was right. There was no way that Holly Stearns would know her Miranda rights were read. All she knew was the cold handcuffs as she was put into the squad car with no explanations or more importantly, no interpreter was provided. *Wow, she is good.* Blake pondered. How does she know sign language? Blake was mystified by Melody's odd knowledge yet grateful.

Holly's hand sprinted fast with her hands and Melody gasped. She turned to Blake. "She really needs a lawyer. She does not understand what is going on. Her friend gave her your number but was unable to come and interpret for her today. You have a huge civil case for you there!" Melody was quite upset that this poor woman suffered due to the ignorance of the officers that arrested her. Melody gave her a reassuring hug.

"Melody, would you please inform Ms. Stearns to accept my apologies and set up an appointment with me for next week. I will file suit with the city of Troy immediately. Have her sign the retainer contract and we will proceed," Blake leaned forward to Melody "and I will need your assistance with this." Blake winked at her.

Holly's face showed obvious relief. She cried. She repeatedly signed "thank you" to Blake and Melody. Holly quickly signed the contract and hugged Melody and Blake thanking them profusely. She left the office smiling.

Blake was stunned, looked at Melody and asked, "How on earth do you know sign language?"

"Oh, it was something I picked up as a child." Melody grinned.

"Well, thank you for that surprise. I really appreciate your help. Hey, I meant to mention this earlier, I usually take new employees out to eat. I like to get to know them better and welcome them to the firm. Would you be available for dinner tonight? I'll understand if you're not, its short notice."

"Tonight? Yeah. I guess that will be fine. I need to wrap up some loose ends and I will gather up my things."

"Great! I just need to make a quick phone call and check on my son."

Blake meticulously reviewed the police report closely and spewed out a dictation which Melody knew he would do. He listened to his dictation and recapitulated a few details. He was satisfied. He stood up and place some files into his brief case. He listened to Melody as she gathered her things and locked up the file cabinet. He wondered how Melody was able to pick up something up like that. He was deeply intrigued by her. He caught himself several times wanting to ask her questions. Melody was quite a mysterious person. She spoke very little of herself or of her past. Her stunning beauty was riveting.

He met her at the back door. "Let me punch in the security code and we can walk down the block. There is a quaint Italian restaurant I usually go to. You like Italian food?"

"Oh yes, I love it."

The Italian restaurant was one of Blake's favorite places to eat. He held the door open for Melody as they entered into the restaurant. The owner of the restaurant spotted Blake, "Hey man, where have you been?" He snapped his fingers and had them seated immediately.

"Well Papa, lately I have been very busy with work. This is my new secretary, Melody. Melody, this is Papa. Everyone calls him that." Blake winked at her.

Melody sipped her water with lemon as she watched Blake eat his salad. He gobbled it up as if someone was going to snatch it away. Soon, Blake wiped his mouth. He asked Melody, "So what brings you to Schenectady? Where are you from?"

"Well, as you know from my resume I did some work in Utica and I heard there were some job opportunities here. I actually grew up in Washington State." Melody shoved salad into her mouth. She knew she should not have said that. She did not want to reveal too much about herself. She was here on assignment to do some investigation of the law firm. She was frustrated due to the lack of any supporting evidence that would even intrigue Hal. She had wondered if she had a case at all. She had decided earlier when she got home to give Joe Rizzo a call.

Blake interrupted her thoughts, "Washington State? That is quite a distance from here! Do you have any family here?"

"Uh, no, just me." Melody laughed nervously. "Yeah, I get around a bit."

Blake could not help but wonder why Melody was guarded. He sensed she did not trust people easily. Melody absently rolled up her sleeves as she ate her salad. Blake glanced at her arms and was startled to see faint scars on her arms. He peered closely at her face and noticed a faint scar on her forehead and on her neck. Blake wondered what horror she had been through. He instinctively wanted to protect her.

"You have any children?" Blake asked. Melody looked up at him. He noticed her eyes filled with pain and emotion, uh-oh, wrong question. Blake admonished himself.

Melody spoke softly, "No, do you?"

Blake's face lit up, "Yes, I have a mischievous 8 year old son named Jake. You might have seen pictures of him in my office. He is the best thing that has ever happened to me. He definitely keeps me on my toes!" Blake rolled his eyes.

Melody laughed. Whatever had transpired a moment ago disappeared. Blake studied her as she ate. He knew Melody was hiding from something. He did not know why, he decided he would make sure no harm came to her.

Blake and Melody walked back to their cars as the humid air began to settle for the night. "Blake, thank you for dinner. I enjoyed it and thank you for taking Holly's case." Melody smiled at him.

"Oh it is something I usually do; I know how crazy it gets with my schedule at times. I do like to meet with new employees and get to know them better. As far as Ms. Stearns goes, thank you for helping me out there. I truly did not understand what she was trying to say. It was difficult to understand her speech."

"That is understandable and I am glad I was able to help out. Especially with the difficult day you had," Melody hesitated, "Do you know why Gus Laurent was in your office?"

"No idea. His case is strictly a DWI. There is nothing in the office that would interest him. That's odd that he did that, nothing was missing, nothing that I can see. I changed the security code and I have instructed Sheila not to let that man onto the premises. Oh, I meant to ask you earlier, how do you know sign language?" Blake inquired.

"Oh, I grew up with a cousin who was deaf." Melody felt a pang of guilt lying to him like that. Truth be known, Will taught her sign language when she was unable to speak in the first few months after she met him.

Melody clicked her keypad on her keychain and reached for her door handle. Blake leaned in and opened the door for her. She smiled at him and slid into the driver's seat. She automatically reached for the seatbelt and clicked it. He shut the door and smiled at her.

"See you in the morning!" Melody started up the car. Blake waved as she pulled away from the parking lot and headed home.

Blake entered his Black BMW and decided to go for a drive. Melody captivated him. He wanted to ask her so many questions. He knew Melody was hiding something. He knew from experience not to push. He wondered was it domestic abuse? What happened to her? How did she get those scars? His hands gripped the steering wheel. He was surprised at himself how he wanted to protect her but he was not sure what she needed protection from or who.

Melody arrived home and peeled off her clothes in her bedroom and changed into her nightgown. She laid herself down on the bed and looked up at the ceiling as her thoughts twirled in her head. What was Gus looking for in Blake's office? Who was he? She thought for a split second, maybe Blake was in danger? She shook her head. He was too clean. She suddenly remembered she forgot to call Hal. She picked up her cell phone and speed dialed Hal. She reported to him the little she has been unable to find on Blake Matarazzo. Hal told her he understood and assured her she was doing a great job. Melody certainly did not feel that way. He told her he spoke to Will and he was doing fine. Melody felt a twinge of homesickness when he mentioned Will.

"Is he okay?"

"Oh, he's fine. I told him you were away on assignment. Baldy still attacked me. Bandit was on the porch with him. I can't believe that wolf still intimidates me!"

Melody laughed at the thought of that. "Okay Hal, long as everyone is okay. I'll keep looking around."

Melody decided to call her right hand man, Joe Rizzo the lab technician in Seattle.

"This is Joe. Name your deal!"

Melody laughed, "Hey, Joe how are you doing?"

"Hey, Arvidia how are you? I miss you girl. When are you coming back?"

"I don't know, the way this assignment is going, probably soon. Can you do me a favor?"

"Girl, anything, what is it you need?"

Melody smiled. They had always had an odd relationship. Joe was very dependable when it came down to the nitty gritty of needing help. "Can you look up some information for me? I need background information on Blake Matarazzo and Gus Laurent."

"Sure thing, I will get right on it."

"Thanks Joe, let me know if you find anything."

Melody clipped her phone off. Her thoughts returned to Blake. He was incredibly handsome. His soft brown eyes were full of emotion. She saw passion in his eyes when he spoke about Holly's case. She was finding it hard to believe this man was guilty of anything. She was starting to doubt she had a case. She suddenly realized, if the law firm was cleared of any charges, her assignment was done and she would have to leave and return to Seattle. She realized she actually didn't want to. Slowly, she drifted off to sleep with the radio playing a quiet country song.

The following morning, Melody hurried against the traffic to get to the office. There was much to do and little time to accomplish it. Melody parked her car and her cell phone shrilled. She noticed it was Joe calling.

"Hey, Joe what's up?"

"I did some checking as you requested. Blake Matarazzo is clean as a whistle. But this Gus dude? Arvidia, he is bad news. Got a rap sheet a mile long." Joe hesitated. He was not sure if he should tell her the following information, "Um. Arvidia, he was paroled from Walla Walla prison a year ago."

"Melody's hairs on her arm stood up, she looked up sharply into the rearview mirror, "Joe, did you say Walla Walla prison?"

"Yes." Joe whispered. He did not dare to tell her about Jim Mason escaping from prison. "How did you come across this dude?"

"Well, he is Blake's client or was. Blake terminated their contract. He was extremely uncomfortable with him. Anyways, Gus wanted him to do something that went against his moral ethics. Joe, I have to go, I'll call you later."

"Okay, Arvidia. Talk to you soon." Joe hung up. He had wondered if he should tell Hal about this.

"Good morning, Sheila!" Melody waved as she walked by the receptionist desk. She pushed open the doors and walked to her desk. She was surprised to hear Blake hard at work on the phone discussing a settlement.

Melody sat down and took a deep breath. She was deeply disturbed by the news of Gus Laurent. *Maybe it's just a coincidence.* She thought. Her gut was saying otherwise.

CHAPTER 8

FBI OFFICE, SEATTLE WASHINGTON

Hal and the Quad sat in the conference room with grim faces as they listened to the Warden of the Walla-Walla prison talk through the speaker phone.

"All I can tell you is that Mr. Mason killed one of my guards, took his uniform and then somehow escaped." The Warden paused, cleared his throat, "It appears he had inside help. We're trying to determine who that person might be. Mr. Sampson, we have never had this happened since I have been at this facility. I apologize for the burdens that have been placed on you and I'm well aware of the gravity of the situation. We do have confirmed reports he has headed west towards Seattle." Todd's stomach churned. "My secretary has faxed a recent picture of him to you, as well as, the security videos from our prison library which was sent priority to your forensic guy, Joe Rizzo. I do hope you find this dangerous man. If I can be of further assistance please do not hesitate to call."

"Okay, thank you for the information. I'll discuss this with my team and get back to you if we need anything further." Hal clicked off the speaker phone, sat back in his chair, and looked at the other members of his team. Turning his head as he heard the fax machine come to life, he leaned over the table and watched as Jim Mason's image appeared before him. He studied it for a moment and then passed it around the table.

"Well, he got older. The evil look hasn't changed." Todd passed the photo around.

"You think he knows where she is?" Mark dared to ask.

"Good question. As you heard the warden say he's been keeping to himself for the past year and spending much of his time in the prison library. I'll check with Joe and see if he has received the security videos yet. I certainly want more information about this Gus Laurent. I find it interesting he's not only been a frequent visitor of Mr. Mason but he was also paroled from Walla Walla prison one year ago. I'll have Joe Rizzo do some research on him as well." Hal tapped the conference table and pursed his lips together.

"You think there is any connection between the Jim's escape and Gus Laurent?" Mark inquired.

"It certainly appears that way." Hal responded.

Todd threw the photo onto the table and thumped his index finger hard onto the table, "I think there is a connection." Todd threw up his hands and pointed his index finger at Hal, "I know, I know—we need proof. But you always told us to trust our inner gut and this is ringing some bells I don't want to hear."

"Hal, I have a suggestion. What do you think of the idea of us going undercover to keep an eye on Arvidia in New York?" Mark asked as he looked around the table. All of whom were nodding their heads in agreement.

"I think that's an excellent idea." Hal breathe a sigh of relief.

"Good. I'm sure Mr. Mason will soon figure out Arvidia is not here and we need to stop him before that happens." Mark tapped his fingers firmly on the table and questioned, "Who is this Gus dude anyway? I thought Mason's M.O. was working alone?"

Just as Hal began to answer his question, the intercom buzzed, Todd reached over and clicked it on.

"Hey, Joe here," Joe was nearly choking on his salvia at the news he needed to report. "Todd, is it true that Jim Mason had a frequent visitor name Gus Laurent?"

"Yes, so we were just discussing that. Why?" Todd's eyebrows knotted together.

"Well, Arvidia called me last night to do a background check on her boss, Blake Matarazzo, and it seems he was unhappy with a client and refused to represent him any further, the client's name is Gus Laurent!" The Quad and Hal paled as Joe continued, "I do not think its coincidence that he happens to show up in the same law firm Arvidia is doing undercover work." Joe's voice was high-pitched as he spoke. Hal suddenly leaned forward and turned his head towards the speaker.

"Joe, did you say Gus Laurent was at the law firm?" Hal's heart was pounding wildly in his chest.

"Yes, Sir. Arvidia said Blake and Gus got into some sort of an argument yesterday and Blake told him to find another attorney. It was something to do with a DWI charge and this Gus dude asked him to do something that went against his morals. I ran a check on Gus and noticed his name on an email from the prison. Turns out he was Jim's former cell-mate." Hal and the Quad looked at each other. The air was suddenly charged with the sense of urgency. "There's one more thing. Arvidia said after she returned to her desk, she walked by Blake's office and found Gus rummaging through his desk, but after informing Blake, he didn't find anything out of order."

"I wonder what the heck he was looking for." Hal stammered then asked, "What was Blake's reaction? Then as an afterthought, Hal interjected, "What else did you find out about Gus Laurent?"

"Arvidia said Blake was quite angry about it. I did some digging on Gus and all that I could find is nothing but bad news. He's got a rap sheet a mile long. Mostly drugs and robberies, he's been in and out of prison most of his life. He is definitely not someone to mess with."

Hal was drumming his fingers on the table, "I do not like this one bit."

Todd felt a chill run down his spine. "It's probable that Mr. Mason knows where Arvidia is. We can't waste any more time, we need to get to New York, pronto."

"I agree. Joe what did you tell Arvidia?" Hal Inquired.

"I only told her about Gus being paroled from Walla Walla prison a year ago. I didn't say anything about Jim Mason. I don't think she suspects anything, but she is having doubts about the assignment she's on. I can tell she's frustrated and feels like she's not doing a good job."

"I'll take care of that. Thank you Joe, let me know if you come across anything else."

"Yes, Sir." Joe clicked off the speaker phone and lightly touched his chest and looked up at the ceiling and let out a deep breath. Hal stood up, deep in thought. He turned to walk out the door, but, as he reached for the door knob, he faced his team, "I will arrange for you men to head out New York tonight. I want a daily report from you Todd. All of you stay in the background. Do not let Arvidia know that you're there. Keep your eyes and ears peeled for Jim Mason and now this Gus Laurent character." Hal thought of Arvidia's file, a file that held many secrets and horrors few knew about, including, Arvidia. His hand shook as he gripped the doorknob.

"Yes, Sir." Todd answered quietly.

The Quad solemnly filed out slowly passed Hal, nodding their heads as they quickly headed to their office to make preparations. New York would be their home for a time. Mark was the last to leave the room. He noticed Hal's hands were visibly shaking. "Sir, are you okay?"

"I will be once you guys are in New York. I got a gut feeling if Gus knows where she is, it's most likely Jim does too. We do not have much time."

"We won't let you down, Sir." Mark patted him on the shoulder as he left the room.

"I know you won't." Hal let out a sign, shut the conference door and headed slowly to his office.

Hal thought of Will's last words to him, "It has begun."

CHAPTER 9

BLAKE'S HOUSE

Melody was busily sending her most recent dictation from Blake, to a local judge, regarding an urgent matter. It was imperative she finish this so it could be messaged over to the courthouse per Blake's request. She felt a gentle tap on her shoulder, turned around to look and it was Blake's newest client, Holly Stearns. Sheila, who could not understand Holly's sign language, must have figured it was easier to send Holly over to her. Bringing her hands together, Melody's fingers sprinted in sign language. She said, "Blake is on the phone right now with the chief of police of Troy. I'll let him know you are here." Melody beckoned Holly to follow her to the small conference room she had been in the previous week. As Holly sat down she looked up at Melody who signed, "Blake should be finished in a few minutes. Would you like some coffee?"

"Yes, please." Holly signed back to her. For a moment, she paused and spoke with a thick tongue, in a loud and unnatural, nasal sounding voice. She said with great struggle, "With milk and sugar please." Holly exhaled as though it took great effort to say the one simple sentence that took her years to learn. She had to learn to use her tongue to pronounce sounds; she practiced for hours with the speech therapist. Then, with her hands on her throat, she was able to distinguish the variations of sound that emulated and vibrated through her throat and nose.

Melody smiled and nodded at her. She signed, "Right away!" She bowed slightly as she exited the conference room. Melody smiled to herself as she headed towards the kitchen and prepared Holly's coffee. Walking back to the conference room, she set the coffee down in front of Holly. "Thank you." She signed. Melody left her alone with her thoughts and walked back to her desk. She would wait patiently for Blake to finish his phone call. Melody finished her dictation and sealed it into an urgent envelope. She delivered it to Sheila and asked her to have it messengered to the court immediately.

Melody poked her head into Blake's office and noticed his face was reddened with anger. "Fine, I will confer with my client and we will file suit!" Blake slammed the phone down, threw up his hands in exasperation then sat back in his chair. "They're denying any wrong doing, of course!"

"Was that the police chief?" Melody inquired.

"Yes." Blake took a deep breath, exhaled then composed himself before speaking. "Is Ms. Stearns here yet?"

"Yes, she is waiting for you in the next room."

"Good. Let's get to work." Blake grabbed Ms. Stearns file, and proceeded to walk towards where Holly Stearns sat waiting for him. Melody followed close behind. Blake's jaw set in determination, he walked with absolute resoluteness all the while setting the legal wheels in motion. Melody knew he would make sure Holly Stearns voice would be heard.

Melody, while closely following behind Blake, instantaneously felt a stirring within her heart she had not felt in years. She was deeply touched by Blake's passion to help his clients. *Wow. He really cares about his clients.* Melody thought. She felt pangs of guilt because of the truth she was hiding from Blake. She had wondered many times why this has bothered her so. She had relationships with men before but she never allowed her personal feelings to interfere with her assignments. It was much too dangerous for her to reveal who she really was. Why was this man any different? Is it because she was away from the Quad? Maybe I'm not ready for this assignment? What am I missing? She admonished herself for allowing her heart to surface in regards to Blake.

Blake, setting her file down on the table, took a seat directly across from Ms. Stearns. Just as previously instructed by Melody, he made a conscience effort to sit facing Holly. He waited patiently until Melody was seated and ready to interpret. He rolled up his sleeves, then placing his hands on top of the conference table he proceeded to calmly explain his legal advice to Ms. Stearns. Melody swiftly interpreted what Blake said. Holly Stearns nodded her head that she understood Blake's explanation and eagerly agreed to file suit against the police department.

"Good. I will make sure they hear your voice." Blake looked at her with a stern face, "What that police officer did was wrong and he certainly violated your civil rights." Blake spoke slowly and deliberately. He eyed Melody whose hands sprinted quickly interpreting to Ms. Stearns who looked at Blake and signed, "Thank you." Holly dabbed at her cheeks with some tissues.

Blake clasped his hands together and stated, "Okay, let's schedule an appointment for next week. I or Melody will let you know what is going on. Is that okay with you, Ms. Stearns?" Melody quickly signed to Holly who nodded her head yes.

Melody reached across the table and picked up her IPAD and pulled up his weekly schedule. "Is next Tuesday at 3:00 pm okay with you?"

Holly signed, "Fine." back to Melody. They stood up with Holly as she hugged both Blake and Melody. She left with a confident smile.

Blake promptly returned to his desk and Melody knew without a doubt he was busy spewing out another dictation for her. She was amazed how accustomed she had become to his every day routine. She completed her work Blake had asked of her and waited for the familiar beep on her computer, signaling the dictation from Ms. Stearns's appointment, was ready to be typed.

Melody awoke early Saturday morning and stretched before arising out of bed. She smelled the coffee brewing and followed the aroma to the kitchen. Making herself a cup before a hot shower would allow her a few minutes to mull over what she would do this morning. Having decided in the shower, she would finish up the rest of Blake's dictations. With a towel wrapped around her head capturing the wet tendrils from falling, she sat cross legged on the sofa and while all was still fresh, she got to work proofreading each one, before emailing them out, for Blake's approval. She chuckled to herself wondering how she always seemed to be amazed how he dictated between clients and other matters that claimed his attention. Who would have thought, a male multi-tasker, that's hard to find. She smiled and shook her head.

Her cell phone shrilled. Melody grabbed it thinking it was Hal calling to check on her.

"Hello?"

"Melody, I am sorry for bothering you, it's Blake."

"Oh, hi how are you?" Melody touched her not so dried hair and wondered for a moment if Blake was going to ask her to come to the office. "No, you are not disturbing me at all, is everything all right?"

"Yes, I'm fine thank you. Do you by any chance have the Stearns file? I thought I put it in my briefcase but I'm unable to locate it."

"I apologize for that, I should've told you I had the file. I wanted to finish up the dictations you left for me. I just finished the dictations and sent them to you for approval. Do you need the file?"

"Yes, I would like to do some legal research on it. Would it be any trouble for you to bring her file to my home? I have my son with me and he's not feeling well today."

No, it's no trouble at all. Where are you?" Melody finished writing down the directions. She tapped her wet towel again, "Is 2 pm okay with you?"

"That would be wonderful. Thank you so much. Call me if you have any problems with my directions."

"Okay, I'll be there in a little while." Melody clicked her cell phone off and pondered for a moment. She looked at her closet and changed into her jeans and taking the towel off her head, she decided to dry it half way then pop it up into a pony tail that would save a few minutes and allow time in case she got lost. Throwing on a casual cream color cable knit sweater, she reached for the Stearns file and headed out. She followed Blake's directions to his home and didn't have any trouble finding the street he lived on.

Slowly, she drove down the street looking for his address 1013 Brier Court. The neighborhood was tidy with well-manicured lawns; the houses were quaint and distinct from each other. She observed the street, busy with neighbors working in their yards. Children running about, people walking their dogs and others were jogging by. Her navigator soon announced she had arrived at her destination. Pulling slowly into Blake's driveway and she parked behind his black BMW. She peered out her windshield and glanced over Blake's home. It was a small two level white house with blue shutters around the windows. The front porch arched giving way to a beautiful oval shaped stained-glass oak door. She picked up the legal file and exited the car.

As she walked up the S shaped side walk, onto his porch, she felt fluttering in her stomach and for a moment, she thought, *I'm nervous?* Now pushing the doorbell, she listened as the bells chimed her arrival. While she waited for Blake to come to the door, she caught a familiar scent of roses. She leaned over the porch and saw the red rose bushes blooming, proudly, alongside his home. Gently, she lifted one of the flowers to her nostrils and inhaled its aroma. Closing her eyes, the memories flooded in. She remembered how hard Will labored over his rose bushes and how every year they bloomed so beautifully. From time to time, he would leave a single rose atop her pillow. She remembered picking them up and devouring the scent before climbing into bed. Melody's eyes brimmed as homesickness swelled within her heart. She missed Will.

"You like roses?" Blake smiled.

Startled, she hadn't heard the door open, Melody spun around. "Yes, I love roses."

Melody felt her cheeks burn, as she saw Blake standing in the doorway. He was leaning up against the door frame with his hands deep into his jean pockets. His jet black hair was tousled as if he had just woken up. His white short-sleeve t-shirt lined his muscular build. His soft brown eyes, sparkled as he smiled at her shyly.

Melody stammered, "Umm . . . . sorry. I couldn't resist smelling them."

"That's okay, I'm glad you like them. I do enjoy gardening." Blake reached down into his gardening box and picked up a shear. He clipped one of the roses and grinned at her, "Would you accept this rose?"

Melody did not miss a beat, she pretended to bat her eyelashes and said in a southern drawl, "Why, thank you kindly, Sir. Yes, I accept." They both laughed.

"Come on in!" Blake bowed at the waist while extending his arm. Melody stepped inside the foyer and handed Blake the Stearns file.

Blake grasped the file and tucked it under his arm. He wished he'd had more time to tidy up the house but with an eight year old acting like a Tasmania devil, it was just easier to let some things be. He headed towards the living room. "Make yourself comfortable."

Melody glanced around the foyer before following behind him into the living room. The living room and foyer were neat and simplistic with some toys strewn about. Upstairs, she could hear a TV blasting a video game and a child's voice yelling in exasperation. Melody suppressed a giggle. The living room walls were lined with elegant paintings. Her attention gravitated to one large one that hung prominently above his desk. She quietly walked over and looked closely at the painting. On the bottom of the painting, she read a familiar bible verse. In beautiful calligraphy she mouthed the words: <u>For God so loved the world that He gave his only begotten Son, whosoever believeth in Him shall not perish,</u>

but have everlasting life. John 3:16 KJB. She gently touched the painting and fondly remembered Will's talks with her about the Great One.

"My mother is an artist. She did all the paintings in here as well as the calligraphy." Blake said proudly as he glanced around the living room.

"It is absolutely exquisite." Melody said softly. She was transfixed by the painting "Is your mother a Christian?"

"Thank you. Actually, myself, and my family are all born again Christians." He walked over to where Melody stood and pointed, "That particular bible verse is one of my favorites. It is a good reminder to me how much He loved us and the sacrifices He made in order for us to live." Blake hesitated for a moment, and glanced at Melody.

Melody was surprised he confessed to being a Christian. He made no references to being one at the office or maybe she hadn't notice?

"Umm, would you like something to drink? I have soda or juice?"

"Oh, juice is fine." Melody turned and smiled at Blake. She continued to marvel at the painting his mother made. She wasn't sure if it was the words that struck her or the painting. There was something about it that Melody couldn't stop staring at. The bible verse was also one of Will's favorites. She gently glided her hand, lightly touching the cross where Jesus had died. Behind the cross was an illuminating light which shone from the sky that had been parted with God's hand. Angels could be seen, as well, throughout the illuminating light. Will would love to see this painting.

Blake poured the juice into a glass and set the carton on the counter. He wondered for a moment if he should ask her about her walk with God then felt in his spirit, it wasn't the right time. He returned to the living room and noticed Melody was still staring at his mother's painting. He set the glass of juice on the coffee table. He announced softly, "Your juice is on the coffee table. Would you like to have a seat?" He sat on the brown leather couch.

"Thank you." Melody set her pocketbook down onto the thick carpet and seated herself. The couch squeaked softly, as she moved, while looking around the spacious living room, she noticed how the sun embellished the windows with its rays. Her attention was soon drawn to the TV. The NFL Buffalo Bills game was in full swing. Melody immediately thought of the Quad sitting around Todd's living room shouting at the TV watching the Seattle Seahawks game. Again, homesickness swelled in her throat. She could picture them and their silly antics especially at the home games at Seattle Quest field. Who would ever guess her favorite four men are the most sought after top FBI agents in the United States?

"I hope orange juice is okay?"

"It's fine." She took a sip and glanced quickly at the TV. Scanning the updated scores of other football games going on the ticker tape across the bottom of the screen she promptly searched for the Seahawks score.

"You like football?" He sat at the end of the couch almost wanting to laugh, she seemed like she was trying to be polite but her eyes kept diverting to the TV screen.

"Are you kidding? I love football!" Melody said a bit too enthusiastically. She really loved football but he didn't need to know he unnerved her just a little.

Blake was taken aback. She constantly seemed to surprise him and yet, he knew so little of her. He had so many questions and yearned to ask her each and every one. He was suddenly and acutely aware of his heightened feelings for her. *Wow. Where did that come from?* He thought.

"I apologize for that. I tend to get a little crazy with football games." Melody laughed.

"No problem, believe me I totally understand," Blake grinned and pointed at his Buffalo Bills jersey lain across the back of the couch.

"Daddy, can I have something to drink?" Melody looked up and instantly recognized Jake from the pictures in Blake's office.

"Jake, don't be rude we have a guest. This is Melody. Melody, this is my son Jake."

With Blake's prompting, Jake shyly walked over to Melody and shook her hand. Much to his astonishment, he promptly sat down next to her and eagerly bragged to Melody about his video game score, he had just got to the next level. Blake quietly went into the kitchen and poured Jake a glass of milk. Out of the corner of her eye, Melody noticed some reflections on the wall. She turned and looked out the window. The hairs on her arms bristled. There was a gold Lexus parked across the street. She wondered if that was the same car she saw outside of the law firm. Melody gut twinge.

"Jake, here's your milk." He barely took a breath between speaking and gulping his milk. Blake observed how taken Jake was with Melody. He usually ignored the dates his father had brought home which were few and far between.

"Oh man, we're losing!" exclaimed Blake "C'mon guys you can do it!"

Melody knew from the obvious football memorabilia throughout his home he was a big fan of the Bills. She could not help but grin as she sipped her juice. She had bet against the Bills.

Jake stood up, "I'll be right back, Melody." He spoke while he was on the run.

"Okay." Melody replied in his wake.

Up the stairs he flew and within moments he returned with more toys in hand. "This is my monster truck he's going to crush the smaller cars, but I'll do it quietly." He caught his father's eye, but he wanted to be close to her. She smelled nice and he was feeling better already.

Blake opened the Stearns file, during a commercial break and started the discussion of the progress they were making with the case. "Melody, what is your experience with this? I have to say I'm intrigued by your knowledge."

Melody instantly became quiet and she knew she could not keep lying to Blake. She always kept up her sign language while growing up on the reservation. After one particular drug bust, she had met a deaf girl who was physically abused by a drug dealer. She had seen the pain in the child's eyes. The hurt and distrust. Melody deeply empathized with this child for she knew what the child felt. She remembered how she knelt down to the child and spoke to in her language. The little girl had literally jumped up into her arms, hugging her tightly. Melody's heart was continually burdened by the fact that not only this child, but so many were unable to tell anyone about the harm being placed upon them by another. Happily, for this little girl, she'd been adopted by a patient, loving family and was doing well.

"Well, my first job with a law firm specialized in discrimination cases. My boss had a soft spot for his clients who were treated unfairly. His daughter was handicapped. He taught me a quite a bit about the ADA act and he was very good in winning cases for his clients."

"Interesting, how long did you work for him?"

"Oh, I think it was for about 2 years." Melody took a quick swig of her juice. Melody felt guilty lying to him. Glancing out the window now, she noticed the gold Lexus was still parked there. She reached down and felt her gun snuggled inside her purse.

Blake was watching her and observed how she became tensed. He mistook her avoidance in answering his question and decided to change the subject. The air in the living room seemed to have changed for an instant. Jake was oblivious to their conversation and played happily at Melody's feet.

"Um . . . What football team do you like?" Blake asked. He reached over and touched her arm.

Melody jumped and turned to Blake. "I'm sorry, what did you say?" she tried desperately to give him full focus.

"Are you okay? I just asked you what football team do you like." Blake noticed she was absolutely distracted but by something. Did I do something or is there a problem outside the window? He had seen her glance that way a few times but he'll wait until she made herself clear.

"Yes, I'm okay, sorry. I got a little distracted there for a moment." She giggled nervously, and then stated with a grin, "Oh, I'm a true blue, or rather green, Seattle Seahawks fan all the way."

"Seattle Seahawks! Wow, I believe we play you guys soon." Blake winked. He quickly glanced at the football schedule that lay on top of the coffee table. "Yup, we do play you guys in a few weeks. That should be a good game. Would you care for more juice?" Hearing the clock chime he directed his next words towards his son. "Jake it's time for you to get ready for bed."

"Can't I stay up for a few minutes longer Pleassssssssssssssseee?" Jake begged on his knees with his puppy dog eyes. He hadn't moved from Melody's feet the entire time he played.

"No, it's time for you to go to bed. Let's go buddy." Blake stood and waved his arm in the direction of the stairs. Jake, getting up off his knees, knew he was defeated again.

"Aw, man, you never let me get to do anything!" Jake stomped upstairs.

Blake rolled his eyes as he went after him. "I will be right back." Then he whispered, "I'm always the bad guy!" Smiling, he headed up the stairs.

"Okay! Good night Jake." She called to Jake's back just as he spun around, nearly knocking Blake over, and jumped into Melody's arms hugging her with all his might but before he could get away, she held his face in her hands. She was just as surprised as he was and simply said, "Sweet dreams, Sweetie." She let him go as he ran back up the stairs to the sound of his dad's voice bellowing for him to get moving.

"Good night, Melody." He thundered up the stairs and into the bath where his father had the water flowing.

Melody waited for both boys to be out of sight before springing from the couch and quickly going to the window. Parting the curtains, but leaving the sheers, she noted the gold Lexus was still parked across the street but was unable to see through the tinted windows. Turning away, she felt a presence and caught a flash out of the corner of her eye. Peering through the window again she gasped. Will. His image was standing on Blake's front lawn, hands ascending up toward the sky and war paint was heavily applied. He was sending her a message and her radar was up.

Blake came downstairs. "Well he's all tucked in."

Melody jumped, as he walked in. "Oh, you scared me! I was just looking to see if it was going to rain." She walked away from the window trapping her thoughts for a moment about what she had seen outside the window; still she asked herself, *What was Will warning her about? It'll have to wait.* Pulling herself together she forced herself to focus on Blake's voice.

"Sorry about that, I didn't mean to startle you. I think the weather guy said it would rain tomorrow." He wondered why she was so jumpy.

Blake picked up the empty glasses from the coffee table and shaking his head in disgust at the final score of his team. He smiled and said, "Well, there's always next week!" She smiled and followed him into the kitchen. Setting the glasses onto the counter he turned and leaned against it, smiling at her.

"Jake is quite taken with you. He hasn't been like that with any other woman since his mother and I divorced."

"I'm honored." She smiled and asked, "Does he see his mother very often?"

"No, she travels a lot due to her business. He doesn't know her very well and I'm afraid their time together is nearly non-existent. It's difficult for Jake. I know he misses her.

"You have full custody of him?" She asked knowing his answer.

"Yes, when she comes back into town I have no problem with her seeing him." He was matter of fact. Blake really wanted to know more about what was on her mind, but he would wait.

"I can see he's a good kid, you did a good job with him." She knew her conversation was too generic, but her mind just couldn't focus with him in such close domestic proximity.

"Thank you. I try." Blake grinned at her.

Both she and Blake reached for the dishtowel at the same time. Their hands touched briefly just as their eyes locked onto one another. The dish towel remained on the counter as Blake casually took a hold of Melody's hand pulling her closer to him. Her waist length, sleek black, hair partially covered her face. He reached up with one hand and brushed her bangs away from her eyes while encircling her waist with the other. He tilted his head slightly and ever so slowly he kissed her full on the mouth. For a moment, he thought she would pull away.

A little taken aback, but strangely, she felt perfectly safe. She allowed him to part her soft lips with his. Closing her eyes, she knew her face burned with the passion she felt. Gently, he caressed her neck and kissed her deeply. Melody moaned and swayed slightly before him as her arms naturally wrapped around his waist and traveled up and across the muscles of his back. She may have imagined it, but she could have sworn he released a slight shudder.

He now sought after her tender neck and while caressing it with his mouth he curiously found the raised scar. Tempted to ask her questions, he instantly knew, if she wanted him to know about the scar she'd tell him about it in due time. For now, he continued to enjoy this wonderful moment. But when she slowly pulled away, he knew why.

"I should probably head on home." Her cheeks still felt aflame with desire. Her heart fluttered and she yearned for more of him, but she had to bring herself back to reality. Her life now, at this moment in time, was a lie. But she would have to tell him the truth sometime.

"I guess you're right." He hesitated then added, "If I've over stepped my bounds, I do apologize." Slowly exhaling, he was at loss for words. He waited for a cue from her to proceed.

"No. No. Really, it's okay." She stepped just a bit closer and explained. "It's been a long time." Melody gave him a quick kiss on the cheek then turned away from him.

Blake followed as she grabbed her purse on her way out the door. Before she could enter the car, he gently reached in for her. Leaning over, he kissed her on the forehead and wished her sweet dreams.

She didn't want him to feel at all put out, but her mind was on that gold Lexus which still remained across the street. She had to leave for that reason, and so many more.

"Thank you." She gave him her sweetest, most apologetic smile. While looking into the rearview mirror she noticed the Lexus had roared to life and drove away. She looked back at Blake and waved to him. While backing out of the driveway, she glanced up to see Jake waving to her from the upstairs window. That made her smile and she wave back. But that alone didn't soothe the sudden panic she was feeling as she drove away. Reaching into her purse, she pulled out her gun and gently laid it on her lap, just in case.

As Melody drove home, she frequently checked her mirrors. There was no sign of the gold Lexus. Her thoughts whirled in her head. *Why was that Lexus watching Blake's house? What was Will warning her about? Blake? What in the world was I thinking? Kissing Blake? What is wrong with me?* Melody felt her nerves coming apart.

Melody hurried into her apartment, kicked off her shoes, plopped down onto the brown suede sofa and clicked on her laptop. She was determined to find out what was going on. She knew deep down Blake was clean. Gus Laurent and this mysterious gold Lexus had her concerned. There is something fishy going on with this Gus guy and there has to be some sort of connection with the mysterious Lexus. What is it?

"Okay," Melody spoke aloud reasoning things out, "Ok, let's say, I have ruled out Blake as a suspect. Then what is the connection with Gus Laurent and the Lexus? Who was watching Blake's house? Why was Gus in Blake's office?" An idea occurred to her, maybe she could stretch the assignment out to figure out this connection with Gus. She'd have to clear it with Hal. Opening her cell phone, she speed dialed Hal.

Hal was surprisingly agreeable to Melody's plan, yet, he insisted she check in with him daily.

She turned off her laptop, picked up her cellphone, walked towards her bedroom, plugged in her cellphone to recharge, changed into her t-shirt and climbing into bed she starred out the window as the stars shone brightly. She felt confused about Blake. She was terrified of her feelings that were surfacing. She wanted them kept down deep within her. She did not want to care for a man and have her feelings interfere with the work she was doing. Her cellphone chirped as she wondered about Blake. She reached over and read the text. It was from Blake. Rest well. She smiled and texted back U2.

On Sunday, Melody kept her eyes out for the gold Lexus outside her apartment. She also took a couple of drives by Blake's house. The Lexus seemed to have disappeared for the moment. She hadn't heard from Blake at all.

It's Monday morning, Melody wondered how Blake would act towards her at the office. What a stupid thing to do! Melody admonished herself. She finished applying her makeup, gathered her purse and headed out to the office.

"Good morning, Sheila!" Melody waved and walked through the double doors.

"Good morning, Melody." Sheila smiled at her.

Melody silently walked towards her desk and promptly decided to take control of the situation. She popped her head into in Blake's office. "Good morning, Blake. How are you?"

Blake lifted his head up from the computer and smiled at her. He had been angry with himself for much of the weekend for kissing her. He was sure she would not show up for work. But, to his delight, she smiled brightly at him. "Good morning, Melody. I'm good and how are you?"

"Fine. How far did you get with the Stearns file?" Melody inquired.

"Pretty far, I'm confident with the legal research that I've done. When does Ms. Stearns come again?"

"Uh . . . I believe its next week I'll double check for you."

"Okay thanks. I've filed a suit against the Troy police department and we'll see what happens next. The media is certainly helping to propel this case. Hopefully, we can settle without going to trial." Blake said confidently. He wanted desperately to go to her but his feet were made of lead, or so it seemed.

"They certainly are. They will regret their ignorance towards Ms. Stearns. There's just no excuse for that." Melody felt anger rise up within her. "Anyways, your dictations are done. I'll get your files ready. Is there anything in particular you need done, now, before I go?"

"Not at the moment. I do have one question though."

Melody froze for a moment, "Yes?"

"Do you have plans Sunday?" Blake asked.

"I don't believe so, why?" Melody smiled.

"Well, I was wondering if you would like to come with Jake and me to our church service. Then afterwards, maybe you would care to join us for lunch and watch a little football? Blake knew this was a long shot but he was one to be bold at times.

"Oh, church?" For a moment, Melody panicked inside, she always felt out of sort whenever Will spoke of the Great One. She was confused deep inside her about the Great One. How can He be real? Her physical scars reminded her daily, yet, even after all these years she still could not remember happened to her. Why would the Great One allow this to happen to her? Why wouldn't He let her remember? Will always reminded her, the Great One is wise when it comes to His timing, and His ways were not our ways. She gulped and much to her surprise, Melody found herself saying, "Yes, I would like to go."

"Great! Why don't you meet us at my house and we'll head to church together. Is that okay with you?" Blake's eyes sparkled as he spoke. He was pleased with her work, and personally, he enjoyed her company. Jake was driving him crazy with the constant question, "When's Melody coming back?"

"Yes, of course. That's fine. I'll make my famous wings." She wondered what Will's reaction would be if he knew she was actually stepping inside a church.

"I do love wings!" Blake's cell phone shrilled on his desk, "I need to answer that."

"Okay, I'll get the files ready for you." She departed from his office relieved the conversation went well.

The following Sunday morning, Melody pulled into Blake's driveway and parked. She glanced around; checking her rearview and she did notice a blue Toyota that had been following her, had disappeared. *Boy, I'm getting paranoid!* Melody heaved a sigh of relief. She took a deep breath then slowly blew it out just as she exited the car.

Closing her driver's door, she opened the back door and reached into the backseat. Chicken wings balancing carefully in her arms she reached the front entrance. She hadn't been sure what to wear and had gone shopping the night before. Buying a simple dress to wear and bringing a pair of jeans and shirt just in case she felt the dress was too much. She leaned into the doorbell and at the same time and heard Jake thundering down the stairs, hollering he would get the door, then flinging it open before she even had a chance to ring it.

"Hi, Melody!" shouted Jake.

"Hi, Sweetie, how are you?" Melody smiled at him "Where's your daddy?"

"He's in the kitchen. Want to see my new game?"

Jake was gone before she could answer.

Melody carefully stepped over the toys that were strewn about. "Blake?"

"Oh, hey, I didn't hear the doorbell. Let me get that for you." Melody handed him the plate of wings she had made.

"Jake opened the door before I had a chance to!" exclaimed Melody. Blake chuckled as he set the wings into the oven.

Following Blake into the kitchen she felt she made the right wardrobe choice. "I'll put the wings into the oven that way they'll stay warm until we get back from church."

"Perfect." Melody watched him as he domestically dominated the space. He righted himself then checked out his suit while adjusting and smoothing his tie. Melody was used to seeing Blake in his suits but he seemed particularly handsome today.

"You look nice." Melody smiled at him.

"You do too! Are you ready to go?" He needed to get out of the kitchen and get them moving out the door and head to church.

The stairs rumbled as Jake came flying into the kitchen with an arm load of video games he wanted to show Melody. He quickly explained how hard each game was.

"Jake, let's get ready to go, you can show her anything you want, later, when we return from church. Okay, Buddy?"

"Okay, Dad." He plopped the games down onto the kitchen table.

Blake talked excitedly in the car about church and how important it was to him and his family. This was a side of Blake Melody had not been privy to.

"My mother is a God-fearing woman and has always instilled God's word into my brother and me. I'm trying to do the same with Jake. Do you attend church?"

Melody wasn't sure how to answer his question and decided to be honest, "I haven't been to church in quite a while. Things happened that made me unsure in my faith."

Blake was not surprised by her answer. "God's door is always open." He said softly. The ride to the church was quiet except for periods of Jake bellowing out a song with his earplugs in while he bopped to one tune or another. Blake and Melody exchanged looks with understanding smiles, as they both shook their heads.

The church building was white with red trim. It was a small quaint building, immaculate lawn and gorgeous flowers adorned all the sides of the building.

"Morning honey, how are you?" A beautiful auburn haired woman in an immaculate dress suit leaned towards Blake and kissed him on the cheek as he shut his car door.

"Morning, Ma. This is Melody Savoy, my secretary." Blake could feel his cheeks burn as his mother's eyebrows arched slightly at Blake. She gave him the questioning eye, which meant she would drill him later on.

"Melody, this is my mother, Liza, and you already know my father."

Melody stuck out her hand to shake Liza's hand and smiled at Stephen.

"Hello, Dear. Welcome! Please come and meet our Pastor." Instantly Melody felt at ease with Liza. She had a warm spirit about her. Liza now locked arms with her and walked her towards the entrance where the pastor stood greeting those who came in.

He bellowed loudly, "Welcome! Please come in!"

As soon as she walked inside the church, she felt the atmosphere inside buzzing with energy. Everyone she met greeted her with a smile and shook her hand. By the time she sat down the worship music had come alive. Melody felt her foot tapping on the floor as the drums rolled through a powerful song. She watched Blake as he unfolded his arms and reached towards the ceiling. Eyes closed he sang the words he knew by heart. She knew Will would enjoy this. Now all were seated and Melody waited and listened as the microphone was passed around and people gave testimonies of what God had done for them that week.

The service itself was pleasant. Melody was quite surprised that she actually enjoyed it. She could see Blake was quite serious about his relationship with God. His hand gently touched her's and as she opened it and he nestled into it. Noticing his closed eyes, he looked as though he were praying for her. Once again, she felt the stirring within.

Once the service ended, he let her go and they silently made their exit.

"What did you think of the service?" Blake broke the silence as he drove back to the house.

"I actually enjoyed it." She shyly looked at her hand while she spoke. "I was surprised how welcoming everybody made me feel. It would have been hard to leave without a smile."

Blake felt the tug at his heart strings and allowed a laugh to escape. "Yeah, we've been going there for quite a while now, but I am glad you enjoyed it."

"Dad, I'm starving!" Jake bellowed from the backseat, breaking the line Blake was about to cross.

"You're always hungry!" This time he bellowed a laugh out from sheer relief of the tension building in his chest. "We'll order pizza when we get home, okay?"

"Yeah, pizza!" Jake put his earplugs back into his ears and continued bobbing to the music.

Blake pulled in the driveway and Jake bounded out of the car and waited for his father and Melody. Blake chuckled, "I'm surprised how fast that kid goes when he's hungry!" They both laughed and walked together towards the front door. Once open, Jake made a beeline for the stairs towards his bedroom and in an instant the video game could be heard.

Melody smiled with Blake who looked exasperated but smiled at Melody.

"Um . . . . I brought a change of clothes." He looked puzzled. "So I can be comfortable while watching the game?"

"Oh, right, sure! I'll show you the guest room and you can change in there. While you're doing that, I'll order the pizza."

"Thanks. I'll just go and grab my bag from the car." Melody jogged out to her car and grabbed her duffle bag as Blake waited for her.

"The guest room is upstairs to the left. It also has a bathroom in there if you need it."

"Thanks. I'll just be a minute." She walked up the thick carpeted stairs and found the beautifully decorated guest room, which she was sure his mother had helped to decorate. It definitely had a touch of her exquisite taste. Changing her clothes, she peered out the window and noticed the blue Toyota slowly driving by; she frowned for a moment, but decided to push the thought aside for now and went downstairs joining Blake in the kitchen.

"I ordered us some pizza it should be here soon." Blake opened the oven door and pulled out the wings Melody had brought over. He set the oval plate, piled high with wings, on the table. Then taking out some celery from the fridge he placed them in the sink. Melody helped wash it and Blake busily cut the celery in halves.

"I did enjoy the service today. Thank you for bringing me." Melody smiled at him. She turned off the water and tore off a piece of paper towel and dried her hands.

Blake smiled, "I'm really glad you came. It's a great church." He set the last of the celery into the bowl and placed on the table. "Melody, could you grab those plates." The doorbell rang. "That should be the pizza." Blake walked towards the front door.

Just as Melody looked out the front window she caught a glimpse of the blue Toyota in front of the house. Instinctively, she hid behind the stairwell, glancing out she watched through the front door and held her breath as Blake opened it.

"Hey! Mr. Matarazzo! Here's your pizza fresh out of the oven. That'll be, $15.95."

"Thanks for delivering that so quickly. I appreciate it. Keep the change and have a good afternoon." Blake waved and shut the door with his foot.

Melody quietly made her way back to the spot where Blake had left her. She shook her hands loose, took a deep breath and slowly exhaled. She was smiling as she heard Blake's footsteps coming into the kitchen.

"Pizza's here!" He bellowed towards the stairs as he carried the box into the kitchen.

Jake bounded into the kitchen and started to grab a slice of pizza. Blake stopped him and asked him, "Jake what do we do first?"

"Oops." Jake reached for Melody's and Blake's hand. He bowed his head, as well as, Blake. Melody awkwardly bowed her head as well.

"Thank you Jesus for this food and this day." Jake paused for a second and looked at Melody real quick and closed his eyes, "Oh, yeah, God, thank you for Melody. Amen." Jake smiled up at her as she blushed by his sweet words.

"Amen! I'm starving let's eat!" Blake pulled apart a large piece of pizza and took a bite. Much to Jake's delight, his dad snarled like an animal, Jake did the same.

"Melody these wings are delicious!" Blake leaned over and kissed her on impulse.

"Ew . . . you guys are gross!" Jake exclaimed.

"You're gross! You're covered with pizza and wing sauce." He handed him a towel. "You definitely need to take a shower tonight, Buddy."

Melody leaned back in her chair and smiled at the bantering going on between Blake and Jake. She smiled and was quiet for a moment. She ate the last of her pizza slice and laughed along with Blake and Jake.

"Melody, tell him my face isn't dirty!" Jake giggled

"Hate to tell you, Buddy, but your daddy is right, you are covered with wing sauce from ear to ear!" She reached over the table and with a napkin she dabbed his nose and showed him the sauce that came off on the napkin.

"Aw man, do I really gotta take a bath?" Jake asked then caught his father's eye. "Ooookkayy . . . . I'll take a bath, geesh." Jake reached for one more slice of pizza and inhaled that before deciding he was full.

"Dad, May I be excused? I want to finish playing my video game."

"Is your book report finished?"

"No."

"Jake, you know the drill. Go finish your book report, bring it to me. I'll check it for you and if there is time you can play your video game until bed time." Blake placed his plate into the sink.

"But, Dad, I have until Thursday to finish it!"

"Jake, Do as you are told!"

"Yes, Dad." Jake arose from his chair, picked up his plate and placed it in the sink. Blake handed him a napkin for him to wipe his face, Jake grinned as Blake tussled his hair.

"Dad!" Jake laughed, "Okay, okay I'm going. At least I liked the book this time!" Jake exaggerated his footsteps on the stairs and he could be heard going to his room. Blake rolled his eyes at Melody, "He's a smart kid just doesn't like to do his homework."

Melody chuckled, "What kid does?"

"You got a point there." Blake laughed. "I'm going to go and check on him. I'll be right back and we can watch the game."

"Okay. I'll wait for you in the living room."

Melody wandered into the living room while she waited for Blake. She was stunned by the openness of Blake's heart. She felt twinges of guilt building up inside her each time she was with Blake. She deflected many of his questions and knowing the line of work he was in, he'd get suspicious sooner or later. He'd know she was not who he thought she was. Peering out the window again she noticed the blue Toyota, parked across the street. She checked her phone for messages. She had called the Quad several times and they had not returned her calls. That was odd. Maybe Hal has them undercover somewhere. She had no idea it was the Quad watching her from the blue Toyota as she stared back at them, and fortunately for them, she couldn't see through the tinted windows.

Melody had half a mind to storm over to the car and demand to know who they were. Her wisdom won out and she decided against it. She made a mental note to check the plate number before leaving.

Knowing her time was running out and suspicion would get the best of Blake sooner or later, she would have to tell him the truth. But, being unsure if he would understand the truth, she was trying to be very cautious about opening her heart to him. There was only one who knew the truth and he was killed in the line of duty while fighting in Iraq. Losing him had torn a hole in her heart and she wondered if she could ever love someone again. But, Blake was different, wasn't he? Yes. He was. She could trust him. She'd felt that today for sure and for certain. She'd wanted to tell him everything and knowing how strongly Blake felt about honesty, how was he going to feel once he found out who she really was. Would he still care for her as Arvidia? Her train of thought proved to her heart just how important Blake Matarazzo was to her.

Blake came downstairs and noticed Melody staring intensely out the window.

"Melody, are you okay?" He moved toward her and gently put his arms around her shoulder tugging her around to face him. When he looked into her eyes, he noticed her lips quivered ever so slightly and her eyes were brimming with tears. He hugged her, but his lawyer instincts kicked in as he read her body language. His face turned serious. He pulled away from her and placing both hands about her face, he said firmly, "Melody. Whatever it is that is troubling you, you can tell me. I promise. I will help you in any way I can." She buried her face close to his as he whispered, "You can trust me, Mel."

Her heart felt like it was breaking in two. With all of her being, she knew his statement to her was true and she knew at that moment, he could not know the truth, not now and perhaps never.

CHAPTER 10

THE OFFICE BREAK-IN

As Blake readied himself for bed, he couldn't shake the look in Melody's eyes. She was scared but, why? Slipping under the comforter he had no idea he'd be tossing and turning throughout the night. He was puzzled by her. She seemed a little nervous when she left so abruptly, and that was only shortly after I had hugged her. He knew something was disturbing her. But all he could do now was stare at the ceiling with his arms nestled behind his head. *What is she hiding? Who is she hiding from?* Blake wondered. The alarm buzzed before he could render any further thoughts. He slowly rose from his bed, and then stumbled into the shower. It's another Monday and his only issue at hand was getting Jake out of bed and off to school.

Pulling the corners of his son's blanket, Blake said, "Rise and shine Jake!" Jake moaned and pulled the covers back over his head. "Jake, come on, I got a busy day today and it's not the time to start messing around."

"Why do I have to go to school?" As he stumbled out of bed and tried to put on the same clothes he had on the day before.

"What?" His father gave him the Italian eye look.

Jake knew better than to say any back talk. He dropped the clothes on the floor, "Okay, Okay, I'll find different ones." Jake reached into his closet and pulled out clean clothes for the day.

Blake headed downstairs shaking his head and he chuckling to himself. He sometimes wondered about that boy. He poured himself a cup of coffee and flipped open his laptop. He scanned his emails and office messages, one email caught his eye, "What have we here?" Blake muttered to himself. There was an email from Gus Laurent.

What are you doing about my case? *The guy can't take a hint!* Blake was exasperated *with this man.* **DELETE.** That should send some kind of a message. After checking over his schedule, he realized it would not allow him time to pick up his son from school. He decided to call his mother.

"Hi, Ma, it's me. Listen, I am going to be tied up in court all day today. Would you be able to pick up Jake after school?"

"Sure, Honey. What time does his school get out?" Her voice was pleasant to hear when he was stressed. I'm sure I didn't think that way when she had to wake me up for school.

"3:15." He let out a chuckle.

"You're in a good mood. What time do you think you will be picking him up?" Liza asked.

"You do that to me Ma. I am hoping to get him by 4:30pm. Is that okay with you?"

"Yes, on one condition, I would like you boys to come over for dinner on Friday. We haven't talked in a while."

"I know, Ma. I'm sorry. You know how it gets crazy with work and Jake. Friday will be great. I'll make it happen."

"Okay, I'll make your favorite. Love you, Honey."

"Love you too, Ma." Blake hung up. He wanted to talk with her about Melody, Friday would be good.

"Jake what do you want for breakfast?" Blake hollered upstairs.

"Pop tarts!" Jake replied. Blake moaned he should have known not to ask. He quickly threw two pop tarts into the toaster and hastily prepared himself for the day. Soon, Jake came running down the stairs.

"Jake, let's go!" Blake was packed up, keys in hand and standing at the door.

"Coming, Dad!" Jake shoved the remaining parts of the pop tart into his mouth and grabbed his backpack. Blake locked the front door of the house and clicked the starter to his car. He walked to the end of the driveway and picked up his newspaper. While he scanned the day's headlines, he noticed a gold Lexus slowly driving by. "Hmmm," he thought, "must be lost. I can't leave Jake in the car too long to ask. I'm sure they'll figure it out."

The morning traffic rush seemed to crawl at a snail's pace. Jake busily listened to his music from his MP3 player.

"Dad, is Melody coming over tonight?" Jake seemed to holler a bit too loud. Blake leaned over and pulled out one of his ear-plugs, "Son, you need to turn that down. I'm not sure. I'm going to be busy in court all day. Grandma is picking you up from school today."

"Oh, ok." He lacked enthusiasm but understood.

"Jake, do you like Melody?"

"Yeah, she's cool." Jake grinned and he flashed two thumbs up at his father. Blake roared with laughter. He pulled into Jake's school parking lot and watched as his son quickly exited the car to meet up with his friends, hanging out by the front entrance of the school.

"Have a good day in school Jake. Remember, Grandma is picking you up today." Blake had to call to the back of his head.

"Okay, Dad. Bye!" He waved backwards at his father while running towards his friends.

And then the heavy rain came down and he remembered he'd left his umbrella in the foyer. *Wonderful* He thought sarcastically.

"Good Morning, Sheila! I brought you some coffee from Starbucks!" Melody chimed.

"Oh, you are a doll. Thank you! I swear the phones know the minute I walk in here."

Melody hurried to her desk. She knew Blake had a full schedule and wanted to make sure he had everything ready before heading to court. She checked the files on her desk and checked for last minute messages from Blake. She was startled to hear a rustle come from within Blake's office. *That's funny, I didn't see his car and why is his door shut?* Melody stood, and walked towards his office, while reaching for the doorknob, the door suddenly jerked open and a tall figure shoved her to the floor.

"GET OUT OF MY WAY!" Melody quickly jumped up and chased after him. She ran close behind him and looked out the lobby window. A gold Lexus sped away. The back end of the SUV seemed to be covered with mud thus covering the license plate.

"What on earth?" exclaimed Sheila "Are you okay? Who was that?"

"I don't know, but I intend to find out!" Melody was breathless as she rubbed her arm where she fell onto the door-frame. She hurried back to Blake's office and quickly looked around. Everything appeared to be in its place.

"What!" Melody heard Blake shouting as Shelia explained to Blake what had just happened. She heard him running toward his office. "Melody, are you okay? Do you need medical attention?" Blake was deeply concerned.

"No, I'm fine. My arm hurts a little." Melody was angry and confused. She did not get a good look at the guy or get the plates off the car. She did find a strange looking moon shape medallion on the floor just as Blake walked in. Quickly, she stashed it in her pocket.

Blake insisted she have her arm examined in the ER at a local hospital. She decided not to argue with him. She could see he was visibly upset. "Okay, Blake, I will go. But, you need to hurry up or you are going to be late for court. I'll call you later."

Melody sat in the emergency room with a cold pack on her arm. Her thoughts were swirling with questions and she thought of Joe Rizzo. She knew he would be able to help her. She was puzzled as to why the Quad had not returned her calls. Her only option left was to call Joe.

Melody looked around to see if it was safe to call. She speed dialed Joe.

"This is Joe."

"Joe, its Arvidia." Arvidia whispered.

"Hey, Girl! Why are you whispering?" Joe became alarmed.

"I am in the emergency room and I don't want anyone to hear. Listen, I need a favor. Is it possible for you to come out here? I cannot get a hold of the guys. They haven't returned my calls. Hal must have them undercover or something. There's something weird going on here."

Joe's stomach dropped. He knew the Quad was watching her. "Why are you in the emergency room? What do you mean something weird is going on?"

"I got to the office and heard some noise in Blake's office, I went to open the door and this guy pushed me to the ground and I hurt my arm. I chased him out of the office and he took off in a gold Lexus. My arm is okay, I'm sure it's just bruised. I checked around Blake's office nothing seemed to be missing, but I did find a strange moon shape medallion by his desk. It appeared to have broken off a chain. It looks oddly familiar to me. I need you to analyze it. Can you talk to Hal and see if you can come out here soon? This situation is getting weirder by the minute."

"Wow! That is strange. Let me clear it with Hal and I will get back with you."

"Okay, Joe, thanks." A nurse came in and told her a doctor would be in soon to examine her.

Joe speed dialed Todd. "This is Todd."

"Todd, Rizzo. I have a quick question. Are you guys driving a gold Lexus?"

"Are you kidding? No, we are renting a blue Toyota. Why?"

Joe quickly explained the conversation he had with Arvidia.

"Oh, I don't like the sound of that." Todd sat up straight and glancing at the other members of the Quad, who looked, questioning the phone call.

"Arvidia wants me to come out there and help her out. I have to admit there does seem to be something strange going on. She didn't mention anything about Jim Mason. I don't think she's aware. I told her I would clear it with Hal."

"Okay, Joe let us know when you get here. I'm sure Hal will clear you." Todd slid low in his car seat and pursed his lips together. They had been keeping watch outside of the emergency room. He explained to the other guys about Joe's and Arvidia's conversation.

"A gold Lexus, Did she get the plate?" Mark asked. He quickly pulled up his phone to check how many Gold Lexus were registered in the state of New York.

"No. She said the back of the SUV was covered with mud."

"Did she give a description of the guy she saw in Blake's office?" Mark asked.

"Joe said he was too fast and she did not get a good look at his face. As we all know Joe, he's busy pecking away on his keyboard as we speak. He did mention Arvidia found a strange moon shape medallion on the floor. That may lead us somewhere. Chris, would you go in and check on Arvidia?"

Chris put on his hat and glasses and exited out of the car. He shuffled his way into the hospital. As he walked down the hallway, he could hear Arvidia's voice. "Thank you, doctor, I appreciate it." Melody nearly bumped into Chris as she walked out.

"Oh, I'm sorry." Melody said apologetically.

"Not a problem ma'am" Chris shuffled ahead. Melody headed out for the exit doors. "She's coming out. Meet me out front." Chris whispered into his blue-tooth.

Joe Rizzo felt awkward sitting in Hal's office. The solace of his lab was where he felt most comfortable. Joe hastily explained to Hal the recent events and his conversation with Arvidia.

Hal was infuriated with himself. He thought by sending Arvidia away from Seattle she would be protected. Instead, it appeared the danger was heading straight for her. He did not like what Joe explained to him especially about Gus Laurent.

"Joe, I want you go out there immediately and help Arvidia. Keep me informed of any developments big or small. You'll go undercover and be her visiting brother."

"Yes, Sir." Joe gathered his supplies in a small suitcase. He headed for Sea-Tac Airport.

CHAPTER 11

THE FAMILY DINNER

The late afternoon sun had begun its descent and sliced through his office blinds. As he flopped down into the high back leather seat, loosening his tie, he briefly recalled the grueling court. He could feel the dark razor stubble as he wiped his chin in thought. It expressed exactly how he felt, rough. At least the judge agreed to a reprieve until Monday. He'd finish the day by checking emails and just as he completed this task, she walked in. Melody set the cup of coffee on his desk and he hadn't even asked for it.

"Blake, why don't you go home and relax? You look exhausted!"

"I would, but I promised my mother I'd go over for dinner." Blake suddenly sat up in his chair and smiled, "Why don't you come with me?" Then he noticed she was rubbing her arm. "Is your arm okay?"

Melody had hoped to finish searching his office. "Oh yeah, it's fine, it is just a little sore. I don't want to intrude on your family's dinner."

"You won't be. Let me call my mother and let her know you're coming. Trust me she will not mind in the least." Blake reached for the cell in his pocket and quickly punched in #2. Speed dial.

Melody knew it was useless to argue with him about it. While he spoke to his mother, she quietly stepped out of his office and returned to her own desk, all the while, hoping she could find time to search his office again. She checked her own cell and noticed there was a text from Joe, stating he was on his way. *Good. Maybe he can help me figure out what the heck is going here.* Relieved, she shut her phone and rubbed her arm. She could see the ugly bruise forming underneath the ace bandage.

Blake poked his head out of his office and grinned, "See I told you it wouldn't be a problem!" Melody laughed and shook her head. *Where does he get his energy from?* Melody wondered.

"You talked me into it, I'll come." Shutting down her PC; she couldn't help but smile.

"Great! Jake will be happy to see you. Give me a few minutes and we'll go."

"Okay." Melody began to gather her things together just as Blake shut down his computer.

"You ready?" Blake twirled his keys around his fingers.

"Yep." She picked up her purse and walked alongside him towards his car. It was decided to leave her car in the parking lot and he'd bring her back later to retrieve it. As Blake drove, he talked enthusiastically about his parent's house. It was a place of fond childhood memories shared with his brother, Kyle.

Blake pulled up and into the family's driveway as it parted ways to beautifully trimmed bushes and gorgeous, huge old oak trees which led the way toward the front entrance. He spoke fondly of the years he'd spent growing up there.

"This is where my brother and I played. We'd climb as high as we could and jump. And before you ask, yes, I've broken a bone or two, much to my mother's distress." He laughed just as Melody did.

"Did you jump or were you pushed out?"

"Both. He had the upper hand and he was bigger than me." He smiled, as he parked the BMW into the crescent shape drive alongside the front entrance.

"Here we are! I'm famished! I hope you're hungry." He didn't wait for her reply he was feeling a little nervous, but in a good way. "She usually has enough to feed an army." Exiting the car he walked around to the passenger side and opened Melody's door. Smiling at him, she reached for his outstretched hand. The wind blew her long black hair into Blake's face. Her Calvin Klein perfume filled his nostrils. He loved how stylish she dressed each day. He smiled and gazed into those piercing blue eyes that made him sway every time, they could see into his soul, he just knew it. Yet, they still seemed to hold much pain and he ached to ask her what had happened, but he knew from experience in dealing with traumatized clients, he'd have to give her time. She'd tell him; at least he hoped she would. He couldn't help but notice she didn't speak of her family or her past. Her conversations were always in the present.

"Thank you." She placed her hands into his and together they walked towards the large oak front doors. She enjoyed the familiarity he expressed. It felt right to be here, to be holding his hand. Perhaps he is the one to be trusted.

"Ma, I'm here!" Blake hollered as he barely knocked on the door while walking through. He gave Melody's hand a tight squeeze as they walked down the corridor towards the kitchen.

"Daddy!" Jake raced from the living room to his father's outstretched arms. "Hi, Melody! Grandma, Melody's is here!" He had told his grandmother earlier that day about how Melody and his father were dating.

"Hey, there buddy! How was your day at school? Did you do your homework? Were you good for Grandma?" He hugged his son before putting him back on his feet.

"Yes, he was! Hi, love," she squeezed his cheeks and kissed him. Like Blake, she had dark black hair and soft brown eyes. Her presence made Melody feel right at home.

"Ma, you remember Melody?" Blake seemed to turn shy as the two women locked eyes.

Liza pretended to hit Blake on the back of his head just as she always did when he was growing up. "Of course I remember her. Welcome, Melody. I'm so glad you could join us for dinner!" Liza promptly put her arm through hers and walked toward the kitchen. She was highly intrigued by Melody. It had been, nearly a century since Blake brought a woman to his parent's home, well at least it seemed that way. "Melody, please call me Liza," Liza pointed her finger at Blake and stated, "Blake your father is in the living room. He wants to speak with you about court today. Jake, make sure you go and wash up for dinner. Melody, come with me and we will chat. Blake, go on!" She shooed him away as they continued into the kitchen area.

Jake pulled on his father's arm and dragged him into the living room. He had to show him the new video game Grandma had just bought him. He could clearly hear his mother chatting up a storm with her newest guest in the kitchen.

"How did court go?" Stephen asked. He peered over his newspaper to look at his son.

"Okay, the judge gave us a reprieve and we'll resume on Monday."

"What time Monday?"

"9 am sharp." Blake stated.

"I will come with you. You can watch your old man wrangle with these guys!" Stephen was a well-respected lawyer who never took NO for an answer. If there was a way, he would find one.

"Dinner is ready! Come and eat!" chimed Liza.

"Let's not keep Mother waiting, you know how she gets." They both chuckled as they made their way into the dining room.

The family gathered around the dining room table and gave thanks. Blake and Melody sat across from one another with Jake next to his father and the parents at either head of the table. Blake would catch a glimpse of Melody throughout dinner and he thought; *I could get use to this.*

Melody found it hard to concentrate when every time she looked up Blake was watching her. *I could really get use to this,* she thought several times. *This is what it's like to have a real family.*

After dinner, Jake pulled Melody into the living room begging her to play his new video game with him. Blake smiled as he watched, from the dining room, as she sat on the floor with a Wii stick, from him and play along. She laughed and giggled as she lost as quickly as she lost a game just as quickly she'd started, and much to the delight to Jake.

"Okay love, start spilling!" Liza quipped at Blake. She had locked arms with him and pulled him back into the kitchen.

"Ma, I do not know that much about her." He did tell her about her physical scars, how little she talked about her past and family. "I care about her a great deal, but I do not understand why she doesn't trust me enough to talk about herself or her past."

"Give her time honey, maybe people in her past gave her reasons not to trust so easily. Be patient with her." Liza handed him a plate full of food to take home. She ruffled his hair as she had always done. "I like her, she'll come around."

"I guess you're right, Ma." Blake recalled another time in his life where mom was always right. She told him he'd break his arm one day jumping out of the trees. He did. The conversation deepened some more and time had slipped by before Melody entered into the kitchen and announced Jake was sound asleep on the couch.

"Honey, why don't you pick him up in the morning? No sense in waking him up now. He's had quite the day." Liza in her dramatically tone swept her hand across her brow and smiled.

"Thanks, Ma." He grinned and kissed her on the cheek and he yawned deeply. "I guess we better get going. If I don't leave now, I am going to join Jake on the couch!" Both Liza and Melody laughed.

"Good night, Ma."

"Good night, love." Liza turned her attention toward Melody. "It was a pleasure having you join us for dinner. Please, come again." Liza hugged her lightly.

"Thank you so much for the extended invitation. Dinner was lovely and the company was exceptional. I really enjoyed it."

"You are very welcome, dear." Back to Blake she warned, "Drive safe. I'll see you in the morning. Say good bye to your father." She gently ushered toward the door.

Stephen reached the front door at the exact same time. He had nearly fallen asleep in his recliner when he heard his Liza laugh. "I'll see you in the morning, Son. Melody, always a pleasure to see your smiling face, you are a wonderful asset to the Matarazzo office."

Waving to his mother from the car as he drove slowly out of the driveway, he felt another wave of tiredness overcoming him and he shook his head to wake up. He even cracked the window for fresh air. Melody broke the quiet spell.

"Your parents are really nice, I like them. Your mother's cooking, was amazing!"

Blake laughed and looked at Melody. "Yeah, she's an fantastic cook. She's been a lifesaver helping me out with Jake especially since the divorce. I'd be lost if it weren't for her." Blake spoke before he thought about what his tired tongue was spitting out. So, what about you and your family? What are they like?"

Melody inhaled slowly. She had never allowed her relationship with men to get this close and Blake was hitting it too close. Absently, she reached up and touched the scar on her neck. She had no idea how to answer his question. She didn't know the truth about what happened to her family for she had no memory of them. Will explained to her he had adopted her when the Quad was not able to find her family. She never stopped wondering where her family was. She always had a twinge of something missing from her life. On occasions throughout her life, she would hear a little girl's voice calling her. She had chalked it up to she was just dreaming.

"Well, my parents died when I was young and I was adopted by a man name Will."

Blake was stunned and wished he thought before he spoke. "I am so sorry. I didn't know. How did they die?"

Melody felt tears burning her eyes and she blurted out, "I...just can't remember!" She wanted to jump out of the car and run away from Blake. It was too much for her. She wanted to run home to Hal, Joe, the Quad and Will. To the ones who knew the truth about her. *Boy I suck at this job. This assignment!* Melody yelled to herself. She angrily wiped the tears before they fell onto her cheeks.

Blake immediately pulled the car to the side of the road and threw it into park. He was quite surprised by Melody's outburst and instinctively, reached for her.

"I am so sorry for upsetting you, Mel. Please forgive me for my rudeness. It was thoughtless of me to intrude on your privacy." Melody felt blood rushing to her cheeks. *Pull yourself together or you will blow your cover!*

"No, it's okay, I'm sorry, I don't know what came over me. I guess I am tired."

"Are you sure you are okay?"

"Yes." She lifted her eyes to Blake's. His were full of concern and compassion. She touched his cheek. "Really, Blake, I'm okay. I just had a mini-meltdown. I just need some sleep and some dark chocolate!" She laughed nervously.

"Chocolate I can handle! Hey, why don't you leave your car at the office? I will drive you home and pick you up in the morning. How does that sound?" Blake started up the BMW and slowly eased back on the road. Melody did not answer him. Blake turned his head to look at her. "Melody?"

Melody's eyes were fixated on the road ahead of them. Will suddenly appeared in the middle of the road. *Danger is coming!* Whispered Will. He held one single eagle feathers in each of his hands and held them up to the sky, then he faded into the night.

All of a sudden. Melody inhaled sharply as she gripped the door. A gold Lexus sped past them with the tires screeching against the pavement. Blake swerved and wrestled with the steering wheel to regain control of the car.

"Boy, some people are impatient!" shouted Blake as he swerved back on the road. Melody felt panic rising up within her. This was not someone who was impatient. This was someone sending a message of warning. She fiddled with her cell phone and wondered if she should call someone. Her heart felt as though it jumped up into her throat. She could feel it pulsating.

"You okay?" Blake noticed Melody was several shades of white and gripping onto her cell phone. "Don't bother calling, it's just an idiot driver. Don't worry about it. Let's get you home and you can get some shut eye"

Blake pulled into the parking lot of her apartment building. "Are you sure you are okay?" Melody looked as though she had seen a ghost.

"Yes, I'm fine. I think I just need a good night's rest. What time in the morning shall I expect you, sir?" Melody teased.

"Nine AM sharp!" Blake laughed and kissed her. "Get some rest. I was thinking after we get some work done at the office, maybe you'd care to join Jake and I for an afternoon of fun?"

"Sure! I'd love that."

"Great. I will see you in the morning." She walked to her door as Blake waited for her to enter before driving away.

She waved to him as she unlocked her apartment door and stepped inside. She quickly shut and locked the door as she expelled a huge sigh of relief. As she flicked on her lights and peered through the window, she waved again to Blake as he drove off. Setting her purse onto the couch she kicked off her shoes. The she heard the toilet flushed. Grabbing her handbag, she quickly drew her gun and shouted, "Who's there?"

Joe Rizzo came quickly out of the bathroom and put up his hands, "Arvidia, it's me Joe!"

"Oh my God, Joe, you scared the daylights out of me!"

"Didn't you get my text? Why are you so jumpy?"

"Yes, I got it except you did not say when you would be here." She replaced her gun and plopped down on the couch. "It's been a long day, Joe." I think someone is onto me. I saw the gold Lexus again. It nearly ran us off the road, not twenty minutes ago."

"What? Are you okay? Did you get the plates? Who's the, US?" Joe took a seat beside her on the couch.

"No, I wasn't able to get the plates. I'm sure it's the same car I saw at the firm. I am fine. Just confused as to what is going on. Right before it happened, Will showed up in the middle of the road. He was warning me about something. I just don't know what it is he's warning me about." Scooting herself into a more comfortable position she knew Joe would be confused. She knew this was going to be a long night.

"Warned you how? What did he say?"

"All he said was, Danger is coming." Arvidia described the evening events to Joe and the vision she saw just before the car tried to run them off the road.

"If Will was in his warrior garb, doesn't that mean war? What is the significance of the feathers?" Joe inquired as he poured himself coffee from the small pot he had placed on the coffee table just before he had to use the bathroom.

"If I remember right, the eagle feathers symbolize the asking of the Great One for protection from harm. The bald eagle, as you know, is federally protected but most importantly it's fiercely protected by the tribe on Lummi Island." Arvidia suddenly stopped speaking and looked around the living room, "What did you do? Bring the whole office here?"

Joe answered sheepishly, "I wasn't sure what I'd need." Joe had every corner in the living room set up with computers and gadgets that would render James Bond green with envy.

"I should've known you would bring the lab with you." Arvidia laughed.

"Don't think I didn't noticed you didn't answer my question about who's US? And did you call and check in with Hal yet?" Joe sipped his coffee and relished the moment.

Arvidia grabbed her cell out of her pocket and quickly dialed. She left him a message. All was okay and Joe arrived safely. She reached for her purse and pulled out the medallion she'd found in Blake's office. "This is the medallion I told you about. The 'US' I was referring to was Blake. I had dinner with him and his family."

Joe raised his eyes just a bit and decided not to get into that at this time. He became instantly alarmed when Arvidia showed him the medallion. He had hoped she hadn't noticed his reaction. He examined it quickly then went to his computer. He sent his lab partner, Rudy an email. Rudy could verify what he suspected. The origin of the medallion was very familiar.

"I'm on it, don't you worry. Why don't you get some rest you look exhausted." Joe needed her out of his way for a time and he was wide awake.

"Aren't you going to get some sleep?" Arvidia asked knowing the answer.

"No, I slept on the plane. Go on and get some sleep." Joe barely glanced up at Arvidia as she shook her head and grabbed her cell and walked into the bedroom. Joe would be working all night. She undressed and got into bed. She saw a text message from Blake. **I hope U r ok. Rest well.**

Melody texted a message back to him. **I am fine. I will, U too.**

The next morning, Arvidia awoke to the smell of coffee brewing and breakfast cooking. She wondered if Joe had ever slept.

"Morning, you find out anything?" Arvidia inquired.

"No, I am waiting on a few things. I made you some breakfast." He pointed and smiled toward the table.

"Thanks, you didn't sleep did you?"

"Nope." Joe's computer beeped a message. He had hoped this was the message he was waiting for. He quickly stepped back to the computer and glanced at the glaring message.

"Joe, Blake is picking me up soon. I left my car at the office, he had asked me if I would help him with some work and he invited me to spend some time with him and his son."

Joe spun around, eyebrows arched, "Aren't you getting a bit chummy with this guy? Does he know anything?"

Arvidia quickly shook her head. "No. He doesn't know anything. I'm being very careful. Joe, I have researched him and his office. I've found nothing! But," Arvidia pointed her finger at Joe, "this Gus dude? There's definitely something up with him. I can't put my finger on it. I keep getting the willies about him. There is some connection somewhere; somehow, I can't put my finger on it."

Joe held his breath. He did not dare tell her about Jim Mason escaping.

"Okay, just be careful. I will let you know once I get something back about this medallion."

"Okay, I'll wait for Blake outside. Call me if you need anything."
Arvidia put her coat on and stepped out into the bitter wind. Fall had
arrived with a vengeance and way too soon. Good thing she didn't have
to wait long. Blake was arriving that same minute.

Once Joe heard the car door shut he peeked from between the
curtains and saw her getting into a black BMW waiting until the car was
out of sight. He went back to the computer and clicked on the message
he had hidden from Arvidia when she came into the kitchen earlier. He
didn't want to take the chance of her reading it. Joe held his breath as
he read the urgent message from his lab buddy, Rudy. Rudy verified his
suspicion. He too instantly recognized the medallion. The medallion was
the same medallion but a smaller version of the one Jim Mason wore
the day he was arrested. The prints from it came back positive for Gus
Laurent but a second unknown print, appeared as well.

"Holy smokes." Joe knew something was amuck and Hal was not
going to like this.

CHAPTER 12

LASER TAG

Blake could see Melody standing outside waiting for him. His heart fluttered as she watched the wind whipped her hair around. He smiled and waved. She wore skin tight Levis blue jeans with her knee high black boots. Her dark, blue sweater just heightened the beauty of her piercing blue eyes.

"Dad, there she is!" Jake waved excitedly from the backseat of the car. Melody smiled and waved back.

"Hey! How are you on this windy morning?" Blake smiled and kissed Melody as she entered the car.

Jake scrunched up his face in disgust. "Ewwww. That is so gross." Then hurriedly, he said, "Dad got you something!"

"Jake. That was supposed to be a surprise!" Blake looked sternly into the rearview mirror.

"Oops." Jake mischievously grinned at his father.

Blake reached back behind the seat and pulled out a red rose and a box of Lindt dark chocolate. She felt the heat go right to her cheeks and her heart.

"Thank you. That's so sweet." She gave him a quick peck on the cheek.

"Can I have a chocolate?" asked Jake.

"May I?" Blake corrected Jake.

"May I have a piece of chocolate?" Jake gave Melody the puppy dog look, Melody laughed. She no sooner handed it to him and watched him inhale the morsel.

"I was thinking maybe we can skip work and have lunch; we can go to Red Lobster? Then we can come back and pick up your car?"

"Sounds like a plan, I like that idea. You're the boss!" She actually winked his way.

"Yay!" Jake yelled and clapped his hands.

"Okay, Red Lobster here we come!" Blake pretended to be racing his car. Melody turned winked and watched as Jake laughed as the engine revved up, a little.

Melody relaxed on the drive and while staring out the window she recognized all the signs of Thanksgivings. Store front decorations were going up as they drove through town.

"Oh my, I haven't even thought about Thanksgiving!"

"I know. Jake has already mentioned taking out the Christmas décor." Melody laughed. "And here we are! I thought maybe after lunch, we." Blake found a spot close to the entrance and parked. He looked sternly at Jake and put a finger to his lips. He knew his son and wouldn't you know it he was just about to blow it.

"We're going . . ." Jake slapped his hands across his mouth and chocolate smeared onto his mouth and cheeks. Blake groaned.

"What? Do I detect another surprise?" Melody asked with a smile.

"Well, I promised Jake I'd take him to the laser tag arena so he could play with his cousins. I thought it'd be a fun activity for all of us . . . to do." He hesitated for a moment until he heard her response.

"Oooo . . . Now that sounds like fun, I'm game!" Melody giggled and clapped her hands.

As they got out of the car she quickly scanned the parking lot and oncoming traffic but could see no sign of the gold Lexus. She did see someone leaning against the tree smoking. *Todd? Can't be him. Boy I must be more homesick than I thought.* Melody shook her head and walked with the boys into the restaurant.

The seafood they ordered was of no comparison to Lummi Island fresh out of the ocean King Salmon and Alaskan king crab legs, there's just something about the seafood fresh from the ocean. She looked at her watch and knew that Will was most likely out on his boat crabbing about now, her mouth watered at the mere thought of the king crab legs fresh and tender and most times you wouldn't even need butter to dip it in. Will was famous around the island for his cooking crab legs and fish. It's smelled wafted throughout the island.

She watched Blake inhale his lunch as did Jake and wondered how he stayed so thin. Now that Jake was full he asked repeatedly when they would leave. Finally, it was time to go, Jake could hardly be held back as he raced towards the car.

"Boy, you can't keep that kid down!" Melody laughed. Blake shook his head, smiling. He slipped his wallet into his pants pocket and casually slid his hand into hers as they strolled towards the car. Melody turned to him briefly and felt her heart skip a beat; she looked down as she felt her cheeks burning. She didn't let go of his hand until they reached the car. As he usually did, he opened the passenger door for her.

When they reached the entrance of the Laser Tag Game Field, she recognized Angelo from the office. He was there with his own two children. The kids talked excitedly over each other and somehow they all understood what the other one said.

Blake helped Melody strap on her vest and helmet. She giggled to herself at the humor of this. The kids had them on before Blake could turn around and ask if anyone needed help.

"Okay kids, let's roll!" The three kids nearly ran over the adults trying to beat each other to the entrance.

Once inside, the kids raced and laser tagged each other. Blake and Angelo played alongside with Melody. Each shot Melody shot was expertly dead-centered in the chest of the "victim". She gathered up the most points and gave the prize to Jake.

"Wow, you shot like an expert in there!" Blake exclaimed. He exchanged looks with Angelo who was just as surprised as Blake was. She was obviously very skilled, unlike the clumsy girl on the Wii game system.

Melody realized she probably should not have exposed her skills like that. She saw the looks Blake and Angelo exchanged. She chuckled and said, "Well, hunting with my father paid off." That part was true.

"Yeah, I guess so." Blake stated. He arched his eyebrow to Angelo who shrugged his shoulders.

The day wore on and after Laser-Tag they stopped by the mall for a few things before returning home. Jake had fallen asleep as soon as the seatbelt clasped. Melody reached over and touched his face as he slept. He was softening her heart. She had noticed that Jake rarely left her side and held her hand as often as he could. Melody fell silent as her thoughts returned to the guilt piling up inside her. Melody looked at Blake and she wondered if she could trust him with the truth. Would his feelings change towards her? Some of her co-workers had told her how he rarely dated since his divorce. This was the first they had seen him this happy since. She closed her eyes and wished everything were different. A simple assignment, right, instead her first time away from the Quad was turning into something altogether different and she had no idea what was in store. What was the danger Will was warning her about? Was it the Lexus or Blake?

Blake carried his sleepy son up to his bedroom and returned to the living room where Melody waited. "Well, I guess we'll have to get your car tomorrow. I'm sorry. The day just flew by! He looked into her eyes and paused, then asked, "Would you care for some wine?"

"Sure. I'd love some." It seemed natural to walk in and relax on the sofa.

"Okay, coming up."

She turned on the TV and noticed the Bills were winning the game. "Blake your team is winning!"

Blake raced back into the living room with the wine toppling out of the glasses. He set them down quickly never taking his eyes off the television set. "Yes!" Blake threw his fists into the air in a touchdown stance, and then plopped down onto the couch. Reaching over he picked a wine glass and handed it to her, then he picked up his own and together, gently, they clinked glasses together and he said, "Here's to a great day. I really enjoyed it."

"I could not agree with you more. I had a wonderful time." She leaned into him and cuddled up close laying her head onto his chest. Blake watched the game as he methodically brushed her hair with his hand. After a short time he gently lifted her face to his lips and softly kissed her. A quiet passion rose between both of them as the game droned on, but it was Blake that brought it to a halt. "It's late and I'm only human." She totally got his meaning. "You're welcome to sleep on the sofa or if you choose, I could call a cab?" He dragged out the cab part in what seemed to be a whisper. She grinned, "I can sleep on the sofa. It's been a long and wonderful day and we're both tired."

Blake was torn whether to stay there with Melody on the couch or sleep in his bedroom. He did not want to leave her side. He softly touched her face as she fluttered to sleep. He knew his son's million questions would be hard to answer in the morning if he stayed on the couch with Melody. Blake clicked the TV off and tore himself away from her. It was getting tougher to do but he knew he must. He removed the glasses from the coffee table and opened a trunk and found a lovely woven blanket, courtesy of his mother's fine craftsmanship; he knew that would keep her warm for the night. She had already seemed to have settled into the soft furnishings as he placed the blanket over her small form, he leaned over and gently kissed her head she slept soundly. He took the wine glasses into the kitchen and headed for the stairs. Leaving the hall light on for his guest, he walked up the stairs while checking his cell for any messages. There was one from Jake's mother. She was in town and wanted to know if she could see Jake the following day. He'd text her and say it was okay. He didn't want her voice to be the last thing he heard before going to sleep.

Melody awoke suddenly to the smell of coffee brewing, and a little boy's voices in the kitchen. She checked her cell and saw several messages waiting for her. Walking into the kitchen she stopped and stood in the doorway. Jake looked very upset.

"I don't want to see her!" he cried quietly with clenched teeth.

"She's your mother and she wants to spend some time with you and you should."

Jake folded his arms across his chest and furrowed his eyebrows together as he stared angrily at his father. He stomped his feet. "I am not going!" He was still trying to be quiet not knowing Melody was behind him, awake.

Melody kneeled down and tapped his shoulder. He spun around and she gently put her arms around him. Then, pulling him away and squatting down next to him, she spoke softly, "Jake, I think you should give your mother a chance."

"You do?" A tear escaped from his eyes and slid down his cheek. She quickly wiped his tears. "What if she doesn't like me?" Melody looked up at Blake who quickly explained it had been a year and a half since he last saw her.

"I think she'll be impressed with how much you have grown! I have an idea, why don't you draw a picture for her?" Melody suggested. She hated seeing Jake so upset.

"Okay." He looked into her eyes, "I'll go this time." Jake hugged Melody and glared at his father. He walked slowly up the stairs as if he were being punished.

"I wish she would see him more often. They really don't know each other very well." Blake shook his head and put his coffee cup into the sink. "Hey, would you like some coffee? Can I make you some eggs and toast?"

"Coffee would be perfect; I'm not a big breakfast person, at least not this morning." She giggled. "He'll be okay." Melody wrapped her arms around Blake's waist; he turned and lightly kissed her on the lips.

He handed her a hot cup of coffee then said, "Well, I guess what we should do is drop Jake off at his mother's and go get your car. I do have to finish up some work at the office."

"Anything I can do to help?"

"No, you take the day off. I just have to do some legal research to do. You have done enough for me. Take some time and unwind today. We'll head out as soon as I get the little monster ready. So, enjoy the coffee and we'll be right down."

They drove towards Glenville, New York where Jake's mother lived. Melody noticed the gold Lexus was back and it was following them. Anger began to build in her. She heard Will's voice echoing in her head. *Danger is coming!*

Blake pulled into his ex-wife's driveway. Jake pouted in the back seat and hesitated before getting out of the car. "Jake, it will be okay." Melody gently reassured him. She looked sharply around for the gold Lexus. It seemed to have dropped out of sight.

Jake's mother stood on the front porch waiting patiently for her son. Blake got out of the car and held the back door open for Jake. He kneeled down and hugged his son, but Jake was still a little miffed with him and ran toward his mother's porch. Blake followed and talked with his ex-wife for a few minutes and then returned to the car.

"I'll see you in a couple of days!" Blake waved and yelled out the carr window. He pointed his finger at Jake "Be good for your mother."

Jake frowned at him as Blake pulled away.

"It will be good for him to visit with his mother." Melody nodded in agreement not daring to take her eyes off the side-view mirrors. Blake turned on the radio just as breaking news was blasting through.

There were reports of increased emergency room visits of young teenagers coming in with strange symptoms from a new street drug called Blue Dust. It had hit the streets hard and had local authorities concerned.

101

Local hospitals reported patients coming into the emergency room with hypoxic-like symptoms. Some of the victims of this new street drug have died, as a result, of severe hypoxia.

Melody was riveted to the news. *Blue Dust?* Where have I heard that before?

Blake interrupted her thoughts, "I wonder what that's all about? I can't stand representing kids who get themselves into drugs. It really messes up their lives. I hate seeing them dragged off to prison. It saddens me to see that happen. It totally ruins them. I feel so helpless when their parents plead with me to help them."

Melody had seen that happen within her own investigations with the Quad. Greedy drug lords causing havoc wherever they go. It was difficult to see the drug lords skip away clean, while the underdogs that work for them get slammed into prison for doing their dirty work. It was a vicious cycle to rectify but when a big break came through and they caught the boss it made all their hard work worthwhile.

Blake pulled into the parking lot and pulled up next to her car. He tugged her in close before she could escape and kissed her passionately. "Blake you are not making this easy!" She managed to say between giggles.

"Okay, I'll settle for another hug. I have piles of work screaming for me to finish. Now you go home and get some rest and I'll call you later." He pretended to shove her off when he really wanted to reel her in.

Melody waved and watched as Blake entered the building. She sat in her car and gasped as she tossed her purse on the passenger seat. There sat a single Eagle feather. *Will!* Melody was starting to get frightened at the chain of events that were rapidly unfolding. She knew Will was trying to warn her and protect her but couldn't figure out from what. As Melody waited to exit onto the main road, she watched as the gold Lexus rolled by. Gripping the steering wheel with the feather in hand she was able to study the license plate and quickly, she speed dial Joe.

"Where have you been?" Joe yelled.

"Joe, run these plates now! NXE-1245 New York."

Joe quickly punched in the numbers and waited for the computer to respond.

"Car is owned by two people, a twenty year old male name Marcus O'Neil. He's had had some minor scrapes with the law. I don't see anything major. "Joe gulped as he read the latter part of the paragraph, "I'm waiting for the information about the other guy to come up, this darn system is running slow again." Joe hoped she didn't detect the panic rising within him.

"I don't recognize that name. Joe, I will be there in a few minutes." Arvidia hung up. The afternoon sun was bright and briefly blinded her. She held up her hand and pushed down on the gas petal as she took a sharp left hand turn. She could see the gold Lexus was four cars ahead. Gritting her teeth she glanced into the rearview mirror, and directed her car into the next lane and inching her way ever closer the Lexus. Muttering to herself she said, "I don't know who you are, but I will find out what you are up to." She crept in and found herself directly behind it. There were two of them. Seeing the driver glance in the rearview mirror, he noticed her and sharply pulled to the left, narrowly avoiding a head on collision with an oncoming car. He sped through a red light and headed towards the interstate. Arvidia knew she wouldn't be able to catch up with them. Frustrated, she slammed her fist into the steering wheel. "Dammit!" she hollered. She took a deep breath and exhaled and decided to head towards her apartment.

Joe wiped his forehead and immediately dialed Todd, "This is Todd."

"Todd! Arvidia just called and had me run these license plates on the gold Lexus. Two names came up: Marcus O'Neil and Gus Laurent!" Todd put Joe on speaker-phone and beckoned the other members of the Quad to listen in.

Joe continued on, "Let me recap what I have found out so far. Last week, Arvidia found a moon shape medallion in Blake's office the same day someone ransacked it. I ran it through for prints and I thought I recognized this medallion. Rudy, my buddy from the Seattle lab double-checked it for me." Joe paused for a moment, then continued, "Get this; the medallion is the same medallion Jim Mason wore the day he was arrested 30 years ago! This particular medallion is a smaller version of the one he had, but it is exactly the same type medallion. I ran the prints. I found one of the prints came back positive for Gus Laurent's. The second print belonged to Marcus O'Neil. I can't talk long, Arvidia should be here soon."

"Who is Marcus O'Neil?" Mark asked.

"He is twenty years old with some minor scrapes with the law. He's also the owner of the gold Lexus." Joe replied.

"Gus Laurent is Blake's client right?" Todd asked.

"Yes, but Blake terminated their contract because Gus Laurent was offering him money to make his DWI 'disappear'. Arvidia said the last appointment Blake had with Gus they had apparently gotten into an argument. She mentioned she did see Gus leave the office. He subsequently must have tiptoed back into the office. Arvidia found him riffling through Blake's desk. She didn't recognize the second dude that pushed her to the floor."

"I bet it was Marcus O'Neil. I wonder what this Gus character is really up to." Todd hummed.

Joe heard Arvidia's car pull up. "Got to go, she's here."

Arvidia opened the door. Joe could tell she was agitated. She sat right on the edge of the couch holding an eagle feather.

"What is that?" Joe point to the feather Arvidia was holding.

"I found this in my car."

"How did that get there?"

"I don't know, but I wouldn't be surprised if this is from Will. There's got to be something I'm missing somewhere. You'd think with all the training with you guys I'd be at least be able to figure this out. I totally suck at this!" She huffed and puffed as she folded her arms together, but all her toughness went out the window, temporarily as her lips began to quiver.

"Are you kidding me? You are one of the best agents in the field! Hal wouldn't have sent you if he didn't feel you could do the job." Joe thought to himself it probably would help her if she knew the truth.

"I guess you're right." She stood up, placed the feather onto the coffee table and announced, "I'm exhausted. I'm heading to bed, good night." Arvidia yawned and walk towards her bedroom.

It wasn't long before she fell into a deep slumber and Will reappeared in her dreams. He was in his warrior armor with the floor length headdress. His face was heavily-painted in black stripes. He crossed his arms across his chest and in each hand, he held a single eagle feather.

"Sqimi, Nyoowa'ls, You are Nttxwte!" (Young bald eagle, strong heart, strong mind, woman warrior!)

Arvidia awoke suddenly and sat up. *Sqimi?* Will had not called her that since she was a little girl. Arvidia's stomach turned. She knew without a doubt something bad was coming. She laid back down and rubbed her hair, I can't withhold the truth from Blake any longer I'm going to have to tell Blake the truth. She knew she was risking her relationship with Blake. Her heart felt heavy at the mere thought of telling him. She knew Blake would be upset with her and probably wouldn't want to see her again. Tears slid down her face, knowing deep within her heart it was the right thing to do.

CHAPTER 13

THE ARREST

Blake was shocked to see it was well past midnight. He sat in his office chair worn and weary. He was pleased with his legal research and had left quite a bit of work for Melody to do in the morning. He turned out the lights in his office then stepped over to Melody's desk. He heaved the stack of files onto her desk to attend to in the morning. *Blake's sarcastic smile said she would not be happy with me in the morning!* He whistled as he set the security code and stepped out into the brisk cold air. He clicked the starter button for the BMW and moved quickly towards it.

Exhausted, he in his car and cranked up his Christian music; he loosened his collar and removed his tie, throwing it into the back seat. For a moment, he thought to call Melody but a quick look at his Rolex watch said it was much too late; it was 12:26 AM. *"Naw, she's probably asleep. I'll call her in the morning."* Blake felt restless so he rolled down the window as he started his journey west on I-90. He missed Jake. He was mystified by Melody. As the tension began to leave him, he began to sing the songs that often lifted his spirits. Blake never noticed the gold Lexus following him.

The following morning, after much tossing and turning, Melody checked her cell phone. She had overslept. Dressing quickly as she stumbled about the apartment looking for her keys. She caught a glimpse of herself in the mirror. It wasn't the baggy eyes that held her attention but her thoughts. They seem to return, fully, about her telling the truth to Blake. Mostly, about past relationships about how they fizzled out because of the secret life she led. She wondered about his reaction.

Joe had made coffee, the aroma smothered her senses and if she could get a couple quick sips she'd be good to go. Seeing he was hunched over the computer, oblivious to his surroundings she stepped behind him.

"Morning Joe." She ruffled his hair.

"Hey, I covered for you. Hal called." Joe ducked and smoothed his hair. "Hey, don't be messing with my hair!"

Melody laughed, "Shoot I forgot to call him! Was he mad? Thanks for the cover. What would I do without you?"

"No, I told him you were busy snoring!" Joe snickered.

"What? I don't snore!"

"Hate to break it to ya Girl, you do, are you going to the office?"

"Yes, I am running late. I'm sure Blake left me a pile of work to do. Did you find anything on that medallion yet?"

Joe quickly looked down and he mumbled "Working on it."

Melody looked at him. She thought it was odd he was not looking at her. "Oh, okay. Well, call me when you find anything out." She hurried out of the apartment and headed for the office.

Melody was annoyed; the traffic was heavier than usual. *Oh! I am going to be late!* She quickly looked at her watch. She was shocked when she drove into the parking lot of the law firm. There were two state trooper cars parked in front of the building with lights flashing. *What in the world is going on?* Melody hurried out of the car and bolting into the lobby she noticed Sheila's face was reddened from, apparently, crying. "Shelia what's wrong?"

"Those state troopers are here to arrest Blake!"

"What?" Melody flew into his office where Angelo and Stephen stood with the two troopers.

"Sir, you are under arrest for the murder of Marcus O'Neil. Place your hands behind your back."

Bewildered, Blake looked at his father who nodded his head. Blake did what he was told. The cold heavy, handcuffs clasped onto his wrists. They read him his Miranda rights and hastily escorted him out of the office and into one of the waiting trooper cars. Melody looked briefly at Blake; he looked as though he'd seen a ghost. Fear riddled through his eyes. Melody's hand flew to her mouth. Murder? Marcus O'Neil? What does he have to do with Blake? Melody's blood drained from her face. She felt weak in the knees. She knew there was something odd and dangerous about this entire mess. Was this what Will was warning her about?

Stephen and Angelo were understandably upset and immediately went into the conference room, whispering quietly behind closed doors.

"Blake would not do such a thing! Who the heck is Marcus O'Neil?" Stephen stammered.

"I know! I can't believe they would think he would do that. I've never heard of Marcus O'Neil. Let's go to the barracks and get some more information. This has got to be a mistake." They both hurried past the onlookers and out to Angelo's car and headed towards the trooper barracks.

Melody had grabbed the stack of files from her desk and returned to the lobby, her legs felt wobbly, "Sheila, I need to go home. I'll be back later."

"Hon, you okay?" Sheila looked on as Melody walked out of the lobby.

"Yes, I'm fine. This is crazy!" She knew deep down Blake Matarazzo was not even remotely capable of murder.

"It most certainly is! Give me a call later and let me know that you are okay." Sheila suspected a relationship was growing between her and Blake and was very happy about it.

"Okay, I'll take this stack of files Blake wanted me to work on. I will call you." Outraged, and determined, Melody walked thru the lobby doors and out to her car.

Tossing the files into the back seat, her thoughts swirl faster than she could absorb them. She gripped the steering wheel and started up the car. She'd go back the few blocks to her apartment and try to piece this together.

Joe was startled when he heard a key turn in the lock. Immediately he reached for his gun. He was surprised to see it was Arvidia.

"What's wrong, Arvidia?" Joe could see she was extremely upset.

"They've arrested Blake for murder!" She tossed her purse onto the floor.

"What? Who arrested him? What murder?"

"The state troopers came to the office and placed him under arrest for the murder of Marcus O'Neil! Isn't he the one that owns the gold Lexus?" exclaimed Arvidia as she reached Joe and stood behind him and his computer.

"Okay, calm down. Let me check," Joe scanned his PC, "Yes, Marcus O'Neil owned the gold Lexus. Let me see what else I can find out here." He immediately was able to hack into the NYS trooper's computer system and found Blake's report.

"Okay, I got it."

Arvidia leaned close to Joe as they both read the report.

35 year old male suspect, Blake Matarazzo has been formally charged in the murder of 20 year old Marcus O'Neil. On the eve of November 20th 2012 Victim was found lying supine with a single gunshot wound to the anterior chest. Victim's body was found near the shore of the Mohawk River by lock 7 in Niskayuna. Evidence was obtained in security video tapes that placed the suspect at the scene and at the time of the murder. Suspect unable to account for alibi. Suspect states he worked at his office until 12:26 am and went for a drive on I-90. ME states victim's time of death approximately between the hours of 2 am to 2:30 am.

Angry, Arvidia paced the living room, her lips were pursed tightly together and her blue eyes were blazing. "Joe, Blake was framed. There is no way he could commit murder. That guy is clean as a whistle! He goes to church for crying out loud!"

"Arvidia, you know how some of these guys can fool many. I guess that's why Hal is always saying be careful who you trust. Are you sure about this?"

"Joe, I am positive. Blake is not a killer!"

"Okay, okay, calm down and let me do some more checking around. Why don't you go check out the crime scene?" Joe knew by the looks in her eyes that is exactly where she was going.

"Yep. That's exactly what I'm going to do!" snapped Arvidia. She abruptly grabbed her keys, scooped up her purse and slammed the front door on her way out.

Joe immediately called Todd.

"Joe, what is going on?" He was hoping Joe would call him. The Quad had observed Blake escorted out of the office building in handcuffs and shortly thereafter, Arvidia storming out. Now the Quad observed her speeding out of the apartment building parking lot.

"You guys need to come here now."

"We're across the street, be right there."

The men piled into the living room and Joe explained the recent chain of events. "Arvidia went to the crime scene. She strongly believes Blake was framed."

"Hmm . . . I think we may have to "come to Schenectady" for Arvidia. Something is not adding up here." Todd rubbed his chin stubble.

"I agree." Mark concurred, "We need to see what is on that tape. This definitely has Mason's signature all over it."

"I agree." Chris imputed.

"Where did she say she was going?" Mike inquired.

"She said she was going to the crime scene. I put a GPS tracker on her car and" Joe clicked on the computer, "it looks like she is almost there."

"Good thinking Joe. You need to go and help her. We will "arrive" tomorrow and we will have to get this sorted out before Jim finds her. She doesn't know does she?"

"No." replied Joe.

"Good. Let's keep it that way."

Joe gathered his tools he felt he would need to examine the crime scene. He placed them into his black briefcase and began to head towards the door. "I won't be long."

"Joe, call us if any problems arise." Todd said. "We'll wait at the hotel and I'll call Hal with the news."

"Okay, will do." Joe left.

Mark's cell rang, "This is Mark."

"Mark? It's Arvidia. I really need you guys." Arvidia's tears flowed down her cheeks. "Where have you guys been? I have been trying to call!"

"What's wrong, Pumpkin?" Mark covered the mouth-piece and mouthed, "Arvidia".

"I tried to call Todd but his phone keeps going to voice mail. You know that I've been undercover working for this lawyer name Blake Matarazzo? He's been arrested for murder!"

"Wow, yeah? You want me to pull up his profile?" Mark pretended and hoped she wouldn't ask for it.

"No, I've already done that. I need you guys here in New York. Hal must be so ticked off at me. It's obvious I'm not able to handle this assignment and I have to admit this case is getting too weird for me to handle." Arvidia cried.

"No, you're doing fine. I'll talk to the guys and we'll come ASAP. Okay, Pumpkin? Hang tight."

Arvidia sniffed, "Okay. Mark, I know he's innocent."

"I believe you. Hang in there. We're coming. Where are you now?"

"I'm going to the crime scene and see what I can find there. I'm sure there's something I can dig up."

"Arvidia, be careful and keep a low profile."

"I will." She closed her cell feeling relieved her Quad would be here soon. This made her feel brave.

Arvidia carefully walked through the field behind the crime scene. She skillfully climbed a tree and listened in on the conversation that flowed below her. Soon the investigators piled into their cars and left. She slid down the tree and hunkered low to the ground. Four of her senses kicked into high gear. The Quad's teachings echoed into her mind, look, listen, feel and smell—they are the biggest clue factors into a case.

It would soon be dusk. Arvidia knew she didn't have much time. She carefully examined the obvious. Bloodied grass where the body had lain. A pool of dark blood centered in the middle of the grass. She clipped and bagged some grass for Joe to examine. As she stood up she noticed an opening in the woods heading towards the Mohawk River. She was surprised to see the area was not blocked off with the yellow crime scene tape. She walked alongside the path, and she noticed a set of footprints. One set of prints were longer than the other and leading the way into the woods. She walked slowly into an opening in the wooded area. Soon, she came upon two sets of footprints going in several directions as if though there was a scuffle. Tire tracks were deep in the wet mud. The Mohawk River rushed by. Arvidia heard twigs snap; she turned quickly with her hand steady on her glock and saw Joe standing there.

"Find something?" Joe smiled.

"You have got to stop scaring me Joe!" Arvidia smiled. She was glad he was there.

"Why isn't this area secured?"

"That's what I am puzzled about too. It looks as if two people were here. The investigators have been too focused on the actual crime scene. This pathway seems relatively new. Are these ATV tracks?"

"I believe so." Joe snapped a picture. Arvidia kneeled and found a leaf with blood on it.

"Joe, someone else was here." Arvidia sniffed the leaf, she smelled a certain cigar. It was very familiar to her. She handed him the bag with the leaf.

Joe looked around, "I think you're right. Arvidia, it is starting to get dark. We probably should head back."

"Okay. Wait, what's this?" Arvidia kneeled down. Joe handed her the tweezers as she picked up a small canister attached to a silver chain necklace.

"I don't know. I'll know more once I examine it more closely when we get back." Joe smiled, "See! That's why you are the best agent in the field!" Joe threw his arm around her shoulders. They both headed down the walkway toward the crime scene.

Arvidia suddenly stopped and looked toward, what appeared to be an abandoned building, alongside it were the faded words **Port of Niskayuna**. She noticed the security camera attached to the side of the ramshackled building and quickly, glancing back and forth at the crime scene, she thought, This must be where the investigators retrieved the video.

"Joe, isn't that a digital security camera?"

"Yes, it is. Why?"

Arvidia grinned at him, "If I'm correct, isn't there a second memory chip in the camera in case of power failure?"

"Woman, you are good!" Joe and Arvidia quickly walked to the building out of the camera's view. Neither spoke a word. Arvidia and Joe carefully climbed the side of the building and Joe cautiously pried the back of the camera off. She was right. He found the second memory chip.

They carefully retraced their steps taking the long way back to their cars.

"Joe, how did you know where to find me?"

"I put a GPS tracker on the car." Arvidia looked sharply at him, "It was Hal's orders I swear!"

"Okay, since you put it that way. I can't get mad at you for it."

"Thanks. By the way, the Quad is on their way." Joe felt guilty lying to her like that. "So what is up with you and this Blake guy?"

Arvidia was relieved of the news the Quad was coming. "Is Hal mad?"

"Heck no! He gave the orders to the Quad to come here as soon as he heard the news."

Arvidia sat on the hood and snuggled her arms around herself. Her breath came out as escaping clouds. "Blake is different from any other man I have ever met. The only problem is I'm not so sure he'll care as much about Arvidia as he seems to about Melody, once he learns the truth." Tears slid down her cheeks.

"Aw, Arvidia, you know I can't stand it when you cry! You know you have to be sure you can trust Blake. That's a lot to unload on a guy who thinks you're just a secretary. Suddenly you are not the person he thought you were. So, think very carefully if you want to tell Blake the truth. You should prepare yourself for his reaction."

"I know I thought about that. I know it comes with the territory and it stinks. I am so torn up about this. However, I do know in my heart, Blake is innocent. I just have to figure out how to clear his name." Arvidia pursed her lips together in determination, then she jumped off her car. "Let's get back to the apartment and see what is on that chip."

Todd called Hal immediately as the Quad left Arvidia's apartment. He briefed him on the situation.

"I was just about to call you. I have been called in to come to the Albany area."

"What for, the murder case?" Todd asked.

"No, I was just informed of a rash of drug overdoses occurring at an alarming rate. The local authorities are having a difficult time trying to find the person or persons responsible for this new street drug called Blue Dust."

"Do you think it's any relation to this case?"

Hal spoke firmly. "It might be the dead guy Marcus O'Neil? He happens to be Gus Laurent's cousin. They both have a history of drug trafficking and I'm suspicious there are some ties here to Jim Mason. The medallion for one speaks volume. Jim Mason is laying low and letting these guys do his dirty work."

Todd let out a low whistle. "He's Gus Laurent's cousin? Maybe it's a drug deal gone bad?"

"Possible. I'll find out more information when I talk to the Albany police chief. I should get there tomorrow morning. Call Arvidia and let her know you guys are there."

"Yes, Sir."

CHAPTER 14

BLAKE'S PLEA

The cell door clanged shut. Blake stood inside the jail cell holding a neatly folded blanket and a pillow resting under his chin. He never thought, in his wildest dreams he'd be wearing a bright orange jumpsuit. The correction officer's keys echoed in the hallway as he whistled his way back to his post. The only sounds left to hear was water dripping from a faucet and someone snoring loudly in the cell across from him. Both emotionally and physically drained, he briefly looked at himself in the dirt stained mirror. His eyes were bloodshot and the five o'clock shadow frosted his drained face. He sat on the cell bed holding his head in his hands. He knew his alibi was weak. How was he going to prove his innocence? Who and why would someone frame him for murder? He wondered with a crushing panic, what Melody was thinking of him or worse, his son. He knew his family would stand by his side as well as many of his friends. He was deeply concerned about what his clients may think of him and how this would affect the firm.

Slowly, Blake kneeled down onto the cold cement floor and clasped his hands together. He lifted his head up towards the small window where the sky lined with stars could peek through. Tears slowly streaming down his face he did the only thing he could do, pray.

"Lord, I come before you for I am in trouble. My heart is heavy with grief. You know I am innocent of these charges. Lord, please cover and protect me. I know this is an attack from the devil. Lord, despite this, whatever the outcome is, I will not let this shake my faith in you. Lord, please help me stand fast in your Word. Give me courage where I am weak. Please help me clear my name. Thank you, Jesus. Amen."

Blake stood up slowly and starred out the window where traffic seemed to speed by the jail. Feeling utterly alone, he lay on the bed and starred up at the ceiling. He thought about Jake and Melody then he soon fell asleep.

"Mr. Matarazzo?" the correction officer clanged his flashlight on the cell bars. Startled, Blake sat up. "Yes?"

"You have some visitors. Please put your hands out to be cuffed." Blake stumbled off the bed and put out his hands.

The correction officer led him down the hallway to a small room where his father and cousin waited for him. The room was dingy yellow with bubbled and peeling paint off the walls. In the center of the room were four worn out chairs and a small table covered with notes and papers.

"Take those cuffs off my son!" Stephen bellowed.

"It's policy, Sir."

"I'm his lawyer!" The guard removed the cuffs and stood guard outside the doorway.

Blake stood and rubbed both wrists where they had been bound and he walked over sitting heavily on the chair provided.

"Blake, what happened?" Stephen paced the room, his face reddened with tension. Angelo sat bewildered. He furiously worked through the stacks of papers as if a morsel of a clue would pop out of them. He was at loss for words as to what to say to his cousin.

"I decided to do some work at the office after I dropped Jake off at his mother's. Melody and I went to the office."

"Oh so, Melody worked with you?" Stephen asked.

"No, I sent her home."

"What time was that?"

"About 4pm." Blake wished now he had kept her around.

"Was there anyone else working in the office?"

"No, just me. I did some legal research on the Stearns case first, some dictations and then left a pile of work on Melody's desk. I set the security alarm and when I got into my car, the clock read 12:26am." *Exactly like that,* he thought it all happened just like that. So where did it all go wrong? Blake was stymied.

"Did you speak with anyone during this time? Melody?" Stephen was hopeful.

"No. It was too late to call her." *Maybe he should have,* he thought quietly.

"Okay, what did you do next?"

"I don't know why I felt so restless, but I was, so I decided to go for a drive."

"Where did you go?"

"I went west on I-90. I did go through one toll that should show up on my E-Z Pass. I got off at exit 3 to Washington Avenue. I decided to take the long way home." He looked at his father and said, "I just needed to breathe."

"What time did you get home?" Stephen wondered why his son was so edgy. It wasn't like him. Perhaps he really liked this girl or perhaps he just missed Jake.

"Around 1:45am. I showered and went to bed." Blake signed, his eyes brimmed with tears as frustration welled up within him until he finally broke down. "I am not guilty of this! I was nowhere near Lock 7! I don't even know the guy!"

Stephen reached over and touched his forearm. He knew his son needed some reassurance. "Blake, your old man will handle this. We know darn well you didn't do this and God forbid, I should meet the person who set you up!" Stephen looked towards Blake's cousin, "Angelo, see if you can get his E-Z Pass records."

"I'm working on it, Uncle Stephen." Angelo clicked furiously against the key board of his laptop.

"We also need to get our hands on that video tape. From what I understand, only the DA has the videotape which, he says, puts you at the scene of the crime. I'm going to see if I can pull some strings and find out exactly what is on that tape."

Stephen placed his hands on his son's shoulders. "Son, we will get you cleared, don't you worry. I know you didn't commit this crime." Thinking again his father asked, "Did you recently have a fall out with a client? Maybe have a disagreement with someone?"

"Well, I did have one strange occurrence." Stephen sat beside him listening intently. "I had terminated my contract with a client name Gus Laurent. He was very odd, wanted to pay me in cash for this DWI charge he got to make it go away." He paused for a moment and continued, "He got quite upset with me. Melody caught him riffling through my desk and then there was the other incident where some guy shoved Melody to the floor when she caught him ransacking my office again."

"Hmm . . . that sounds really interesting, Angelo." Stephen knew his nephew was listening just as intently.

"I'm way ahead of you, Uncle Stephen." His fingers were busily tapping the keyboard.

"Okay, your bail hearing is in a few minutes. Let's get that taken care and see if we can get you home by lunchtime. There is one tiny matter we need to address."

"What?" Blake looked at his father.

"It's the news media. They've left numerous messages for interviews. I think it would be most appropriate if we release a public statement. We need to refrain from saying anything publically that could possibly contaminate the case."

Blake's eyes implored his father's eyes. "Pop, I am so sorry for all this. I'm so worried how this might affect the firm."

"Blake, it's okay. This is just another storm we're riding out as a family. God's got it. Have faith! We shall prevail!" Stephen stood as he shouted to the guard as he gave the door a quick pound. The corrections officer came in quickly and handcuffed Blake again, as he escorted him to the courtroom.

Blake sat on the bench with an correction officers seated on either side of him. He rubbed his wrists where the handcuffs were and watched the clock tick. More than an hour had passed since he'd seen his father or Angelo. They had gone to speak to the judge. He thought the halls were oddly quiet. He turned his thoughts and ruminated about his son Jake. He was aching to call him and tell him everything would be okay. He looked around the hall almost, expecting Melody to come walking in.

Suddenly, heels echoed in the hallway. They grew louder as they approached Blake. It was Stephen and Angelo. They both looked nervously at each other.

Blake's stomach sunk, he knew something was drastically wrong.

"What? What's going on?" Blake noticed the officers disappear just as the judge ducked into the back of the courtroom. The prosecutor walked past them, he seemed to look at Blake with concern for a split second, and then he quickly went into the courtroom.

"What's wrong? What took so long in there?" Blake's anxiety rose up a few notches.

Stephen sat down onto the bench and looked directly at Blake. He bluntly stated, "Jake is missing."

"What!" Blake stood up and paced the hallway. "What? When? How?" Blake cried.

"Your ex-wife said she went to wake Jake up this morning. His bedroom window was open, his backpack was gone and she can't find him. She said Jake was very upset when he saw you on the news. The state troopers think it may be possible Jake has ran away. They've issued an Amber Alert. Judge Cavallaro has agreed to an emergent bail hearing. We must get in there now."

Blake could hardly stand up. He felt like his world was collapsing around him.

Stephen and Angelo helped walk Blake into the courtroom. He sat stunned in his chair and stared blankly ahead of him. The words of the Ten Commandments that hung on the wall behind Judge Cavallaro blurred.

"All rise, the Honorable Judge Cavallaro presiding. New York State versus Matarazzo." the bailiff announced, he glanced at the judge. She nodded at him. "You may be seated." stated the bailiff.

"Would the defendant please rise? Mr. Blake Matarazzo you are hereby charged with murder in the first degree of Marcus O'Neil. How do you plead?" Judge Cavallaro peered down through her glasses and stared at Blake Matarazzo. She was quite surprised to see the Blake Matarazzo, the man who fought so vigorously for his clients, now standing before her as a criminal.

"Not guilty, you're Honor." Blake said meekly.

Evan Lighton, the prosecutor for the state of New York stood, "Your Honor if I may, I ask the court to remand Mr. Blake Matarazzo in custody. I fear he is a flight risk."

"You're Honor!" Stephen interjected, "My son has no priors, not even a parking ticket. These charges are ridiculous!"

"They may be ridiculous, Mr. Matarazzo. However, these charges are quite serious; nonetheless, I do agree, Mr. Blake Matarazzo is not a flight risk. Bail will be set at $25,000.00. Due to the extenuating circumstances, I will notify both parties of a trial date. Mr. Matarazzo, I am sorry about your son. I do hope he returns home safely. Court is adjourned until further noticed." Judge Cavallaro slammed her gavel and exited the courtroom.

"All rise!" The bailiff commanded.

"Thank you, You're Honor." Blake whispered.

"Sir, you can come with us and retrieve your personal belongings. There are some papers you need to sign. Your father can pick you up on the other side of the court building." ordered the correction officer.

"Okay, Pop, I will meet you outside."

"Okay, I have your mother's car." Stephen was already on his cell reassuring Liza that Blake was okay and coming home. He knew darn well she was already cooking up a storm in the kitchen. Angelo and Stephen headed outside.

"Sir, if you would, follow me to the elevators so we can expedite this quickly for you." the correction officer extended his arm towards the elevator doors. Blake stepped heavily into the elevator. He hung his head deep in thought. His first priority was Jake. He had to find his son. The elevator doors shut. Blake did not see one of the men approaching him from behind and forcefully put a white cloth over his nose and mouth. Blake fought vigorously against the four men. Soon he felt weak and blacked out. Blake thought he heard one of the men say, "Sorry man, had to do that." He gently laid Blake down onto the carpeted floor of the elevator.

"Okay, guys we have exactly five minutes to get him out of here. Mark is the plane ready?" Todd commanded.

"Yes, crew is ready and the pilot is a go."

"Okay, Chris, Mike, you guys need to disable the power and create a diversion. Bring the car around quickly. We have five minute tops before someone figures out he's missing. Hopefully, by then we'll be ascending 30 thousand feet into the sky."

The elevator doors swung open to the basement, there Chris and Mike were able to overpower the two engineers working in the basement. They quickly disabled the power to the courthouse and Mike floored the car out of the garage and peeled up the street as fast as he could.

Todd and Mark helped the unconscious Blake whose feet dragged against the sidewalk and his head hung low.

"Come on man, you really need to stop drinking so much!" Todd snorted at the two women who walked by who had looked at them strangely. Then they understood.

"Another drunk." Todd winked at them and they laughed and walked away. Mark gave Todd a quick look. "What? What was I supposed to say?"

"No, look down there, his father is waiting for him. We need to get him out of here before he sees him. Where are Chris and Mike?"

Chris screeched the brakes behind them. Todd and Mark quickly put Blake into the car. He slumped over between Todd and Mark. Mark quickly threw a blanket over Blake.

"Go! Go! Go!" Todd hollered. Chris floored the gas pedal and made an illegal U-turn. He sped towards Glenville Airport.

"What in the world is holding Blake up?" Stephen demanded.

"I don't know Uncle Stephen but there is something going on over there." Alarms were sounding and correction officers scurried about.

Angelo walked quickly towards the correction officers. "What is going on?"

"Well, Sir, we're not sure. We suddenly lost power. Two of my staff members were overpowered by a couple of men and they were knocked out. Whoever they were, they took Blake Matarazzo."

Stephen felt faint. Angelo quickly walked over to his uncle and gently sat him down into one of the chairs. "First my grandson is missing, now my son?" Stephen stammered in shock. "What in God's name is going on here?"

CHAPTER 15

JAKE'S DISAPPEARANCE

J oe drove quickly away from the crime scene with Arvidia following close behind. They had to get back to Arvidia's apartment. He hoped that whatever was on this security chip would help them solve the mystery.

They quickly threw their coats onto the couch as they entered her home and settled in front of the computer. Joe carefully placed the disc into the computer and eventually found the video. They both leaned in and Joe slowed the video down. He replayed it several times.

"Arvidia, I don't know. It sure looks like Blake. Look here. Here is his black BMW. His hair, coat and the suit are all the same outfit he wore the last night when you saw him right?" Joe pointed to the computer screen.

"Yes, but it can't be him. I mean, it looks like him, but I know it's not him! It is only a partial view of the car and we can't see the license plate." Arvidia pushed back her chair and paced the living room. "Something is not jiving. There's is something off about the tape. Play it again."

Joe detected by the tone of Arvidia's voice she was onto something. She had a knack for looking where no one else did. "Okay, I'll slow it down and we can go frame by frame." Arvidia walked slowly behind Joe and sat next to him.

The video showed Marcus O'Neil exiting the gold Lexus. He was pointing to someone who was not shown in the video. The voices were mumbled and difficult to understand. Marcus appears to be arguing with someone. Then suddenly, Marcus facial expression changed to shock and he abruptly put up his hands. It is clear Marcus is mouthing the word NO! Shots are fired and Marcus fell clutching his chest.

"Okay, slow down right here. I need to study this particular frame." Arvidia scrunched her brows together. This particular frame disturbed her. Who was Marcus arguing with?

Joe had expertly slowed the video down. Blake's back is facing the camera. The video consisted of a partial view of the front end of the Black

BMW. "Joe! The tire rims are different. Blake doesn't have that brand of rims on his car!" Arvidia inched closer to the screen. There was something in the video that was nagging at Arvidia but she could not put her finger on it.

"Joe, can you freeze it there?" Joe slowed it down. The video slowed to show Blake standing at an odd angle. Arvidia noticed he was rocking back and forth on his feet. Blake walked very tall and took long strides. The man in the video appeared shorter. Suddenly, Arvidia sat straight up and pointed at the computer. She excitedly grabbed Joe's arm.

"Joe! Zoom in onto the back of that guys neck." Arvidia backed away from the computer. "Joe, that is not Blake, he does not have a tattoo on the back of his neck!"

Joe strained to see what Arvidia was talking about. He quickly enlarged the video. Joe immediately saw what Arvidia saw. The video showed a tattoo identical to the medallion found in Blake's office.

"That is Gus Laurent!" Arvidia stood up and stretched. She looked down at the screen. Arvidia suddenly realized why the video was not jiving right. She slowly sat down and starred at the screen.

"Arvidia, what is it?"

Arvidia remembered when she saw Gus at the office she noticed he had a snake tattoo on the back of his left hand. The tattooed left hand was holding a very expensive revolver. Arvidia recognized it as a Ruegers. A specialized gun made for left-handed people. "Joe, that gun's a Ruegers."

"Okay, so?"

"That gun is only made for those who are left-handed. Blake's right-handed and he does not have a snake tattoo on his left hand. Blake was set up! I knew it!" Arvidia jumped up and walked angrily around the living room.

The computer suddenly beeped an urgent message. "Oh, my dear sweet, Lord." gasped Joe. He quickly glanced at Arvidia. The prints from the canister found in the woods from the crime scene came back positive for Jim Mason. His picture flashed onto the screen.

"Joe? What is it?" Her energy was spent. Joe looked as if though he'd seen a ghost. Her eyes searched the computer screen.

"What! It can't be!" Arvidia felt the room spin and she swayed. Joe leapt up from his chair and caught Arvidia as she fainted. He guided her down onto the couch. His heart beating fast, he wished Hal and the Quad would hurry up and get here.

"How can it be him?" Arvidia felt light-headed as she tried to focus her vision.

"Arvidia, I gotta be straight with you. The truth of the matter is Jim Mason escaped from prison four months ago. That's why Hal sent you here undercover to keep you away from him. The Quad has been here for several weeks watching you."

"What? You mean that was Todd I saw across the street from Red Lobster?" She didn't know whether to be angry or relieved.

"Yes, that was him. There hadn't been any sign of Jim Mason until now. One other thing, Gus Laurent is Marcus O'Neil's cousin."

"His cousin!" Now, she felt sick.

There was a knock at the door. Joe quickly answered it. It was Hal and the Quad. They looked at Joe quizzically when they saw Arvidia pale on the couch.

"She knows. Prints from the canister we found at the crime scene came back positive for Mason. It's also positive for the new street drug, Blue Dust. We were able to retrieve the video chip from the crime scene. Blake Matarazzo is innocent. The man posing as Blake is actually Gus Laurent." Joe said quietly.

"Wow, this case is getting stranger by the minute." Todd said quietly.

Hal walked towards Arvidia and sat beside her. He gently picked up her hand and clasped both of his hands around them. "Arvidia, I did not want you to find out about Jim Mason this way. I was trying to protect you. I thought sending you here was safer for you than keeping you in Seattle. I am so sorry."

Arvidia sat quietly and looked around at the six men who had taught her everything she knew, and what she knew now was, how they were trying to protect her. Still, anger boiled within her. Will warned her many times, she may have to face her wrath with Jim someday. She suddenly realized what it was he had been warning her about. Her voice gritted with anger, "This whole thing was a complete set-up and I walked right into his trap. Blake became a target because of me. This is about Jim seeking revenge against me. I'm putting the people I love and care about at risk because of me." Arvidia suddenly gasped and stood abruptly. "Oh my God, Jake! We have to get Jake out of here!" Arvidia scrambled to grab her coat and gun.

"Jake?" Mike questioned.

"I thought Jim was seeking revenge against you?" interposed Chris.

"Jake is Blake's son and I would not put anything past Jim!" Arvidia swung her coat over her back punching her hands through both sleeves.

"Point taken." Chris blushed wishing he hadn't said that.

"Arvidia is right. We need to take proper precautions and escort Jake out of New York State ASAP." Hal pointed at the Quad. "I want you guys to go with Arvidia assist her in getting Jake. I'll have a plane ready for him at the airport. Jake's staying with his mother in Glenville which is not far from the airport. Coordinate your actions and be swift. We do not need to raise attention."

"Yes, Sir." the Quad quipped at Hal.

"Hal, I want Jake to go to Lummi Island and stay with Will. He'll be safe there." Arvidia stated.

"That's an excellent idea, except, you will be joining him as well." Hal turned towards the Quad, "In addition, not only do Jake and Arvidia need to get out of New York. I'm thinking, Blake will be needing protection as well. Let me know what your plan of action will be. I'll meet with Jake's mother and explain as best as I can." Hal said sternly.

"Yes, Sir." They answered in unison.

Arvidia, Joe and the Quad quickly gathered around and made plans. Joe quickly made some phone calls and worked on the computer. Hal sat down in one of the chairs and exhaled slowly. He prayed silently things would go according to plan.

Todd killed the engine to the car as they sat outside Jake's mother's house in Glenville. "Which one is his room?"

"Jake told me there's a huge tree in front of his window. I believe that window must be the one he was talking about." Arvidia, using her night vision goggles, looked closely at the tall oak just outside the bedroom window.

"Okay, Guys let's roll." Arvidia and the Quad pulled the dark ski masks over their faces. The house was dark. Chris quickly exited the car and looked into the living room window. He saw that Jake's mother would not be an issue. He heard the TV drone on as she slept.

"Jake's mother is asleep on the couch. According to Joe, and the setup of the house, his bedroom should be back here." They proceeded behind the house.

"I think it is." Arvidia looked up at the enormous tree limbs climbing its way almost to the roof. "I'll go ahead and climb up. Hopefully Jake won't be too frightened by my waking him up. I'm sure his father's arrest upset him a great deal." Arvidia sighed.

"I'm sure he's upset, especially, with his father's picture flashing all over the news." Mark stated.

"Okay, I'm going." Arvidia quietly and skillfully snaked up the tree and carefully climbed the branch close to Jake's bedroom window. Arvidia could see him sleeping soundly on his spiderman bed. She quietly pried open the window and climbed through. She carefully stepped onto the thick plush carpet and she quickly pulled off her ski mask shoving it into her back pocket.

"Jake?" Arvidia whispered and gently shook Jake a few times.

He finally opened his eyes and rubbed them. "Melody?"

"Yes, Jake it is me." Melody whispered. She gently touched his cheek. Jake sat up and hugged her neck tightly. Then pulling away he whispered, "Something bad happened to Daddy." Jake look down sullenly.

"I know that's why I'm here. Daddy will be okay I promise." She hugged him tight.

"You promise?" Jake muffled into her shirt, he was afraid to let her go.

"Jake, I pinky swear it!" Melody pulled him away from her body and held up her pinky. He linked his with hers and the promise was sealed. Letting go, she looked him right in the eye and took his hand in hers and said, "Jake, I need you to listen carefully. We need to talk." She waited for confirmation.

"Okay." Jake clasped his hands tighter into hers and looked right back at her. She kneeled before him and looked deeply into his big brown eyes.

"Jake, first of all, I am an FBI agent. My real name is Arvidia Miles. I was assigned to protect your daddy from some bad guys."

"Are the bad guys coming after me?" Jake asked wide-eyed.

"Not if I can help it. Do you trust me?"

Jake shook his head vigorously in confirmation.

"Okay, you and I are going on a special trip far away from here. Daddy will be coming along, shortly, after we get there. There are some special men outside waiting for us, they are all FBI agents, and I call them the Quad. Their job is to keep us safe." Arvidia smiled.

"How come you call them that?" In his child like curiosity he made Arvidia smile.

"The four guys are my heroes and I have always called them the Quad."

"Where are they taking us?"

"They are going to be taking us to Glenville airport and we are taking a private plane."

"Oh, but what about my Mom?"

"My friend, Hal, he's also an FBI agent, will be coming tomorrow afternoon and explain to your mother where you are."

"Oh, OK." Jake quickly grabbed his backpack and headed for the window. He stepped out onto the branch with Arvidia stepping close behind him. Jake quickly looked around and saw Arvidia's glock revolver that rested in her holster. He smirked at Arvidia. "So that's why you shot so good at laser tag!" He grinned as he skillfully climbed down the tree much faster than Arvidia.

Jake met Todd at the trunk of the tree. "Hey there, Big Guy, if you're going to ride with us, you are going to have to become one of us!" I'm Todd. This is Mark, Chris and Mike. The four of us are known as the Quad." Todd handed Jake a black ski mask. He gleefully pulled it over his face.

Arvidia had just come down from the tree, "How do I look Mel—I mean Arvidia?" Jake asked.

"You look cool Jake, now you're one of us!"

Todd piped in, "We've got to get going the plane is waiting."

They all piled into the car and quietly drove past the living room window.

"My mom will be okay, won't she?" Jake looked worried.

"Yes, Jake she'll be fine." Arvidia assured him.

The long white airplane waited quietly. The pilot turned on the propellers and started up the engine. "Arvidia, you be careful. You have your stuff?" Todd asked.

"Yes," She touched her gun. I'll call you the minute we get there. Please be careful with Blake."

"You do know once he is awake you'll need to tell him the truth?" Todd searched her eyes; he knew there would be no way of escaping Blake knowing the truth. Too much had evolved and too much danger loomed not to tell him.

"Yes, I know. That's going to be tough. But their safety comes first. Let's take care of Jake, and then I'll deal with Blake later."

"Okay, Jake we'll see you soon!" Todd waved, Jake held onto Arvidia's hand tightly as they entered the plane. He settled quickly into his seat. They looked out the window as he waved back to the Quad. She hoped this plan would go off without a hitch but for now, Jake was safe and soon Blake would be too. It wasn't long after take-off that Jake fell asleep in her lap. His gentle breathing pulled at her heart-strings.

"I sure hope this plan works." Mark said as they entered back into the car. "Now we have to kidnap Blake! We have to make it look real."

"Yes, Hal said he would speak to the judge soon. He's to be arraigned quickly."

"You think they'll release him?"

"Why wouldn't they, he has no priors, all his family is here. He wouldn't be a flight risk."

"He will be, when we kidnap him!" The guys roared with laughter. The mood turned somber as they drove back to the hotel. They only had a few hours' sleep before duty called.

CHAPTER 16

BELLINGHAM, WASHINGTON

Arvidia poured herself a cup of coffee and stared out the kitchen window. The view of Bellingham Bay teemed through the kitchen window. She quietly walked over to the sliding glass door and stepped out onto the deck. Sipping her coffee and gazing into the blue green water as the seagulls cawed above; she listened closely, to the ocean lapping against the rocks on shore. Off in the distance, Orcas playfully splashed about. A tapping on the glass disrupted her nervous tension. It was the physician who had come to examine Blake.

She turned to see the physician who apparently had completed his observation of Blake.

"Is he okay?" Arvidia was anxious and being very cautious with Blake's health, after all, he didn't ask to be put to sleep for nearly twenty-four hours. Her nerves were a little frayed. She stood just inside the glass sliding door.

"Oh yes, he's fine, he's starting to come around now so I left some Tylenol for him to take when he is fully awake, he'll have quite the headache. He'll feel the after effects of the chloroform, and might even experience some nausea, but that will wear off quickly. He should be waking up soon, probably in an hour or so. If you have any problems, don't hesitate to call me." The doctor stepped to the side as Arvidia walked through to escort him out. Bag in hand he followed her.

As she approached the door, she turned, took his hand in hers and said, "Thank you, Dr. Benjamin. I appreciate you taking the time to come and check on him."

"Not a problem Dear. Have a good day!" Arvidia showed the doctor to the front door and said a prayer of thanks. She walked back through the house and went out onto the deck again to finish her coffee. She smiled at the thought of her conversation with Jake earlier in the day. He'd adjusted rapidly to his temporary home. Will assured her he was safe. He had told her many tribe members had been taking turns watching over Jake. She felt blessed that her family so willingly took to him. She fidgeted with her watch. *The time is coming. Soon Blake will know the truth.*

She heard a low bark and turned to see Bandit. "Hey, Bandit!" He gleefully loped towards her then playfully turned on his back for his favorite belly rub. Arvidia marveled at the beauty of this wolf that graciously protected her from the cold night as she laid in the woods so many years ago, dying. She named him Bandit for the white markings that covered his eyes. His thick fur was a beautiful blend of grey and black striped throughout. His enormous paws were no match for anyone who dared to challenge him. His golden brown eyes spoke volumes and he was one hundred percent dependent upon her trust and Bandit trusted few. Arvidia knew he was the Alpha of his pack whom he roamed with them nightly in the nearby woods. He always sensed when she needed him, just as Baldy did. *What an odd pair these two are.* Arvidia thought.

"Come, Bandit." He bounced onto all fours and followed her through the glass doors and into the living room, taking command of his one corner of the couch. She flopped bedside him and flicked on the TV to catch the rest of the Seahawks game as she waited.

Blake groaned and put his hands to his head, it was pounding. He sat up and a wave of nausea hit him hard. He paused, allowing to pass and while his vision blurred for a moment, he lifted his head and look around slowly at an unfamiliar bedroom. Cautiously, he sat up and mindful of the dizziness, he swung his feet to the side of his bed, gingerly placed his feet onto the thick carpet and glanced at the clock. He noticed a glass of water and a bottle of Tylenol. His head felt foggy. He touched his wrinkled suit, it was the same one he wore in court the previous day. All he could remember was walking into the elevator. Checking the clock on the nightstand, he had no idea who the clock belonged too. Becoming vaguely aware of loud waves hurling against the rocks, he wobbled towards the big bay window. He was amazed to see ships floating by in the ocean and seagulls flying about. He heard a low murmur of a television in the distance. *Where the heck am I?* Blake wondered. He made his way through a door on his left and glanced into a mirror in the bathroom. His hair was a mess and he was in serious need of a shave and, after catching a whiff of himself, a shower. Then he noticed some clothes hanging in the closet with the tags still attached. It was clear to him someone wanted to make sure he was comfortable, but who and why?

He stepped into the shower and allowed the warm water to bring him to life. After fifteen minutes or so, he stepped out and found a new razor and shaving cream had been placed on the sink, so he put it to use before getting into a pair of jeans and a shirt. Blake carefully stepped out into the hallway and cautiously took to the stairs. He looked over the banister and walked quietly down the carpeted steps. As he reached the bottom he saw a woman sitting on the couch engrossed in a football game, he thought for a split second to bolt out the front door until he heard a low growl. He turned to see Bandit, growling and baring his teeth, Blake froze.

The startled woman suddenly stood up and "signed" for Bandit to sit. She spoke some unfamiliar words. Bandit promptly sat. He bore his eyes into Blake.

Shock revered throughout Blake's body, "Melody?" Blake's face paled.

Arvidia spoke softly, "Hello, Blake, how are you feeling?"

"My head hurts and I feel like I'm in a fog."

"The doctor said that will wear off. He left you some Tylenol to take. Did you take any?"

"Yes I did." Blake paused and spoke, "Melody, Where am I? What happened to me? The last I remember is being in the elevator and some guy put a cloth over my face."

"I know."

Arvidia walked towards Blake and gently took his hand and walked him to the couch. He looked around the living room. The decorum was exquisite. He looked out the huge bay windows that lined up with the incredible view of the ocean. She noticed his hands were shaking and his eyes bore confusion.

"Blake, let me get you something to drink." Arvidia walked quickly into the kitchen, her hands shook as she poured the two glasses of water. She could see he was scared and confused.

Blake carefully sat on the couch as Bandit eyed him suspiciously. He could feel his heart pounding in his chest. He felt strange, like something was going to happen. He asked the Lord to help him understand what was transpiring. The Seahawks game roared a touchdown, as he nervously rubbed his legs he glanced down onto the coffee table and noticed a thick manila file marked Arvidia Miles. He wondered *who is Arvidia Miles?*

Arvidia returned with his glass of water. He gratefully, took the glass and down the drink quickly, his mouth was dessert dry. She sat down next to him, as he finished his drink, and looked directly into his eyes. Gathering her nerve, she spoke slowly, "Blake, there are some things you do not know about me and I need to tell you the truth. I am not who you think I am." He looked puzzled, but allowed her to continue. "My real name is Arvidia Miles. I'm an FBI agent." She paused and at the same time reached for the manila folder on the coffee table and handed it to Blake. "Before I explain any further to you, I think it might be best if you read the contents of this file. I'll answer whatever questions you have, and I'm sure you'll have many. So, I'll answer them the best I can. I just want to make one thing clear, I don't know nor do I want to know what is in this file. I know it is my life story, I just don't remember what happened to me."

"Wait! What?" Blake gasped. "You're an FBI agent? What's going on? Where am I?" Blake's mouth again went dry. Arvidia gave him her glass of water. He inhaled it once again. Arvidia knew by the vein bulging out of his neck his Italian blood was at boiling point.

"Yes, I'm an FBI agent. You are in my condominium in Bellingham, Washington." Blake glanced around the living room.

"I am in Washington State? How did I get here?" Blake demanded.

"Do you remember the four men in the elevator?" She winced as she asked him this.

"Yes, that's actually the last thing I remember."

"Those guys are FBI agents and my partners. They're part of a special division known as the Quad from Seattle, Washington. They took you and brought you here for your safety."

"Why because of the murder? Melody, I'm sorry I mean, Arvidia I swear to you, I did not kill Marcus O'Neil. How much trouble am I in?" His anger subsided and panic settled in.

"I know you're innocent, and I'm happy to report you have been cleared of all charges. My boss, Hal Sampson, whom you will be meeting shortly, spoke with the judge. She is aware of your whereabouts and dismissed all charges."

Blake eyes suddenly welled up in tears. He put his face in his hands and felt a huge weight taken off his shoulders, he sobbed. He mumbled into his hands, "Thank you Lord. Thank you." Blake suddenly jerked his head up, his eyes wide with fear.

"Blake what's wrong?" Arvidia reached out and touched his arm.

"My son is missing! How could I forget my own son?"

"You have so much going on and I know this is quite a shock to you but I assure you Jake is fine."

"You know where Jake is?" He stood up suddenly, Bandit jumped up and snarled at Blake.

"Bandit, SIT!" She was nervous and frustrated with herself, and Bandit didn't know what was going on, but she didn't have the strength to soothe her wolf's ego right now. She had to allow Blake to drink in what she needed to tell him. "Yes . . . . I know where Jake is . . . . and please trust me to know that he is safe." Blake started to protest but calmed, even though he was unsure as to her identity, he trusted her instinctively. She allowed her statement to develop and she could see by his expression he did trust her, why she had no idea, but he did and that was good. He shifted gears and listened to her go on.

"I, or rather, WE, felt Jake was in danger and had to take drastic measures to keep him safe. Don't worry his mother knows where he is, too. We didn't want there to be an all-out search for him. She'll make up a story, but we won't worry about her right now, she too, is safe. My boss felt you needed to be brought here as well." She waited for his response; it was a lot to take in.

"Where's Jake? I want to see him!" He stood now demanding to know where his son was but his body was revolting against him and he sat back onto the couch, his strength and courage in confusion.

Arvidia talked in slow monotone sounds, so first not to upset him further and second, she knew the chloroform hadn't completely worn off yet. "Jake is on a reservation called Lummi Island. It's about eight miles north of here, and you will be with him shortly. He's with," she hesitated briefly, "my father, Will Miles. You'll read about him in that file on the table. He's very safe. There are only two ways onto the Island; one is by boat and the other a dirt road. The entire tribe is watching over your son and protecting him with their lives."

"Tribe? What do you mean tribe? Who are you?" He was perplexed but intrigued as well.

"My father is an Indian, he's Chief of the Lemaltcha Tribe." She was very proud of this and before he could say anything she stood and clicked her tongue and Bandit stood at her side then she directed him. "Read the file. I'll give you some privacy. Then we will talk."

Before she reached the door he spoke aloud, Bandit turned warily and glared at Blake. "I don't understand, if I'm cleared of the murder charges then why am I here? Do you know who framed me?" And why?"

She petted the raised fur on Bandit and as he calmed, she answered, "It's complicated. But, I promise, everything will make sense. Please, read the file and it was Gus. Gus Laurent framed you. Read! We'll talk after." With that she left with Bandit walking out onto the deck.

Blake glanced at the thick file with her name emblazoned on it. He knew whatever was in the file it wasn't good. He lowered his head and spoke softly to God. He asked the Lord to give his mind wisdom to understanding, and peace to calm his spirit and trust, He prayed for trust and that his son was safe.

Blake's hands shook as he slowly opened the file. The pages were obviously graced with age. He gradually looked through the pages and read the reports. He covered his mouth with his hand. The pictures were grotesque and the story that unfolded before his eyes, of Arvidia's life, were very disturbing to say the least.

Turning briefly, he watched Arvidia through the sliding glass doors. She was sitting in her Adirondack chair scratching Bandit's ears. Her long black hair swayed in tune with the wind. *She survived this?* Blake thought.

He became acutely aware he was not alone in the living room, and as he turned back around, there were six very large men watching him. He'd never heard them come in. The older looking gentleman was the first to speak.

"Mr. Matarazzo, my name is Hal Sampson. I'm the director of the FBI division here in Seattle. These four men are part of a special division called the Quad. This is Todd Riley, Mark Smith, Mike Lawson and Chris Magin. Over here, is Joe Rizzo, he's Arvidia's right hand man and he's is our Evidence Specialist."

Hal walked over and sat down next to Blake.

"Is this file true, this happened to her?" Blake felt as though the room was spinning. "Yes, besides me, you are the only one who has read her file. She wanted you to read it because she has no memory of what happened to her. She only remembers what she refers to as 'blips'. She's called them that since she was a wee one."

Blake suddenly recalled the day she got upset in the car when he inquired about her family. *No wonder she got so upset!*

"Why am I here?"

"Arvidia can explain that to you. I wanted you to be aware of us. Did Arvidia tell you the charges have been dismissed against you?" Blake shook his head, yes. "Good. I also took the liberty to speak with your father. He is fully aware of the situation and relieved you and Jake are okay. He is deeply concerned about what I told him concerning Arvidia."

"He knows the truth?" Blake asked.

"Yes, he was quite surprised but understood why we had to take you and Jake out of New York. I have taken some precautions and stationed some men for your mother and father. I do not believe they are in danger. Jim Mason only wants Arvidia. He will, however, will kill anyone that gets in his way, including those that are close to her. You are aware Gus Laurent killed Marcus O'Neil?"

"Yes, Arvidia told me. Why did he set me up?"

"Gus Laurent was paroled from Walla Walla Prison one year ago, and as you can see from the recent notes in the file, we found out he was Jim Mason's former cell mate. Furthermore, Marcus O'Neil was Gus Laurent's cousin. From what we can gather, Jim Mason, somehow, found out Arvidia was in New York and sent Gus there to locate her. Gus came to you under false pretenses to get to Arvidia. We believe something went down and their plans went awry."

"Where's this Mason character now?"

"He escaped from prison several months ago."

"Escaped?" Blake was appalled and concerned for Arvidia.

"We've learned that Jim Mason has been planning his revenge for a very, long time."

"Arvidia can explain more of this to you. Did she tell you where Jake is?" Hal liked this guy, and he felt bad to have had him mixed up in this mess.

"She said an army would not be able to get through where he is." Hal smiled and the five men chuckled. There was much truth to that.

"As of now, you, Jake and Arvidia are under federal protection until Jim Mason and Gus Laurent are in custody. Until then, these four gentlemen will be with you twenty-four seven."

"Why was Marcus O'Neil killed?" Blake wanted to know.

"We are still working on that, but we believe he was killed for drug money. We know for sure Gus Laurent killed him. Arvidia knew you were innocent from the start and fought vigorously to clear your name."

Blake felt the anger growing in him. "Why did Gus frame, me, in particular? Why didn't he go after Arvidia? I'm not saying that I wanted that to happen, but he certainly had opportunities to do so."

"I'm not sure. Jim is very a meticulous planner. It is my guess, Jim told Gus to stay away from her until the "right time". I'm afraid I'm responsible for her chaotic assignment in New York. I thought that was the safest place for her to go so I sent Arvidia to you on a dud assignment so I could keep her safe. She didn't have any knowledge of Mason's escape. He somehow figured out where she was and sent Gus to watch her by, pretending to be your client. We didn't make the connection between the two, until, the prints from the medallion came back positive for Gus Laurent." Hal paused and pointed at Joe, "Joe, here made the connection between the two men. He found out about him being Mason's former cellmate." Hal stopped for a moment, allowing some of this to sink in, then he continued on, "Anyways, when we found out Mason escaped, I called in some favors and she was immediately sent from here to Schenectady, New York. Some of my colleagues kept an eye on her there. I'm inclined to think that Jim was planning to kidnap Arvidia. Fortunately, we were able to figure out what was going on and got her away from there. It won't be long before he figures out where Arvidia is. I have no doubt Mason and Laurent will be heading in this direction in the near future."

"This, um . . . Jim Mason, is he is responsible for what happened to her? Is that why she has those scars?" Blake wasn't completely sure he wanted to know the answer, but the question was out.

"Yes. We only know what Will has told us, he found her in the woods. She was in bad shape. He's a very evil man." Hal looked as though he was going to spit nails.

Blake sighed heavily and closed the file. "He sure is."

Arvidia opened the sliding glass doors and entered into the living room. Hal stood up and briskly walked towards her, kissing her gently on her forehead. "Tell him everything." he whispered.

"Okay." Arvidia whispered back.

The Quad quickly disassembled and went to their posts. Joe Rizzo left minutes before and headed upstairs to a hidden room called the stat room to do more research on the evidence. He wanted Jim Mason caught as badly as the Quad did.

CHAPTER 17

ARVIDIA'S PAST REVEALED

"Are you okay?" Arvidia asked softly.

"Yeah, I think so." Blake exhaled slowly as he leaned in and threw the file on top the coffee table then reclined back into the couch.

Arvidia silently sat next to him. Bandit had followed her, his head swayed back and forth as he stared, hard, at her guest, as he was still wary of him. Blake leaned forward and placed his head in his hands, just as he had done several times this day.

"Does your head still hurt?" Arvidia asked softly.

"A little bit, I don't understand why didn't you just tell me the truth? I'm overwhelmed with this. My head is swirling with questions and I don't even know where to begin!" Blake raised his voice slightly higher then he should have, given the headache situation. Bandit suddenly stood and let out a low growl. Blake pulled back, heart racing. Arvidia immediately spoke softly in Bandit's ears. He cocked his furry head and settled into her lap. She petted his head, grateful he had calmed down as well as Blake.

"Arvidia, huh? What was that you said to him? Is that some sort of dog language? Have you noticed he is quite large for a dog? What else do you have to tell me?" Her name was foreign across his lips.

Arvidia laughed and curled up on the couch. Bandit promptly jumped up onto the couch and parked himself between her and Blake. He stared hungrily at him or so Blake thought. "Ahem . . . um . . . Bandit is what you'd call a grey wolf. Their breed dictates the male to be quite large. He's the one who found me in the woods and kept me warm, until Will found me."

Shock glazed across Blake's face. He looked warily at Bandit, who happily panted in his face. "That's a wolf? What do you mean he found you? Is Will the man mentioned in your file, the Indian man who adopted you?"

"Yes, he is my adopted father. He's the chief of the Lemaltcha Tribe on Lummi Island. It's an Indian reservation where I spent the majority of my life. The words you heard me speak to Bandit are a language known as Salish. It's the native language spoken in the Lemaltcha tribe. Bandit does not trust easily, but he won't hurt you. He's just protecting me, it's his natural instinct. He wants to be sure you won't hurt me."

"Well then, I will be sure to work on not upsetting him." Blake was as unsure of Bandit as the wolf was of him. His heart was still pounding fast and he was careful not to lick his lips or blink too quickly. He cleared his throat and carefully reached for the file, once again, from the coffee table.

"According to this file, you have no recollection of what happened?" Blake stated in a form of a question.

"I vaguely remember the night of the fire. I do remember, vividly, the day Will found me." Arvidia put her head up against the warmth of her protector and as her voice quivered slightly, she began to reveal the past she barely remembers.

"Bandit was with me the day Will found me. His fur kept me warm throughout the night. I think there were several other wolves around me. I could hear them panting but Bandit was the only one who would lie beside me to keep me warm. I'm not sure where they all were, but I knew they were close by. I remember hearing the rustling leaves and the wind whistling through the evergreens. The ground was hard and cold and I could actually hear my teeth chatter, I recall my entire body hurt head to toe. I couldn't see a thing but blackness. Will told me my eyes had been swollen shut because of the severe bruising and remained that way for several weeks. But, I just can't seem to remember, exactly, how I got my injuries but I definitely remember seeing the moon before my eyes swell shut. I'd been staring at the glow of the full moon. I know this may sound odd but, the illumination of the moon was so huge and bright I thought I could reach out and touch it, but my arms hurt too much to move. I could smell smoke and feel this intense heat." Arvidia shivered at the thought, but knew she had to go on, because if she stopped now she'd never through with it. "Later I found out, that was the smell was the cabin that had just burnt down. I am not sure why Bandit didn't just kill me. He'd attacked Jim, tearing up his left arm. Then Jim, simply disappeared, into the night. The next thing, I know Bandit was standing over me breathing real hard. I thought for sure I was his meal. Instead, he just lay down as close he could and stayed by my side until Will found me."

"How long were you there?" Blake was so tender, he couldn't imagine this child, hurt and left alone to die.

"I don't know, I can't remember." Arvidia sighed and buried her face into Bandit's fur.

Blake's face reddened and his eyes brimmed with tears, "I think God sent you an angel, by way of a wolf to protect you." Blake voice wavered emotionally. "It's simply incredible you survived at all." He carefully reached over Bandit and lightly touched the scar on her neck. "Did he do this to you?"

Arvidia looked down at her hands, "Yes."

"What happened to your family?"

Arvidia sighed deeply and looked away as her eyes filled with unshed tears. "I don't remember. Will had informed the authorities, Hal, and the Quad, searched in vain for my family. I was unable to give them anything to go on. The only thing I knew for certain was my name, Arvidia . . ."

Blake lightly reached up and with a tender touch; he brushed a tear from her cheek. "It's a beautiful name, you know. I like it." Blake swore his hand was going into spasms passing by Bandit's mouth.

"Will told me my name means Wanbli Isnola which means Lone Eagle. Ironically, his nickname for me was Sqimi, which means young bald eagle. He hadn't called me that in years except in some recent visions over the past few weeks. He's been warning me about something, I had thought it was you, but now I know, it was Jim Mason he was warning me about."

"What visions?" Blake sat on the edge of the couch, intrigued.

"Will is a very spiritual man. Like you, he's a born again Christian. He speaks daily with whom he calls the Great One, sometimes several times a day. He often goes to the Ancient Rock or Mt. Baker to pray and read scripture. He feels closer to God when he's there. Sometimes he'll meditate and appear like a vision when I least expect it. You remember the night we were going home from your parents?"

"Yes. I remember that."

"Well, Will was standing in the middle of the road in his warrior armor. Shortly after that is when the gold Lexus nearly ran us off the road."

"Wow. God was using him to warn you. I would like to meet this man." Blake exclaimed.

"Oh, you will. There is no avoiding Will." Arvidia smiled and laughed. "The men you just met have known me since before Will adopted me. They lived on the reservation with me until they were able to capture Jim Mason. They, as did Will, taught me everything I needed to know to be an FBI agent." She hesitated then reached over to touch his hand, "I am very sorry I wasn't able to tell you the truth. I was following orders."

"I understand. I just wish you'd trusted me enough to tell me sooner. Hal explained to me your assignment was to get you away from here to protect you from Jim Mason. I do feel God's hand was on this from the beginning, how odd we met under such unusual circumstances." He was receptive to her touch. His heart ached for her.

"I wanted to. I didn't know Mason had escaped from prison, until a few days ago. Hal confirmed to you that the charges against you have been dropped, right?"

"Yes, he did. He tells me you figured out who killed Marcus O'Neil. How did you ever figure that out?" He was being drawn to her in a whole new light.

"The video chip from a security camera at the crime scene, usually, in a digital camera has back up chips. Joe and I managed to obtain the second chip and review it. We watched the video and it was convincing on the surface, but when you watch it frame by frame, well, that's when I noticed something just wasn't adding up. Once that clicked in my head, I was able to figure out the man in the video wasn't you, but Gus Laurent."

"What was it you were able to see?" Blake liked the fire that sparkled in her eyes.

"Well for one, Joe enlarged one framed and I noticed the tattoo on the back of the mystery man's neck. That neck belonged to, none other than Gus Laurent. I almost missed it. Secondly, he had a snake tattoo on his left hand, I knew you didn't have that on your hand but the real tipoff was the gun in his hand. He shot with a Ruegers." She could see he was a little confused.

"What is odd about a Ruegers?" Blake asked.

"Well, for one, it's an expensive piece to own and two, because of the cost, few are made. The company that makes this particular type of gun is one of five gun companies in the world. What makes them unique is they specialize in making handguns for people that are left-handed. I knew you were right handed. Once I figured that out, I contacted Hal and he immediately told Judge Cavallaro about the new evidence and she cleared you. You were already on your way here, to Washington State when this happened. Hal also met your mother and father and informed them." Arvidia continued. "Remember that day I was shoved and hurt my arm when your office was ransacked?"

"Yes. I remember. That really upset me. You could've been seriously hurt!"

Arvidia smiled at him, it was touching how protective Blake was of her. Even with all this information dumped on him, he sat beside her and didn't run off. She searched his eyes before continuing, she knew deep down she could trust this man with her life. She decided to continue. "Just before you came into your office. I'd found a moon shaped medallion by the corner of your desk on the floor. I had Joe analyze it for prints. The finger prints came back positive for Gus Laurent. The tattoo on the back of his neck is identical to the moon medallion. The most important factor here is that, that particular medallion is same exact medallion Jim Mason wore on the day he was captured by the Quad. Furthermore, Jim Mason and Gus Laurent were cell mates at Walla Walla state prison."

"What! They were cell mates?" Blake exclaimed.

"Yes, Gus was paroled a year ago."

"Have they been planning this from the beginning?"

"We believe so. Jim had been studying up on me by using the prison library. I'm sure he lured Gus into working for him."

"So how did Gus end up as my client?" He was listening to this incredible story as if it were a movie on the big screen.

"I believe Jim figured out Hal sent me away, how he got the information as to my whereabouts I'm not sure. This man is very manipulative when he wants something he knows how and where to get the information he needs. Once he figured out I was in Schenectady, New York he sent Gus out to become your client under false pretenses. I believe he showed up to watch me and report back to Jim of my whereabouts."

"What meaning does this medallion have?"

"I am not sure. I know my father will explain it to me. It has something to do with a curse and the full moon. The medallion is supposed to protect them from this curse and there's some kind of special significance to it, but I just can't remember what it is. I'll have to ask my father about it."

"Arvidia, in my experience as an attorney, repressed memories usually come back by some sort of trigger and it usually happens when you least expect it. Sometimes they come back in bits and pieces or all at once. The more intense this situation becomes don't be surprised if you start remembering things. When you do, will you talk to me about it?" She absently nodded to him. "But for now, I just want to focus on you. Before we proceed any further, I do have one question, when can I see my son and is he okay?"

"Oh yes! He's fine. Will is keeping him busy. We can see him now! We don't know why, but Mason won't set foot on the reservation. I knew sending Jake there would be the safest place for him. The tribesmen have been taking turns watching over him." Arvidia swiftly jumped off the couch, "Come with me. I'll show you how we can see Jake."

Arvidia held Blake's hand as she led him upstairs into her bedroom. Bandit raced ahead of them, she touched a panel that appeared to look like a switch plate only she held up her hand and the wall gave way to a special room called the stat room, it's where Joe sat studiously at work. "This is Joe, our evidence tech."

"Hey, Blake, pleasure to meet you." Joe shook hands with him.

Arvidia sat down and punched a phone number on the keyboard and instantly Will's face appeared on the computer screen."

"Hello, Father." She grinned at him.

Will's face broke into a grin, "Welcome home, Sqimi!"

Arvidia beckoned Blake to sit next to her. "Father, this is Blake, Jake's father."

"Hello, Blake, Jake is fine. Let me fetch him. Jake!" Will hollered.

Jake breathlessly bounded into the house and noisily sat before the screen.

"Daddy, Guess what? I caught a fish! A real one!" Jake beamed. "See!" He held up the fish to the screen as he grinned from ear to ear. "Will, what's it called again?"

Will leaned over and whispered into Jake's ear. "It's called a King Salmon."

"Oh yeah, it's a King Salmon. Isn't that cool, Dad? Dad, they are still fishing out there, I'm going back out and catch some more! Bye, Dad, love you!" Jake was blemished with dirt and twigs but he did not seemed to mind as he raced back outside to the wonders of the ocean.

Blake was relieved to see his son was safe. He never thought he would ever lay hands on a fish yet he seemed to be thrilled about it and his new whereabouts. "Thank you." Blake said with relief. "All of you." He felt blessed.

Arvidia noticed Bandit was whining and pacing. "What's wrong, boy?" She stood and followed him downstairs. Bandit growled at the sliding glass doors, she immediately grabbed her gun and slowly pulled the sliding glass doors open. She glanced quickly above her front entrance doorway. A red light was flashing. Someone had tripped her silent alarm. Bandit launched down the steps and off the deck at full speed. She could see the Quad searching the area with their guns drawn.

Joe thundered down the stairs and whispered, "Arvidia! You want me to call Hal?"

"Not yet, I see the guys out there. Keep Blake upstairs."

"Done!" Joe quickly ran back up the stairs, blocking Blake from leaving the room.

Stepping cautiously, down the deck stairs, she could hear Bandit snarling and growling. Additional growling, *ah,* she thought, *his pack had joined him.* Suddenly, Todd and Mark hollered freeze as several shots rang out. She heard someone cry out in pain and simultaneously, she heard a waiting boat roar to life and move away from the docks.

Blake spun around back into the room just as the shots rang out. Joe was puffing in the doorway. "Arvidia said to stay put."

"What's wrong?" Blake paled as the upstairs door closed.

"Someone tripped her silent alarm." Joe said.

"Was that gunshots I heard?"

"Yep. Trust me, she's is an excellent sharpshooter. I would never want to be on her bad side. She'll come back when it's all clear." He wasn't sure he convinced Blake, but he had his orders.

Blake remembered the day at laser tag. She shot everyone dead centered into the chest. He knew Joe wasn't kidding. He carefully peeked through the small window and noticed a pack of wolves joining Bandit, obviously his posse.

Chris and Mike met up with Arvidia at the head of the docks. Before long, Todd and Mark joined them. Todd spoke first, "He took off in a boat. There was someone waiting for him, I couldn't get a good look at either one of them. I'll tell you what, Bandit took a good chunk out of that man's leg."

All looked towards Bandit and his pack who stood proudly on the beach. No one messed with them.

"Bandit, you did well." Arvidia snuggled into his fur. When she looked into Bandit's eyes she suddenly saw a blip in her mind. She stood up confused. He cocked his head to the side and whined. "I'm okay Bandit." Arvidia quickly caught up with the Quad and walked back to the condo with them. Bandit and the pack stayed behind as if they expected the intruders to return.

"Arvidia, I don't think it's safe for you to stay here. You and Blake are going to the rez first thing in the morning. We'll get your boat ready." Todd spoke firmly.

"I agree. We'll leave at first light." Arvidia looked at her boat swaying slowly as ripples of waves gently splashed against it.

"Don't worry. We'll be on guard," Mark glanced at Bandit who cocked his head at him, "I'm sure they will be too."

Arvidia glanced at the sky. The moon was half full. The blip she saw with Bandit minutes before reappeared in her mind. The hairs on her arms stood up. She felt confused and bewildered. Will warned her this day would come. "Whoever it was is not coming back. Jim never does anything unless the moon is full."

The Quad quickly glanced at each other.

"What?" Arvidia stared at them.

"That is the first reference you have made about him since you were a little girl!" Todd exclaimed.

Arvidia was just as surprised. Maybe Blake was right. A trigger does need to happen before remembering anything. Joe and Blake came downstairs when they heard her and the Quad entering in the condo. All were talking at once.

Blake immediately went to Arvidia's side. "Are you okay? Where's Bandit?" Blake was surprised he was actually concerned about the wolf.

"Yes, I'm fine. I'm pretty sure it was one of Jim's men. Bandit bit him on the leg, but he managed to escape into a waiting boat. Bandit and his pack are out there. They'll probably stay there until they feel he will not return."

"Do you think it was Jim Mason?"

"I doubt it. I'm thinking it may have been Gus."

"What!" Blake stood rigid and paced the kitchen.

"Blake, Todd suggested we leave for Lummi Island in the morning. I think that might be best for the both of us. I don't think it'll be safe for us here. Plus, you'll be able to be with Jake." Arvidia gave him the bright side to the entire fiasco.

Blake looked out the kitchen window amazed to the see Bandit and his pack guarding the beach. He nodded his head, "Okay! My son is okay?" Blake asked anxiously.

Arvidia flew to Blake's side and placed her hand on his chest, "Trust me, my father, will not let anything happen to him. I assure you he is safe." Arvidia gently kissed Blake on his cheek.

"Arvidia, sorry to interrupt, but two of us will stay inside and Mark and I will stand guard outside." Todd glanced out the sliding glass doors. Bandit and his pack had not moved an inch since parking themselves on the beach. Todd always felt safer around Bandit.

"Ok, that's fine." Arvidia was exhausted as she took Blake's hand and headed upstairs to her bedroom. "I'm so sorry about all this, Blake." She examined her gun to make sure the safety was on as she placed her glock on her nightstand. Her hands trembled as she rubbed her legs, and for the second time in her life, she was frightened to her core.

"Blake, I think I remembered something." Arvidia almost whispered.

He sat next to her and wrapped his arms around her. He could feel her trembling. He brushed her black tresses away from her face with his own trembling hands. Arvidia leaned into his chest, she wanted to cry but no tears would come.

Blake deeply concerned, spoke gently. "Arvidia, tell me what you remember."

"I'm not sure if I understand it. Bandit bit one of the suspect's legs at the beach before he jumped into the boat. I went over to Bandit and hugged him. I told him what a good job he did. I scrunched up his fur like I usually do but Bandit had traces of blood around his mouth and the blood had stained his fur. It happened so fast, so quick that I'm not sure of what I saw or whether I can understand it. You had a name for that, what was it again? I call it blips."

"A flash back?"

"Yes. That's it! In this blip, on the night of the fire, I heard Bandit snarling and he jumped and bit into someone's arm. I could hear screaming and I also kept seeing something shiny but I can't figure out what it is. That's all there was. It was a quick one, crazy, huh?"

"No, but it is interesting. Your mind is trying to open up what you've been repressing for so long. This is a good thing."

"I'm not so sure if I want to remember!"

"It will help you heal. You weren't ready before, but now you are. God will help release these demons that have bound you for so many years. He has protected you with extraordinary gifts. You must believe that." Blake pointed gently to her chest. "God lives within you. Look how He sent you Bandit to protect you from harm. I am simply in awe of what you've survived! I've been meaning to ask you about this, where is your relationship with God? Do you love God?"

"To be honest, I'm not sure. Will has spoken to me about God many times. I've been too angry at Him for the losses I suffered at the hands of that man. Will told me told me someday I will need to forgive Jim. I'm still having a hard time with that. Maybe it's because I can't remember. I don't know." She looked lost.

"That's understandable. You're human and it's natural for you to be angry at God. Even so, you're acknowledging Him as God. So in one sense, you do believe in Him. Will is right. I know it isn't easy having a relationship with God; even I get confused about Him from time to time. However, God's wisdom is not our wisdom. Will sounds like a wise man." Blake said softly.

"He is. You will like him. He's very kind and gentle. No one knows exactly how old he is." She giggled. "Hal has been trying to figure that out for years. The man never seems to age!" Arvidia laughed again softly. She slipped away from him and reclined back and she stared at the ceiling. She slowly slipped away into the plush pillow, and before she knew it the sleep deprived sharp shooter was out.

Blake smiled and kissed her on her forehead while gently pulling her blanket over her. He quietly stepped out of the bedroom and headed into the guest room next door. He didn't want to undress. Standing by the window, where the moonlight streamed across the dark ocean, rippling over each wave in silence, he realized just how exhausted he was, physically and emotionally but spiritually he kind of felt enlightened. He said a small prayer, "Lord, I have no idea where all of this is leading but I simply ask for tonight, give Arvidia a sweet sleep as well as Jake and myself. Tomorrow will take care of itself with you as its Guide. Amen." Blake lay on the bed, fully clothed as he fell fast asleep.

CHAPTER 18

LUMMI ISLAND, WASHINGTON

B lake awoke early in the morning as the sun had just begun to rise above Bellingham Bay. The morning's mist slowly receded into the fog now, blanketing the ocean. Fog-horns had blasted through-out the night. He tiptoed to Arvidia's bedroom door and cracked it open. Bandit immediately raised his head up and away from her bed then slowly rolled off. He slid past Blake and headed downstairs. Arvidia was sleeping soundly. Blake shut her bedroom door and nervously walked down the carpeted stairs. While, quietly walking into the living room, he observed Bandit lying beside the sliding glass doors. Blake was not sure if he should head back upstairs or try to see if the wolf would eat his hand. "Umm . . . morning, Bandit." Blake stammered.

Bandit sat up and cocked his head to one side. A little startled, Blake slowly approached the kitchen when it dawned on him, Bandit might be hungry. "Are you hungry?" He quickly opened the kitchen cabinets and scrounged around for dog food. Bandit whined at the sliding glass doors. Blake slapped himself on his forehead, "What am I crazy? Duh, he is a wolf. You don't eat dog food do you?" Bandit stood wagging his tail as Blake quickly went and slid the sliding glass doors open and the wolf bolted down the deck stairs. As Blake stood watching him move, he was in awe of the enormous wolf whose feet barely touched the ground as he headed into the woods. Somewhat relieved, he returned to the kitchen counter and poured himself a cup of coffee then checked the front door to see if there would be a daily newspaper. Waving at Todd and Mark all the while he looked for the paper. "Aha, there it is." He bent down and grabbed it from under the deck chair. He felt comforted by the Quads presence. They had stood guard all night. He inhaled deeply, and realized despite all the stress he had slept quite soundly. He shut the front door and headed towards the sliding glass doors. He tucked the paper under his arm and grabbed his hot coffee from the kitchen counter and stepped out onto the back deck.

The fresh ocean air filled his lungs. He sipped his coffee as he observed the unbelievable view that was unfolding before him. He wasn't sure but he could've sworn he'd seen a whale flipping in the ocean. He made himself comfortable in one of the two Adirondack chairs that graced the deck. Crossing his legs and unfolding the Bellingham Herald newspaper, he stole another sip of his coffee. The ocean, furiously lapped against the rocks as the seagulls cawed above him. He'd never seen this kind of beauty; it almost made him forget what had been transpiring in his life recently. He scanned the headlines and began to soak himself into the current news.

He relaxed and sipped his steaming cup of coffee just as the stocks caught his attention. He carefully eyed the numbers and was pleased with what he'd seen . . . Suddenly, a large massive bird swooped down, snatched the newspaper out of his hands and dropped the newspaper into the ocean. Blake, startled, had spilled coffee all over himself and he stood up quite angry and thrust his fist at the bird. All of a sudden, the massive bird turned and headed straight for him.

Blake's eyes widened. He bolted down the deck stairs and ran towards Todd and Mark. He ran flailing his arms, screaming for help. The massive bird dove and pecked at his head. Mark and Todd howled with laughter. The massive bird, Baldy, was making her presence known.

"Yo, Blake, that's Baldy!" Todd hollered back at him as he ran up and down the shore of the beach while Baldy continued to fly and dive after him.

"Who the heck is Baldy? Make it stop!" Blake shouted and ran as fast as he could past them and into the water. Baldy flapped her wings furiously above his head and cawed loudly making known her sheer displeasure of Blake. Todd and Mark roared with laughter.

Arvidia stood watching from the deck barely able to contain her laughter as she watched Blake endure the wrath of Baldy. Baldy never did like any of the men in her life. Arvidia reached under the bench and pulled out an arm length heavy-duty glove. She screeched the sound she knew Baldy would know and held up her arm. Baldy immediately turned away from Blake and headed towards Arvidia.

Blake collapsed on the beach gasping for air, as Todd and Mark approached him. Blake muttered, "Biggest damn bird I've ever seen!" Mark assisted Blake up from the beach. He stood wobbly. His coffee stained clothes were soaked with sea, sand, twigs and even seaweed hung from his head. He quickly checked his hair. He was sure the bird scalped him.

Blake turned and pointed back toward the deck. Blake's jaw dropped as he saw the bald eagle proudly perched on Arvidia's arm. She appeared to be talking to her as she gently stroked her. "What in the world?" Blake stood astonished with his hands on his hips astonished, "Is that a bald eagle?"

"Yeppers, that's, my friend, is a bald eagle and somebody you don't want to mess with. Her name is Baldy. As you can very well see Baldy is quite protective of Arvidia. She's almost as bad as Bandit."

Blake was stupefied, "First a wolf! Now, a bald eagle?"

Todd's cell chimed and he answered laughing. "Yes, Hal. We're almost ready. Baldy apparently does not like Blake."

Hal understood all too well what Todd meant, and he smiled.

Blake slowly walked up the deck stairs and Arvidia covered her mouth barely able to contain her laughter. Baldy cawed and flapped her expansive wings. Despite his misgivings towards Baldy, she was the most beautiful, fearful bird he had ever seen. her golden eyes pierced into Blake as though she were reading his soul. Arvidia stroked Baldy and spoke softly to her.

"You might want to change before we head out." Arvidia grinned at him.

"Yes. I probably should." He looked down at his battered clothing and he walked slowly past Baldy who squawked loudly as he instinctively ducked, covered his head and bolted upstairs.

Arvidia and the Quad waited for him in the boat. They chuckled as they watched Blake craning his neck looking for Baldy. "Guess he doesn't know Baldy will be leading us to the Island." Mark laughed.

Blake sat down in the stern of the boat with the others and wrapped his arms around Arvidia. Todd stood at the helm and skillfully steered the boat slowly away from the docks. Baldy cawed, loudly, from above in the sky; she swooped skillfully around the boat. Stunned Blake opened his mouth then just ducked out of the way.

Arvidia giggled, "Baldy is leading us to Lummi Island. Don't worry about her. She's just protective of me. She does that to everyone especially Hal. Right, guys?" Todd and Mark smirked at the mere mention of Hal.

"What's her story?" Blake did not like this massive bird.

"Well, the night of the fire, Will told me Baldy was very persistently flying around Will's house and only his house. He strongly believes animals have spiritual souls. He also believes they are gifts from God and he told me if the animals connect with a human, it is considered a great and honorable gift from Him. It was extremely, unusual for the bald eagle to be flying around his house like that. Once the bird realized, Will was following her, she took him deep into the woods.

Confused, Blake asked, "Wait. I thought Bandit found you?"

"They both found me. Bandit stayed by my side while Baldy searched for Will. Will believes Baldy and Bandit saw what happened to me. He also believes God sent Baldy to him to lead him to me. He told me Baldy had perched herself in a tree right above me. One of her feathers had fallen on top of Bandit. That is how I got my Indian name Sqimi. He originally thought Bandit was injured. Will has the greatest respect for the wolves. He said Bandit didn't even growl or snarl when he approached him. It was, almost as though, he was expecting him. He signed with his hands to Bandit that he'd come in peace. Bandit moved gently away. Will was shocked to see me laying there. He then understood why he didn't move and how it was, and why, Baldy had come to acquire his attention."

Blake's innards grew with anger. "Do you remember that?"

"Barely, I remember hearing Baldy screeching and the branches bending from her landing on the tree limb. Then Bandit moved and I was afraid he would leave me. Then I smelled different scents. I tried so hard to see, but my eyes were swollen shut. I remember a gentle touch on my arm and then jerking my arms back in pain. I hadn't realize I had burns on them and my legs. The pain was awful, intense. I remember crying and Will was singing softly into my ear. He, gingerly, lifted me and I immediately felt safe as he cradled me in his arms, as he carried me home. Baldy and Bandit followed along and they have been with me since."

Blake fell silent. He had represented many clients with horror stories of their own but none close to Arvidia's. He now understood why he felt the urgency to protect her when they first met. He glanced at her arm and tenderly put his hand on her. Arvidia looked deep into his eyes and he confirmed, once again, she could trust him without reservation.

Blake inhaled the fresh ocean air and the salty smell stung his nostrils, in a good way. He looked around the incredible lines of evergreen and aged rocks that lined the way as the boat's wake carved its way into the sea as they headed toward the island.

"Blake! Look!" Arvidia stood and pointed ahead. Blake heard a barking noise and looked into the binoculars. Among the rocks laid many sea lions who barked as the boat drifted past them. They all seemed to bark in unison.

"Wow, there sure are a lot of them!" Blake said.

"We should be seeing the pods soon." Todd searched through the binoculars. He immediately slowed the boat down as required by federal law.

"Pods?" Blake asked.

"The pods are the Orca whales. There are three families of them that frequent these waters. They're very well known in this area." Arvidia explained.

Stunned, "You mean that really was a whale I saw this morning?" Blake asked.

"Yes, you probably did see one."

Suddenly, a rip roaring sound split into the air. A large Orca whale jumped, twirled about into the air and splashed heavily into the ocean. Dolphins swam swiftly side by side as they too leaped into the air and squealed as though they were welcoming Arvidia. She squealed with delight. She never tired of seeing them.

Blake was in awe at the power of nature. He had been on vacations, but never in his life had he ever thought he would meet a wolf, get attacked by a bald eagle, see an Orca whale and dolphins all in one day. He pulled Arvidia close to him, wrapped his arms around her and gently kissed her on the cheek as they watched the wonders of the ocean pass by.

Soon the boat turned into an inlet where Lummi Island came into view. The boat pulled up against the dock and the tribesmen quickly tied them in. They greeted the Quad, Arvidia and Blake with much enthusiasm and welcome to Lummi Island. Blake looked around and he noticed at the end of the docks stood two intimidating totem poles. He stopped and looked at them. They were obviously handmade, so much artistic details. He lightly touched the crevices and curves. He was mesmerized by the beauty of them. One of the tribesmen, who made the totem poles explained to Blake how each one of them are made, a story carries with them. At the top of the totem poles large eagle wings spanned out from within the two totem poles. Blake heard a familiar laugh. He turned quickly and watched his son sprinted towards him. He was waving enthusiastically nearly falling into the water. "Dad!"

"Jake!" Blake dropped his things and kneeled, just as Jake leaped into his arms. He hugged his son tightly. Tears flowed freely down his cheeks. Jake nestled his head into the crook of his neck.

"I missed you, dad."

"I missed you too, son."

"Dad, you're are choking me!" Blake laughed and wiped his tears quickly.

"What happened to your cheek dad?"

The unpleasant meeting of Baldy made Blake look up in the sky. Sure enough Baldy flew by as though she were warning him. "Uh . . . . I cut it shaving." Blake stood up to gain his composure.

Jake pulled on his father's arm. Blake leaned down as Jake whispered into his ear. "Dad, don't be mad, I am not supposed to tell, but Melody's real name is Arvidia. She's a real FBI agent!"

Blake winked at his son, "That's okay son. She told me." Jake looked relieved.

"Hi, Arvidia!" Jake hugged her tight.

"Hey, Jake, I told you I'd be back soon! Where are Trista and Caleb?"

"Over there." Jake pointed towards the docks.

Arvidia turned to see her kids running to greet her.

"Who are Trista and Caleb?" Blake asked.

Arvidia looked softly at Blake, "They are my twins."

"You have children?" Blake stammered. "You never mentioned them."

"I usually don't due to the nature of my job. I'm rather overprotective of them. I had married one of the tribesmen and he enlisted into the armed services. He was killed in action in Iraq. The twins were very young when it happened."

"I'm so sorry." Blake said softly. He turned and looked at the kids, they, especially the daughter, were a spitting image of Arvidia. "Do they know what happened to you?"

"I haven't said much to them mainly because I just don't remember much. I do suspect Will told them a few things. One of my biggest fears is Jim finding out I have kids. Will had warned me Jim may seek revenge against me. I would not put it past him to bring harm to my them; it's why I kept them here on the reservation. My daughter's name is Trista and my son's name is Caleb. They're 9 years old."

Blake starred ahead taking in his surroundings. He watched the men drift their boats to the docks and busily empty the fish into large bins. He was astonished at their skills and the teamwork of the tribe, men and women working about, kids running around playing. Some of the kids were pulling crab buckets out of the ocean. He wondered which one of them was Will.

"Blake these are my children, Trista and Caleb." She was so pleased and proud to present them to him knowing this was a very special and personal moment.

The children timidly, shook Blake's hand. "Ok, you can go ahead and play guys." Arvidia shooed them away knowing they would overcome their shyness once they got to know him.

Arvidia shouted to one of the men on the docks, "Where's Will?"

"He's at the Ancient Rock."

Arvidia glanced at the Quad. "Would you guys mind showing Blake the way to Will's house? Blake, I'm going to head over to Ancient rock and talk with my father. Do you mind?"

"No, not at all." Blake quickly kissed her as she walked away. Baldy flew close by and Bandit appeared from the woods, now trotting bedsides her as they headed down the beach. It was an odd sight to see. Concern welled up inside Blake; he did not miss the looks exchanged between Arvidia and the Quad.

"She'll be fine." Todd stated.

"Maybe, but she's still in danger, isn't she?" Blake said with apprehension.

Todd looked in the direction Arvidia walked and hesitantly said, "Yep."

As they approached Will's house, a car pulled up. Hal exited the car and walked towards them. Baldy appeared out of no-where and squawked over his head. Hal dived towards the ground and cussed up a storm. "Ya think that bird would know me by now!" He muttered and wiped the dirt from his suit. He never seemed to remember to make sure he had a change of clothes whenever he came to the reservation. Everyone laughed hysterically, even Blake.

Todd placed his hand on Blake's shoulder. "I told you, Baldy don't like anyone."

"She sure doesn't." Blake shook his head and looked towards the direction Arvidia had walked. He could not help but wonder, what trouble was looming ahead for her and how he even think about protecting her, she was a trained agent, she could probably kick my butt, yet, I still want to protect her.

CHAPTER 19

ANCIENT ROCK

The Ancient Rock was an enormous boulder with half of it cemented into the sea, while the top protruded enough, out of the water, to cause this to be the perfect spot for Arvidia to have grown up near, it was her favorite escape place, to just sit and drink in her surroundings. Its name, Ancient Rock, refers to the remembrance of the generations of tribe members that would come and pray. It was also known to evoke many tears, sorrow and lamentations of the wonders surrounding them, naturally.

Baldy screeched from her perch above Will's head and waited on a protruding tree root from between the cluster of rocks, high above the sea. Will knew Arvidia was coming before he could see her walking towards him. She soon appeared with Bandit at her side. He waved hello and as she smiled her beautiful smile. He'd been praying to the Great One for her safety. He felt fear in her life as well as for her life, he just couldn't shake it, he knew his prayers would be of protection. He held tight to the leather necklace he'd made for her, it was a feather from Baldy. He wanted her to wear it as part of her protection.

He reached out his hand, to his blessed daughter, and helped her up, to sit with him, upon the Ancient Rock. She hugged him tight saying, "Hello, Father."

"Hello, Sqimi." He waited, just a moment, and then gently placed the necklace around her neck. "Please wear this. It will protect you from harm." Baldy flapped his wings loudly as if he understood what Will was saying.

She didn't question his actions, she knew his heart and simply said, "Yes, Father." She looked into his eyes and felt the distance they recently shared. "I've missed you."

"I missed you too, Sqimi." He held tightly to her hands and they both sat on the boulder and watched as the sun slowly sank into the sea.

Will waited, and then said, "Sqimi, You know Jim Mason is coming for you. The day will come when you will have to muster up your will and courage to face him. I feel in my spirit to share this with you. Will opened his tattered dog-eared bible. I read a passage this morning in Ephesians (KJV) 6:11. It said, "<u>Put on the whole armor of God, that ye may be able to stand against the wiles of the devil.</u>" He paused a moment then, still holding her hand he said, "I know I have spoken with you about God many times, and Sqimi please, think to accept Him into your heart. This verse is exactly the storm that is coming your way."

Arvidia looked down at her hands. She simply did not feel God loved her as much as Will claimed He did. Truthfully, she was still angry with Him, why did He allow the horrors and losses she still suffered? What God would allow that? Will never wavered from his faith. He always believed there was a reason for everything that happened. She felt confused. Even Blake shared Will's beliefs about God.

"Sqimi," Will raise her chin up to meet him. She starred into her father's eyes. "God will never leave you astray. You are strong, like the wind. With God, all things are possible. Remember that verse?"

Arvidia smiled; it was the first biblical verse Will taught her. "Yes, I can do all things through Christ which strenghtheneth me." (Phil. 4:13 KJB)

"See. You survived. God healed you."

"Actually, Father, Blake has been talking to me about God too. He's also, a born again Christian. He's been slowly teaching me some of the ways of the bible." Will's eyebrows arched a bit, his heart fluttered. He prayed for many years for this day to come. Arvidia was opening up to God! He rejoiced inside. He knew heart had hardened over the years from the losses she had suffered and understood why.

"Tell me about Blake. Is he good to you? Does he know the truth about you?"

Arvidia's face softened at the mention of Blake's name. "Father, he is a very kind, passionate man. He cares very much for his clients and he fights hard for justice. He and his father operate a law firm out of Schenectady, New York."

"Is this the man you're were working for?

"Yes, I didn't know it at the time, but it was a dud assignment, but strange complications arose. Hal was so upset, he just wanted to protect me, yet the danger came straight for me."

"Well, Hal could not have predicted that. Obviously, God's hands was in on it otherwise, you would not have met Blake. Does Blake know who you really are?"

"Yes, I told him the truth last night. In fact, last night, I let him read the file."

Will's surprise was evident as he looked at Arvidia. "You let him read the file?" She had never let anyone read that file except for Hal.

"Blake is very inquisitive. I knew he would have many questions that I probably would not be able to answer. I was not sure how he'd handle the truth once he knew who I really was."

"How did he take it?"

"Well, he was a little angry and confused, and obviously, he was deeply concerned for his son, but once I told him where he was and that he was safe, he calmed down. We spent most of the night talking. I was so sure he would head out the door once he heard the truth." Arvidia looked off into the evening sky.

"Why did you think that?"

"Well, look at my past previous relationships, except for the kids' father, nobody could handle it."

"You didn't trust them enough to tell them the truth Sqimi. With Blake, it's obviously, different. You care very much for this man don't you?"

"Yes, Father, I do." She looked into her father's eyes.

They both fell silent for a moment then Arvidia spoke up.

"Father, I need to ask you a question. You remember how I called those weird memories "blips"?" She looked at him to see if he really remembered or if he was just humoring her.

"I remember." He really did.

"Well, Blake told me that they're actually repressed memories trying to resurface. He said it usually happens in times of stress and sometimes all it would take is a trigger, such as a smell, touch or an object to bring them to light." She paused, then said, "The other night someone tripped my silent alarm. Bandit and I, along with the Quad, chased someone down to the docks. Bandit bit him on the leg but the suspect escaped into a waiting boat. I had hugged Bandit and when I looked into his face his mouth was covered with blood. My mind had a blip moment. Blake told me it was a flashback I had." Reflecting for a moment, before she told him of what she recalled from that night, she spoke softly. "The night of the fire, I remember Bandit snarling, and I remember him leaping into the air and then biting someone on the arm. I could see the arm was bloody, the moon was full that night but one thing I keep seeing was a shiny object. I now know, it was some sort of a moon shaped medallion he had worn around his neck." She directed her face right to Will and asked, "Father, that medallion is the same one I found in Blake's office the day Gus Laurent broke in. What does this medallion mean?"

Will puffed his mouth and slowly exhaled. So the legend was true, he thought, "My great grandfather told me about that legend. The Legend of the Medallion, when worn on the night of a full moon, gave permission to evil spirits to roam and cause chaos about the islands. The only exception to that would be when there's a Blue Moon or even worse, a double Blue moon."

"What happens if there's a Blue Moon?" Arvidia was very intrigued.

"According to the legend, a curse could be as simple as a cough, constant rash, boil, cough or an inflammation of the skin. A more severe curse, would be, the death of a family member on a yearly basis or even deformation of their own body. We've have never taken this lightly and it's why we obey the Great One and offer up our warrior dances and praise and worship with our songs and drums. We are warriors of God. He keeps the evil from our paths. Those that believe in a moon medallion can protect them are trusting a false god, they believe they are safe from the Blue Moon Curse, but the just call out to the evil and chaos will erupt without peace or direction." Will paused and looked up to the sky. He waited a moment to let it all sink in. Now, watching Arvidia as she gazed into the ocean, twirling the feather from the necklace he'd made her around her fingers, he had no idea she was remembering again. Will took a slight breath and continued, "That night of the fire, we'd heard terrible screams coming from deep in the woods. As you know, we'd gathered to play our drums and pray for God to protect us from harm." Will gently touched Arvidia's arm and pointed at Baldy. "Baldy was very persistent. She kept flying around my house. I remember asking God to give me strength to follow her into the woods and He did."

Arvidia fell silent. She leaned her head onto Will's shoulder just as she did when she was a little girl. Will told her of this legend before, but it seemed as thought she'd only heard it for the first time and it riveted her attention. She remembered the drums he spoke of, they had been comforting. The legend was becoming more of a reality. They both sat on the boulder as dusk gave way to darkness.

Will spoke first, "You are strong like the wind, do not forget that Sqimi." He lightened the mood and said, "We'd better get back to the house before they come looking for us."

"Yes, we better head back." Will extended his had to her as he stood and leapt off the rock. She smiled at him always grateful for his words of wisdom.

As Will locked arms with Arvidia, Will stated, "By the way, I hear Blake met Baldy."

Arvidia laughed. "Oh, you should have seen it; it was very funny to watch them."

They made their way back to the house walking across the beach with Arvidia's arm in the crook of his arm. The minute she saw Blake standing on the porch she recalled him just in the same position, the first night she'd gone over to his home. Hands deep in his jean pockets and he watched as she came towards him. Her heart fluttered in her chest. She knew he was something special.

"Hi, Blake," They reached him just as he stepped off the porch. "This is my father, Will Miles." They extended hands. "Father, this is Blake Matarazzo."

"Please to meet you, Sir thank you for taking great care of my son."

"Blake, please, call me Will. Jake is a wonderful boy. He hit it off with my grandkids as you can very well see." The children had been playing around Blake most of the day.

"Thank you." Blake stood proud.

"Blake, have you ever tried king salmon?" Will was all smiles.

"Uh, yes sir I've had it before. It's quite delicious."

"Not the processed fish," Will scrunched up his face as he stepped inside his house, "Have you ever had FRESH king salmon, right from the ocean? Best you will ever taste!" Will promptly headed into the kitchen.

"Shall we join everyone?" Arvidia knew he must be hungry.

"Yes, let's." Blake's stomach had rumbled earlier as he paced the house waiting for her to come home. The aroma of the fish tempted him badly enough to think about opening the oven door and taking a bite like he normally did at his mother's. To his surprise, the kids, even Jake, quickly set the table and assembled themselves in their proper seats. Hal, the Quad and many tribe members stood and filled the house with their presence. Will brought the piping hot fish to the table, while Arvidia followed with a plate of clams and Alaskan king crab. Blake's mouth watered at the sight of it all. Arvidia prayed he would at least hold back before attacking the food.

"Can I pray Will?" asked Jake.

"Yes, Son you may." Jake quickly said a prayer of thanks. All said "Amen."

Blake's rumbling stomach overtook his hand as he reached for the food. The salmon melted in his mouth, he'd never tasted anything like this, and the crab was tender as can be. He didn't even use butter.

"Arvidia, why don't you take Lexy and show Blake the mountains tomorrow?" suggested Will.

"Oh! I haven't done that in ages! You will love it Blake!"

Blake stopped munching his food. He was afraid to ask who or what a Lexy was. "What is a Lexy?" Blake asked.

They all laughed, especially Hal. "I'd ask too after meeting Baldy."

"Lexy is my horse. We have Appaloosa's in the stable. They're awesome to ride. You needn't worry; I'll ask Sara if you can use Blacky. Do you know how to ride?" She reined herself in to allow Blake to catch his breath.

"Umm . . . . no. Blacky is a horse too, I presume?" Blake looked at Arvidia apprehensively. Meeting a wolf and a bald eagle in one day, not to mention they that tripped the alarm and got away, is one thing, explaining this to his mother would be another. He'd spoken to her earlier and told her most of his adventures. She spoke so fast, and asked so many questions he didn't know how he would get a word in edgewise but he got through it.

"Yes, Blacky is a horse. She's sweet and gentle. It's a piece of cake. Trust me." Arvidia grinned at Will who winked at her.

Blake was nervous about this venture, but decided if this would be his last meal it was perfectly ok by him. He patted the slight bulge on his stomach and stated, "The food was fabulous!" He ate heartily while the others giggled.

CHAPTER 20

BAKER MOUNTAIN

The morning sun warmed the land but the air was brisk. Arvidia went to the stables to ready the horses for the trek into the mountains. The horses whinnied, excitedly, as she spoke to Blacky while tightening the saddle belt. "Blacky, you need to be gentle with Blake. No teasing okay girl?" Arvidia gently patted the horse's snout and checked again to make sure the saddles was secured.

Blake nervously pulled a pair of boots on and then the coat, Will had loaned him. He wondered why he was doing this. He'd never stood close to a horse let alone ridden one, he considered himself an adventurer, but this was out of his comfort zone. He stepped onto the porch and watched as Arvidia stood in front of the house holding onto the reins of the two horses they'd be riding. He was awe struck by her beauty and those blazing blue eyes, completely, held his heart. He glanced at the horses and gulped, he thought he detected a hint of mischief in her eyes this morning.

"Are you ready? Blacky promised me she'd be gentle with you." she grinned. Blacky neighed, bobbed her head while scuffing her hooves in the ground.

"Yeah, I guess I am. I take it this is Blacky?" Blake awkwardly walked towards Blacky as though she would charge him. The mare stood quietly while Arvidia explained the reins. He insisted on getting himself into the saddle.

"Suit yourself." Arvidia stepped away and easily mounted into her own saddle.

She watched him as he lay, sideways, on top of Blacky. She stifled the giggle begging to escape her. He finally pulled himself up and gathered the reins. Blake was surprised Blacky didn't move an inch nor utter a sound. "Uh, Arvidia, now what?" He helplessly looked at the reins and wondered what to do.

"You don't have to do a thing, Blacky knows the way." Slowly, Arvidia pulled on Lexy's reins and Blacky followed. They headed slowly up and into the mountains. She occasionally looked back at Blake, who at first looked bewildered, but now looked in amazement at the beauty of the woods. The woods sang with so many sounds. Pine needles rustled as the tall evergreen leaned into the light wind. Squirrels raced up and down to the tops of them, and all kinds of birds whistled a tune. After an hour of riding up through the mountain paths they finally reached an area nearly as well known as the Ancient Rock. This was a burial ground for the tribes' members.

The crest of Baker Mountain was a peaceful area overlooking a serene small lake. The scenery was truly indescribable. Arvidia spoke softly, "Will often came here as well, to pray and to bury those who had passed on. It was believed, that when you were buried in the mountains, you'd be closest to heaven."

Dismounting now, from their horses, they could see Bandit sitting tall on a large rock where it overlooked the crystal, clear lake. The sun's rays sparkled as they pass through the still waters. The snowcapped mountains lined up into a crescent shape as they stood high across the blue sky. Blake's mouth dropped opened as Blacky came to a halt. Arvidia smiled and pointed, "We're on Baker Mountain and that over there, and the largest mountain of all is, Mountain Rainier." The mountains were peaked with snow and stood tall in the sky.

"Wow, I've never seen anything like this!" The air seemed to clear his lungs and his mind. It was easy to forget troubles once you stood on this peak. Arvidia sat down while the horses wandered and nibbled on the grass. Bandit lay down to nap. Shortly thereafter, Baldy screeched by and soared over them. Blake ducked his head, he was still unsure of her. Arvidia laughed as she opened their picnic basket. She had spread the thick blanket onto the ground; she and Blake sat close together and soaked up the breathtaking view. He wrapped his arms around Arvidia and gently kissed her neck. "This is absolutely incredible. You can almost feel God's presence here!"

Arvidia smiled, "I know, you can't describe this, it's the kind of thing you definitely have to see for yourself." She noticed Blake touch his backside, "So the horse ride wasn't too bad?"

He rubbed his legs now, as they did ache a little. "No, it wasn't too bad. I was a little nervous at first, but Blacky there sure knew where she's going! I can't get over this incredible view!" Blake held her close to him, and kissed her lips gently. "Being with you makes it all worthwhile." Arvidia smiled shyly at him.

"It has been awhile since I've brought someone up here. Trevor and I use to come up here all the time before the kids were born."

"I can see why this place is special." He felt honored and wanted to know more about the children's father. "How long ago did your husband pass?"

"The kids were almost a year old when I got the news he'd been killed. It was quite a shock. I just stayed busy with the kids and decided to shorten my maternity leave, so I could return to work with the Quad." Bandit had lumbered over to Arvidia and plopped his head into her lap. She scratched behind his ears; it was his favorite spot and it usually lulled him to sleep.

Blake laughed when he saw Bandit's eyes loving the massage on his head, "Bandit sure is a unique wolf. Where does his pack go when he's not around?"

"Oh, they're never far from him." She gently patted Bandit's belly. She pointed quietly toward the edge of the trees and looked at Blake and nodded her head. Blake looked in the direction of her finger he could see a pack of wolves, nestling, beneath the trees.

"So we are well protected." He stated. "Now we can eat." He looked into the picnic basket and pulled out some sandwiches Will had made for them. They were both silent, while eating slowly and deep into their thoughts, just taking in the view.

After a short time, it was Blake that broke the silence. "Did you say Will comes up here too?" He spoke practically, in a whisper.

"Yes, mostly to pray. This is considered a sacred place for us; it's quiet, tranquil, and a peaceful place to seek wisdom through prayer and meditation."

"It sure is." Blake nodded in agreement then hesitated before asking, "Arvidia, What did you and your father talk about last night?"

"We talked about Jim Mason and Gus Laurent. The tribe members have reported that they've been spotted the two around in the woods. We also talked about God, and he pretty much said the same thing you said, about facing Jim Mason soon."

Blake swallowed hard. "They're here already? How do you mean, face him?" He was immediately, uneasy about her going anywhere near those guys and was surprised Will let her come up here alone with him while they are on the loose.

"I knew they would come eventually. Jim is like a hound dog and Gus is doing his dirty work for him. Will is right;. I do have to face him. He'll keep hunting for me or threatening to harm the people I love. I'm terrified he'll go after my kids, when I say kids, I also mean Jake. No one will ever touch a hair on those kids." Arvidia shuddered at the thought.

Blake knew by the expression on her face she meant every word, "But what do you mean by facing him?"

"I'm not exactly, sure." Arvidia pointed at the sky, "It is not a full moon yet. Jim is waiting for the right time and I have no doubt he will attack. I just have to be ready when he is."

"I do not want you to do this. It's much too dangerous." Blake implored her. "Todd told me what happened the day they arrested Jim. I don't want that for you."

"I know you don't. It is why I have to do this. He will harm or kill someone if I don't." She knew he cared but she was trained for this. Well, mostly.

Bandit suddenly snapped out of his nap and stood up barring his teeth and he let out a menacing growl. He stared past Arvidia and Blake. Arvidia's hairs on the back of her neck stood straight up. She knew Jim was near. *She felt him.*

"What? What's wrong?" Blake looked at her. She didn't answer but she slowly, crouched down besides Bandit; slowly she reached for her holster, and pulled out her glock. She glared hard as Bandit did towards the trees.

"He's here!" Arvidia whispered to Blake. "Go to the horses!"

"Who?" Blake realized who as soon as he said it and stumbled back towards the horses. Fear rumbled through his body.

As she kneeled beside Bandit, he snarled, loudly and stared straight ahead, she watched him closely. Suddenly, a gunshot rang out and struck Baldy. As she fell from the tree limb, Bandit charged into the woods.

"NO!" Baldy!" Arvidia screamed, "Baldy!" She ran towards her injured protector and kneeled beside her. She squawked loudly, in pain. Picking Baldy up, she cradled her in her arms. Blood stained her wings. "Blake, she's hurt! We need to head back down fast!" Blake was at her side in a moment.

"What about Bandit?"

Arvidia knew Bandit would chase Jim down. She knew deep down he would always protect Baldy. "He'll be fine, I hope."

The horses neighed when the shot rang out, but stood firm until Arvidia whistled for them. "Blake you are going to have hold her while Lexy and I lead the way back." She gently wrapped Baldy in the thick picnic blanket and her coat and she gently placed Baldy into Blake's waiting arms. Blake stared down at the enormous bird that lay helplessly in his arms. Baldy whimpered. "Shh, it will be okay." He awkwardly, stroked the bird's head before taking hold of the reins just as Blacky reared and raced down the mountain behind Arvidia and Lexy. He felt nauseous as the tree branches whip by his face. He could barely blink as he watched Arvidia booting Lexy down the mountain. She looked back at them as Blacky raced behind them. He held Baldy close to his chest and he fervently prayed to God to help this enormous bird who had pecked at his scalp. Baldy seemed to be barely breathing.

"Mom's back!" hollered Trista. Will looked up from reading his newspaper and noticed Arvidia was riding Lexy at a rapid speed. Something's was wrong. He stood up and quickly ran to meet her.

"Whoa!" Arvidia quickly dismounted Lexy like a child coming down a slide. She ran towards Blake and Blacky. Blake gently handed Baldy to her. Will reached them and looked down into her arms. "Jim shot Baldy!" Tears streamed down her face and anger welled up within her. Will smoothly. took the injured bird from Arvidia and carried her into the house.

Will gently examined Baldy with much care. He observed Baldy moving her feet and cawing lightly. The bullet was a through and through. He let out a low whistle. "Baldy you are lucky, God had his hands on you!" He gingerly wrapped her wing with kling wrap and gently set Baldy onto the floor, on her good side. She cawed weakly. "You will have to stay here until you are well." Baldy seemed to understand.

Will went to the porch where he knelt down beside Arvidia as she held her face in her hands. "She'll be okay; the bullet went through her wing."

"Will she be able to fly again?" Arvidia sniffed.

"I believe so, yes. I'lll need to fetch her some food. Perhaps I'll give her some of my healing herbs." It didn't seem as though Arvidia was convinced, she he said, "Baldy is fine, she just needs time to heal. She is a feisty one; She kept trying to stand up!"

Arvidia, laughed and wiped away her tears. She was more surprised that Baldy didn't bite anyone.

"She's fine, Arvidia. What happened up there?" Will, gently, stroked her hair.

Gritting her teeth, she looked at Will and said, "I felt *him*. Bandit woke up suddenly and snarled. I haven't heard that particular snarl since the night of the fire." Suddenly, Arvidia looked around anxiously, "Has anyone seen Bandit? Oh God." Before anyone could answer, she bolted from the porch and ran towards the woods. Bandit limped towards Arvidia. He lay down and whimpered. His left front paw was badly injured. Will came up beside them and examined the wolf.

"We need to get him inside the house. I need to look at this more closely." said Will. The tribe members looked at each other unsure if Bandit would let them near him. Arvidia whispered into Bandit's ear. She and Will gently picked up Bandit as did the other tribe members. They carefully carried him into the house and set him on the floor near Baldy who squawked loudly at her loyal friend lying nearby. The tribesmen quietly exited the room.

Arvidia methodically, stroked Bandit's head as Will sutured his paw. "It is deep, appears to be a hunting knife. He'll be fine." He finished stitching him up and asked, "Well, Bandit, I hope that blood around your mouth means you got a piece of him?" Will, knew Jim was still alive. Will set down his surgical tools and sternly looked at Arvidia. "Arvidia, you do know why this happened?"

"Yes, he's eliminating those that protect me so he can come after me." She pursed her lips tightly together. "I will not stand by and let him hurt anyone else I love!"

Will was angry; he knew the tribe members were too. Jim was encroaching onto their territory. "This is *plstwe`xw! (War)*. We will do the war dance tomorrow! I'll go and speak with the others." Will touched Arvidia's shoulder as he left the room and exiting outside, he spoke with the other tribe members waiting for his word.

They were very upset and agreed to the war dance. Blake was most agitated, he felt totally helpless. He listened closely to the members as they discussed the next evening's plans, then went inside to be near Arvidia. The Quad stood on full alert and Hal talked busily on his cell phone.

Bandit whimpered. "I know Bandit. It will get better. I promise." She lay on the floor and put her head on Bandit's stomach as the tears slid down her cheeks. She simply, stroked his fur. She could see his pack outside the bedroom window. They all lay beneath the window. Blake sat next to her and felt her compassion as real as her anger.

Arvidia spoke to Bandit and Baldy. "Guys, it's time. You have protected me all these years. Now, it's my turn to protect you." Bandit whimpered and Baldy squawked. Arvidia heard the men outside talking about the war dance. She knew if she didn't do something soon, he would come after her or worse, her kids. Blake knew she was trained to protect and kill, but he still didn't like it.

The next day, Will examined Baldy and Bandit. His healing herbs did wonders. Baldy was able to stretch her wing, but obviously she was not ready to fly. Bandit was able to stand but limped painfully when he walked. Will prayed over the two gentle giants who had loved and guarded Arvidia all her life. He had never seen Arvidia so upset and was concerned when he saw her drive off into town alone.

"Where is Arvidia?" Blake asked as he entered the room where Baldy and Bandit rested. He stood in amazement as he watched Baldy sitting on a homemade rail, perch with her left wing still bandaged. She squawked loudly as Blake came close to her. "Hey, you look a lot better!" Baldy swayed back and forth. She seemed pleased to see him. Bandit was able to sit with his wounded paw pulled up close to his trunk. He leaned his head into Blake's leg and rubbed his head against him.

"It appears these two have accepted you. They haven't liked anyone before you." Will lower his voice. "Arvidia went into town."

"Alone?" Blake stammered. "Why?"

"I don't know. She's very upset about what happened yesterday." Blake nodded his head. He noticed she slept with her protectors. He too had been checking on them several times but had fallen asleep sometime just before dawn.

"I don't like her going alone either, but she was determined to go. I told her she must be back by noon. Todd and Mark followed her." Blake was relieved.

"Why is Arvidia going into the library?" Todd asked Mark as he peered through the binoculars.

"I am wondering the same thing. You think she's okay?" Mark pondered.

"Well, I've never seen her upset like this. I think what happened last night set her off. I just can't figure out what she could possibly be doing in a library!" They could only wait outside for her. They wouldn't lose her.

Arvidia approached the librarian. "Hi, I was wondering if you could help me."

The woman at the front desk turned and smiled at her. "Sure, what can I do for you?"

"Do you have any information and maps of the Lummi Reservation?"

"Yes! It's right over here in our historical area, but I'm afraid this material cannot be checked out." Arvidia followed her to the area she was talking about.

"Thank you, I just need to do a little research." Arvidia scanned the various materials before her and found a few selections and set them on the table and took a seat. She carefully read a document which contained The Point Elliott Treaty. She set it aside and reached for the maps. She found one in particular from the year of 1885 when the Treaty was signed. *I was right! The boundaries were changed!* Arvidia took out her cell phone snapped a picture of the map. She folded the maps up, sat down at the computer, and for the next hour she researched more information about Lummi Island.

"Thanks for your help." Arvidia left and walked towards her car. She knew Todd and Mark had followed her.

She sped off and took some side streets she knew Todd and Mark wouldn't know. She needed to get them off her tail. Once she returned to the reservation she immediately got Lexy ready for a ride. As she rode by Will's house, she saw Bandit with his head cocked and he'd smeared his nose onto the window, whimpering. Arvidia stared at him and Baldy.

"I know boy, but you need to stay, I won't be long I promise."

"Where are you headed Sqimi?" Will leaned over the porch railing. He knew she was up to something.

"I'm going for a ride. I promise I won't be long. Todd and Mark should be here soon. I need to be alone."

Will eyed her carefully. "One hour otherwise, the Quad is coming after you. Have you said anything to Blake? What shall I tell him, he's concerned about you?"

"That is all I need. Thanks, father. Please just tell Blake I need some time alone." She rode off.

She took Lexy up the coastline, stopping now, she studied the cell phone picture. *It should be around here.* Arvidia thought. Her brows furrowed together and she jumped off Lexy. She walked towards a section of the woods she'd never ventured into before then finally she reached a valley engorged by cliffs and evergreen trees. Arvidia kneeled and touched the ground. *This is it. Dead Man's Point!* According to her studies at the library, Dead Man's point was where one of many battles was fought. The Lemaltcha Tribe fought hard for this land. The Point Elliot Treaty changed the course of history of the Lemaltcha Tribe. This field was all but forgotten was the sacred war ground where the Lummi ancestors fought and died.

Arvidia kneeled, and looked up to the sky. She clasped her hands together and prayed. Lord, I know I am not worthy of your great Love. My heart has been made hard and cold. I know. I know I must forgive Jim for the wrongs he has done to me. I just ask for forgiveness for shutting you out of my life. I kneel before you, and I accept you Jesus, as my Lord and Savior, into my heart. You sent me people and even animals that love and protect me. I would not be alive if it weren't for them. I know it was you who sent them to me. Lord, I really need your help. I do not know what to do. The wind caressed her long black hair as she stayed kneeled until she heard His whisper into her ear. Thank you. Arvidia stood, and she knew what she had to do.

She quickly jumped into her saddle on Lexy and tugging on the reins and clicked her heels hard into Lexy's ribs. Lexy knew to gallop at a quick pace, and she did all the way to Will's house. She had been gone just a minute or two over the hour time limit he set. She knew he would send the Quad out if she didn't return on time.

She rode Lexy back into the stables before going over to the house. Blake was standing on the porch while the children were running about. She could hear Bandit howling and Baldy squawking most likely from boredom, or they knew she was near.

"Where were you all day?" Blake studied her. He too, could tell Arvidia was up to something. Todd and Mark came back a while ago and told Will and Blake how she went to the library and purposely lost them.

"I needed to be alone." Arvidia hugged him.

"Okay, I understand. Are you okay?" Blake searched her eyes. He felt she was holding something back.

"Yes, I'm fine." She turned and looked at him, "Want to go for a walk later?" she asked.

"Sure." He was cautious and curious.

"First, let me go check on Baldy and Bandit."

"Sure." Blake took her hand as they entered the house but soon let go as she ran into the room where Bandit and Baldy were healing. She was amazed at their progress. Bandit's paw was nearly healed, he snorted and stomped when she scratched his head. Baldy's wing spread wide when she entered the room. She squawked loudly until Arvidia spoke softly to her so as to soothe her.

Will smiled a crooked smile and stated, "I think she may be ready to fly in a day or so. Bandit's limp is barely noticeable. It's simply amazing. The Great One is healing them quickly." Will stated. He had wondered if the Great One was healing them quickly for a reason. Time was running out for Arvidia. The war dance was going to occur at dusk. "I need to go check and see if everything is in order for this evening."

"Okay, father, I'll be out shortly."

Blake heard a commotion outside and went out to see what was going on. He stood among the many tribe members, who were dressed in their warrior armor. One of the tribesmen's wives painted war stripes onto Blake and Jake's face. Many drums were being set up and Will explained to Blake what would happen.

"The purpose of the war dance is to send a message to the eyes of the woods." Will continued, "Legends passed down through our ancestors, have told the story how the war dances keep the evil spirits away, The Great One protects us and keeps us from harm."

"Will, I'm worried about Arvidia. I know she's hiding something." He noted his concern.

"She may have a reason for not saying anything. She will, in due time, she will." Will patted Blake's shoulders, grateful for his concern for her, it was a good sign.

The thunderous wails of the drums in harmony were amazing. Many danced and shouted in their native tongue. The bonfire roared high above them. Hal and the Quad stood guard nearby. Bandit howled while his pack crouched beneath his window. They too were standing guard.

Arvidia slid her hand into Blake's hand and they walked towards the beach. They walked silently hand in hand until h felt he had to ask, "Arvidia, what's wrong?"

"What happened to Baldy and Bandit really hit too close to home." Arvidia stopped and turn to face him. "Blake, I felt *him*."

"What do you mean?" He looked into her eyes for an explanation.

"Remember when Bandit stood and snarled towards the woods?"

"Yes." He was very curious about what she did and didn't remember and was hopeful she'd regain all of her memory while being here on the Island.

"I hadn't heard that snarl since the night of the fire. It was the first time since that night I actually felt *him*."

Suddenly, Blake had an idea. "Arvidia, I think I may have a way to help you."

"Help me? What do you mean?" She couldn't imagine how he could help her.

"I've dealt with many clients who were traumatized by a tragic event in their life. When I talk with them I try to help them remember by asking specific questions and taking them through the event step by step. Sometimes it works, other times it doesn't. It all depends on if they are ready to cope."

"Okay." Arvidia was not sure she was ready, but she needed answers and she trusted him.

"Okay, sit here on this rock," she did as she was asked. "Now close your eyes." She hesitated but, again, did as he asked, "Listen to the waves of the ocean. Relax. Calm your spirit and just listen to the sound of my voice. Focus on the last thing you remember, now, tell me what you remember, even the smallest details can trigger another memory." He spoke in soft tones.

Arvidia sat still on the rock and she felt herself just listening to his voice. "Okay, I'll try."

Blake kneeled down on one knee to face her equally. "Okay, go back to the night of the fire. What do you see?"

Suddenly as if she had been taken back through time, the vision that once had been blackened swiftly came into sharp view. Arvidia scrunched her nose up and shook her head. "You're safe Sweetie. No one will harm you. I promise you. What do you see?" Blake kept a sharp eye on her and kept a certain distance. He wasn't sure what she would remember or how she would react.

"I smell smoke and feel an intense heat." She closed her arms around herself and she slid off the rock and huddling her knees together. She whimpered.

"What happened before the fire?" He was eyeing and circling her.

"Oh, my." she gasped then repeated the words she heard in her mind's eye.

"You will be punished for this!" It's Jerrill from behind the bars." She recalled, "it's a jail cell, but it's in a cabin. There's a woman and child cowering in the corner. Jim cackled and laughed. He checked the lock and threw a lit match on the floor as he walked out. The fire was spreading quickly towards them." She continued with her vision, "Quick we must get her out of here! I heard Jerrill shout, we don't have much time! He was scared and quickly started to pull the rocks away from the wall. It gave way to a hidden tunnel. Jerrill lifted me up and pushed me through the tunnel. I climbed quickly through the hole until I was outside. When I looked behind me and called, "Papi, Mama? They didn't come. The tunnel wasn't wide enough for them. I started coughing, harshly for the smoke was thick and the fire's heat was intense.

Arvidia coughed a little, but; Blake touched her arm to reassure her safety. "It's okay . . . go on." He whispered.

"I can feel a sharp pain in my arm as I lay on the ground, I turned around and Jim Mason is standing there, snarling at me with a knife in his hand. He's reaching for me," She leaned into the rock as if to get away. Again, Blake touched her for reassurance. Arvidia relaxed and continued. "He's picking me up and purposefully flinging me against a tree." Wooshh . . . she let out some air, but still continued. "I fell sharply to the ground, but I'm getting right back up again. My arm is dripping with blood. The full moon shone brightly as I ran. A piercing pain on my neck caused me to trip and fall. Jim's screaming at me. I'm thinking, why does he hate me so much? Then he's saying I ruined his plans and how I would suffer the consequences because of this. He swung his foot high in the air, kicking debris at me. I simply, turned my head towards the cabin and watched it burn, furiously, and long into the night. I writhed in pain, until a wolf barring its teeth lunged for Jim biting, viciously, into his flesh. He screamed as the blood dripped heavily, from his arm. The wolf snarled so more and Jim running away. My head and eyes were screaming in pain. I could feel the wolf's warm breath upon me and felt it was my moment to die. Instead, to my surprise a wolf gently laid beside me and his fur was so nice and warm, but then more wolves came from within the woods and lay in a circle near around me. I could hear them breathing. I could hear the screeching of a bird high above me as the large wings clipped lightly above my head. The wolves howled throughout the night, and the far off sound of drums, it was like a lullaby. Despite all that happened I knew I was safe.

Blake was sure he wanted her to continue, tears were already streaming across is face and he could see sweat building around her upper lip. But just as he was about to stop her she continued on. She seemed determined to remember it all and have it be heard.

The morning came and went. She felt the afternoon sun warming her face. I continually, reached for the wolf; he was by my side, continually. I tried and tried to open my eyes, but they were swollen shut. But before they were shut I remember seeing the masked marking on the wolf. I decided to call him Bandit." Arvidia smiled at this and that made Blake happy as she continued, but now her face scrunched into despair. "I called for Papi and Mama, but I think I knew they were gone, into the sky, where mama said angels took people to heaven. Suddenly, I heard leaves crunching and twigs snapping and I gripped onto Bandit. But when I recognized the screeching, I relaxed, it was the bird again. But, I still felt someone was near. And I thought it was strange that Bandit didn't growl. I felt him move slowly, away from me, but I still clung desperately to his fur and when I felt something fall on my chest, I touched it and it was an eagle feather, the bird's feather.

I could actually, feel, kindness kneel bedside me and touch me with a gentleness I hadn't known in days. I can hear the person gasp and mumbling some worlds, so I tried again, to open my eye. But I couldn't, and I got scared, so I jerked back my swollen burnt arm as the stranger touched me. He began to sing softly in my ear and then he gently wrapped something soft around me. I felt safe again and as I was being slowly lifted from the ground I could remember moaning in pain and then nothing. I must've lost consciousness.

Arvidia started to recoil, Blake touched her arm and said, "You're safe. Open your eyes." Blake knew she had remembered. He carefully reached for her and asked, "Arvidia, who were the people you spoke of?"

She clutched onto Blake. "They were my parents. He killed my parents! Arvidia's sobs echoed deep into the woods and raked through her body. Blake held her close as they sat for a time.

She leaned heavily into his arms feeling weak and worn out but she finally knew the truth about her family. She was ready to go. She looked at him and said, "Let's go back to the war dance. I have to finish this." They walked slowly back to the war dance.

Will suddenly sat up as Bandit howled. He heard Arvidia's sobs. *She remembers. He knew this day would come.* He pounded hard on the drums and the dancers fiercely stepped up their charge of their ritualistic dance.

He walked quickly to Arvidia's side as they came into sight. "Come child, we will pray." He took her from Blake's arms and she went willingly.

"Father, I" Arvidia tears streamed down her face.

"I know. You remembered." Wisdom spread over his gentle face. "The Quad and I went back to the area where I found you. We thought that was where you went for your ride. Joe found some human bones deep in the rubble."

Arvidia closed her eyes. She knew she would not have to wait for Joe's answers. She spoke softly, "They were my parents." She stepped away from Will. Blake started to walk after her. Will stop him, "Give her time Blake, and tell me what happened."

Arvidia stepped into the room where Bandit scuffed the floor and howled. He whined at the sight of her until she sat beside him. "You saved my life. Both of you did." She laid her head on Bandit's trunk and checked his paw.

Her thoughts returned to where she found the ancient war ground. She remembered the words whispered into her ear as she prayed.

"Mom?" Trista walked quietly into the room. "Are you okay?" She kneeled and petted Bandit as she looked into eyes that mirrored her own.

"Yes, I'm fine. Where is Caleb?"

"He's outside with Jake."

"Can you go and bring him here? I want to talk to the both of you."

Trista quickly went and told Caleb to come. Jake followed behind. They went into the room where she laid next to Bandit. Jake hesitated before entering but when. Caleb waved him in he knew it was ok. He and Jake had bonded just as brothers should.

Arvidia gently touched their faces and spoke softly, "I'm sure you have noticed so many things have been happening lately. I want all of you to promise me something. I'm going to give each of you a special job to do."

"Even me?" Jake quipped.

"Yea, man, you're our brother!" Caleb's face grew serious as did Jake's.

"Jake, you're very much part of this family." Arvidia whispered and touched his cheek.

Arvidia explained to them, in kid terms, what had happened to her and why a bad man was looking for her.

Caleb stood with his arms folded across his chest, "Don't worry mom. We'll take care of you."

"That goes for me too." Jake harrumphed and folded his arms like Caleb.

"Good. Your special jobs are to look out for each other. Do not go anywhere alone." Arvidia pointed her finger at each one of them as she spoke.

Blake stood outside in the hallway and leaned against the wall. He had heard the conversation. *I knew she was up to something!* He heard the kids moving around and he quietly left the hallway and returned to the porch to watch the warrior dance. He felt Arvidia's arms encircle his waist and turned her toward him just as he kissed her on the forehead. They both watched the bonfire rise high into the sky as the tribesmen dance furiously to the beat of the drums long into the night.

CHAPTER 21

JIM MASON

Jim Mason slammed his fist on the table. "What is it about those animals?" He spoke to Gus as he rubbed his heavily bandaged arm where the wolf had bitten him. He'd hoped he had injured the wolf enough that he didn't make it back to old Indian's house.

As irony would have it, the injured arm was the same arm he had taken a chunk out of when he attacked Arvidia. Bandit was no match for him.

"Did you say she has kids?" Jim asked.

"Yep, twins, a boy and a girl. They looked to be about 9 or 10 years old. I saw them playing with some boy on the beach." Gus Laurent moaned as he stood from the chair. His leg still throbbed from the bite he took at the docks. He had wished he shot that damn wolf.

"Hmmm . . ." Jim pondered, "That info may come in handy."

"Yeah, well, if you're thinking what I think you are thinking, they are heavily guarded by the tribe and those FBI guys and don't forget the animals."

"Well I'm not surprised by that. Get as much information as you can about them." Jim rubbed his chin.

"What is so important about this Arvidia woman anyway? I can just shoot her from the trees and boom, problem solved." Gus was the ever practical one.

Jim suddenly reached over and grabbed him by the collar. His towered over Gus, to his advantage; he could sneer down at him. "No! You leave her to me!"

"Okay man! Relax! I won't do it." Gus stepped away from him. Panic rose within him, he immediately changed the subject. He could see, much clearer, how the man loathed Arvidia. "What time on Friday do we meet at the docks?"

"The boat is docking at midnight. I heard of this dude through my other contacts. He wants to discuss the possibility of partnership. I'm not too sure about that." Jim leaned towards Gus, "I don't want to have too many hands in the bucket, but I've heard his money's good. He pays cash, but, I want to make sure this dude is what he says he is."

"What's his name?" Gus inquired.

"Buck Taylor." Jim grinned at him.

Gus whistled, "The Buck Taylor?" Gus had heard about this guy. He demanded top quality stuff and paid promptly when his demands were met. However, word had it; he could become easily enraged if he thought he was being double crossed by anyone. The consequences weren't pretty.

Jim scoffed at the breaking news just coming on the TV the voice was reporting about the mysterious deaths rising in numbers due to the street drug Blue Dust. "Come on. We need to go check the lab and make sure we're on schedule. We've got a deadline." Jim walked abruptly towards the door.

"You're the boss." Gus grabbed his jacket. They both headed out the door as the TV droned on about the dangers of Blue Dust.

At the reservation, Hal was updating the Quad about the spread of the street drug, Blue Dust.

"There has to be a connection between Jim Mason and this drug, Blue Dust!" Todd raised his voice slightly and glanced around. "I mean, first it appeared in Albany, New York and now it's here, and so is he."

"I totally agree with you," said Hal "We need proof linking the drugs to him. The only one we have is his fingerprints on the canister found at the crime scene in New York. For all we know he could be using the drug. Not necessarily making and distributing the drug. I have sent Chris and Mike to track Jim and Gus. I want solid proof to bust this case wide open. Jim is very slick and covers his tracks carefully. He's got Gus doing his dirty work, and also has whomever else he has working for him, making the drug. Remember he's good at disguising himself."

"He's right. I found part of a wig up on the mountain. Joe ran the hair strands and the drops of blood through the CODIS. The DNA matched Mason." Mark added.

"That only tells us he's here." Hal sighed "We have no proof that he attacked the animals and he's making the drugs. We need to use extreme caution in gathering evidence and watching our backs. He'll do anything to protect himself and get at Arvidia." Hal was very sure of all he said.

"Not if we can help it." Todd stated angrily.

"Okay. Keep me posted. I'm going to head back to Seattle and meet with the higher ups about this situation. The local hospital has reported 2 more deaths linked to Blue Dust." Hal moved, unceremoniously, through the door and back to his car.

Todd's phone shrilled, "This is Todd."

"Hey, there's an incoming boat named **The Lurk** coming in on Friday at the harbor." Mike stated.

"What's so unusual about that?" Todd asked.

"Well, for one thing, it's never docked in Bellingham port before, and, rumor has it, that Buck Taylor is on the ship."

Todd swung around and looked at Mark." Buck Taylor!" Buck Taylor was Todd and Mark's first drug bust before they were hired by Hal to be part of the special division in the FBI. "How did he get out?"

"His sentence was reduced due to good behavior. He hasn't been seen or heard from since his release."

"Hmmm . . ." Todd mumbled. "So no connections between him and Mason?"

"Not that we can find. I'll keep you posted."

"Do that. Thanks." Todd shoved his cell deep into his pocket.

"What was that all about? Are you talking about the Buck Taylor I am thinking of?" Mark's face was shocked.

"Yep. He got out two years ago. Nobody has seen or heard from him since. He obviously has been keeping a low profile. There's a ship called **The Lurk** docking at Bellingham Port on Friday night. Chris heard rumors he maybe on it."

"Okay," Mark tensed up. "We know Buck is big into selling drugs, I bet you anything there is some sort of connection between him and Mason."

"I agree. We need to find the link that connect these them. Hal wants an airtight case and we have to watch our step. Buck is another dangerous dude."

Mark shook his head. "I think we need to call in some favors."

"I was just thinking the same thing! You don't think Buck would go after Arvidia do you?"

"No, I doubt it. He's too concerned about himself and making money." Mark suddenly looked at Todd. "Hey! You think Blake might be able to help us? Maybe he can use his connections from New York?"

"That's a great idea!" Todd waved to Blake "Hey, Blake!"

"Is everything okay guys?" Blake quickly walked towards them.

"Yeah, hey, listen can you help us with something?" Mark asked.

"Sure, whatever you need." Blake felt an excitement building.

"We need your expertise to help us pin Jim Mason to this street drug, Blue Dust."

"Blue Dust? Oh, yeah, I heard about that on the news. I just heard it again on the radio you think Jim Mason's connected?"

"We have reasons to believe he's making and distributing it, but according to Hal we don't have enough solid proof to bust him for it. When Arvidia was searching the crime scene she found a small necklace, canister type that had particles of the drug Blue Dust inside. His finger prints were on it." Mark explained.

"But not enough evidence to touch him right?" Blake asked.

"Exactly. We need to find the people that work for Jim. It seems the leads we had, people aren't talking or can't and that means they are either dead or they've mysteriously disappeared."

"Okay, give me some names let me make some phone calls. I'll see what I can find out."

"Thanks man we appreciate it." Todd jotted down a few names, on his IPAD and then shook his hand. Blake quickly walked away and speed dialed his father. "I have to admit I do like that Blake. I can see why Arvidia is so protective of him."

"Yeah, he's a good guy." Mark concurred.

"Hey Dad, it's me Blake. How's everything going out there?"

"Blake! How are you? Everything is fine. I just got word we're set to go to trial for Holly Stearns in 6 months."

"Excellent. No response from the defendants?" Blake was thrilled he was holding down the fort.

"None at all." Stephen said firmly, "I am quite sure they will come up with a response."

"Yeah, I'm sure they will. The city cannot afford any negative outlook on the police department. Listen Dad, the reason I'm calling, I was wondering if you can find out some more information about this new street drug, Blue Dust. The guys from the FBI think there's a connection to this guy, Jim Mason. The only evidence they have against him is his fingerprints on a canister found at the crime scene where Marcus O'Neil was killed. I've got a couple names here for you."

"I believe I can make some phone calls and see what can be found. Is, oh, I've forgotten her name again, what is it again?"

"Arvidia."

"Yes, Arvidia. What an unusual name. How is she doing?"

"She's doing okay." Blake hesitated whether to tell his father what happened on the mountain. "She's still shaken up about Jim Mason escaping from prison."

"Oh that poor child! Uh. Blake, your mother said you are on some island that is an Indian Reservation? What on earth are you doing there?"

"Well, it is an amazingly long story. Arvidia grew up here. I'll explain it all when I get back there."

"Okay, Son. I will call you when I get some information. Take care and please say hello, to Arvidia for me."

"Thanks, Dad, oh and she has two kids, they're actually twins, Trista and Caleb. They're nine years old, great kids. Jake gets along with them very well."

"Oh? That reminds me, what is this I hear about a wolf and an eagle?"

"Yeah. Um . . . I'll explain that too, later. Bye, Pop." Blake knew his father was going to keep asking questions if he didn't hang up. He knew there would be many questions to answer upon his return; Blake moaned.

Jim Mason and Gus Laurent glanced around quickly as they walked into the abandon warehouse at the harbor where the makeshift lab stood. "How's it going?" Jim roughly slapped Roland on his shoulder blades, "Will we have enough to make the delivery?"

Roland nervously stood and looked at Jim. Three lab scientists hired before him were killed for not meeting the deadline. He desperately needed the money Jim offered him. "Yes. We'll definitely have enough made in time for Friday."

"Good. I knew I could count on you." Jim smirked at him. "Show me what you've finished."

"All right," He nervously led Jim into the back of the warehouse where several people were scurrying about. None dared to look at the man that entered into the room. "This is what we have so far. Two more loads are coming up. We're right on schedule."

Jim slapped his hands together and sadistically exclaimed, "Wonderful!" His meeting with Buck Taylor should go smoothly. He just had one more detail to take care of. He smiled at his plan for that.

CHAPTER 22

THE LURK

Arvidia carefully walked outside with Baldy on her heavily gloved arm. "Okay, Baldy, time for you to fly!" Baldy squawked, flapped her wings and with a gush of air, soaring high above the rooftops she flew back and perched herself on Will's rooftop, and majestically scanning her surroundings, just as it should be.

Arvidia heard Bandit howling, she went into the bedroom and held on tightly to the scruff of his neck, but he literally bolted out of the house, dragging Arvidia behind letting go she allowed him to run straight for the woods, she could see his pack waiting for him. Bandit stopped, turned and trotted back to Arvidia. He rubbed his enormous head against her leg. She laughed and standing up she wiped the dirt from her jeans and said, "Boy, don't be thanking me, you need to thank Will! Now go, shoo. Your family is waiting for you." Slowly, she walked back to the house. Her heart tingled with happiness that Baldy was able to fly and Bandit was able to run. She ran up to Will and hugged him tight. "Thank you, Father, for saving them."

Will smiled as he watched Baldy on the roof screeching as if she were announcing her return to the wild. "They will be fine. Sqimi."

Blake watched in amazement at the incredible healings of these two animals. He knew God's hand was on them. He was in the midst of walking back to the house and catch up with Arvidia when his cell shrilled in his pocket. "Hello?"

"It's me, Son." Blake's father announced.

"Hey, Pop!"

"Blake. I found out some information for you. One of my contacts was able to locate an individual who was selling and using the drug himself. He said he nearly died from it. He said he never heard of Jim Mason or Gus Laurent. However, he was able to identify a picture of Gus Laurent who he only knew as Luke. My contact also located another person who had dealings with Gus Laurent. She apparently developed some sort of relationship with Gus and has kept contact with him. Their last conversation was him bragging about a big load coming in Friday in a town called Bellingham, Washington. There seems to be plenty of evidence pointing towards Gus Laurent."

"And none towards Jim Mason." Blake interrupted.

"You got it. Gus Laurent is doing Jim Mason's dirty work. This one knows exactly what he's doing."

"Sure sounds like it." Blake turned back and looked at Todd. He beckoned him to come over to where he stood. Todd whistled at Mark and they quickly walked towards Blake.

Arvidia noticed the three of them huddling together. *Something is going on.* She had noticed Chris and Mike seemed to have disappeared. Todd and Mark seemed particularly agitated, Hal abruptly left for Seattle and Blake seemed rather distant.

Blake spoke rapidly to give them all the information his father had given him.

"Gus said there's a load coming in Friday?" Todd whispered.

"He has to be referring to the boat docking on Friday!" Mark said excitedly.

"What boat?" Blake asked and lowered his voice, "Arvidia is coming."

"Talk football!" Todd ordered.

Arvidia stepped lively over to where the guys were standing. "What's going on here?" Arvidia demanded.

"We're just talking football."

"No, you are not. Something's going on here and somebody better start talking. Where are Chris and Mike? Why did Hal suddenly take off?"

Todd looked at Mark and decided to tell her part of the truth. "You ever heard of Blue Dust?"

"Yes. Joe Rizzo found Jim's prints on a canister that had some residue inside. It came back positive for Blue Dust. Why?" She watched them carefully to assure there were no secret signals.

"Well, Blue Dust has popped up here, we're suspicious that Jim is making and distributing the drug, but you know how Hal is. He said in order for the charges to stick, we need hardcore evidence to link him to it. He also said hospital sources are telling him this drug is extremely dangerous."

Arvidia did remember a broadcast flashing some news about some recent deaths linking to the use of Blue Dust. "Oh, yeah, I do remember hearing something about that." Now calmer she still felt they weren't telling the entire truth.

"My father did some digging and I was just passing some information to Todd and Mark." Blake glanced at Mark and Todd. He was just as curious as to why Todd and Mark were excited about the "boat" coming in. Arvidia knew these guys were holding back and was about to rip into them when her son ran up to her and grabbed her arm.

"Mom, Look what we caught!" Caleb and Jake ran up to Arvidia proudly showing a basket of fresh crabs.

"Good job guys!" Arvidia smiled at them.

"Come see how we caught them!" Caleb pulled on Arvidia's arm.

Jake pulled on her other arm. "Yeah, come, we made a neat basket!" Jake said excitedly.

"All right, I'm coming." Arvidia glanced back at Todd and Mark. "I am not done with you two." Then looking at Blake again she said, "Three."

Blake waited until Arvidia was far enough away. He turned and looked at Todd and Mark. "What boat are you guys talking about and why didn't you tell Arvidia about it?"

"We found out there's a boat coming into port on Friday called **The Lurk**. A long time ago, Mark and I worked on our first drug case that took two painstaking years to bust. It was a huge drug ring. The kingpin of that was Buck Taylor. We just found out he was paroled two years ago and has been keeping a low profile. Chris heard rumors that Buck Taylor maybe on that boat. If we are right, I am betting Jim Mason is meeting up with Buck Taylor. This has to be the payload Gus was bragging about." Todd explained.

"Is it enough to bust them then? Then will Arvidia be safe?"

"Hal wants us to back off as much as possible until we have all the evidence to connect Buck, Gus and Jim. Remember we only have Gus connected to this and he's not the type of guy to handle this operation alone. He's more of a follower." Todd interjected.

"In other words, he's doing the dirty work for him." Blake rubbed his chin as he often did whenever he was in court or deep in thought about something.

"You got it." Mark snapped his fingers at him.

"I know Chris and Mike are setting up video equipment across from the building where Hal thinks they're making and disturbing the drug. They've seen Gus and Jim coming and going from the building, Mike is going to try and get inside and place bugs when the boat docks. Gus had said they would be meeting at the docks and would head out to Dirty Dan's." explained Todd.

Blake was listening and absorbing all the details coming out. His brain worked quickly at the possible scenarios that could be happening. He didn't like what he was thinking or hearing but he knew the Quad would do everything they were trained to do, to serve and protect, Arvidia. He looked over at her standing and listening to the long winded explanations from Caleb and Jake about their "invention". He felt raw emotions of anger and fear trying to surface; he fought to keep them down by curling up his fists.

CHAPTER 23

BUCK'S ARRIVAL

"We have docked, sir." a nervous deckhand carefully, shook Buck Taylor.

Buck Taylor stirred slowly awake, "Is he here?" he stated gruffly. He stood up in his cuddy and looked at the cracked mirror that hung crooked on the wall.

"No, Sir. It's 11:30pm He should be arriving soon."

"Okay. I'll be up shortly. You can go." Buck waved him off.

The nervous deckhand left quickly and sought out the captain. He'd heard rumors about this guy and wanted to steer clear of him. "Captain, he's awake. He said he'll be up shortly."

"Okay." The captain was weary and glad to have the boat finally docked, at least for a couple of days. Buck Taylor insisted on no stops while they headed straight for Bellingham Port. He had no idea what the shipment was they were picking up, other than it was important. He was informed not to ask any questions about it. Buck Taylor paid him a handsome sum of money that quickly squelched any suspicious he'd had about Buck Taylor. It wasn't long before he heard footsteps on the docks. Peering over the railings, he noticed two men approaching the boat.

"You guys looking for Buck?"

Jim quickly looked around and nodded his head.

"He'll be up shortly."

"Wow. Buck Taylor is on that boat!" Chris whispered while watching through the binoculars. "Is it recording, Mike?" They both peered through a cracked window of an abandon warehouse.

"Yep. Joe said this baby should capture their conversations on the boat as well." Mike held the camcorder up and recorded the action on the dock.

"Good. I think that's him!" Chris whispered.

"Hello, Gentlemen! I'm Buck Taylor." Buck stuck out his hand towards Jim. "Let's get down to business. Is the delivery ready?"

"Welcome to Bellingham!" Jim cracked a crooked smile. Soon the cash he longed for would be his. His golden ticket out of Bellingham for good, once he took care of Arvidia that is, and of course, Gus. Got to make sure there are no loose ends. Then it's off to Brazil. "Yes, the shipment is ready to be loaded first thing in the morning."

"Good. I'll pay as soon as the package is delivered."

"Fair enough. How about we go and celebrate our new partnership? I know a great restaurant we can go and further this discussion."

"That sounds good." Buck looked around the eerie dock and walked with them towards the car.

"We better go and follow them." Chris whispered. They quickly covered their equipment and inaudibly snuck out of the warehouse. Chris quickly dialed Joe's number, "Joe is he on the tracker?"

"Yep. I got him. He just turned left onto Bayview Street. I also got all the data you guys have recorded."

"Good."

"I'll be here in the lab if you need me." Joe sat back and observed the large screen before him. He had hoped these three men laughing up a storm in the car would be having their last laugh. He shook his head as he looked down at the three very thick files of criminal activities that had spanned over their lifetimes.

"Thanks, Joe. We will check in with you later." Chris placed his cell back in his pocket. He wasn't sure if Joe heard him say thanks or not. "It looks like they're pulling into Dusty Dan's. I'm going to call the waitress I know who works there and see if she can seat them in the window seat. He looked at Chris in his mischievous way and added, "After being stationed so long on a island, you get to know people. We should be able to see and hear everything they say." He reached again for his cell, and punched in her number.

"Good Idea." replied Mike, with a smirk on his face.

"Hey Michelle, need a quick favor from you, there'll be three men coming through the doors. Can you can seat them in the window seat and steer clear of them except to take orders?"

Michelle loved a mystery. "No problem, Chris. I see them now. Need a bug placed?"

"No, we should be able to hear them." Chris smiled to himself.

"Okay will do."

"Thanks!" He replaced the cell once again back into his pocket.

Chris and Mike followed Jim's car until it parked in front of Dirty Dan's. The three of them glanced nervously about as they entered the restaurant. Directed to a booth with a window view, they slid in. Chris and Mike could hear their conversation. The three men ordered their drinks, and it wasn't long before the conversation turned serious about the deal.

"I'm willing to pay you 2 mill for the first load, if all goes well, I'll increase it to 3.2 mill. depending on how things go." Buck leaned back confidently and stared and Jim. Jim rubbed his hands together. The amount was more than he had hoped for. It would be enough for him to escape out of the country, *how sweet life will be in Brazil.* Jim thought. "That sounds like a good deal, but my price is 2.5."

Buck's eyes flashed with anger. He'd heard about his careless respect for human life. He stared at his cold black eyes. He was greedy, like him. "I need to know more about this drug? What is it called again?"

"Blue Dust. I'll lower my price to 2.2 million and throw in some extra kilos and if you like the profit it brings you, we can talk more down the road. It's a real deal, you won't be disappointed!"

"Deal." Buck put his hand out and Jim firmly shook his hand, pleased with the big payload this would deliver. He glanced at Gus, "When we get back, check on Roland and make sure the delivery is done and loaded onto the boat by tomorrow morning."

"Okay Boss." Gus looked out the window and stared at the car he had seen earlier. "Consider it done."

"What would I do without you?" Jim slapped his shoulders. He had no intentions of keeping Gus around. He knew too much already.

"Yo, Chris we better hightail it out of here, he keeps looking over this way."

"Yeah, I noticed that." Mike put the car in neutral, fortunately, in the part of town they were in, Ole Fairhaven; there were plenty of hills around. Mike was able to slowly back the car down and around the corner as they disappeared into the night. Gus looked out the window and noticed the car was gone. *Guess I am getting paranoid.* He thought to himself.

Mike's heart was pounding. He glanced in the rearview mirror. There were no signs of them coming after them. Mike let out a low whistle, "That was close."

"Joe!" Chris hollered into his blue tooth, "Are they still in the restaurant?"

"Yeah man. You guys are clear." Joe eyed the large computer screen of the three men still deep in conversation in the restaurant.

Chris was relieved. "We are going to head back to the warehouse."

"Okay. Check in later. I have to run some more tests and I need to speak with Hal about the bones we found by the cabin that burned. Arvidia was right, they were her parents."

Chris sucked in his breath. "Wow. Well now we know why we couldn't locate her parents." He glanced over at Mike.

"That stinks. How did you think she'll take this?"

"Truthfully, I think deep inside her, she knew it was them. At least she'll have some sort of closure. Maybe this will help jog her memory a bit."

"Yeah, it might help her. I had hoped we would be able to find someone who'd be able to tell her what happened."

"Are you going to tell her, Joe?" Chris asked.

"I'm not sure if I am the right person to tell her this type of news. I called Hal. He should be here soon."

"Okay buddy, talk to you later." Chris clicked off his cell and placed it on the dashboard. He leaned back into his seat and slowly sighed as did Mike. The ride back to the warehouse was silent as they both thought of the day they first met Arvidia.

Joe hung up and recharged his cell phone. He furrowed his brows together. He was agitated. He paced quickly around the lab. *This cannot be right!* The results of the DNA test stunned Joe. *No way, this cannot be right!* Joe reran the test several more times and he got the same results. The DNA from the bones did confirm that Jerrill and Marilyn were in fact Arvidia's parents. The test also confirmed Arvidia and Jim were half brother and sister. "Wait until Hal hears this." Joe whispered.

"Hear what?" Hal boomed as he walked into the lab startling Joe. Hal saw that he looked as if he'd seen a ghost. "Joe, what's wrong?"

"Uh. Sir, I got the DNA results from the bones." He hesitated, feeling sick to his stomach.

"Okay, so, is it her parents or what?" Hal couldn't get a read on him.

"Or what, Sir." He took a deep breath, "I mean, yes, they were the bones of her parents. Sir, their names were Jerrill and Marilyn" Joe stopped for a moment and almost whispered, "Mason."

"Mason!?" Hal's face puffed into a surprise. "You mean Arvidia and Jim are?"

"They're half brother and sister, Sir."

"Oh my, I certainly did not see that coming." Hal sat down in the nearest chair. How was he going to tell Arvidia this? "Did you find out anything about them?"

"Well, according to the CODIS files, her parents were born again Christians and kept to themselves. According to records, they moved frequently. Jim's trouble seemed to have started shortly before his biological mother died in a mysterious fall down stairs in their home in Atlanta, Georgia. The death was ruled accidental. Jim was home alone with her and his father Jerrill, was working in a local factory. He met and married Marilyn Secore two years later. It seems Jim became more violent after his father married Marilyn. Not long after they married, Arvidia came along. Apparently, Jerrill and Marilyn feared for their safety and had planned to take Jim to a place that could provide psychiatric help. Jim found out. He took his parents and Arvidia prisoner in the woods until the fire." He watched Hal nearly turn green. He continued, "There is one other thing sir."

"What?"

"It appears Arvidia has a twin sister somewhere."

"A twin sister?" Hal rubbed his reddened face with both hands, before speaking again. He had to be 110% sure of this information, so he instructed Joe. "Research more on his biological mother's death. Search more on this "twin". I don't want to tell Arvidia anything, until all the facts are positive and we are absolutely sure. She was sure about the bones being her parents so I don't think she will be shocked about that. Are you positive that Jim Mason is her half-brother?" Hal asked incredulous.

"I personally ran the tests several times, Sir. Jim is definitely her half-brother."

"Okay." Hal was stunned. "What doesn't make sense is the twin. Why spare her?"

"I don't know, Sir. I assure you, I will research this further."

"Yes, please do. Don't say anything to anyone, not even the Quad. Call me immediately when you have more information. I'll speak with Will in a bit. Maybe he can shed some light on this."

"Yes, Sir." Joe spun around in his chair and busily clacked the keyboard as fast as his fingers would let him. He was afraid of what more the computer would unlock about Arvidia's past, and wondered how much more she could handle.

Hal walked quickly back into his own office, picking up the drink he had left on his desk, he blindly took a sip and let his mind wander. He was in shock. *Arvidia was Jim's half-sister? Why did he hate Arvidia? Who and where is this twin?*

CHAPTER 24

IF BONES COULD TALK

Hal slept fitfully throughout the night. His conversation with Joe disturbed him a great deal. He decided to get up and get ready to head up to Lummi Island; he quickly showered and changed. Lumbering into the kitchen, where the already made coffee awaited him. He fingered the well-worn file of Arvidia's life, he'd added the information he had learned from Joe the previous night. Slowly he sipped the hot coffee and starred out the kitchen window. His thoughts slipped back to the day when he first heard about Jim Mason. He had often wondered where the profound rage from Jim Mason toward Arvidia had come from. It never crossed his mind the two might be related. None of Jim's files from the prison ever mentioned any family. He reviewed the photographs of them. There were no familiar resemblances between them. He thought about the tough job Joe had sifting through the evidence in the bones found in the woods. Hal thought, *if bones could talk, then again, they can.*

Hal gathered his things, and placed her file in his briefcase, taking a deep breath, he walked toward his car. It didn't take long before he was on the freeway heading to Lummi Island. The hour and twenty minute drive went by quickly and soon he was parked in the front of Will's home, which still, to his amazement, tilted to the left. Todd, Mark and Blake were sitting on the steps of the porch waiting for Arvidia and the kids. "Todd, is Will around?" Hal asked.

Todd pointed towards the beach, "Yes, Sir, he is at the Ancient Rock."

"I can show you where to go!" Caleb jumped over the men sitting on the steps. "Come this way!" Jake bounded out of the house and tried to jump like Caleb but managed to find himself tumbling down the steps just as his father caught him. He was off and running before his father could say anything to him. Baldy flew over Hal's head but spared him his usual torture. She seemed to understand the urgency of Hal's walk toward Will.

"Something's up." Blake starred after Hal and the two boys who were racing each other toward the beach.

Todd followed his gaze and stood. "I agree. Chris called me this morning. He said Joe told him the bones found in the woods were positively Arvidia's parents. Didn't she say she thought it was her parents? Something else is brewing. Hal rarely brings that file anywhere. He knows Arvidia hates to even see it."

"You think Joe found something?" Mark asked. "Then again, why would Hal not discuss it with us?"

"Because it's personal." Blake turned his gaze on Todd and Mark. Blake did not like the look on Hal's face when he first saw him. It was a look of pure shock. He'd seen this look many times before. Sometimes he relished the thought of shocking witnesses on the stand. It was often what they deserved whenever they got caught lying under oath.

"What's personal?" Arvidia walked onto the porch with Trista. All the men turned and looked at Arvidia. She looked stunning in her dark blue dress. It mirrored her blazing blue eyes.

"Oh, nothing, you look fantastic! Happy Birthday!" Blake leaned over and kissed her on the cheek. Arvidia glanced at Todd and Mark. She knew instinctively something was off. She knew Mark and Todd well. Glancing over she noticed Hal's car parked. "Hal's here? Where is he?"

"He went to talk to Will." Todd fussed with his hands;, he did not seem to know where they belonged. He chose to fold them in his lap.

"Hal went to talk to Will where?" Arvidia was surprised. Maybe it was about the bones. She knew the bones belonged to her parents. Why would Hal not talk to her about it?

"The kids walked him over to the Ancient Rock."

She felt a wave of concern even though she knew the news had to be about her parents. Maybe Hal thought it was proper to let Will know first before letting her know.

"Sweetie, why don't you and Trista wait in the car and I'll go get the boys." Blake replied

"Okay." Arvidia held Trista's hand and walked away.

Todd leaned over to Blake, "Give them a few minutes. We'll follow behind you in the car."

"Okay, sounds good, I'll go and see if the boys are ready." Blake headed towards the beach just as the boys located Will sitting on the Ancient Rock.

"Grandpa, Hal is here!" Caleb was running and waving towards the Ancient Rock. Jake was close behind him, Hal desperately tried to keep up with them. He was huffing by the time he reached the rock.

"Thank you. Boys, please go check the crab baskets and empty them."

"Yes, Grandpa, let's go Jake!" The boys bounded off to their hidden crab baskets that bounced playfully in the sea.

Once they were out of ear-shot. Will turned slowly and looked at Hal. He helped him up onto the rock. I have been expecting you. I've been feeling something in my spirit all morning."

"Somehow I knew you would be waiting for me." Hal awkwardly maneuvered his way onto the ancient rock and sat heavily next to Will. He set Arvidia's file onto his lap.

"I take it you know the identity of the bones?" Will inquired.

"Yes. It came back positive for Arvidia's parents. According to Joe, they appeared to have died in the fire. I have to say, Will, I've been at this job for many years and I've had some shockers, but Arvidia's case is so highly unusual."

"I do not believe Arvidia will be surprised it was her parents. She said since she started remembering some things, pieces of her 'blips' are starting to make sense to her. Blake has been tremendously helpful with her on that. I believe all the people that fell early into Arvidia's life, you, myself, the Quad, Blake, and the kids are all part of God's plan for her." Will looked at Hal and realized there was more news to come. "What is it, Hal?"

"Joe discovered not only were they Arvidia's parent's but Jim Mason's as well. From what I can determine, Jerrill Mason is his father. Marilyn was Jim's stepmother. They were both Arvidia's parents." Hal paused.

Will's head turned ever so slowly towards Hal as the shock slowly spread across Will's face. "Mason? Jim and Arvidia are . . . . related?"

Hal spoke softly, "Yes. They are half brother and sister." Will muttered something unintelligible and yanked an eagle feather off of his necklace and through his fingers he let the feather slip through his hands into the ocean. "We must give her parents a proper burial."

Hal sighed, "There's more. Joe is actively confirming this and I do not have much information at this point, but it appears Arvidia has a twin sister."

"Arvidia did mention several times she felt like a piece of her were missing. I always thought she was referring to the loss of her family, but perhaps she was talking about that?"

"Possible. I wanted to discuss this with you first. I respect your leadership here with the tribe and you are Arvidia's father. I haven't discussed this with the Quad, yet. I want to be sure we're taking every step possible to build a strong case against this man."

"I agree."

"Will, do you want me to tell Arvidia or do you want to tell her?"

"Knowing Arvidia, this news will greatly upset her. I would like to tell her privately. I'm not sure when the right time will be. Since it's her birthday, I will wait until later."

"Of course, I respect that. Would it be okay to discuss this with the Quad? I have no doubt in my mind Jim will come after her. I just wish I knew where the hatred for her comes from."

"Yes that is fine to discuss it with them. I just ask they respect my wishes to let me tell Arvidia. As for Jim, he may not even know where it is coming from except that he is consumed with hatred."

"You're probably right."

"It is sad though, to watch someone be so consumed with hate that they wither away from life as a result from it." Will looked out toward the children, they were close but they couldn't hear.

"I see that all the time in my job. It is incredible." Hal's face turned serious, "Will, I'll do whatever it takes to catch Jim Mason, dead or alive. I just have one request, after all this is said and done, I want to burn this wretched file." Hal held the file tightly, his knuckles whitened.

"Absolutely, we can definitely do a fire burning ceremony with it. I know you fellas will catch him. I feel it in my spirit. I also feel Arvidia will be in the twist of things. I am not sure what that means, but that is all what the Great One has revealed to me."

"Okay, I'll go and discuss this with the Quad. Chris and Mike have been at the docks watching Mason. He's doing his drug deals but I still want to make sure we have enough evidence to close this case for good. I want Todd and Mark to keep watch on Arvidia."

"Yes. I agree. I think you should inform Blake as well."

"All right, I'll include him." Hal slapped himself, "I've been so wrapped up in this case, I completely forgot about Arvidia's birthday!"

"Oh I'm sure she is fine with it. She has been feeling 'old' lately. I do not know what she is talking about she is the most beautiful woman I have ever seen. She's my daughter!"

Hal laughed softly. "That she is. Now, I'm off to go talk to the guys. Again, Will, I'll do my best to catch this wretched man."

Will placed his hand on Hal's shoulder and said, "I know you will and together we will burn that wretched file. I have faith in the Great One and in you, my friend." Neither man had noticed the boys were no longer in sight anymore.

Caleb and Jake were hiding behind the boulder and overheard Will's and Hal's conversation. Caleb was quiet, his face was serious. He whispered to Jake "Why does this man hate my mom so much? I know mom said he did bad stuff, but she can't remember what happened to her. If those bones were my mom's parents that means he killed my grandparents."

Jake looked at Caleb, "It sure sounds that way. We can go talk to my dad, he knows all about this kind of stuff. He and my grandfather are lawyers back home. He'll know what to do."

A tear escaped from Caleb's eye. He quickly wiped it away with the back of his hand. "Well, the Quad knows what to do, too. Why don't they want my mom to know? Shouldn't she know?"

Jake shrugged his shoulders, "I don't know stuff about that, but my dad does. Come on let's go talk to my dad." Jake jumped up and pulled Caleb up. They abandoned the crab baskets they had brought to show Will and ran over the hill in the trees hiding from Will and Hal as they hurried back to Will's house.

"What are those boys up to now?" Blake saw the boys sneaking around the trees waving fervently at him. Blake could only think they had got into some sort of trouble.

"Okay boys, what did you do now?" Blake folded his arms across his chest.

"Dad, if someone overhears something important we should tell you right?" Jake said quickly.

Blake saw the look on Caleb's face. These were not the typical uh-oh we are in trouble looks. Blake kneeled down and gently placed his hand on Caleb's shoulder. Caleb stared down at the ground and kicked the ground lightly. He liked Blake but was not sure if he could trust him.

"Caleb? What's wrong?" Blake looked sternly at Jake, "What do you mean you overheard something? Were you listening in on Hal and Will?"

"Yes, Dad we were, It was an accident. I swear! Will told us to bring the crab baskets back to him and we heard them talking. I'm sorry, Dad."

"Okay. Jake, you know better than to listen in on grown up people's conversations!" Blake replied firmly, Blake turned and looked at Caleb, he became concerned. Caleb was usually a happy go lucky kid. He had not seen him this serious. "Caleb, whatever it is, you can talk to me."

Caleb spoke softly, and barely in a whisper, "Jim Mason is my mom's half-brother and Hal said something about a twin sister. The bones that were found in the woods were my grandparents."

Blake felt his blood drained from his face. "What? Are you sure you heard that right?"

"Yes, I heard him too dad. They're both are going to wait to tell her. Hal said something about they're watching Jim, something about drugs? I forgot the name of it. He also said Jim is waiting for Arvidia."

"Do you mean Blue Dust?" Blake inquired. Both boys nodded their heads yes.

"Why does this man want to hurt my mom?" Caleb's face flushed with tears brimming along his eyes. His lips quivered as Blake gently encircled Caleb and hugged him. Jake threw his arms around his father and Caleb. Arvidia peered through the back window of the car and noticed them hugging, she could only see Blake's back. *Hmm . . . . maybe Blake is praying.* Arvidia thought.

"Mom, what are they doing?" Trista look in the direction of her mother's view.

"I don't know. Maybe they did something they shouldn't have. I'll ask Blake later."

"Boys, look at me. Let me talk to Hal and Will." Blake glanced quickly in the direction of the car and indicated he would be right there. "Do not say anything to Arvidia. Okay boys?"

Caleb sniffed, "Okay, Blake. Is my mom going to be okay? He sounds like a bad man."

"Yes, I promise you. You have your family and friends here, we'll do everything in our power to protect your mom. Most importantly, God

197

will protect her. Yes. Jim is a very bad man. So, don't go anywhere near him. Both of you, understand?"

Both boys wide eyed and shook their heads in unison at Blake. "Good. Let's go and have a nice dinner and celebrate your mom's birthday. Go wash up quickly and get in the car."

"Ok Dad." said Jake, He and Caleb weakly waved to Arvidia and walked quickly into the house.

"Don't worry, Caleb," Jake did a quick splash under the faucet and wiped his pants with his wet hands. Caleb looked at his hands, shrugged his shoulders and did the same. "My dad will help your mom. You guys have the Quad, the tribe and as my dad would say, how can you lose with God on your side?"

"I know, Grandpa taught us not to be afraid and trust the Great One. But Jake I'm scared, why does this guy want to hurt my mom?"

"I don't know. I'm sure my dad will find out." Caleb and Jake headed towards the car.

Blake walked quickly over to where Hal and Will were standing. Hal pointed towards Mark and Todd beckoning them to come over. "I wonder what's going on now." Todd whispered to Mark. They urgently walked over to them.

Arvidia debated whether or not she should step out and join the meeting as well. She knew something was going on. She stepped out of the car just as Caleb and Jake piled into the car both were talking at once.

"Boys, what's going on? What did you two do?"

"We lost the crab baskets. We didn't secure them tight enough and they must have floated out to sea." answered Caleb using hand gestures to strengthen his point.

"Oh." Arvidia was not quite sure if she believed him. "Is that true Jake?"

"It was my fault. I didn't tie the baskets down tight enough. I'm sorry, Caleb. Really I am."

"It's okay, man. I'm cool." They both did a fly handshake and smiled at her. Both of the boys hoped she was buying this story. Arvidia studied the boys closely.

"Well. I'm going to see what they could possibly be meeting about." She partially opened the car door to step out knowing something was amiss.

"No!" Caleb and Jake shouted a bit too loud.

"Why not?" Arvidia was surprised at their reaction.

"Uh . . . It's a birthday surprise!" Jake threw his arms up. "Tada! You can't tell dad we told you."

Relieved, Arvidia laughed, "Okay. I'll pretend to look surprised."

Caleb ribbed Jake and whispered, "What surprise?"

"I don't know but we are going to have to think of something quick!" Jake whispered. "I'll ask dad."

Hal looked sternly at the Quad and Blake while Will walked up to the porch and sat in his rocking chair. Bandit laid down bedside him. They gathered around at the side of the house out of Arvidia's eyesight. "Gentlemen, I have some news. Last night Joe came across some information about Arvidia's past. First off, the bones that were found up in the woods are in fact, Arvidia's parents." Hal's eyes glanced at the file, "Their names are Jerrill and Marilyn." Hal puffed his face and slowly exhaled, "Mason."

"Mason!" Todd looked sharply at Hal. Blake looked down at the ground. He was hoping the boys misheard what they said.

"How can that be?" Mark asked.

"Jerrill was Jim's father and Marilyn was his stepmother. Secondly, Joe found out Arvidia is also Jim's half-sister." Hal put up his hands to quiet the men. "Shhh . . . Lastly, Joe also found out, she has a twin sister. We don't know if she's alive or dead. Joe is working on that. I don't want Arvidia to know any of this information yet. It's her birthday and I am positive she knows the bones are her parents, I'm just not sure how she'll handle the news of Jim being her half-brother or the fact she has a twin sister." There, he got it all out without choking up.

The men carefully looked at each other and fought hard not to look in the direction of the car where their once very young charge sat in wait of her birthday celebratory dinner.

"Wow. I didn't see this coming! What do you want us to do?" Todd stood with one hand on his hip and ran his hand through his hair. Todd had seen this man in action and he knew Jim would kill anyone that stood in his way. Mark looked as stunned as Todd.

"For now, I want to continue as we are. Chris and Mike are still at the pier watching Jim, Gus and Buck. I want you two to stick close to Arvidia. Do not let her out of your sight. Remember this is an armed and dangerous man, not to mention a wanted man. Will believes, from what Arvidia remembers, he will strike when the moon is full."

All glanced towards the sky, the moon was half-full. "We have about two weeks to catch this guy before he strikes."

"Why not get him now?" Todd asked.

"I want to make sure this case is overwhelmed with enough evidence to put this man away in prison until he dies and meets God's wrath for his wrongdoings!" Hal's face flushed with red.

Todd knew he should not have asked that, but he knew as long as Buck Taylor, Gus Laurent and Jim Mason hung together and were milling about, Arvidia's fate hung heavily upon the men to keep her safe and sound.

"I want this guy locked up as bad as you guys do, but we have to do this right. We're trained professional agents and we need to follow this by the book. We cannot afford any mistakes. Now, knowing Arvidia, she's is probably getting suspicious." Hal glanced around the house and waved at Arvidia. "Blake, tell her we are doing something for her birthday. I know she's going to ask questions."

Will leaned over the porch, "Beat you to it, we're going to have a party here waiting when you guys return from the restaurant."

"Okay, problem solved!"

"Sure, no problem I'll keep her busy!" Blake replied as his thoughts were crowded with worry and concern.

"Todd and Mark I want you to go with them. I will stay and uh . . . help out." Hal looked at Will.

Blake walked to the porch and leaned over the railing. He looked at Will carefully, "What happens when the full moon appears?"

"He becomes very evil." Will was careful to maintain his facial expression to cover a fact that suddenly surfaced in his brain as he spoke. He needed to be sure before he spoke of it. "Try not to worry, go and enjoy dinner and we can talk more about this later."

Blake walked towards the car, spinning his keys around his fingers. Todd and Mark went to their car and waited to follow them. Jake jumped out of the car, "Dad, we have to think of a surprise for Arvidia. She was grilling us with questions and we told her you had a surprise for her."

Blake laughed and rubbed his son's head. He leaned down and whispered, "There is going to be a surprise party for her when we come back."

"Oh, good," Jake relieved, "Me and Caleb can't handle any more of her questions!"

"Caleb and I." Blake corrected him, "Its okay son. Get back in the car."

"Okay guys, anybody hungry?" Blake's eyes glinted with mischief and grinned at Arvidia. He could see the questions swimming around in her eyes. "Where are we going my dear?"

"I have the address punched into the GPS. I think you'll like the place." Arvidia winked at him. "So what were you guys talking about?"

"Oh nothing, really. Let's just relax and enjoy the dinner." Blake smiled at Arvidia; she couldn't help but notice how tightly Blake gripped the steering wheel as he drove.

The GPS led them to a windy street that lined itself up with the shore of Bellingham Bay, Blake turned right into the parking lot of a well-known restaurant: Guspitto's. He paused after parking just to the capture the beauty of the ocean as the sun quietly rests atop of the waters.

"Wow, this is really a beautiful spot! Oh . . . it's an Italian restaurant!" Blake grinned from ear to ear as they exited the car in front of Guspitto's restaurant. "Arvidia, this was supposed to be your night!" He felt like it was a gift for him.

"I know. I'm very grateful to you and Jake and I know being away from New York must be hard. So I thought I would bring a little Italiano to you guys." Arvidia giggled and hugged Blake as they walked into the restaurant. The kids were perfectly behaved and followed. Todd and Mark showed up shortly after.

After Blake and the Quad left, Will hurried into the living room and clicked on his computer. He told the others to hurry and get the party set up. "Running Bull, do you have a second?" Running Bull, set down the table and walked with Will into his house. They both sat down and Will showed him what he had found at on the computer.

"Are you sure about this?" said Running Bull.

"Yes, those fellas from the Quad mentioned something about how Jim usually does things when there's a full moon. I suddenly recalled my great grandfather talking about this particular type of full moon." Will excitedly pointed towards the computer, "This coming moon is a rare one, it only occurs once every 19 years and it will be a full blue moon! You have any idea what this means?"

"So the legend is probably true then. The question is, does this guy, Jim, know about the legend? If not, we will have to plan this very carefully."

"I feel in my spirit, he does not know about this. I agree we must be very careful." Will and Running Bull, now more informed, went about setting up for the festivities with a more watchful heart and preparedness.

CHAPTER 25

TRISTA

"That was a splendid meal!" Blake patted his bloated stomach and kissed his fingers in delight. I'm not sure if I have enough room for dessert!" Laughter rang from the table. Todd and Mark did the same as Blake. Arvidia was amazed how much these men could pack away.

"Mom, can I go to the bathroom?" Trista asked.

"May I, and yes. I'll go with you as well."

Arvidia held onto her daughter's hand. They both turned into the ailse headed toward the women's restroom. Suddenly, someone with a large tray of food crashed into them. They both fell to the floor. Arvidia turned to check on Trista when she heard her scream. To her dismay, Arvidia saw Gus running out of the restaurant with Trista tucked under his arms. "TODD!" Arvidia screamed and ran behind him. Todd and Mark stood up quickly, and jumped over the tables and ran towards the entrance. They ran towards the parking lot. Gus threw Trista into a waiting white van which sped off quickly. Todd jumped into his car and sped off, and stopping only long enough to allow Mark to jump through the passenger side of the open window.

"You get a look at the guy?" Todd spewed out as he drove fast to catch up with the white van.

"Yep. It was Gus. I'm punching in the plates." Mark exclaimed, "Big surprise, it was reported stolen this morning. Sure looks like they're heading towards the docks." Mark gripped onto the door as Todd swerved between cars and lanes to catch up with the speeding white van.

Todd could only grunt as he drove angrily to catch up to the van. He was very angry. He wanted to personally wrap his hands around Jim's throat.

Arvidia panted heavily and screamed, "Trista!" Panic rose up within her. She kicked the car.

"Arvidia, Are you okay?" Blake was bewildered by Todd's and Mark's sudden exit toward the door, until he heard Trista screaming under the arms of a man who looked very familiar to him. "Don't worry, Todd and Mark are chasing after them."

"Is that Baldy?" Mark craned his neck to see the swooping bird flying close to their car.

"No, that one is smaller than Baldy. Trista told me about her the other day she had noticed a smaller, younger, bald eagle hanging around her the past few weeks. Will thinks this is Baldy's daughter. She has the same markings on her chest as Baldy does."

"Well, we need all the help we can get! Does the bird have a name?"

Todd chuckled. "She calls her Gulp. Because of the way she eats her food."

"Gulp? Okay . . ." Mark grinned.

Todd suddenly slowed down. "I'm going to back off, Looks like Gulp is perched in a tree up there." He craned his neck looking up into the sky and noticed a boarded up building near the tree where Gulp sat. "Isn't that where Chris and Mike are hiding out?"

"I think so. Let's check it out, I'll send them a text." Mark quickly texted them a message.

Todd and Mark parked the car close to the old Georgia Pacific plant. Gulp screeched loudly as though she was warning them. Mark spied the white van parked in front of the warehouse. Trista could be seen fighting them as she was being dragged into the building. *Arvidia and Trista are two peas in a pod. Both are feisty!* Mark thought to himself.

"We better call Hal." Mark looked at Todd who looked as though he was going to run into the building after Trista. Mark's cell shrilled. He grabbed it quickly so as not to attract attention.

"Hey, what's going on? Was that Trista being dragged into the building?" Chris inquired.

"Yep, it was. Where are you guys?"

"We're in the next building over. We'll meet you at the door."

"Ok. We'll be there ASAP." Todd and Mark quietly made their way towards Chris and Mike.

Mark whispered to Todd, "I hope Arvidia is okay. She's probably ripping heads off by now."

"I wouldn't doubt that." Todd whispered back.

CHAPTER 26

THE WAREHOUSE

"He will not hurt my daughter!" Arvidia was enraged. She paced around the parking lot, clueless as to what to do first. She searched the skies for Baldy. She reached the waiting car and yanked the driver's car door open.

"Arvidia, Todd and Mark went after them. They will find her!" Blake placed his hand firmly on top of her hand and slowly removed it from the car door. "I'll drive." Blake said firmly. "Boys get into the car." Caleb, was very angry as both he and Jake both filed quickly into the car. They couldn't believe this was happening.

"Dad, is Trista going to be okay?" Jake said with a worried face. Caleb had not spoken a word since the kidnapping of his sister. He almost looked as if he could spit nails. How dare they take his sister! He muttered something unintelligible under his breath.

"Yes, Son." Blake looked anxiously into the rearview mirror. Arvidia punched numbers furiously into her cell phone, trying to reach the Quad to no avail. All of their cells went to voice mail. Frustrated, she then tapped #1, Hal's speed dial connection.

"This is Hal." He sounded relaxed. He didn't know yet.

"Hal he took Trista!" Arvidia cried into the phone.

"What? Who? Slow down Arvidia, what happened?" Hal sat up in full alert. She had his attention.

"Gus took Trista!" Arvidia's voice went up an octave, "Todd and Mark went after them, I can't reach either one of them. We're heading back to the reservation now." Arvidia jutted her jaw out in anger and breathing rapidly as she waited for Hal's response.

Hal felt his gut tighten as he gripped the cell phone tighter. He calmed himself and said through pursed lips, "Okay, we'll be waiting. I'll inform Will immediately." Hal locked his jaw and through gritted teeth he said, "Arvidia, we'll get him."

Will knew immediately something was wrong. He anxiously looked at Hal as he shoved his phone into his shirt pocket. "What happened?" Will asked, cautiously.

"Gus kidnapped Trista from the restaurant!" Hal's face reddened as his blood boiled within him, "Todd and Mark are in pursuit. He's in a white van. I do not want to call them in case they're still chasing him. I'll give them another 20 minutes to report."

"Trista?!" Will became very upset. He wringed his hands together, "I'm going to gather the elders, this is plstwe'xᵂ!" (war) Will promptly walked out of the house before Hal could reply. He followed behind him wishing the cell would ring. He knew they were highly skilled agents but even with Hal's years in the field it had always been said you never knew what danger lurked around every corner. He was sure they had a good reason why they hadn't contacted him. Silently, he prayed no one was hurt.

Chris and Mike met up with Mark and Todd close to their hideout. Todd pointed out the building where Trista had been taken. "Are they armed?" asked Mike as he squatted down next to Todd. Mark busily scanned the area through binoculars.

Mark whistled quietly, "They're armed like Fort Knox. I can barely see Trista, but she's sitting in a chair and clearly voicing her displeasure. Just like someone else we know." Mark grunted.

"Oh, boy." Todd rolled his eyes, "We need to get her out of there, tonight. Mark do you see Buck anywhere?"

"I only see Gus and some of the guards."

Chris piped in, "Buck headed back to his boat about an hour ago. They're meeting later tonight on the docks. Did he make any demands yet?"

"Doubt he's going to. He knew there was only one way to get a rise out of Arvidia and that was to take something very precious from her." Todd said slowly. "She's got to be out of her mind about Trista."

Mark beckoned the men closer to him. "We need to get Trista out of there. We can't take any chances. We'll go in pairs. You guys cover the roof." Todd pointed at Chris and Mike. "Mark and I will go through one of the windows and take care of the guards in there. You guys have any more weapons?"

"Yep, I'll go and grab them." Chris quickly ran towards the warehouse and gathered more ammo, guns and the gears they'd need.

Before returning to the others, he took a minute to kneel and pray for protection.

Trista looked around the dusty warehouse. She noticed the armed men walking around and a funny smell that made her stomach weird and her eyes tear. She was more angry than scared. She knew the Quad would be looking for her and she noticed Gulp by the window just as she was yanked inside the warehouse. She decided to speak up to cause some distraction, "Where am I?" she was demanded.

Jim stood to the side as he allowed the shock to wear off. He was stunned by how Trista was the spitting image of Arvidia at that age. "Shut up kid. Your mom is coming. Trust me." He walked around her staring at her. "What's the matter, you hungry?"

"Stupid. I was kidnapped out of a restaurant, no, I'm not hungry! Now let me go!" She wiggled the ropes that bound her hands. Out of the corner of her eye, she saw Gulp sitting by a cracked window.

Jim's anger welled up quickly within him and he grabbed her shoulder, "You will not speak to me that way!" He then flicked her shoulder away.

Trista shrugged him off, "You don't scare me. Everybody is looking for me!" Jim knew that was true. He needed Trista to bring Arvidia to him, and then his final wish will be complete.

"Gus, Keep a close eye on her. I'll be right back." Jim hastily walked into his makeshift office and there he pondered his next move. He knew Arvidia would move swiftly and do anything to protect her daughter.

Gus moaned. He didn't anticipate babysitting some kid. He hadn't quite figured out the deal with Jim's hatred for Arvidia, but he figured as long as he paid him it was none of his concern. He didn't want to know what was going on inside that twisted mind of his. He was hungry and all he had was a banana so he turned a chair backwards and straddled it as he sat, groaning a little while rubbing his bandaged leg. He studied her as he slowly peeled and bite into the banana. He like Jim couldn't believe how close she resembled her mother. "How old are you anyway?"

Trista glowered at him, "Nine."

Todd kneeled and peered through his binoculars. "Okay, from what I can see, there are two guards up on the roof and there appears to be six guards inside. Gus is guarding Trista. Jim is sitting in his office. Gulp is sitting by one of the windows. She has not moved from that spot."

"Who is Gulp?" asked Chris he looked curiously at Mike.

"Will thinks it is Baldy's daughter. Lately she's been hanging around Trista. Baldy must have sensed something was going down and sent her for protection. That is one amazing eagle." Todd chuckled and shook his head.

"Yes, she is. I wonder if she'll attack Hal." They chuckled quietly then suddenly became serious, "We'll need to spread out and take the guards out one by one and work our way inward. We have to do this quietly otherwise, Buck, Gus and Jim will take off." Mark spoke with a serious tone.

"Anybody get a hold of Hal yet?" Mike questioned. All the men realized their phones were turned off and knew by the red angry blinking lights they were probably messages from Hal and Arvidia.

"We don't have time to answer them. We need to get this done now. Remember to use the code words." Todd stood up and loaded his gun.

"Okay, I'm loaded, is everyone ready?" Todd stood tall as if war was about to commence. The Quad members all nodded their heads quietly. They skillfully scaled down the side of the hill behind the warehouse and spread out. Mike and Chris headed up the side of the building to take down the guards on the roof. Todd and Mark edged around the building and carefully climbing through a side window. Once inside they cased the building behind a tall stack of pallets. "I think we can take these dudes down, what do you think Mark?"

Mark carefully looked around. He noted the six men standing around the perimeters of the warehouse. They were heavily armed and wearing the infamous medallion around their necks and with their backs turned to them it was plain to see the medallion tattoos at the napes of their necks. "Let's check in with Ant and Roach." (Chris and Mike).

"Ant and Roach—what's your nine?" Mark whispered into the cell.

"Yo, Slug, we got the two dudes on the roof. We're waiting for your signal to throw our ropes down." Chris whispered back.

"Good job. Just hang on a minute." Mark gave thumbs up to Todd.

"Gotcha Slug." Todd returned the thumbs up.

"Ready Spider?"

Todd packed a wad of gum into his mouth. Arvidia was always on him about his smoking. He decided to quit two years ago. Lately he'd been fighting the urge to smoke again. "Ready as I'll ever be." He inhaled and screwed the silencer onto his gun.

Todd and Mark carefully came from behind each one of the six guards and silenced their life one at a time and they were now able to descend towards Trista. Gus was still sitting across from her unaware of the activity going on around him. He held out his gun, twisting it aimlessly. Trista had wondered where the Quad was until she watched Todd and Mark climb through a window and disappear and all of this without Gus catching on.

Jim hastily came out of his office. "Has Stu checked in yet? I called him on the walkie but he's not answering. Go check on him." Jim ordered. He didn't have time for people who goofed off on the job.

"Okay." Gus stood and walked slowly past Trista with a sneer.

"Pshaawww." Trista was very smug.

She really annoyed him. He walked over to where Stu was supposed to have been and found him slumped over on the desk. Gus tapped him on the shoulder, "Stu, come on man quit goofing around. The boss really hates that." Tapping again with more force he noticed his skin color was turning ashen. "Stu?" Gus stared at the lifeless body of Stu and then quickly drew his gun and spoke quickly into the walkie talkie, "Boss we got trouble. Stu's dead."

Quickly, Jim jumped up and grabbed Trista off the chair. He hastily dragged her with him to his office as he gathered his things. Trista knew the Quad was near. Chris and Mike suddenly rappelled down a rope from the roof, and swiftly unhooked themselves with weapons drawn. Sprinting towards Jim, Chris felt sharp pains in his back and he fell hard onto the concrete floor. Gus then fired at Mike, who returned fire. Mike dove behind stacked pallets.

"Ant you okay?" Chris did not respond. "Guys cover me while I get Ant, he's not responding."

"Go ahead Roach, Spider and I will cover you."

Bullets rained as Mike dove and rolled towards Chris. He quickly checked for a pulse. It was weak, but he was alive! Pulling Chris by his pant legs, he threw him over his shoulders and made a mad dash out of the nearest window. Mike was almost completely out the window when he felt a burning pain in his left leg. He gritted his teeth to keep from screaming. His main concern was his partner, Chris.

"We better back off!" Mark shouted.

Gus fired angrily around the building. The confused scientists from the lab could be seen huddled under the tables. Jim stuffed stacks of money into his briefcase and grabbed Trista by her arm. She tried to wiggle away. He shouted into the lab area, "Make sure that shipment is done by tonight!" He walked quickly out the side door toward his car. He popped opened the trunk using his keypad and hissed at Trista; "Get in!" She glowered at him but did what she was told. Just as he shut the trunk she saw Gulp right behind Jim. She knew Gulp would protect her and let the others know her whereabouts.

Gulp soared high above Jim's car and kept close tabs on the fast moving car headed toward the mountain.

At the warehouse, unaware Jim had made his escape, Todd noticed Gus's oddly bandaged leg, then remembered Bandit had taken a bite out of someone's leg at Arvidia's condo. He eyed Gus and slowly lowered his gun toward the injured leg and pulled the trigger. Gus shrieked in pain. They swiftly arrested him and dragged him to a chair, cuffing him to it as they searched the area before, running around to the side of the building, where Chris laid on the ground barely breathing and Mike was wincing in pain. Todd instantly dialed 911 he could see Chris was not doing well.

Mike gritted through his pain, "Jim took off with Trista, she's in the trunk of his car!"

Mark quickly dialed Hal. "Hal, shots fired, two agents down. Chris was shot in the back and Mike in the leg. Todd and I are OK. Gus has been arrested and Jim took off with Trista." Mark hardly breathed while he spoke.

Hal winced as he heard two of his men had been shot. "I'll be right there." Hal quickly walked towards Will and Arvidia. "Jim took off with Trista. Chris and Mike have been shot. Todd and Mark are okay. They have Gus. I need to go and assess the situation."

Arvidia gasped, "They've been shot? I'm coming with you and I am not taking no for an answer!" Arvidia promptly headed towards Hal's car ahead of him.

Blake was stunned. He feared for Arvidia and Trista. He looked around at the tribesmen who were quite agitated and talking in their Salish dialect. They put on their war armor. They gathered their war drums. A bonfire was promptly started and faces were painted furiously with black stripes. He observed Will holding up his headdress and feathers towards the sky. He was speaking unfamiliar words. Blake fell to his knees in the midst of the bustling activity and prayed.

CHAPTER 27

THE HOSPITAL

Arvidia jumped into the driver's seat. Hal started to argue then hesitated against waging a war of words with Arvidia he knew he'd lose. When she set her sight on something nothing stood in her way. He quickly got in and buckled up. He unknowingly gripped the handle of the door as she gunned the car and spun out onto the dirt road and hit the gas hard. Hitting the gas hard she wouldn't waste another minute in the matter of her daughter's safety.

Hal hung on while he called the Quad for an update. "Todd, what's the status?"

"Well, the ambulance just left with Chris and Mike. Chris was shot in the back and Mike was shot in the leg, Sir, we have Gus Laurent in custody." He looked at Gus who hung his head low while being taken in. His leg was wrapped where Todd had shot him. "We're trying to locate the scientists that were here but they quickly dispersed once the shooting started. I've sent out an APB on the scientists. How's Arvidia?"

Hal glanced at Arvidia as she stared straight ahead with her hands gripped to the steering wheel. She looked as though she could rip someone's head clean off. "She's, uh, okay considering. Put Gus in the cage and record everything. Do everything by the book. We'll go to the hospital and check on the guys. Good job men."

"You got it!" Todd clicked off his cell and placed it into the pocket of his jeans. He walked over to where Mark stood with his gun close to Gus's head. "Hal said to record everything and put him in the cage."

"How are Chris and Mike?" He did not dare ask about Arvidia.

"Hal is heading over there with Arvidia."

Buck Taylor angrily watched from afar from on his boat. He had seen Jim leave with a little girl and a large briefcase under his arm. That held the money he had just paid Jim for delivery. He drummed his fingers onto the glass and mulled over what to do next.

"Arvidia, Todd has the crime scene secured. Go to St. Joseph's. That's where the ambulance took Chris and Mike. Todd also said Jim took off with Trista. I'm going to issue an Amber Alert. Todd is positive Gulp is following them." Hal gently touched Arvidia's hand. "Trista will be okay."

"All I know is, he better not touch a hair on my daughter's head." She turned the car around sharply and headed toward the hospital. She drove quietly for a few miles. Hal glanced at her. He loved her as if she were his own daughter. He'd never married or had kids of his own but he watched Arvidia grow up to be a beautiful and intelligent woman. She trained hard at the academy and due to her unusual skills, she was one of the most highly sought after agents but she'd decided to stay with Hal and the Quad.

Hal marveled at Will's wisdom, for he did warn him this day may come. He had no clue what thoughts turned in Arvidia's head. He could literally see the wheels spinning. She suddenly stomped on the brakes and the car screeched to a halt. Arvidia parked the car sideways, not caring who noticed how she parked in the ambulance bay at the ER entrance.

Hal quickly approached the front registration desk and flashed his badge as did Arvidia. "I'm Captain Hal Sampson, and this is agent Arvidia Miles. We are here for agents Chris Magin and Mike Lawson!"

A doctor stood behind the clerk and quickly looked up from his clipboard at their announcement. "Oh, hi, I'm their doctor," Doctor Stan held out his hand and Hal firmly shook it. "Come this way." He led them into a conference room and silently shut the door, a nurse followed behind the doctor. "Chris Magin is a lucky man. The bullet hit his back hard but the vest saved his life. However upon removing the bullet it does appear to be an unusual one. I've not seen one like it."

"Do you have it?" Arvidia asked.

"Yes, I was able to retrieve it. Judy, will you get the specimen cup with the bullet?"

"Yes, Doctor." The nurse immediately left the conference room.

She returned just as quickly with the specimen cup that held the bullet inside. Handing it to Arvidia she watched as she held it up to the light. She instantly recognized the bullet. She spoke rapidly to Hal. "Hal, this is the same bullet we found at the crime scene in New York. These bullets only come from a Ruegers. This particular type of gun is made for people that are left handed. We can connect Gus Laurent to the murder in New York! Hal, remember I told you the suspect in the video was left-handed? Gus Laurent is left handed. This had to have come from his gun."

Hal knew she was right. "You're absolutely right. Send that right over to Joe." Hal glanced at the doctor, "Is Chris okay?"

"Yes, we'll observe him for a few days and if he does okay, he can go home. His back will be badly bruised but it will be fine. Your other agent, Mike Lawson's left lower leg was shattered by the bullet. He'll need a procedure called ORIF (open reduction internal reduction) surgery to repair his tibia and fibula. The orthopedic surgeon is examining him now and most likely will be taking him to the operating room shortly. I can take you to him if you like."

"Thank you, doctor. Yes, we would like to see him." Hal stood and shook his hand. Arvidia lingered behind them as they walked down the hall to the room where the two partners lay in wait.

Dr. Stan opened the door and waved them in. Arvidia flew to Chris's side and glanced at Mike. "I hear you guys are gonna live!" She leaned over and hugged Chris. He winced in pain as she hugged him. "I'm sorry, Arvidia. He was this close!" Chris showed his hands and smacked his forehead. "I almost had Trista. Then Gus started shooting like a wild man." Chris touched her arm, "Trista was not hurt." She hung her head with relief.

"Yeah, uh hello? I'm alive and well over here." Mike almost sounded drunk. Arvidia went to his side as the techs came into the room to take him to surgery.

"Mike, how you feeling?" Arvidia knew that was a stupid question considering how his face grimaced in pain.

"Peachy." Mike grinned and gave a thumbs up. Arvidia leaned down and kissed him on the cheek. "Thank you for everything." tears escaped from her eyes as her lips quivered. She quickly turned away and hid her face into her hand. "Honey, Trista will be fine. Remember, she is tough like you. Todd and Mark are not going to give up looking." he gently touched her arm.

The door opened quietly as the nurse walked in, "We need to take him up to surgery, you can wait in the family room if you like." She put the IV bag on to the IV pole of the stretcher and maneuvered him out of the room.

"See ya!" Mike waved weakly as he was wheeled out of the room.

Hal put his arms around Arvidia. "Mike is right, Trista is tough like you plus she has Gulp. She won't leave her side."

"He's right Arvidia." Chris tried to sit up but the pain reverberated to his brain that his body would not allow that.

"I know. I am just upset people are getting hurt because of me."

Chris piped, "You know darn well that is the risk that comes with the territory. We are all doing our jobs. I understand this has become very personal, but we will get this dude. I know we will." The door suddenly opened and a young medical technician entered the room.

"Hi, I'm Sandy I'll be taking you to your room."

Arvidia reached over the stretcher and kissed him. Chris grabbed both her cheeks and stared into her blazing blue eyes, "Arvidia, we will get him. I promise."

Hal slowly drove back to the reservation. Todd and Mark were busy at the headquarters of the Bellingham Police department questioning a mum Gus. Hal knew that Gus would not spill. Todd hustled him back into the cell. Frustrated, they too headed back out to the reservation.

Arvidia broke the quiet spell that hung heavy in the car "Hal, Are Blake and Jake safe? Should I have them moved? I don't want any harm to come to them." She was very concerned.

"No, they'll stay where they are. You know as well as I do they are in the safest place."

"Yes, I guess you're right about that." Arvidia trembled inside. She knew there was more trouble looming on the horizon. She prayed silently for the Great One to protect her daughter.

CHAPTER 28

CALEB AND JAKE

Angry conversations about Trista's kidnapping and the injured agents spread like wildfire throughout the reservation. Voices became hushed when Caleb and Jake wandered through a conversation. Caleb was quiet, deep within him he quivered in anger. He had always admired his mother's toughness, watching her kick her car in anger and lose control was something he had never witnessed. His mother was scared to her core. Her blue eyes blazed in an anger he had never seen before.

"You okay man?" Jake asked, he too was frightened by what had happened at the restaurant. His father rushed him and Caleb home. He tried to asked questions but he could see his father was deeply upset.

"Yeah, I guess so. I've never seen my mom so angry. She's always so cool even with the toughest criminals she had to arrest. I have many questions about what happened to make this man hate her but she doesn't remember." He angrily scuffed his feet on the ground kicking up some dirt as well.

"Yeah, I heard my dad say something about that. I can't remember the word he used, but I've heard him talk before about clients and he said when bad things happened their head blocks it from remembering it. Don't worry Caleb, my dad will protect her." Jake boasted.

Caleb angrily replied, "She has the Quad and they can't protect her!"

Jake fell quiet and he stopped walking, "I'm sorry," he looked down then said, "I care too, ya know."

"I'm sorry too but I'm really scared. My sister is missing and my mom is really scared. She was crying this morning." He paused then said, "Come on, I'll race you!"

They both ran toward the ocean where they threw rocks into the far depths of the perils of the sea. They laughed quietly and soon their conversation resumed.

"You think those guys from the Quad are going to be okay?" Jake asked.

"Yea they will, they've been shot at many times." He threw the rock hard into the ocean.

Jake's eyes grew wide, "Really? Wow. Well, I hope they're okay. We shouldn't stay here too long, dad said to come right baaaccck." Jake looked in the direction Caleb was looking.

"That's Gulp!" Gulp soared closely over their heads. "Come on, she knows, she knows where Trista is!"

"How do you know that?" Jake looked nervously around. "What about my dad?" Jake ran after him.

"She doesn't usually circle around like that or make that funny noise. Gramps says it's a way of communicating and to always respect it. We won't be gone long. Here you better put this on." He strapped the soft leather necklace with the single eagle feather crested on it around Jake's neck. "Gramps said this will protect us." Caleb puffed out his chest and touched his necklace. He pointed the feather towards the sky. He shouted some Salish words of prayer. Jake awkwardly did the same although he had no idea what he said or why he was doing it.

The boys followed Gulp deep into the woods. Caleb followed as though he had taken this route many times. Jake was overwhelmed with the mysterious path they were taking, the trees even seemed to talk to each other. Suddenly, Caleb put his hand out. He put his finger to his lips; he turned slowly to Jake and pointed. Gulp was sitting next to Baldy. Not far was a small cabin which was dimly lit and smoke could be seen billowing from the chimney.

"I think they're in there. I'm going to look in the window. We have to be very quiet."

"Okay." Jake's voice was trembling.

They both softly approached the window while Baldy and Gulp looked on from the trees. Jake kneeled down so Caleb could stand on his back and peer through the window. Caleb could see Trista sitting in a chair with her hands tied behind her back.

Jim was agitated and pacing back and forth. He was tired of listening to Trista who had a mouth the size of a whale. She showed no fear whatsoever toward him. This seemed to annoy him a great deal. He was more concerned with Buck Taylor. Jim had taken Buck's money as he escaped.

He knew the illegal drugs were seized by the FBI agents. He was not sure of Gus's whereabouts and he was sure Buck was watching the chaos from his boat. He'd heard about Buck Taylor's reputation of verdantly silencing those that dared to double-cross him. He had to figure out a way to escape but he was not going to leave without finishing his final piece of his plan and Trista was the key to finalizing that plan.

The rotted wood from the window frame gave way and Caleb fell. Jim reared his head and stormed outside where he spied the two boys. Caleb ran into the cabin and quickly cut Trista loose and together they ran out the back door. Gulp soared after them. Jim grabbed Jake by the scruff of his shirt. Baldy screeched and dived towards Jim who was wrestling with Jake to pull him into the cabin. Jim was furious as the bird attacked him. "I should've shot you when I had the chance!" Jim shouted. Terrified, Jake scrambled into the corner of the cabin and drew up his knees. He prayed the Salish prayer reverently even though he felt like he was speaking in many different languages; he just hoped God understood one of them.

"He has Jake!" Trista stopped running and looked behind them. Gulp perched nearby Trista's head. "Thanks Gulp, I knew you would save me." Trista gently kissed Gulp. Gulp soared off towards the reservation.

Caleb felt torn whether to stay and try to get Jake out or run back and get help. He felt his heart pounding hard in his chest. "Don't worry Baldy will keep an eye on him. She won't let anything happen to him. We have to hurry and get help. He may try to escape again." Caleb was terrified for Jake. *That was one mean looking dude.* He thought as they both ran as fast as their legs could carry them.

"Jake! Caleb!" Blake hollered up and down the beach. There was still no sign of them. He grew weary with concern. He was exasperated with the boys. He was deeply worried about Arvidia and now he couldn't find the boys. He threw up his hands and headed back to Will's house. He saw some children playing nearby the leaning house. "Have you girls seen Caleb and Jake?"

The older one stood and pointed towards the woods, "Gulp took them into the woods."

Surprised, Blake asked, "Gulp? Who is Gulp?"

The two girls looked at each other, "Gulp is an eagle. Will says its Baldy's daughter. Gulp led them into the woods."

"There's another one?" Blake rubbed his hands through his hair and muttered, "Oy. These animals are something else. No one back home would ever believe this!" He walked briskly towards Will. Just as he asked about Gulp, he saw Caleb running towards the house with Trista in tow. They were both shouting and waving. Jake was nowhere to be seen. His stomach suddenly lurched.

Will ran towards them. Blake's feet seem stuck to the ground. Hal's car came up the dirt road just as Todd and Mark did. Arvidia jumped out of the car, "What happened?" she looked at Blake who had paled and gone to the ground. Todd slammed his brakes as he saw Caleb and Trista running towards Will. "What the heck is going on?" Todd said as he jumped out of the car.

Will kneeled before his grandchildren who, breathlessly, talked at the same time. Arvidia grabbed her daughter and hugged her tightly. "Are you okay? Are you hurt anywhere?"

"No Mom. But," Trista anxiously looked at Caleb.

"But what?" She looked around, "Where's Jake?"

"That bad man has him." Caleb said bluntly.

"What!" She looked towards Blake. "Tell me exactly what happened."

They both quickly explained what happened and how Baldy was attacking him. "Okay. You guys go ahead into the house while I talk to Will."

"Yes, Mom." They quickly retreated into the house not daring to look into the direction of the woods that held Jake hostage. Gulp sat nearby in the tree, closely watching.

Arvidia's eyes were blazing; she quickly threw her hair back into a pony tail. She snapped her glock into the back of her pants. She spoke to Will, "Father, this is it! He has brought harm to my family and now to Blake's! No, I will not stand for this!" Before he could reply, she walked away and down the hill toward Will's house. Her cell was ringing. She snapped it out of her pant pocket answered angrily, "What!"

"I'm willing to trade. Come alone." Jim sneered.

Her heart raced at the sound of the voice that revered fear deep into her soul. She glanced around and looked up at the sky. She smiled slyly. "Deal, meet me tomorrow at 5 pm at Dead Man's Pier. I'll trade me for the kid. If any harm comes to him, don't even think about underestimating me. I will not hesitate to use full force." Jim knew of her sharp shooting skills and also knew she wasn't bluffing.

"Agreed." Jim hung up and smiled. Finally his big day would come. His smile provoked evil intent toward Jake, who prayed reverently God would come quickly. He looked out the window and to his amazement, Baldy sat nearby on a tree branch.

Arvidia slowly closed the cell phone and looked at the full moon in the sky. She felt deep within her spirit it was time. She knew she had to plan quickly and execute it to ensure Jake's safety. She would not forgive herself if anything happened to Jake or Blake. She stood still with her chin resting on the edge of her cell phone. Her heart raced at the mere thought of Jake and how frightened he must be. *I have to do what I have to do to protect Jake.* Arvidia knew Jake meant the world to Blake. She never thought of sacrificing herself in order to let someone live. Her job put her life on the line many times, but this was personal and painfully close to her heart. She slowly turned her head and stared at Blake whose feet were still stuck to the ground where she first saw him when she jumped out of the car. She knew then and there despite all the turmoil surrounding her, she was in love with Blake. Will told her a day would come where she would have to face Jim's wrath. She never quite understood what he meant by that. She did now. He meant Sacrifice. She would have to sacrifice herself for Jake. She knew of Jim's hatred for her, she also knew she'd have to fight to save Jake.

She slowly walked up to Blake and hugged him tightly, fighting the tears that threatened to spill down her cheeks. She gently raised her hands on his face and looked deeply into his fear ridden brown eyes. Tears slid down his cheeks and his lips quivering as he spoke, "He has my son?"

"Yes." Arvidia's piercing blue eyes bore deeply into Blake's eyes. "I assure you, as an FBI agent, I will take care of that tomorrow." Arvidia said sternly. "Jake is safe, Baldy is sitting out there with him, I know Bandit and his pack are close by. They will not allow harm to come to him." Blake noticed Arvidia's eyes were blazing, She clasped his hands into hers, "Blake, I promise you, he will be fine. I will make sure of that."

Blake knew Arvidia well enough to know she was hiding something. "What are you up to? Who just called you?" Blake's eyebrow arched and he stared at her, she didn't flinch. She dropped his hands and stuck hers into her back pocket. Looking towards the ground her long black hair fell partially over her face. She reached up and flicked her hair away.

Her lips pursed tightly, "It was one of the guys, and it was nothing important." Her blazing blue's said otherwise. "I need to discuss some matters with Will and the Quad."

"Okay." Blake didn't quite believe her. He grabbed a ahold of her hand as they walked back to Will's house.

They walked silently into the house and prepared for bed. Blake lay awake praying for the safe return of his son. He reached up and touched the feathers that dangled from the dream catchers. His son spoke enthusiastically about the teachings behind the dream catchers. A single tear slid down his cheek and dripped on to his pillow, he prayed, God, protect my son. Blake whispered. He slept fitfully.

In the room next to Blake's, Arvidia laid awake and stared at the ceiling. She decided to wait until dawn to launch her plans. She arose just as the sun was peeking through the woods. She tiptoed to look into the guest bedroom where Blake snored lightly, and then she quietly walked past his door in her stocking feet with her riding boots in hand. Once she was on the porch, she quickly strapped on her boots and headed towards the barn. Lexy snorted, shuffled her hooves into the dirt and whinnied. Arvidia knew she could trust her for her agility and speed. She needed exactly that for this mission. She quickly threw her saddle on Lexy and walked her outside of the barn. Arvidia did not want anyone to hear them so she walked Lexy towards the edge of the woods. She heard wings flapping lightly behind her and she knew it was Gulp. Expertly, she mounted and bolted up towards Mount Baker.

Blake stood quietly in the window watching Arvidia as she flew through the woods. He desperately wanted to go after her and wondered why she headed into the woods alone. He was afraid for her as well as for Jake. It was just then he spied the motorcycle leaning up against side of the barn. It has been years since he last rode. He pondered if he should go after her. The sun was just peeking through the mist that hung over the ocean.

"Blake." Will gently patted his shoulder. "I assure you Jake will be fine." Blake continued to stare out the window. "Do you know where she went? I wanted to talk to her."

Blake pointed out the window, "She left a short while ago on Lexy."

"Lexy? How did I not hear her?"

"She walked Lexy over there by the woods."

Realization spread over Will's face. She's heading to Mount Baker. There was only one reason she would go there, "Come, we must wake up the Quad. That darn Sqimi is up to something." Will hurried to the rooms where the men lay and quickly awoke all of them. They also had barely slept.

Blake was curious as to what Will meant. The men were wide awake now. They knew when Will demanded their attention something was askew. They gathered quickly together into the living room. Todd literally had to slap himself silly to wake up. He had been without sleep the past few days.

He sleepily asked, "Chief what's wrong? Where's Arvidia? If we're up she should be too."

"She is and she left early this morning with her horse. Blake said she headed over toward the woods."

Hal, Todd and Mark looked at each other silently. "I was afraid of that." Will said anxiously, "She was very angry last night about Jake. I should have said something to her. I just thought it was best to leave her alone."

Blake suddenly remembered her cell phone had gone off before their conversation and how she never answered his question about who it was that had called her. "She did take a phone call just before we came back into the house last night. I asked her who it was. She said it was one of you guys."

"I didn't call her, did you?" Todd looked at Mark who shook his head no. Hal also denied talking to her on her cell.

"I'm going to have Joe check her phone records." Hal immediately dialed Joe.

"Joe, trace a phone call received at approximately 9:30pm on Arvidia's cell."

"Okay, give me one second," He quickly clattered the keyboard, "Uh-oh . . . Hal, It was Jim Mason." His voiced quivered as he spoke.

"What! How did he get her number? Never mind don't answer that." Hal growled into his cell then slapped it shut. He angrily turned and looked at the men, "Blake was right. Arvidia did get a call. It was from Jim."

The Quad took a sharp stance. Todd spoke first, "That can't be good, especially if she didn't tell any of us about it. He must have threatened her with Jake!"

"Will, where do you suppose she went?" Mark asked.

"I believe she went to Mount Baker."

"Isn't that where Baldy was shot?" Mark looked at Will surprised.

"Yes, but I don't believe they're meeting there."

"Why do you think that? It has to be where they're meeting."

"First, the area she is heading to is sacred. She would never desecrate that. I believe she went there to pray." Will did not dare explain any further. The holy land was also an area where tribe members go to prepare to die. "Secondly," Will pointed to the sky, "It's not yet time."

"Arvidia Pray? She never spoke about God." Todd's face flushed as he stammered, "I mean we all do before our missions right guys?"

"Arvidia knows about God. She just never opened her heart to Him."

Mark's head whipped up and suddenly he remembered, "Wait a minute. Todd, you remember a few weeks ago, Arvidia went to the library and studied some maps?"

Todd snapped his fingers and looked at Mark, "Yes! Whatever she was researching that's got to have something to do with her direction."

"What maps?" Hal inquired.

Mark held up his hand and quickly punched in the number to the library, "I'm calling the librarian and see if she remembers what Arvidia was looking at." Mark hoped the same woman was there that day and would be able to remember what she was looking for. "Okay, thank you. Please have her call this number as soon as she gets in? It's very important. Thank you." Mark closed his cell, "She won't be in until later."

Will's forehead crested with concern. He paced lightly about the living room floor. He was quiet and deep in thought. Blake went over and sat next to him. "Will, are you okay?"

"Yes, I am fine. It's just that I think I know what Sqimi is up too." Will suddenly recalled that day as well. He did notice Arvidia rode to the north of the beach instead of the south where the Ancient Rock was. He had wondered for days where she went that day.

"You do? Where did she go?"

Will suddenly stood up and walked over to his computer. He goggled Lummi Island maps. "Hmm . . . Mark, can you try and call that librarian again?"

"Sure." Mark quickly pulled out his cell, and called the Fairhaven library. "Okay, great thank you! You've been a big help!" Mark turned and spoke to Will. "She said Arvidia was looking at the Point Elliot Treaty and some of the old maps of Lummi Island."

Will slowly folded his arms across his chest. He now understood what Sqimi was doing. He stood and explained to the men about Dead Man's Point.

"The Point Elliot Treaty was signed on January 22 in 1855. The treaty caused the original boundaries of the Island to be changed. If I am correct, I believe she went here." Will pointed to an area on the map on the computer. "This is called Dead Man's Point. This is an ancient war ground. It is very sacred to our tribe. Many of our fore fathers fought to save this island from the white men who felt it was their right to take. It has been said, if you stood silent on a windy day, you can hear the echoes of the war calls from where they fought and, many of our ancestors, died. Due to the war, many are buried there as well. My great-great-great grandfather felt it was proper to bury them there and to honor their memory. However, as legends have been foretold, only true warriors can stand on this land, no blood can be shed. If so, curses can be brought upon the person that kills. I am sure Arvidia knows this. I have told her all the legends of our tribe." Will pondered if he should further explain about the moon.

"Why on earth is she going there?" Blake's chest pounded and heaved as panic set in.

Running Bull stood large in the door frame, stated, "For sacrifice." Will nodded his head in agreement.

"Sacrifice? You mean her life?" Blake stunned, looked around at the others. They did not look surprised by this news.

"She is upholding honor." replied Running Bull.

"What are you talking about? What is she going to do?" Blake demanded. His face reddened.

Hal hollered from outside for Will, Baldy was screeching loudly and flying in an agitated state. Will quickly went outside. He looked up as Baldy flew into the rays of the full moon that shone brightly. Will knew instantly what Arvidia was doing. He looked at Running Bull. It was the war call.

"She knows she can't kill? Doesn't she?" Running Bull whispered as he leaned down to Will.

"Yes, she does. That's what is confusing me! I totally trust Sqimi. She would never jeopardize the tribe." Will whispered back.

Exasperated, Blake shouted to whoever would listen, "What is Arvidia thinking? Isn't she leaving herself wide open to be killed?"

"It looks that way yes. Blake, this is Arvidia we are talking about. I believe she may have outwitted us. Look up in the sky." Will points towards the sky.

All heads turned up into the sky, Blake looked up, "it's a full moon so what?" Blake huffed.

"Blake, you are not seeing look at it again."

Blake again spied the motorcycle and fought the impulse to run and jumpstart it. Annoyed he looked up, *was that moon blue?* Blake quizzically looked at Will. Will smiled.

"That is a rare full blue moon. It only happens once every 19 years. According to legend, the blue moon emits special protection for true warriors. It will only stay blue for a short time. Therefore, we must hurry and get to Dead Man's Point."

As if on cue, Baldy soared into the sky, screeching against the giant moon that shone powerfully over the sky.

"Why must we hurry?" Blake asked. "Will it protect my son?"

"I know Arvidia will protect him. Dead Man's Point has been virtually left untouched since the treaty was signed in 1885. We need to retrace exactly where that land is before she gets herself into a situation."

"I thought you said you can't kill there?" Blake asked, just as the rest of the men were about to say that.

"You're right. I do not know exactly what Sqimi is doing. I do know I totally trust her and she will feel our presence there. Blake it might be best if you stay here."

Blake started to object but knew Will would not allow otherwise. He decided to respect his decision.

"I do have something I want you to do. I will show you. Come." Will walked quickly into the house; he wanted to show Blake his bedroom. Will lit candles around the room and then dimmed the lights in the bedroom. He lined the floor with eagle's feathers. He gently put his bible in the center of the floor. "Blake, I know you are a strong Christian man. Would you mind praying while we are out there?"

Blake stood tall, "I most certainly will. I know just the verse to read and pray." He immediately kneeled and without hesitation opened the bible to the verse he wanted to read and began praying.

"Good, knowing you are praying for us will give us that much greater power of God's protection."

Blake looked at Will, "Please bring Jake back to me and Will, I know this is probably the worst time to ask you this, but I want to ask your permission to marry Arvidia. I have never in my life met a woman like her. I wanted to tell her how special she is to me and that I love her before all this chaos broke out. I never got a chance to tell her that. If she dies . . . ." Blake's voiced choked up and he turned away.

"Blake you didn't even need to ask. I knew you were the one for her. You pray for us and we will do what needs to be done." Will hugged Blake and left the bedroom to talk with Running Bull.

"What is Arvidia up to?" Hal scratched his head, and he stood in disbelief at the conversations he was hearing. He never discarded the tremendous faith Will had in his historical culture and his religion, as far as he knew, everything he said, had stood true.

Will stood on the porch and looked up at the powerful moon. He knew without a doubt Arvidia was heading to Dead Man's Point. He nodded his head at Running Bull and walked away with him. Hal, Todd and Mark gathered and discussed strategies of how they could capture Jim Mason.

"Why do you think Arvidia is at Dead Man's Point if she knows she can't kill him?" Running Bull whispered.

"I know Arvidia. She is beyond angry. Once she sets her mind to something, only the Great One can have His way with her! She is so stubborn! She never does anything without a plan. The mere fact she researched this area shows me she is up to something. I strongly believe she will sacrifice herself for Jake. Once she knows Jake is safe, she will face her wrath with Jim. Have you noticed Baldy has been screeching up there and circling?"

"Yeah, I noticed that too. You think it's a war call from Arvidia?"

"No, I think Baldy is giving us a war call. Round up the others, I will give the signal. We will head there in peace. This is her war."

"Yes, chief." Running Bull quickly strolled away, whistled loudly and as if on cue, Baldy stopped circling, and she flew in the direction of Dead Man's Point.

CHAPTER 29

ARVIDIA'S PRAYER

Lexy shook her head as Arvidia pulled the reins and brought her to a halt. She slowly inhaled the fresh clean scent emulating the air. Sliding off Lexy she landed lightly on her feet and headed over to the area where Baldy had fallen when Jim shot her. Spots of blood still remained on the rocks. Lexy hung back and nibbled on the grass. Arvidia slowly kneeled beside the rock, touched the dried blood then she clasped her hands together. Closing her eyes and hanging her head low she began to pray.

"God, I know I haven't had a heart to heart talked to you in a while. God, I ask forgiveness for my sins. I am sure you know the reasons why I am here today. I am afraid the spirit of hate has gripped onto my heart so deep, I'm actually afraid for myself. My earthly father told me about the great love you have for your children. I kneel before you, for my heart is troubled. I do not know what to do. There's a little boy being held hostage by that man, Mason. I'm sure you know all about him. I told Jim to meet me at Dead Man's Point. I know I can't kill Jim there because of the curses believed by Will and the tribe. I wouldn't do that to them, but it's likely I may die trying to save Jake. As long as Jake is safe from harm then I know it'll be worth the sacrifice. However, I do know about the legend of the Blue Moon. I do not know how much truth there is to it but I know I'm not a true warrior nor am I worthy of your time but I really need your help. Please, help me save Jake."

Eyes closed, her tears flowed unchecked down her cheeks. Her body trembled as she prayed. Her knees ached against the cold hard ground. A sudden, strong, breeze blew through her hair. She felt His presence as a gentle touch against her face. The fear that had rippled through her heart throughout her life suddenly disappeared. She felt a serene and a profound sense of peace. She opened her eyes slowly and heard His whispers in her ear. Arvidia felt as though she could kneel there forever listening, to His voice. She could see clearly for the first time in her life why Will came to the mountains to pray.

"Thank you, God, for listening to me." She felt humble and strong at the same time.

She knew, without a doubt, in her heart what she needed to do. She slowly stood up, she again grazed her hands over the blood stained rocks where Baldy had fallen. Clenching her fist she thrust it momentarily towards the sky, she turned and whistled for Lexy.

Lexy neighed and almost marched up to Arvidia as though she knew about the mission the two of them were about to embark upon. Grabbing a hold of her mane Arvidia hoisted herself into the saddle. They slowly headed down the mountain towards Dead Man's Point.

"I found her." Joe almost whispered into his cell phone.

"Found who?" Hal's voice sounded worn and strained.

"Arvidia's sister, Kelia. She's alive and well in Stony Creek, Virginia."

"Wait, she's alive? Are you sure it's her sister?" Hal was cautious about everything but even more so when it came to Arvidia.

"Look for yourself. I sent a picture of her to your cell phone. Other than the blond hair, they look exactly alike." Joe sounded just as surprised and cautious as Hal.

"Joe, I want you meet with her. See if you can talk her into coming here to meet Arvidia. Call me and let me know. I'd rather do it myself, but I don't think I should leave under these circumstances." Hal knew he couldn't leave until he knew his girl was safe.

"Yes, Boss, I understand. I'll handle this with the utmost respect." Joe hung up and picked up his already packed bag with airline ticket in hand. He headed out of his office and down to the waiting cab to take him to Sea-Tac Airport. Joe was ecstatic for Arvidia, he stared at Kelia's photo again, *finally a piece of her past has surfaced!* Joe thought. I hope she is as kind as she looks in the photo.

Hal's hand shook as he studied the picture Joe had sent. There was no doubt. This was Arvidia's sister. Her piercing blue eyes spoke the truth. He felt excited for Arvidia but wondered if this would bring her more pain or happiness?

Somewhere along the coastal beach, Arvidia finally arrived at Dead Man's Point. She had ridden Lexy around the island so as to avoid being seen by anyone from the reservation. She felt the need to do this alone.

She'd hidden her backpack under a rotted fallen tree. She squatted down to pray once again. She felt calm knowing whatever would happen, Jake would be safe. She looked up to the sky and knew dusk would soon fall. She waited patiently, *God, please be with me and Jake. Let him be safe.*

Jim grabbed Jake up from the cabin floor and roughly pushed him into the car. "Finally, I can be done with this and head to Brazil!" He looked into the backseat and patted the bag of Buck's money hidden in its lining. He aggressively threw the car into reverse, then purposely into drive. Jake was afraid for Arvidia. His hands were bound, his mouth gagged, his forehead beaded with sweat and his eyes were wide with fear. He began to pray in his heart. He would always remember what happened the night before. He had listened to Jim pace about the room as he spilled his guts about how he hated Arvidia and Kelia to Jake. Jake was puzzled as to who Kelia was. Jim spat in anger about how they were favored and pampered. His father no longer paid attention to him. He spat on the ground whenever he mentioned his father. "I didn't mean to push her down the stairs she just made me so mad! He shouted this out loud. "I know my father blames me for her death. I just get so angry I can't control it."

Jake nodded and fought to stay awake. He was afraid to close his eyes. He had never seen someone so angry and hateful.

Jake had no idea where they were going now but they were heading very fast down the mountain. It didn't take long before they pulled into an area he had never seen before. The car rocked heavily as they pulled into the center of Dead Man's Point and Jim suddenly slammed the brakes and yanked Jake out of the car. Jim rested his gun on Jake's back while cowardly, holding him as a shield. He searched around the gorge. It was dead silent.

"Arvidia Show yourself or he's dead!" Jake shook in fear. He looked around quickly and up in the sky. He didn't see anything. It appeared no had come to save him. He hung his head. As he looked at the ground he thought it was odd there was a perfect circle of beach sand in the middle of the gorge. He looked up into the woods. Jim gripped his shoulders tight. He could feel him breathing down his neck with cigarette smoke billowing from his mouth. Jake coughed nearly silent.

Arvidia slowly walked from the woods towards them. "Let Jake go. He has nothing to do with this. This is between you and me!" Arvidia shouted and twirled around with her arms above her head, "I am not armed. Let him go!"

Arvidia stopped at the edge of the beach sand. Jim shoved Jake forward. Arvidia kneeled down to Jake and quickly pulled the tape off his little hands and the bandana out of his mouth.

"He's going to kill you." whispered Jake. Tears slid down his dirt stained face. His body trembled in fear.

"Shh . . . Listen to me," Arvidia hugged him tight and whispered into his ears. "Look over to my right into the woods. Do you see a white Bengal tiger?" Jake's eyes widened and he quietly shook his head. "Her name is Maleka. Go to her, she will protect you. Do not look back. Okay? If anything happens to me, please tell your father, I love him very much." She looked sternly into Jake's eyes. She was ready. She lightly touched Jake's nose with her finger and tenderly kissed him on the forehead. His lips quivered. He fought back the tears stinging his eyes and walked quickly towards the mammoth, Bengal Tiger. Her yellow eyes seem to penetrate through Jake resting heavily onto Jim. She let out a low growl. Jim quickly looked around nervously but didn't see anything. Darkness was setting fast and soon the blue moon would be full. Maleka gently nudged Jake onto his hip and walked behind him.

"Well, I'm surprise you were stupid enough to come unarmed." snarled Jim.

"According to Tribal Law, we cannot kill on this land otherwise curses will be brought forth."

Jim snorted and laughed. "Well, you're making this quite easy for me then. You always had a soft spot for them kids." He twirled the gun around his fingers then checked the bullets. All six rounds were accounted for. "There's one thing I should inform you of before I kill you. Your adopted last name maybe Miles," A sly grin spread slowly over his face as he tilted his head sideways and stared at Arvidia. "but . . . your real last name is Mason." Hesitating for emphasis he grinned and said, "Hello, Sis!" He nearly bellowed but held back until it registered.

Arvidia's blood ran cold. He's just playing head games with you, keep yourself together!

Jim's evil laugh taunted her; "Yep, that was Papi and Mama in the cell I built for them. They were going to send me away! Can you believe that? Me? They pampered you and the other one like you were gold or something. It was sickening. Well, I took care of that problem didn't I? But no, you had to go and escape and spoil my plans. But now I can finish them." Jim aimed the gun towards Arvidia's head as he walked closer and closer to her, until they were face to face. She had closed her eyes and prayed her death would be quick and painless.

Jim placed the cold gun against Arvidia's temple. She heard the gun click as he pulled back on the trigger. She squeezed her eyes shut. The ground suddenly rumbled and shook. Loud growls roared past them. Arvidia opened her eyes seen sets of yellow glowing eyes peering from throughout the gorge, there were too many to count. Looking up she could see the tribe sitting on their horses with their spears by their side just atop the gorge. Her relief was deep. Now she heard the wolves howl, knowing it was Bandit's pack, the growls grew louder and closer. Suddenly the wolves launched from all directions onto Jim. Baldy and Gulp were frantically screeching from above. Arvidia sprinted away from Jim as fast as she could, but when she dared to looked back, she fell, striking her head. She turned onto her side but the pain was fierce and she felt blood trickling down the side of her face. She breathed heavily at the sight before her. It was unlike anything she had ever seen before. The beach sand had funneled furiously high around the wolves and Jim. It was difficult to see anything. All that could be heard were the fierce growls of the wolves and Jim's screaming.

Will, spread his arms towards the sky. He understood why Arvidia wanted to meet him there. God told her to go there. He knew Arvidia finally accepted Him into her heart. He prayed for many years for her to accept Jesus, into her heart, but he knew it had hardened with the sufferings and the losses.

Suddenly, it was over. Bandit strode over to Arvidia and gingerly licked her face. She grasped onto Bandit who leaned in to help her stand. She looked ahead and watched as the funnel of sand calmed. Serenity took over a land once cursed. All of the wolves sat in a perfect circle around the strange looking beach sand. There were no signs of Jim anywhere and strangely enough, no sign of blood. Arvidia knew deep down inside her, Jim Mason was gone. She looked up to the gorge where the tribe stood with their spears raised in silence.

It worked! When Arvidia researched the Tribal Law, it clearly stated only man could not kill on Dead Man's Point otherwise the curses would come forth. It did not state animals could not. Arvidia knew Bandit would not hesitate to protect her if he sensed she was in danger. She did not expect the whole pack to show up. She was not sure about all of what had happened.

Arvidia breathed heavily then sat down. She lightly touched her head where the blood still oozed. She looked at her hand and it dripped slowly on the ground. *Did he say we were brother and sister?* Arvidia felt numb inside. She began to shake uncontrollably. Bandit sat nearly on top of her, licking her and nudging her. She held tightly to Bandit, and looked around, wondering if Jake was okay.

Will looked down on Arvidia, "Let us go and help her," Will ordered. He could clearly see she was not well. They clicked their horses and turned down towards the valley.

Meanwhile, Todd and Mark found the cabin where Jim held Jake hostage. They forced their way into the cabin. "All's clear!" Todd shouted. He holstered his glock. Inside the cabin, it looked like someone had an temper tantrum, and then some. Furniture tossed, bookshelves turned, kitchen table broke, broken glasses strewn about.

Mark whistled as he stood alongside Todd. "What happened here? I hope Jake is okay." He looked quickly around for any signs of blood, grateful not to have found any.

"Your guess is as good as mine. This doesn't make sense, why toss the place? He had Jake as his bargaining chip and I'm sure he had an escape plan and,"

"Todd, look!" Mark walked quickly over the broken glass and looked at the mirror. "Recognize this?" There they found a symbol scribbled onto the mirror which meant death. They both knew danger was eminent.

"Holy . . . We've got to find Arvidia!" Both Todd and Mark ran out of the cabin. Unable to get a signal for the cell phones, Todd raced the car down the mountainside. They both looked at each other and hoped it wasn't too late. Mark gripped onto the door as Todd gripped tight to the steering wheel.

"Maleka, that didn't sound so good." Jake was terrified when he heard the loud roars rumbling through the woods. He stepped closer to her. She turned and looked at him, nudging him gently. As intimidating as Maleka seemed, Jake felt strangely safe with her. He had no idea where she was taking him but he promised Arvidia he wouldn't look back. "Maleka, is

Arvidia okay?" He shuddered at the mere thought of losing her. He knew his father would be very upset if anything happened to her.

Blake was unable to stay at the reservation. He paced inside and outside the house. The reservation was like a ghost town. Will told him it would be better if he stayed behind in case Jake showed up. I have to do something! Blake thought. He eyed the motorcycle, again, leaning up against the barn. It had been years since he had ridden one. It was either that or ride Blacky. There was no way he could just stand around. He dodged toward the motorcycle, hopped on and headed towards Dead Man's Point. He throttled the motorcycle as fast it would go; he could barely breathe as the branches from the trees whipped by his face. His chest tightened, panic rose through him when he felt the ground shake. He had difficulty controlling the bike. The loud roars made the hairs on his neck stand up. Blake, terrified, throttled the motorcycle full thrust and sped through the woods. *Please God, cover and protect Arvidia and Jake.*

"Dad!" Jake shouted. Blake roared by skidding to a stop, when he heard his son's voice. He dropped the bike and ran toward Jake falling to his knees, placed his hands onto his sons face and hugged him tightly. Tears streamed down both their faces, relief flooding in.

"Jake, I'm so happy you are safe!" Blake opened his eyes to see him and saw Maleka just sitting there. It almost seemed like she was smiling at him. Blake's eyes widen, "Uh, Jake, wh . . . What is that?"

"Oh, that's Maleka. Arvidia told me to go with her and she would protect me. She did, dad. You should have seen her. She's some kind of tiger."

"What? A tiger?" Blake looked again, Maleka was gone. "Where did she go?"

"She was just here a second ago." Jake looked around as if for the first time and realized Arvidia wasn't there yet. "Dad, is Arvidia okay?" Jake started to shake violently. Blake circled his arms around his son opening and wrapping him under his coat. He was just as frightened as his son.

"I don't know son." He was still kneeling beside him, holding him.

"Dad, we have to go get Arvidia!" Jake broke free of his father and ran toward Dead Man's Point.

"Jake! No! Come back here right now!" Blake ran after his son and caught him. "It's too dangerous out there. I don't know what's going on out there, but, Will said specifically to stay at his house. He will know what has to be done."

"But Dad, we have to find her!" Jake sobbed into his father's arms. "I don't want to lose her!"

"Shh . . . . I don't want to lose her, either but she knows what she's doing. I know the tribe is there and I'm sure we'll hear what happened soon. I'm sure she's fine." Blake looked around the woods, even the trees didn't seem to be moving. It was a spooky silence. "Come, Jake, let's go back to the house and wait for Will." He picked up the bike and they both walked back to the reservation. Blake fought the temptation to go after Arvidia. He was terrified something awful had happened to her.

"What the heck was that?" Mark gripped onto the side of the car door.

"I don't know, maybe it was an earthquake? Do they get those here? Sure is a fine time for one!" Todd shouted and fought to gain control of the steering wheel. The dust from the dirt road caked the windshield. Todd quickly turned on the wipers only to smear the dirt. "Great! Now I can't see!" He clicked the wiper fluid and the windshield soon became clearer. They were almost to Will's house.

"Mom!" Caleb and Trista shouted as they dismounted their horses. They ran toward their stunned mother who seemed unable to focus or stand. Caleb protectively wrapped his arms around his mother.

"Mom, you okay? We sent the wolves just like you asked us."

"You guys did an awesome job. How did so many wolves come? Is Jake okay?"

"I don't know, mom, it was weird. Bandit seemed to know what was going on, it was almost like he was waiting for us and then he let out this loud weird howl and they came running. Who was Jake talking to?"

Surprised Arvidia asked, "You guys didn't see her?"

"Who?" Caleb asked. "There was nobody there except Jake. Mom, you must've hit your head pretty hard."

"You guys didn't see the white tiger? It was Maleka. Remember her? Oh, that's right, you guys haven't met her. She just showed up here today. I was so surprised to see her; I haven't seen her in years. I wonder if Will had seen her."

Will slowly dismounted his horse and kneeled before her. His spirit within him softened at the mere mention of Maleka. "Maleka passed away while you were in training at the FBI quarters." Will said quietly as he spoke.

Arvidia gasped, "She did? Then who was that?"

"Oh that was definitely Maleka. The Great One sent her to protect you and Jake."

"I had no idea. I was sitting here praying earlier before Jim came and suddenly she appeared before me. I touched her and hugged her. She was real!" Arvidia exclaimed.

"I do not doubt that. The Great One must have returned her to Earth to protect what was taken from her." Will recalled a time she had saved him as well; he felt serene peace and serenity flow through him. Dead Man's Point tranquility remained. He never told Arvidia how Maleka entered into his life. She had fought Jim off while protecting Will. It happened while the Quad was actively searching for Jim and Will was pondering whether or not to adopt Arvidia. No family members had stepped forward to claim her. He had decided one day to take a walk in the woods and pray for the Great One's blessing for him to adopt Arvidia. Jim suddenly jumped down onto him from a tree limb and dared him to fight. Will had seen the blood splattered all over his clothing and he had a deranged look spearing from his eyes.

They locked arms and fought. Will slipped to the ground and Jim held his knife tightly against his throat. Will showed no fear. Out of the corner of his eyes, he saw the most unusual white Bengal tiger with thin black stripes alongside her ribs, approaching Jim. She snarled, bared her teeth then she knocked him off of Will. Will escaped Jim's grip and quickly climbed up into a tree just as Maleka attacked Jim. Jim managed to stab her before running into the woods.

Will jumped down from the tree and cautiously approached the white tiger. He had never seen such a beautiful creature. He lightly touched her wound as she breathed heavily. Will swiftly worked on her, and then he immediately noticed why she had attacked Jim. She was a mom and her cubs were nearby. They would never have left their babies unless someone attacked them. He looked around quickly for her cubs. He'd seen how none had survived Jim's senseless attack. He gently picked up the injured animal and brought her home.

He was amazed how calm she was around humans, she healed quickly. After a time, Will wondered where she had come from. White

Bengal tigers are from the Middle East. It didn't take him long to figure it out. A circus had come through Bellingham and a Bengal tiger had escaped shortly after a parade through town. Time went by and because the wooded area was so vast, she had disappeared. Will believed she was pregnant and she didn't want to continue the life with the circus so she ran away, but he also believed, Maleka was sent directly to Lummi Island just to save him and Arvidia.

She was accepted by Baldy and Bandit without hesitation. As soon as she was well, Will knew she would head back up to the mountains where she belonged. She often appeared when Will went to the mountains to pray. She'd always lay nearby him. Will was amazed at her powerful beauty. He felt a strong bond with her. Then one night, he felt a pressing need to go to Mt. Baker. There he found Maleka in the spot where he prayed so often, he knew she was dying. He gently lifted her head onto his lap and sang songs to her. She passed peacefully.

"Maleka, I sure miss you." Will whisper into the air. He placed his arms around Arvidia. "Arvidia, we must get you home." He gently lifted her and whistled for Lexy. She came immediately. He lifted her weight easily and allowed her to rest her head onto Lexy's mane while he mounted. He held onto the reins and led them all home.

"This calls for a celebration!" Running Bull shouted and thrust his spear into the air as did the others. They whooped and hollered in celebration. The horses neighed loudly and thundered into the woods.

Blake and Jake stood on the hill watching for the tribe to return. They soon heard the hollering and whooping as the tribe members began to appear on the beach. Blake searched in vain for Arvidia. He felt his anxiety rise high within him. Blake did not know the members well enough to ask. He was terrified something horrible had happened to her.

"Dad, there she is!" Jake jumped up and down pulling on his father's shirt. Blake could see Will was leading her horse down the beach. As they got closer Blake was startled how pale, bloodied and bruised she was. Blake approached her horse and helped her off. He hugged her tightly. Arvidia groaned. "I'm sorry, are you okay?" Blake was deeply concerned, especially how pale she looked.

"That's okay." She turned to face Will, "Father, thank you."

"For what, Sqimi?" For the first time since the day Will found Arvidia in the woods, he felt profound peace. The Great One finally answered his prayers. Arvidia was finally safe from harm.

"For loving me and believing in me, I am so honored to be your daughter. I'm so sorry I didn't tell you what I was planning, but I went to Mount Baker and God came to me. It was surreal and now I know and understand what you have been trying to instill in me for many years."

"Sqimi, the Great One told me you would someday accept Him into your heart. I sure did wondered at times, you are so stubborn!" Will smiled proudly and hugged her.

Blake stood awkwardly aside. He was excited Arvidia had accepted Jesus into her heart. He too had prayed for her. Will walked over to Blake and hugged him as well.

As he was hugging him, he spied Jake running fast towards them. "Jake is coming." Arvidia smiled and she kneeled with her arms spread out for Jake.

"Arvidia You made it! You made it! What was that horrible sound?" Jake threw his full weight onto Arvidia. They both laughed and fell to the ground.

"Maleka was cool, Dad even saw her. Then she disappeared."

"Well, I'm going to have to explain that to you later." Arvidia jumped up and hugged Blake and kissed him gently with her sore lip. "You are a sight for sore eyes! I was afraid I would never see you again. I hope you understand I had to do what I did to protect Jake. There was no other solution or so I thought."

"Arvidia," Blake's voice choked with emotions, "I may not understand why you did what you did, but I know you did it out of love just as God has shown His love for you. He spared you so that you may live. I have never met a woman quite like you. I love you." Blake's soft brown eyes starred deeply into Arvidia's blue eyes.

Arvidia looked away when he spoke the three little words she worked so hard to avoid hearing again. She looked up at Blake and smiled, "I love you too."

Blake smiled, and wrapped his arms around her and together they headed over the hill to Will's house. She held onto Blake's hand, and was elated to finally feel free of the long nightmare, Jim Mason. She no longer had to keep looking over her shoulder.

Blake spoke softly, "What happened back there? Is he?"

"Blake it was amazing, God was there and Jim is gone, gone for good. I just want to tend to these cuts and bruises and I can tell you later what happened out there."

"Okay. I can't wait to hear about it but honestly, I'm just glad you're safe."

Arvidia smiled and walked with Blake as the children ran about. Many of the tribe members were excitedly talking about what happened at Dead Man's Point. Arvidia noticed Baldy soaring about screeching and Bandit seemed to be pacing back and forth. She knew immediately something was wrong and stopped walking. Blake looked around confused; He could see the tension in Arvidia's face.

"What's wrong?"

"I don't know Baldy and Bandit are acting strange. Something's wrong." Arvidia's gut instinct agreed with Baldy and Bandit. But what was it? Did Jim escape? Arvidia turned and looked at Will who was noticing the same thing. He too sensed an ominous presence. Suddenly Will shouted at Arvidia and ran towards her. Confused, she looked toward Will. Everything seemed to move in slow motion. Suddenly, gunshots reverberated from within Will's house. Arvidia felt a sharp burning pain in her chest. The jolt of the bullet knocked her to the ground. She clutched the left side of her chest and was shocked to see blood pumping out. She was instantly dizzy and fought hard to talk to Blake.

"Arvidia, you've been shot!" Blake quickly scooped her into his arms and ran towards a row of trees. He fought the wave of nausea as he watched the blood stain her shirt. Arvidia was gasping to breathe. "Shh. Don't talk." She grabbed Blake's hand and placed it hard onto her chest. She winced in pain.

Caleb, Trista and Jake immediately went to her side, "Mom you okay?" Caleb was frightened as were the other two kids. she noticed their voices seemed to drift away and was surprised how sleepy she felt.

Arvidia smiled and weakly touched her son's face, "Yes, I am fine."

Caleb knew his mother was not fine, "Gramps! Mom's been shot!"

Chaos broke out as people ran about confused. The tribesmen hid alongside of whatever they could find. Will ran quickly through shouting orders to the tribesmen. He finally saw Arvidia sitting up against the tree, with Blake and the kids surrounding her and blood covering Blake's hand.

Will knelt down to look at her. He knew by how fast the blood was oozing out and how pale Arvidia looked, that this was beyond his skills. He immediately dialed 911.

"Where's my money!" Buck Taylor shouted in a drunken rage. He stumbled out onto Will's porch. He twirled his gun aimlessly around in the air and in his other hand was a bottle of whiskey when Buck seen Arvidia had arrive hatred consumed him. He knew Jim was dead, he could care less. It's his millions he was missing. "I'm not leaving here until I have my money!" He saw the children huddled protectively around Arvidia. Blake glowered at him. Hmmm, maybe if I shoot lover boy, maybe my money will appear. He chuckled and aimed the gun at Blake.

"Blake!" Arvidia could barely shout. Caleb saw Buck aiming the gun at Blake, Caleb jumped over Arvidia and pushed Blake out of the way just as the shot rang out. They both rolled around on the ground but neither was hurt. Blake immediately covered his body around Caleb. Suddenly, rapid gunshots fired and a loud thud hit the ground. Todd and Mark stood firm with their firearms drawn. They both fired at Buck Taylor who fell over the porch railings onto the ground, dead.

"Arvidia!" Blake scrambled back to her as she was gasping for air. Will had taken his shirt off to keep pressure her Arvidia's chest and talked rapidly with a 911 operator who said the police and ambulance were on their way.

"Sqimi, stay with me!" Will shouted at Arvidia. "Blake, keep her talking." Will desperately exerted more pressure onto Arvidia's chest. Arvidia winced in pain. "I'm sorry Sqimi I have to do this."

Soon the ambulance arrived with the state police in tow. Will knew by looking at Arvidia it was bad. He listened for the vitals the paramedics shouted out, he shut his eyes and prayed silently, he knew she was unstable. The paramedics worked quickly to establish an IV access and placed a nonrebreather mask over her mouth and nose. They hastily hurried the stretcher into the ambulance. One of the paramedics told Will to come with him, "I don't think she'll make it."

Will looked at Blake who looked as if he was going to faint. He firmly gripped his hands, "You must not lose faith, PRAY!" Will commanded, then turned and jumped into the ambulance and in an instant they were gone.

Stunned, Todd and Mark raced to their car, "Blake, come with us. We're going to follow them!" shouted Todd. Blake jumped into the car as Todd screeched the car in front of him.

"Can we go dad?" Jake asked anxiously. His tear stained face was beyond description. Caleb and Trista stood along either side of him in shock. Running Bull stood behind them.

"No, Stay here with Caleb and Trista. I will call as soon as I can." Blake rapidly kissed each of the children and jumped into the car as they raced off. Mark dialed Hal and again got his voice mail. "That is really weird. I have not been able to get in touch with Hal. It keeps going to voice mail! Come to think of it, where has he been?"

"Huh? Now that you mention it, yeah where is he? I know he had talked with Joe the other day and said he needed to go back to Seattle for something." Todd pressed the accelerator down to catch up to the ambulance racing down I-5 towards St. Joseph Hospital.

"I think we better call Joe and let him know what happened." Mark slowly ran his finger over the screen until he spotted Joe's number. He paused for a second before touching the screen to dial his number. He looked at Todd who briefly took his eyes off the road and nodded as Mark raised the phone to his ear and waited for Joe to answer.

"This is Joe."

"Hey, Joe," Mark cleared his throat before speaking again, "You need to come home."

Joe sensed immediately something was not right, he excused himself from Kelia's living room and walked quickly to the hallway. He whispered, "What's wrong?"

"It's Arvidia. She's been shot in the chest and Joe, it's not looking good. You need to come home ASAP."

"What? She was shot? How? What happened?"

"Buck Taylor shot her in the chest. Don't worry, Todd and I fired back. He's dead."

"Oh, my, God I'll be on the first plane." Joe leaned against the wall and peered around the corner where he could see Kelia leaning on her husband's shoulder.

"Plane? Where the heck are you?"

"I'm in Virginia." Joe whispered back.

"What the heck are you doing in Virginia?" Mark looked at Todd who shrugged his shoulders.

"It's a long story, but I found Arvidia's twin sister, Kelia." Joe whispered.

"Oh, man . . ." Mark let out a low whistle. "Talk about bad timing!" Mark hesitated for a moment to tell Joe about Jim but Joe interrupted his thoughts before he could say anything.

"You said it." Joe leaned his head against the wall. He stared up at the foyer chandelier's sparkling lights. "I'll be there as soon as I can."

"Okay, bro. We'll keep you informed." He clicked off his cell and looked at Todd. "I'll tell him about Jim when he gets here. He's got enough going on at his end."

"Yeah, he sure does. Why is he in Virginia?"

"He found Arvidia's twin sister, Kelia."

Todd let out a low whistle, "Wow, you are right, talk about bad timing. I hope they get here in time."

CHAPTER 30

KELIA DOVER

Joe swallowed hard as he peered around the corner of the hallway. He saw Kelia sitting on the couch holding her husband's hand while her two year old son played with his toys on the living room floor. Her face was still showing signs of shock from when Joe informed her that her twin sister was alive and well. Now, how was he going to tell her that her sister is dying?

Joe's eyes stung with unshed tears. He inhaled deeply and he took long strides into the living room. He muttered, "Umm . . . . I got some bad news." Joe's stomach felt tight and hard as he spoke. He fiddled with the cell phone in his pocket.

Kelia sat straight up when she noticed his eyes were brimming with tears. "What's wrong?" She stood up and gently placed her hand on his shoulder.

"That was one of my partners in Seattle, Washington." Joe's tongue felt thick and he could feel the tears he could no longer hold in, rolling down his cheek. He wiped them with the back of his hand. "He uh . . . . informed me that . . ." His voice squeaked and he fiddled nervously with his cell phone. "Arvidia's been shot and it's not good."

Kelia's hands flew to her face, "Shot?! Is she okay?" Kelia's husband, Dr. Thomas Dover stood up immediately from the couch and stood behind Kelia who appeared as though she would faint.

"You just told me she's alive, and now you are telling me she's been shot?" Her husband held her.

"I'm not exactly sure of the circumstances of how this happened, but I do know I have to be on the plane ASAP. I know we just met, but is it possible you can come with me? He thrust his badge at Kelia, "You can call my boss, check out my credentials, I assure you, everything I have told you is true and I have no doubt in my mind, you are Arvidia's sister. It might be your last chance to see your her alive if we make it in time. I promise, I'll answer all of your questions." Joe knew he was pleading with her but he felt he had no choice.

Kelia paused for a moment, "Why are you so sure I'm her sister?" She looked at her husband who was studying Joe's badge.

"Except for the blond hair, you guys look exactly alike. There's no question about it, you are Arvidia's twin sister." Joe answered as he glanced at his watch.

"I think you should go. You've always said you felt a piece of you was missing. Joe, what hospital is Arvidia at? I'm a doctor and I'm sure I can find out some more information."

"She's at St. Joseph's Hospital in Bellingham, Washington."

"Thank you, I'll be right back." He paused and spoke lovingly to his wife, "Honey, you should go with him and meet your sister. I'll stay here and take care of Austin." Their son chose that moment to let a reassuring coo escape.

"Are you sure you're okay with this?" She asked with a caution she didn't really feel necessary.

"Yes, go pack. You don't have much time. While you are doing that, I'm going to make a couple of phone calls." He glanced at Joe then swiftly walked into his office and shut the door.

Joe didn't blame him for being suspicious. It was a rather wild story to tell someone. I'd be suspicious too. Joe thought.

Kelia went upstairs to her bedroom and packed a few things. Her hands shook as she packed her clothes into the suitcase. She sat on the bed; her brain felt like it was swirling faster than it could process her thoughts. Arvidia is my twin sister and she's alive? She had no doubt Joe was telling her the truth. She stood and walked to her closet, turning on the light she shifted a few boxes around and found the aged red shoe box she had carried with her for so many years. She sunk down to her knees and lifted the lid. The box had a few black and white photos of Mami and Papi, her aunt, a doll and a letter from her mother, the last letter. She unfolded the letter and read the neat cursive writing. It was a letter to her mother's sister, Margaret.

September 19ᵗʰ 1980

My dear sister,
We have finally arrived in a quaint little town called Bellingham, Washington. Jerrill and I are quite exhausted.

Our appointment to have our son Jim committed is on Monday. Margaret, he is so in need of help. Please pray for this child. I've never seen such an angry child such as this. He literally hates Arvidia and Kelia. Can you believe that? They look up to him yet he spats at them. Jerrill and I are weary. We are at our wit's end trying to help him. I sure hope this doctor will be able to help. The only thing is we have to leave him there for one year. The doctor told us the therapy is very intense and he preferred we not keep in contact. He did say he would keep us informed of his progress. His violent temper tantrums are quite difficult to manage and are quite frightening. Jerrill is beside himself. He's terrified for Arvidia's and Kelia's safety. Speaking of which, how is Kelia feeling? Please give her kisses for me. I miss her so much! I feel so bad leaving her with you like that. She's so prone to fever. I didn't want to risk making her sick.

Arvidia is doing fine. I think you are right I should've left Arvidia with you as well. I didn't want to burden you with the twins. I sure don't like the way Jim looks at Arvidia. Well, I best be going, we have a long day tomorrow. Jerrill says we should be home on Wednesday. I hope so; I think we need this year apart from Jim so we can focus on Arvidia and Kelia. I don't feel we've been giving them much attention lately. It's time we be a family again. Give Kelia hugs and kisses for me. See you soon!

Lovingly In Christ, Marlene

Kelia wiped a tear that trickled down her cheek. This was the last letter her mother sent to her aunt. Whenever she questioned her aunt about her family she would become sad and say she didn't know what happened to her family. She had more questions than answers. Whatever those answers were her aunt took them to her grave. She read this letter many times and had wondered who Arvidia and Jim were? Kelia knew Arvidia was her twin sister but who was Jim? She stood up and gingerly packed the red shoe box in her suitcase. She looked at her watch but before she could reach the door she prayed quietly. "Lord please cover and protect me on this journey." Kelia felt urgency in her heart and knew she could trust Joe. She'd go to Seattle with him and meet her twin sister; at least she hoped it was her sister.

She carried her suitcase down the stairwell and met her husband at the bottom. Joe stood by the doorway, patiently waiting. Thomas held out his hand to take her suitcase and leaned in to whisper to her.

"I checked him out, his boss, Hal confirmed everything and your sister, Arvidia is in critical condition. You must go and see her." He kissed her.

"I will. Joe if you're ready, I'd like to go with you."

Relieved, Joe said, "We don't have much time. Hal sent us a private jet. I just hope we get there in time." His voice faltered.

"I spoke to her doctor, her vital signs are stable and she's in an induced coma to help her breathe better, but she's critical. I'll pray she comes out of this okay." Thomas stuck out his hand towards Joe and they firmly shook hands. Joe could see in his eyes he was concerned for the woman he never laid eyes on and he was grateful he took the time to call the hospital but a word of thanks could not come out. "Honey, call me when you get there."

"I will, Bye-bye Austin. You be good for daddy, okay?" Austin stood wobbly on his feet chewing on one of his toys. He waved goodbye to himself and Kelia laughed. She kissed her husband as she entered the waiting cab. Joe urgently told the driver they needed to get to the airport as quickly as possible. Kelia waved to her husband and son as they drove away. She turned and looked at Joe who held his face in his hands. He muffled his cries into as he soaked his palms in tears.

"Joe, she'll be okay, she has to be." Kelia said softly.

"She's my best friend, my best partner. She's been through so much and now this?" Joe cried. "I don't usually break down like this but you have no idea what has transpired over the past 6 months."

"Well, time is what we have right now." She patted his hand. "Perhaps you can tell me on the way to Seattle?"

Joe sniffed and looked at Kelia. Her stunning beauty and stark likeness of Arvidia amazed him. There was a soft hue about her and her countenance was translucent of innocence and pureness. "I'm sorry for staring at you. I can't get over how much you look like Arvidia. You both even tilt your head the same way."

"What?" Kelia laughed and flung her long blond hair back just as Arvidia did. Joe shook his head. Yep, she's definitely Arvidia's sister. Joe thought.

Kelia gently placed her hand onto Joe's, "Tell me more!"

"Sir, we're here." The cab driver interrupted Joe before he could answer her.

Joe saw one of the suits standing nearby the entrance, "Here, keep the change." He quickly opened the door and assisted Kelia out of the cab. The cab driver was quick to get her bag and they both hurried to the man waiting.

"Hey, Joe, follow me. The plane is ready for takeoff."

"Thanks, man." The three of them hurried through a secured hallway and soon the roars of planes could be heard. A small lone white aircraft could be seen waiting with the door wide open. The pilot had his badge clipped onto his hip and glock exposed in his holster. His face was serious.

"Mrs. Dover, this is Frank, our pilot. He's an agent as well."

Frank, stunned by the likeness of Kelia looked at Joe puzzled, "She's looks a lot like Arvidia!" He whispered to Joe.

"I know. That's her twin sister. How is Arvidia?"

"Same. Don't you worry; I'll get you guys there as fast as this baby can fly."

"Thanks, Man." Joe buckled himself into the leather seat across from Kelia and stared out the window. He inhaled slowly, fatigue was overcoming him, but he knew he needed to answer Kelia's questions. He looked into similar blue eyes and said, "So to answer the question, what is Arvidia like? Well she's one amazing woman. I don't know of anybody who could've survived what she went through."

Like Arvidia, she tilted her head and with concern in her voice, "Joe, what happened to my sister?"

"Well, in the fall of 1980 my boss Hal received a phone call from a Whatcom County Sheriff asking for help. So he and my four buddies, Todd, Mark, Mike and Chris went on an assignment to find out the identity of a little girl. Little did any of us know, she would become a major part of our lives."

"Are you her partner?" She was intrigued.

"Well, no, I'm a forensic specialist. Arvidia calls me her right-hand man." Joe puffed out his chest. "My four buddies, she calls them the Quad and Hal, well, he's Hal." He cracked a half smile. Kelia giggled.

"Joe, I have to ask this question. Are my parents, alive?" Kelia heart pounded as she asked.

Joe shook his head, "No, they died in the fire." He said softly.

"Fire?" Kelia's hand flew to her mouth. "Joe what on earth happened to my family?"

"That's how Arvidia came into our lives. She was badly burned in a cabin fire in the mountains on Lummi Island. Her adopted father, Will Miles found her and nursed her back to health but when no family members stepped up to claim her he called the sheriff's department, who in turned called us and that is how we met Arvidia."

"Oh my." Kelia looked down at her hands and looked for a tissue in her pocketbook. Joe promptly place one in her hands.

"I'm so sorry about your parents. I know it's not what you wanted to hear."

"Where is this, Lummi Island?" Kelia said between tears.

"It's a little island approximately 8 miles north of Bellingham."

Surprised, Kelia lifted her head up towards Joe, "Did you say Bellingham?"

"Yes why?" Joe leaned in towards her. He rested his elbows onto his knees as Kelia dug through her suitcase and found the red shoebox. She gingerly opened the aged box and lifted the letter and handed it to Joe.

Joe read the letter written by her mother as Kelia sobbed. Arvidia was indeed her twin sister. Joe looked at Kelia, "Wow, was this the last you heard from her?"

"Yes. Who is this Jim she mentioned in her letter?"

Joe did not want to answer that question. Just hearing his name made his stomach lurched. "I'll have my boss fill you in about him, but I can tell you he is your father's son which would make him your half-brother."

Kelia gulped and asked, "I have a brother? My aunt never mentioned I had a brother. Why wasn't I told about this? What is all the secrecy about?" Kelia shook her head, unbuckled her seatbelt and paced around the plane.

Joe unbuckled his and he stepped beside her. Standing in front of Kelia, he looked into her eyes and gently placed his hands onto her shoulders, "Kelia, your brother, Jim is a very evil person. He killed your parents and nearly killed your sister. If it wasn't for a wolf, an eagle and an Indian chief who adopted her she would not be alive today."

"What? He killed them? Oh my god. So that's what my mother was talking about, committing him." Kelia sat down trembling. Concerned, Joe wasn't sure if he was overwhelming her with too much information.

He lightly touched her knee, "Yes. Your parents were trying to help him and somewhere, somehow his little mind snapped." He paused then said, "I'm not one to mince words so I apologize, but being in forensics I only know one way to talk straight."

Kelia flinched at the word, 'snapped', "What about this wolf, eagle and an Indian chief you spoke of?" She was actually grateful Joe didn't mince words as he said.

The plane dipped her wings to the left and Joe looked out the window, recognizing Lummi Island. He said, "That is a story that will blow your mind," He pointed his finger towards the window, "You see that?" Kelia nodded her head, "That's Lummi Island. That is where Arvidia survived enormous obstacles and now, she again is fighting for her life."

The intercom crackled, "Joe, we'll land in five. Hal is waiting for you. He'll take you both to the hospital."

Joe pressed the intercom button. "Thanks, Frank."

"No problem, anything you need you give me a holler. Prepare for landing."

Kelia and Joe buckled their seatbelts, leaned back, and waited. The landing gears unfolded and hit the pavement as the plane roared to a stop. Joe could see Hal.

Kelia asked before she stepped off onto the steps of the ladder, "Is that your boss?"

"That would be him, Hal Sampson."

The door unfolded and they both walked quietly toward Hal.

The dark clouds hung low and ominous. Kelia pulled her sweater close around her while walking behind Joe. She felt anxious and nervous as they approached Hal.

"Hello Sir." Joe set Kelia's suitcase onto the concrete pavement. He held onto his briefcase.

When Hal saw Kelia step off the plane he was taken aback by the striking resemblance to Arvidia. He too, had no doubt in his mind, this was Arvidia's twin.

"Hal, this is Kelia Dover. Arvidia's sister."

Hal stuck his hand out to shake hers, "Welcome to Bellingham, Washington. I wish we were meeting under different circumstances."

Kelia shyly responded, "So do I Mr. Sampson."

"Please, call me Hal. Let's get you to the hospital. Arvidia's condition is the same. Blake, The Quad and Will have not left her side since last night." Hal opened the car door for Kelia and nodded for her to sit in front. Kelia looked at Joe apprehensively. Joe nodded his tired head, "He ain't the one you got to worry about." Joe smirked at Hal. As they piled into the car Hal drove towards the gate. Joe asked, "How in the world did Arvidia get shot?"

Hal looked into the rearview mirror to look at Joe, "From what I understand, Buck was inside Will's house waiting for her."

"Wait a minute. Buck was inside Will's house? Where was Will? I'm surprised he got by Bandit!"

Hal realized Joe didn't know what had happened. "Did Todd or Mark tell you what happened?"

"Yeah, he said he and Todd killed Buck. Am I missing something here?"

"Yep, but I'll explain it to you later. Buck realized Jim stole his money and thought he could take Arvidia in exchange for the money. He didn't know what happened at Dead Man's Point."

"Whoa, wait a minute. I know I'm tired, but I feel like I'm missing something here."

Hal glanced knowingly in the rearview mirror and said bluntly, "Like I said, I'll explain much of this to you later but rest assured, we no longer have to worry about Buck or . . . . Jim."

Joe's eyes flew wide open, "You guys got him too?"

"Nope, Bandit's pack did."

"What? Bandit's pack? How?" shocked, Joe rubbed his face, "He's really gone?"

Hal shook his head yes. He looked over at Kelia, who hung her head and had not spoken since leaving the airport. "Are you okay?"

"Yes, I'm just a bit overwhelmed, just how bad was this Jim?"

Hal responded as compassionate as possible, "He was a very evil person. I don't know you, but I wouldn't even let you near him."

"Ok, so what's this Bandit's pack?" she felt she had so much to learn.

"That would be Bandit, the wolf. I didn't get a chance to tell you about him and Baldy."

"Baldy?" Kelia looked at Joe in the backseat.

Joe smiled, "Baldy is an eagle."

Kelia looked at Joe and Hal like they were crazy. "How interesting, an eagle?"

"Remember when I said to you, this story would blow your mind?" Kelia shook her head yes. "Well, wait until you hear how Arvidia was found. We probably should let Will tell you."

"Will is the Indian chief you spoke of?" Kelia thought she was beginning to catch on.

"Yes. He's the man that found Arvidia, Baldy and Bandit. Actually Baldy led him to Bandit and there he found Arvidia. Out of respect for Will, I'll let him tell you about that." Joe leaned forward at the same time he heard Hal's phone.

"Yes, let Will tell her." Hal's phone chirped, he fumbled and pressed speakerphone. "Yes, Todd go ahead."

"Sir, Just checking in with you. There's been no change in Arvidia, has Joe arrived?"

"Yep, He's with me as well as Arvidia's sister, Kelia. We're almost at the hospital. Is Will there?"

"He hasn't left her side sir."

Not surprised, "Good, how's Chris and Mike?"

"They're are doing great, sir. They're here with us right now."

"Good. We'll be there shortly."

"Welcome home, Joe, and we're looking forward to meeting you Kelia."

"Thanks, man." Joe raised his voice just enough to make Kelia jump.

Kelia awkwardly tried to utter some words but none came out.

Hal clicked his phone off. Joe yawned and stretched. "So Sir. Again, how did all this go down?"

Hal looked up toward an ominous cloud as it parted to reveal a full moon, though no longer blue. Dusk would soon settle in. "Well, Joe, it started about twenty-four hours ago."

CHAPTER 31

ARVIDIA

An ambulance pulled into the bay and quickly pulled the stretcher out carrying a barely alive Arvidia. Rushing her in into the emergency room, a trauma staff awaited her arrival. They quickly went to work.

"BP 80/60, she's tachy and respiratory rate 30." shouted one RN. The nurse noticed Arvidia's face grimaced in pain, her legs were restless as were her arms. The nurse applied a nasal cannula to her nostrils and for a moment her patient settled. "Doctor, shall I give her morphine?" She expertly inserted an IV hepwell into the back of her right hand.

"Give her 0.5mg of morphine." He clapped his hands and shouted, "Okay, let's get a STAT chest x-ray, CBC, WBC, Chem profile, IV normal saline wide open" He glanced down at Arvidia's pale body and added, "and get an ABG! Let's go people we are losing her!" ordered the emergency room doctor.

"Morphine is in Doctor." She glanced up at the monitor and watched her vital signs.

"Doctor, her hematocrit and hemoglobin are low." shouted another nurse.

"Okay, do a cross and type match. She'll need a blood transfusion STAT."

"X-rays ready!" The x-ray tech quickly handed them to the doctor. The doctor hung the x-ray and immediately saw that her left lung bore a large hole and she had some cracked ribs. He quickly dialed the OR and explained to the cardio-thoracic surgeon the emergent patient he had his care.

"I will be right down. Have the chest tube tray ready." The surgeon hung up and briskly walked away. He turned to one nurse, "Get OR 2 ready."

"Yes, doctor." She immediately set to her task.

The emergency room nurse opened the door to the family waiting room. The room was high with anxiety and worry for Arvidia. They feared the worst. Hal managed to join them as soon as he got the frantic messages on his cell.

"She's critical at the moment and will be going to the OR." concern waned over the nurse's face. "Are there family members here?"

"We are her family. I'm her sister, Kelia." Kelia shyly looked about the room. Joe filled had her in about her sister's life. She marveled at the gentlemen that were in the family room. Their love for her was obvious. She had always felt a piece of her was missing. She didn't understand until Joe sprang into her life and suddenly the veil, once blinding, had parted and everything made sense. Her memories were vague about her early childhood and her aunt could only fill in bits and pieces and she lived the rest of her remaining life in near despair of not knowing what happened to her sister. She had always been wary of the little boy Jim. He seemed to seethe with hatred especially towards the girls. Her aunt eventually told her she had a twin sister.

"Okay, we will keep you informed." The nurse turned and quickly exited the room.

They kept vigil throughout the next few hours sitting in the family room. They held hands and prayed for Arvidia. Soon, they saw the tired surgeon emerge from the operating room doors. He stood and quietly stated, "She's stable for now. The next 24 hours will be absolutely critical. I cannot guarantee she'll pull through. She lost an enormous amount of blood; however, we were able to repair the hole in her lung. I will be monitoring her closely in ICU. You may see her, but she is in a medically induced coma. She's also on a ventilator so the machine will breathe for her to give her lungs a chance to heal."

"Thank you, Doctor." Blake felt his mouth go dry. He and the others prayed feverishly for Arvidia.

The doctor escorted Will, Blake, Hal and Kelia to ICU and pointed towards Arvidia's room. A nurse was in there closely monitoring her. She seemed to be sleeping peacefully, despite the numerous tubes and the machine that breathed for her. Blake gently rubbed her pale face and softly kissed her forehead. Gingerly picking up her hand, he leaned in and whispered into her ear, "We're here. Your sister has come to meet you. So hang in there."

Kelia reached down and gently stroked her other hand. A tear slid down her cheek, she wondered if she would ever be able to talk to her.

"Hey, Sis it's me." Kelia choked back tears and looked away. Will gently touch her shoulder, "Kelia, your sister has always been a fighter. She will pull through." He knew instantly Kelia was her twin.

"I am sorry, but she really needs to rest now." the nurse had entered quietly to administer care and medications.

"Yes, of course." Will spoke up. They walked out quietly into the hallway. Everyone seemed to be deep in thought. It was Hal who broke the silence.

"Has anyone told Chris or Mike what's happened?" They were still in the hospital recovering from their wounds. Hal was beside himself, he had never seen Arvidia so fragile and pale. He was visibly shaken.

"No, Mark and I were just talking about that. I will go upstairs and tell them." Todd was weary and exhausted.

"I'll go with you man. I can't go home just yet." He gently slapped Todd's shoulder and together they went into the elevator. Todd, Joe and Mark had waited in the waiting area of the lounge in ICU. Only a few at a time were allowed to visit but they didn't mind waiting.

"Kelia, you're welcome to come and stay with us in my home. You can meet your niece and nephew, Caleb and Trista."

"Thank you. I would like that. Joe told me I had a niece and nephew." Kelia spoke softly.

"I'll drive you two guys back to the reservation." Joe's voice quavered. He wished he'd been able to get to Arvidia in time. He feared, despite gaining a new friend, he may be losing his best friend.

Blake was on his cell updating his father about Arvidia. He in turn informed Blake his mother had immediately booked a flight to Seattle once she heard the news. "Blake, you know your mother, once her mind is made up, there's no changing it. Besides, she'll be landing in Seattle soon."

"Will she be coming to the hospital?" Blake was surprised at his mother's boldness.

"Yes, she reserved a rental car and she actually requested one with a navigation system. I'll come as soon as possible. We have a hearing Monday for the Stearns case."

"Good. That's good news. What time is her plane landing?" Suddenly Blake's cell buzzed the other line was beeping. It was his mother.

"Wait dad. She's on the other line."

"Go ahead and talk with her. Please keep me informed." Stephen hung up.

"Thanks, Dad." Blake quickly answered, "Ma?"

"Blake, I'm here in Seattle and I'm heading north onto I-5. How's Arvidia?"

Blake voiced cracked as he spoke. "It's not good, Ma. She's in critical condition."

"Well don't you worry, God is healing her. I've been praying for her." Liza spoke softly. She wanted to reach through the phone and hug her son. He sounded weary and exhausted. "I'll be there as soon as I can. I made reservations at the Hotel Bellwether. I'm in room 220."

"Okay, call me when you get to exit 5 the hotel isn't far from there. I will meet you at the hotel. Thanks, Ma. I love you." Blake felt his mother's comfort.

"I love you too, Honey. See you soon." She clicked off the phone and focused on the road.

CHAPTER 32

ARVIDIA AND KELIA

Arvidia stirred from her deep slumber, slowly opening her eyes. Her vision seemed a bit blurry and when she tried to lift her head she winced in pain. As her vision became clear she saw the wall in front of her was riddled with get well cards. Each movement brought pain. Arvidia tried to focus, but she felt dizzy and very weak. Suddenly she remembered her last conversation with Jim. *"But your real last name is Mason. We are brother and sister"* Jim's words echoed deep in her brain. Arvidia tried to speak, something was in her throat. She could see a woman sitting nearby her bed, she was reading a book. It was Blake's mother. *Why is Liza here?* She wondered.

Liza saw Arvidia move and immediately went to her side, "Arvidia, are you okay? You are in a hospital. You had surgery and you have a tube down your throat to help you breathe. Are you in pain?" Liza asked. Arvidia shook her head yes. "I'll get the nurse. Hold tight sweetie." Liza touched her hand gently and promptly buzzed the nurse. The nurse came immediately.

"Oh, good she is coming around! Good!" She was pleased with her progress. Only an experienced ICU nurse has the gift of knowing if a patient may make it or not. She had wondered about Arvidia. "Her vital signs are exactly where I want them to be." The nurse quickly checked her chest tube and made sure it was draining properly. "Arvidia, my name is Sue. I'm your nurse. Are you having any pain?" Arvidia shook her head yes. Sue pulled a white chart with some faces and numbers printed on them. She explained, "This is our pain scale. Zero being no pain and a ten is the worse pain. Can you show me where your pain level is at?" Arvidia pointed to the number 10.

"Okay, I will get you some medication that will help ease the pain." She went to the side of the bed where the medicine cart was and drew up some morphine into a syringe. She wiped her port with an alcohol wipe and slowly pushed the IV morphine into her IV tubing. She eyed the monitor and kept a watchful eye on her vitals as well as watching Arvidia relax as the morphine took effect. "There you go honey, relax and get some sleep."

Liza quickly called Blake. He'd gone to the cafeteria to get some fresh coffee. "Blake she's awake!"

"I'm on my way!" Blake paid for the coffee and made a mad dash upstairs. It had been a tortuous week waiting for her to come around. She'd been up and down in stability, she spiked a high fever and Blake had stayed with her all that night. He bathed her forehead while she sweated out the fever. He bounded quickly up the stairs.

"Arvidia. It's okay. Shh . . . ." Liza rubbed her hand and wiped a tear that floated down Arvidia's cheek. "Blake is okay, he's coming."

Blake entered the room and rushed to her bed. He stared down into hers eyes and could see her cheeks were wet with tears, softly he kissed her forehead, "Shh . . . it's okay, Arvidia. Everything is okay. Jake is okay, Look, he and the kids made you pictures." Blake pointed to the wall of pictures made by the kids.

Arvidia looked at Blake. She almost did not recognize him. He hadn't shaved and looked like he had not slept in days. He looked haggard and tired. Blake sat in the chair and leaned over the bed rails and gently kissed her hand. He noticed Arvidia seemed agitated and watched her hands. He recognized she was signing to him. "Ma, is there any paper in here?"

Liza promptly reached into her ever ready pocketbook and pulled out a pen and a pad.

"Arvidia, I don't understand what you are saying? Can you write it?"

Arvidia took the pen and pad. Her hands shook violently as she wrote: **Is it true? Was Jim my brother?**

Blake felt his blood drain as he read what she wrote. He slowly looked at Arvidia.

"Yes, I'm sorry, Jim was your half-brother." Blake whispered. Arvidia squeezed her eyes tight. *"No, he can't be my brother!" Arvidia screamed inside her head.*

Blake immediately stood and placed his hands onto her face and said firmly, "Arvidia, look at me. Your brother was very sick. What happened was not your fault. You see this blood?" he pointed at the pint size IV bag of blood that dripped into her vein. "This blood came from your sister, Kelia. Joe found your twin sister and she's here. Joe went to her and explained everything to her and she came to meet you the day you were shot." Blake stroked her hair as he spoke.

Her eyes widen and she looked at Blake with confusion. "Yes, you have a sister. Ma, can you grab that picture?" Liza was already one step ahead of him. She quickly placed the picture in front of Arvidia.

"Honey, this is your sister, Kelia." Liza pointed at the picture. "She's really sweet. Like you."

Arvidia's hands shook as she held the photo in her hand. She couldn't believe it, she had a twin sister? A tear made its way down her cheek as she stroked the picture. She tried hard to remember her face, but the fragments of her memory were still blocked. Though the name, Kelia was somewhat familiar. *Kelia. Yes, I remember!* She repeated her name several times until her memory produced a blip. Yes, she remembered the name. She was so young. Why had they been separated?

Later that evening, Kelia slipped quietly into Arvidia's room. Blake and Liza had gone back to the hotel to eat and rest for the night. She gently touched her sister's hand. Arvidia's eyes fluttered opened and she weakly gripped Kelia's hand. It was like they had never been apart.

"Hi, I'm Kelia, your sister." Kelia spoke with a southern drawl and smiled shyly at her. She was enthralled to be reunited. "I guess we have a lot to catch up on."

Arvidia had been extubated earlier that afternoon and her voice was raspy due to the tube having been in her throat. "You still have that doll? I remember you holding on to a doll that day. Wasn't her name Twiggy?" Arvidia tried hard to remember her sister but all she could remember was seeing her on the front porch of some house with a woman. She had remembered a doll she had dragged all over the place.

Kelia was amazed she had remembered that. Blake told her of her memory block and warned her she may not remember her. She giggled, "Yes, her name was Twiggy! Our aunt saved it for me all these years. I found it in the attic after she passed away. She said I used to drag that poor thing around."

Arvidia touched Kelia's hand. "I'm so glad Joe found you. I used to have dreams of a little girl with blond hair, but I never understood the dreams until now." Arvidia smiled at her. "We do have much to catch up on."

"Blake mentioned to me the trouble you might have remembering me. I admit I was a bit apprehensive, when I met that guy Joe guy and he told me about you. I wasn't sure what to believe then Joe showed me a picture of you and I knew. I knew you were the piece missing from my heart. I am so grateful to God for protecting you from that evil man." Just like Arvidia's eyes, Kelia's deep blue eyes saddened. "I am sad for our parents. But at least now we know what happened to them and we finally have found each other again." Kelia lightly touched Arvidia's scarred arm. She couldn't believe her sister survived the trials and tribulations that God had set forth. She felt a profound love and respect for her sister. She could easily see why Blake was fiercely protective of her. Once he finally understood her dark past, he was amazed at her inner strength and her will to live. Kelia learned from him the scars she carried were inflicted by Jim. They talked extensively during the week.

"Yes, we do have each other. So tell me whatcha been up too?" Arvidia grinned at her.

Kelia laughed, "Oh, not too much. I'm married and I have a ten month old son. His name is Lucas." Kelia pulled out a photo of her husband and son. "This is my husband, Mark and this is Lucas."

"Lucas is a cutie! What does your husband do?"

"He is a pediatrician. He's a great guy. I can't wait for you to meet him and our son."

Arvidia and Kelia spoke half the night talking and laughing. They had much in common for two sisters who spent half their life without one another. Eventually, sleep overtook Arvidia and Kelia slipped out of the room to let her sister rest. The doctor had stopped in earlier and told Arvidia she could go home in a couple of days.

Kelia had phoned Liza with the news. Blake had been resting at her hotel room. He knew when he saw his mother sprang up from her chair she was up to something. "That's great news! Yes, I'll tell Blake. Talk to you in a bit." She clapped her phone shut. Pursed her lips together and Blake knew she was plotting something.

"Ma, what are you up to?" Blake eyed his mother suspiciously.

"Arvidia is going to be released in two days. We have much to do!"

"What exactly are we doing?"

"We're throwing her a welcome home party!" Liza stated. She clapped her hands together in excitement she gathered her pen and paper. She went to work writing ideas down Blake was oblivious to her. Blake shook his head and lay back down on the bed and slept.

CHAPTER 33

ARVIDIA'S HOMECOMING

Blake held onto Arvidia's hand as he drove slowly down Salmon Road leading to the reservation. He gave her a gentle squeeze and asked, "You feeling okay?"

"Oh, yes. I am just happy to be out of that hospital! I can't believe all that has happened. Wow, I'm still overwhelmed with the news of Kelia. You were right, once you open your heart to God, He pours out blessings upon blessings." She smiled at him. "It's been great getting to know Kelia. I just wish I could remember everything about her, It feels like we've never been apart, yet, I still only remember blips."

"That's understandable considering the trauma you have endured. Don't try too hard, let it come naturally. God is amazing and I'm just so thankful for you and Kelia to have found each other."

"Okay." She gripped his hand, "Thank you for being there for me. It meant a lot to me and I am touched your mother has come. That was very kind of her."

"She likes you." He kissed the back of her hand lightly, "And I wouldn't have it any other way."

Blake pulled on to the dirt road that led to Will's home, Arvidia noticed many of the tribe members lined up on either side of the road welcoming her home.

"Oh, my goodness." She was surprised as she stepped out of the car. She waved to the many people that held signs and the kids were holding balloons.

They were standing in front of the crooked house, Kelia, the Quad, Hal, Joe, Liza and Stephen who had flown in the previous night. It was a perfect spring day, unusually warm but glorious. Blake helped her stand. Bandit howled and Baldy flapped her wings as loud as possible as did Gulp.

"Welcome home, Sqimi." Will hugged her and without hesitation he placed a leather necklace, laced with eagle feathers around her neck. Caleb and Trista raced to their mother's side. Jake stood awkwardly on the side with sudden shyness. Arvidia eyed him and broke free of the circle. She limped her way towards Jake and as best she could she spread her arms wide. Jake grinned and ran into her arms nearly knocking her to the ground.

Blake turned away and wiped his eyes. His emotions were still raw.

"We will now start the ceremony!" Will stated. "Sqimi, come. I have a surprise for you." He walked with her toward the side where a group of tribe members stood around a large object covered with a tarp.

The tribe members gently pulled the cover off and Arvidia gasped. It was an enormous totem pole made from red cedar. There were smiles all around, it was a tribal moment. Arvidia was stunned. It was simply gorgeous. She limped around the totem pole admiring the works and smiling at Will. She knew what this totem pole meant. She wondered how long they had been working on this.

"This totem pole represents the history of what our people have gone through with the Blue Moon legend and how the Great One proved once again, evil was not to win!" Will pointed to some faces that had been carved. "This also includes you gentlemen. The sacrifices all of you have made for us didn't go unnoticed." Will nodded his head towards the Quad and Hal "Hal, would you like to speak?"

Arvidia suddenly realize what was so different about the Quad, Joe and Hal. They all had on their Sunday best. She laughed to herself. She was so used to seeing them in jeans and beat up shirts.

"Yes," Hal stepped forward. He turned to Arvidia, showing her the battered, aged pages of the time whipped file. The file she refused to read. "I think this would be the appropriate time to burn this." Hal pointed to a hole already dug. He knelt down and set the edges of the papers on fire and dropped the burning file into the hole. Arvidia and the others clapped as the file fell in. The tribe members quickly pulled on the ropes to erect the totem pole into the hole. Arvidia gasped as she saw it stand full and tall. It was beautiful. At the top of the pole were large eagle's wings in full extension, she glanced at Baldy, who seemed to approve. A wolf's face carved underneath. Bandit scuffed his paws into the ground. Many happy faces carved towards the bottom of the pole. The last face was an upside down evil face which she knew represented Jim. That part of the pole would be inserted into the ground. Finally, the totem pole was erect. The carvers that had worked on it day and night danced around the pole wielding their carving and singing their prayers of peace.

Will touched the totem pole as he spoke. "This will tell our story for many years to come. The Great One defeated Evil. As we all know today's moon is Paschal moon which determines the date for Easter which is a week from today. We need to remember what the Great One did for us." Will bowed his head and held Arvidia's hand. All followed. As he prayed the circle closed in tighter.

"Thank you God, for the blessings you have poured out among us. We are ever so grateful. Thank you, O, Mighty One." The moment was serene and peaceful. Will knew God was there among them.

Jake's stomach rumbled loudly as the smell of the food became unbearable. "Thank you, Jesus. I'm hungry!" Jake stated loudly as he looked at his red-faced father. All laughed as they parted hands and Will headed to his seat on his porch.

"Jake!" Liza covered her mouth in shock.

"What?" Jake looked around innocently. Caleb and Trista giggled.

Will was still laughing along with the others, "Jake, before we eat I would like you to come up here."

"Sure!" Jake bolted up the steps, where Will whispered into his ear, Jake reached inside the entrance way and put on the headdress Will had made for him. Will reached up to him and lightly touched his face declaring, "You are hereby an official member of the Lemaltcha tribe." Jake grinned from ear to ear. He puffed up his chest and folded his arms across it.

Blake beamed inside and out. He looked around the island and felt a pang of guilt. Despite his initial misgivings, he had come to love the island and the people, including Baldy and Bandit. But he would soon need to head back to New York and attend to the many cases that were stacking up his desk. He knew he would have to talk with Arvidia. They hadn't spoken a word about their futures.

"Okay, chow down!" Will exclaimed. People scattered about and ate.

Arvidia whispered into Blake's ear. "Blake I need to talk to the guys I'll be right back." She walked slowly towards the Quad. Chris and Mike had been released from the hospital and were recuperating well, Mike on his crutches. She felt emotional as she hugged each one of them. She had spent the previous evening thinking about Hal, Joe and the Quad. Thinking how much they had sacrificed for her. They'd all taught her everything she knew but she was still amazed how they had stuck by her side. It was hard to believe. Her case was finally sealed, closed and buried. She saved the last hug for Hal. She looked into Hal's face whose years of hard work were ingrained on his face.

He spoke first, "I am so glad to be rid of that file. That file haunted me for years. I may not have been able to seal and shut as many cases as I would've liked, but I'm sure glad this one's is over. I am so proud of you. You've grown into one amazing woman." He spoke fatherly.

"Will told me how hesitant you were about taking my case, thank you for all the sacrifices you have made to help me survive." Arvidia had often wondered if she were the reason Hal never married or had kids. Truth was, as he had told her time and time again, that his job was very demanding and time slips away. Hal hugged her tightly and quickly walked away. She could see the emotions flooding his face.

Arvidia turned around and watched the people mingling about. She could see Kelia talking with Blake. She was still grappling with a sister she never knew about. "Thank you, Lord for my sister, Kelia." She observed Liza intently listening to Will as he spoke of a story she was sure he was sharing. She smiled to herself when she recalled Blake telling her of his parent's first meeting Baldy and Bandit. Like Blake, they too were wary of Baldy and Bandit. Amazingly, Baldy didn't display her usual dislikes with new strangers and Bandit was on his best behavior. She turned her gaze on her kids and Jake. She was overcome with gratefulness for the mercy God showed her. All she could do was look up and whisper words of thanks.

Arvidia was in the middle of explaining the symbolism of the totem pole to Blake's parents when Blake approached her.

"Arvidia, may I have a moment with you?" Blake lightly touched her arm. Arvidia looped her arm into Blake's. Blake's parents smiled at each other as they walked away.

"Sure. What's up?" asked Arvidia

"I think you should go home and rest, you look a bit peaked. You've had much excitement the last few days!"

"I am a bit tired. It's been quite a day!"

"All right, I'll gather my parents and drop them off at the hotel and I'll take you to your condo. You need to rest, doctor's orders! Do you want Kelia to stay with you tonight and I'll stay here with the kids?"

"Yes, that is a wonderful idea. That will give me more time with her."

Blake dropped his parents off at the Bellwether Hotel and drove to Arvidia's condo. He looked over at Arvidia who was sound asleep. He looked in the rearview mirror and could see Kelia nodding off as well.

He pulled in the driveway and parked the car. He gently awoke Arvidia as Kelia stirred awake. Once inside, Arvidia yawned, "Kelia, I'll see you in the morning, I'm beat. Blake, would you mind showing Kelia the guest room? It's the smaller room at the end of the hall upstairs."

"Sure." He leaned in and kissed her on the cheek. "Sweet dreams. I'll check on you." She felt pampered. She limped her way up two steps before she heard scratching at the sliding glass door. Blake held up his hand, stating, "I'll let him in." He opened the sliding glass door and Bandit wandered in, sniffed Kelia, snorted and was at Arvidia's side on the steps. Together, they went to her bedroom.

"Wow, I can't get over the size of that thing. He's sure a big wolf." Kelia's heartbeat slowed down to a normal pace.

"Yeah, he wasn't too thrilled with me at first, but I think I have his blessing now." They laughed. "Kelia, before I show you your room, do you have a minute?"

"Sure." Blake beckoned her to sit on the couch.

"I just wanted to discuss with you something that has been on my heart. I've discussed this with Will and received his blessings and,"

Kelia cupped her face with her hands and giggled, "You don't even need to finish you have my blessing to marry her." Blake grinned.

"Okay, that settles it. But don't say anything just yet. I still need to talk to the Quad and get their blessing as well as the kids. I want to do this right."

"Oh, I'm sure they will. How will you do it?"

"I'm not sure yet. I've got a few ideas."

Kelia reached over and hugged him, "I've not only gained a sister, but a family as well."

"You are right about that." Blake yawned and stood up, "Well, let me show you to your room and call it a night."

"Yes, I'm bushed myself." She stood as Blake picked up her suitcase and headed upstairs. As promised, he looked in Arvidia's room and could see she was sleeping soundly and Bandit snored loudly across her legs.

"Good night." Kelia opened her door and went in.

"Good night." He turned and headed into his room. He starred out the bedroom window and as the moon light rippled quietly on the ocean surface. He pondered his thoughts. He had realized the past few days he had no desire to return to New York. He knew he wanted to marry Arvidia, but did she? How was he going to tell his parents? Jake? He sat on his bed and opened the nightstand drawer and picked up the jewelry box and opened it. He held up the ring and all he could think of was how much he loved her, the kids and surprisingly, the island life. He heard his door creak open and a large black nose peeking through. Surprised, "Come on in Bandit." Bandit lumbered and stuck his head between his legs and looked at him, curiously.

"Well, I guess I better start with you, do I have your permission to marry Arvidia?" Bandit looked over at his hand holding the ring and gently rubbed his head on his arm. Blake was stunned at the gentleness of this animal, "I'll take that as a yes." Then he thought for a moment about Baldy. She's going to be a tough one.

"Well, Lord if it is your will for me to marry her, I have much to do tomorrow." He put the ring back into the box and shut the drawer and laid down listening to the ocean waves lap at the rocks. Then he heard snoring, he sat up and looked over the edge of the bed and saw Bandit sprawled out sound asleep.

Blake chuckled and shook his head, "Amazing, a wolf sleeping in my room."

CHAPTER 34

THE BEACH

"Okay, it's been two days, Will. I'm thinking today is the day. What do you think?" Blake asked as he paced the porch while he and Will had their coffee. Will had invited them up for breakfast. Blake hadn't been able to sleep knowing what his plans were.

Will thought he'd have a little fun. "Nope, I don't think it's today. I think you might have to wait another week." Blake nearly choked on his coffee and Will laughed as he watched him wipe his chin. He slapped his knee, "That was fun." He laughed heartily.

I'm glad you find that I amuse you." Blake was actually starting to relax a little.

"Just trying to loosen you up." he smiled and added, "So I thought I'd show your parents around before they head back home."

"I spoke to ma last night and she was thrilled, even my father is enjoying the downtime. I never thought that would happen."

"I'm sure they would love a tour." He looked out over the porch. "It sure is a beautiful day."

"It sure is." Blake starred at the beach. The wheels were spinning in his head.

Arvidia stepped out onto the porch and smiled at them. She felt rested and alive. "Father, thanks for the breakfast, it was delicious." She leaned in and kissed him. "Did I interrupt something?"

"Not at all, Sqimi, I was just going inside to call Blake's parents and see if they would like a tour." He stood and snapped his fingers, "I'll ask Kelia as well." He stood up to leave.

"That's a great idea, I'll come with you."

Blake saw Kelia in the window giving him thumbs up. "I don't think so; I have other plans for us today." Arvidia turned around and gave Blake a curious stare.

"Its okay, Sqimi, I've got it covered." He kissed her cheek, winked at Blake and went inside.

"Should I be worried?" she giggled. "So what should I do?"

"Just grab a jacket and I'll do the rest." Blake ordered lightly.

"Where are you going?" She asked just as she shut the screen door. "Blake what are you up to?"

"It's a surprise! Now, come." Blake looked at her mischievously. She was surprised to see Lexy had been saddled up by Caleb and Bandit sitting nearby. He and Blake helped her onto Lexy. Blake took the reins and started to walk ahead of Lexy.

Blake spent much of the past few days talking with Will, his parents, the Quad and Joe. He wanted to be sure they were all okay with his decision.

"Bye Mom." Caleb raced back into the house excited as well. He, Trista, Caleb, Will and Kelia peered out the window as they went by.

Will ushered the kids outside, "Remember be quiet and listen for Blake's cue."

"Okay." Caleb answered. "Come on, we have to take the back way."

As Blake walked towards the beach leading Lexy he thought about his parents reactions to his news. He really wanted to take Arvidia up to Mount. Baker but he knew she wasn't strong enough. He wanted to show his parents the beauty of the mountains, the woods, and the gorgeous lake but he knew his mother would never ride a horse. He'd had enough trouble trying to convince her that Bandit was just a wolf who protected Arvidia. It wasn't until a couple of days before Arvidia came home from the hospital that Bandit suddenly plopped his head onto his mother's lap. Liza froze and screamed. She was sure Bandit was going to harm her. He then put his large paws onto her lap. Blake was sure his mother would faint but Will rushed to Liza's side and gently explained that this "beast" was nothing but a gentle giant and was showing her acceptance. After that and much to Blake's surprise, he noticed his mother didn't seem to mind Bandit following her around. He'd even seen her patting his head from time to time, but a belly rub would not be to her approval, yet.

Blake chuckled to himself. "What's so funny?" Arvidia asked.

"Oh, nothing, I was just thinking about my mother and Bandit. No one back home would believe this."

Arvidia laughed, "Kelia told me about their encounter. I'm surprised Bandit took to her so quickly, then again, he does have a good judge of character."

"That he does have." Blake laughed.

As they came over the hill, the ocean roared to life. Arvidia sniffed the air and inhaled. Her lung was only sore now. "This was a good idea, a ride out to the beach. I feel so refreshed."

"Good." Blake stopped as did Lexy. He stood for a moment and starred out into the ocean. Off to his right, he noticed the boulder Arvidia sat on the night she recalled the fire. He hung his head for a moment and fingered the box in his pocket. Out of the corner of his eye, he'd seen the kids hiding behind the trees.

"Blake, are you okay?" She started to dismount but grimaced slightly. Blake eased her off the horse and led her to the boulder. She sat down and looked up at Blake who was kneeling down before her. She gasped.

Blake cleared his throat and regained his composure. He gingerly pulled out of his pocket, a heart shape diamond engagement ring with sapphires circled around it. They matched her blazing blue eyes. "Arvidia Miles, will you marry me?"

Baldy and Gulp soared high above them squawking loudly then perched themselves on a nearby branch. Bandit kneeled like Blake. He drew up one paw, and cocked his head to one side. Arvidia wished she had her camera, she laughed hysterically. The kids soon appeared behind Blake giggling.

Arvidia thought for a moment, "Well let me see . . . ." She teased and reached for his hand. "Yes, Blake Edward Matarazzo, I will marry you." Blake grinned and slid the ring onto her finger and kissed her. The kids wrapped their arms around them and they hugged as a family.

Blake and Caleb helped Arvidia back onto Lexy while Jake held the reins. They headed back to Will's home. Many had gathered in front of Will's knowing what had happened. Once the excitement died down, many questions surfaced, which Blake knew Arvidia would ask. The kids were playing, Will and Blake's parents were in a deep discussion and Kelia had gone home with promises to return.

"How are we going to do this?" Arvidia finally found time to talk with Blake about their future.

"Arvidia, I've given this a lot of thought. I even asked Will, Hal, the Quad, and the kids for your hand in marriage. I know they've known you a lot longer than I have, but I can honestly tell you I have never loved anyone like you." He kissed the back of her hand and smiled at her. "I've also talked to my parents. You know the empty plot by the beach?"

"The Peterson plot?" They had made their way into Will's house to talk quietly.

"That would be the one. I talked to them and made an offer to buy it. Arvidia, I know deep down this is your home, and I could never ask you to leave. So I have plans to build us a home and open up an office here." Blake unfolded the house plans and showed it to her.

"What about your family, how do they feel about this? What about the firm? What about the kids?" She looked at the house plans. "Blake this is beautiful! But . . . the kids . . ." She knew Trista and Caleb would be thrilled, but Jake was used to the city.

"I discussed this with them. They are actually all excited to be living together. I'm so amazed at how they have bonded. I was concerned about Jake being selfish due to the fact he's an only child. He sure proved me wrong!"

It was then the kids made their presence known. They had waited just outside the screen door. Caleb was the first to speak.

"Mom, we just want you to be happy now that we don't have to worry about whatshisname." Caleb continued, "Gramps told us a while back, Blake would be our new father."

"He did? When did he tell you this?" Blake and Arvidia asked at the same time.

"A while ago." Caleb was proud to know something they didn't.

"And I finally get a brother and sister!" Jake shouted.

Blake and Arvidia looked at the children. Will's wisdom never ceased to amaze them.

"Now we can be with Gramps!" Trista said happily.

"Does this mean we're staying and we will be a family, dad?" Jake chimed in again.

"That's exactly what it means son. Plus," He looked at Arvidia for approval as he spoke, "If it's okay with Arvidia, your grandparents might have a condo to stay in for long visits with all of us. What do you say?"

Jake looked at Arvidia and asked, "When can I call you mom? Now, that I have 2 moms."

Blake realized grandparents weren't the top of his concern.

Arvidia was overwhelmed with tears in her eyes. She looked at Caleb and Trista for confirmation, they both shook their head yes. "It's your call, whenever you want." He grinned and asked, "Can we go out and play, mom?"

Arvidia smiled and said, "Yes absolutely." She sniffed as they ran out the door. Blake hugged her and while she looked over his shoulder she noticed something about the plans. "What's this?"

"Oh, in that area I'm going to plant trees for Baldy and Gulp where they can make their nests and Bandit had a place to himself so he can come and go as he pleases. I doubt they will be leaving Will's side for long."

"They will love it. The Peterson's were okay with these plans?"

"Oh yes, they're moving to their daughter's land. She's expecting their first grandchild and they are building a house nearby."

"That's fantastic, I didn't realize she was pregnant, I must remember to congratulate her." She took a deep breath and slowly let it out. She felt little pain. "There's so much to do, where do we start?"

"There's more news, my parents are so impressed with the island and the tribe they decided to make a significant donation to help preserve this area as much as possible. My mother cannot get over the beauty of this island, to be honest with you, neither can I."

Stunned, Arvidia's voice squeaked with excitement, "Blake, that's wonderful news! Will must be thrilled!" She knew Will had been praying for a financial blessing for a long time to preserve the island and wild life. She was so happy at the turn of events.

"He doesn't know about it yet. They want to tell him tonight. Will only knew I would be proposing to you."

Arvidia giggled and looked at the ring.

"Oh, one last thing, I did speak with Kelia, she is going to discuss it with her husband but it's quite possible she may be able to move out here, but if not, they definitely will be purchasing a condominium to visit." Arvidia's heart couldn't get any fuller.

"She told me, she lost you once and she'll not lose you again. So my sweet, dear, Arvidia, have all your questions been answered?"

"Yes," She squealed, "We have a wedding to plan!"

"Yes, we do, let's go outside and share the news, especially Will's news."

They both walked out onto the porch with their arms around each other's waist. Arvidia looked up at the sky, "Wow, look at that moon!" Arvidia pointed. "Isn't it brighter than usual?"

Will looked up at the moon and smiled, "Yes, it is." He had just been informed by Blake's parents of their donation to help preserve the historic island and the tribe. He prayed for many years for financial blessings. He felt truly blessed.

Blake gently pulled her close to him for a kiss. "I love you, Arvidia." "I love you, too."

Not too far in the distance, The Lurk chugged quietly out of Bellingham Bay after the captain was questioned and let go by the Quad. He was flustered when he found out that Buck Taylor and Jim Mason were dead. He wanted to high tail it out of there as fast as he could. He found millions of dollars hidden in Buck's room. He tapped the box he sat on where he had hidden the money; Brazil was looking to be a good place to head towards.

The Quad found the bags Gus was trying to escape with. Jim never knew he switched the money bags. He never would reap the rewards as he was safely put away for a long time. After a period of time, the money went unclaimed, which they were sure it would be. The Quad felt the money would be put to good use by adding to the gift Blake's parents to Lummi Island.

CPSIA information can be obtained at www.ICGtesting.com
Printed in the USA
LVOW06s0101250713

344448LV00008BA/893/P